THE OSIRIS WAR

Matthew P. Schmidt

O&H Books LLC

MARTINS FERRY, OHIO

O&H Books LLC
Martins Ferry, Ohio
https://matthewpschmidt.com

Publisher's Note: This is a work of fiction. Names, characters, places, and incidents are a product of the author's imagination. Locales and public names are sometimes used for atmospheric purposes. Any resemblance to actual people, living or dead, or to businesses, companies, events, institutions, or locales is completely coincidental.

While this is indeed political commentary, no culture, faction, character, issue, crisis or event is a direct correspondence with those in the real world. The closest you can get is the guy who dies in Chapter 18. Sometimes you have to make an exception.

Book Layout © 2017 BookDesignTemplates.com
Formatting by Karina Fabian
Cover designed by MiblArt. miblart.com

The OSIRIS War/ Matthew P. Schmidt. -- 1st ed..
ISBN 978-1-959703-07-5

This book is dedicated to St. Josemaria Escriva. Pray for the dead of the Spanish Civil War, on both sides!

CONTENTS

IF CALAMITY COMES TO A CITY 7
ENDURANCE PRODUCES CHARACTER 9
MADE BY HUMAN HANDS 27
ALL IS VANITY 45
A WORD WAS REVEALED... 61
THE LAMB OF GOD.. 75
THE FURNACE OF HUMILIATION 87
A COLLAR OF IRON 107
THE LOVE OF MONEY 115
SLAVE TO THE LENDER.. 133
THE TWO OF THEM SWORE AN OATH....................... 147
THE OTHER MARY.. 153
I HAVE SURELY SEEN THE AFFLICTION................... 163
WHERE THE TRIBES GO UP 173
NOW I WILL TELL YOU THE TRUTH 183
A GOD THAT CANNOT SAVE 195
AND THE EARTH HAS WITHHELD ITS CROPS 209
A HANDFUL OF FLOUR IN A JAR 223
MINGLED WITH THEIR SACRIFICES 231
IN CHARGE OF ALL HIS POSSESSIONS 237
AN ACCOUNT OF YOUR STEWARDSHIP 251
IN THE DAYS OF LOT 263
THIS THING IS FROM ME 275
WHOSOEVER SHALL NOT COME FORTH.................. 287
WAR WAS IN HIS HEART 297

THE INNERMOST PART OF THE HOUSE 307
WARS AND RUMORS OF WARS 323
TREASURE ON EARTH 333
YOU WHO LIVE UNDER SIEGE 343
OF FIRST IMPORTANCE 351
YOU HYPOCRITES! 357
LET YOUR COLLECTION OF IDOLS DELIVER YOU! 367
HE WHO LIVES BY THE SWORD 379
THE GREATEST OF THESE IS LOVE 385
A NEW COVENANT 391
WHAT HAPPENED TO EVERYONE? 397
GLOSSARY 411
ACKNOWLEDGEMENTS 431
WANT MORE? 431
ABOUT THE AUTHOR 432

PREFACE

IF CALAMITY COMES TO A CITY

If you are reading this, I have long since left this world, beyond even OSIRIS's power. I have set this book to be released a hundred years after my soul's eternal departure. The wounds of the war are still too raw to release it now, both thosc in thc world and in myself.

Future reader, I know not who you are or what world you live in. Perhaps this book will seem quaint and shortsighted to you, as the diaries of the Divine Architects seemed to us. Surely some historian of your age has already sifted through the data, examined previous works, and come to an objective conclusion.

My only authority is that I saw the sufferings of those who were trapped within our broken society's broken systems with my own eyes, and I helped them as best I could with my limited pow-er. You may know the events of the OSIRIS War as a series of dry facts, but I watched the world around me crumble, and I dared hoped that things could get better.

Is my story objective? No. Nonetheless true? Yes.

That future historian will have any number of dates to pick for the beginning of the end of the Athanasian League. Perhaps I should begin at the attack on the Necropolis, or the Solstice Riots, or Fimbulwinter, or perhaps the day I met Alan

Jaranjair. But, after many attempts to start this book, I have decided to begin at my graduation.

CHAPTER ONE

ENDURANCE PRODUCES CHARACTER

December 1st, 1042 AGDR

Technically, it was not a slave auction. Technically, we had consented to all of this. Technically, we could walk, at this very moment, off campus and never return. Technically, we could have even chosen not to attend the graduation, and let come what may.

The Athanasian League functioned on the basis of such technicalities. If, future reader, you wonder why our society reintroduced slavery, know that we called them bakts, not slaves. The Debt Reform Amendment was welcomed as merciful even by the indebted, as by giving bakts a name they gained rights. But once the division between free citizens and bakts was made, those rights were ever ground away.

We, the 323 graduates of the Steelriver University class of 1042, had no say in the matter. And like any other group of young men and women faced with something far beyond our control, we did our best to ignore that fact.

The DJ played too-loud remixes of tunes that were popular three generations ago. The students laughed and joked, eating and drinking from the many folding tables set up with treats and strong drinks. The faculty, RAs, and a good number of student lifeweavers kept a close look out for alcohol poisoning. Now and then, one would escort a stumbling student to the bathrooms.

I couldn't blame anyone for his excesses, at least today. My foster father had been a drunkard in his third life, and he had not quit his habit by his fifth, so I detested the stuff myself. Some joker had spiked the punch, but Alan had found me—blessed be the True God—actual water. I sipped slowly from the bottle as Amy drunk herself silly, and Charles had one too many.

There were only twenty-four of us twenty-two-year-old mage graduates, all crowded in the same corner of the gym, slowly shrinking as our names were called. All the other mage graduates at Steelriver University were on their second life or later, and most of the first life students had chosen some degree where a first life could (hypothetically) get a job. But us twenty-four first lifes had, by welfare, credits, loans, and sheer force of will, managed to snag some kind of magic degree.

Of us, seventeen were necromancers, including myself, four were lifeweavers, two were elementalists, and the lone augur had made it through all four years without quitting like his two fellow would-be augurs. Though hypothetically we had more in common with our fellow disciples, the fact that we had tried—and for the most part succeeded—in the impossible was a stronger tie than discipline.

But today we would learn if we had truly succeeded. And deep within each of us, we knew the outlook was grim at best.

Alan rested a hand on my shoulder. The spiral tattooed on the right cheek of his ocher face, combined with his cycle number, made him the sort who would get touted as more proof the Athanasian Dream was real. Or it would if he got a bond. But his mustached smile was unmoved, even slightly amused by his surroundings, as if the worst the world could throw at him was a trifle in comparison to what he would do if he succeeded.

"Mary?" he asked. "Do you need more water?"

"I'm fine," I said. "With the water, I mean." The fact that we had somehow ended up as a couple had the campus scratching its back, and I couldn't explain it either. We had jokingly discussed how much it would cost for me to have my own spiral, but in reality, unless we were bonded to the same place we were doomed, no matter how much we loved each other.

"We all..." Amy hiccupped. "We all know what'cha means." She hiccupped again and stumbled towards the table. My best friend and roommate was also a polar opposite to me: bright, cheery, and willing to do whatever it took to keep the pain away.

The music dimmed. "Sarah Starblueking!" a voice called.

One of the four remaining lifeweavers with us sighed. "See you all. If I ever will."

"Good luck," Alan told her.

"True God's blessing," I said.

"Already tired of gods," Sarah said and walked off. "Best of luck to y'all!"

Amy groaned. "Purge me," she said to the remaining sober lifeweaver.

The campus allowed any party short of a riot or outright orgy, but they made one strict rule: There had to be at least two sober lifeweavers at all times. While there were lifeweavers everywhere, we had gotten used to relying on ourselves rather than getting *another* lecture on our cycle number.

Taylor took Amy by the hand and helped her towards the women's bathroom.

"Charles," I told my other best friend, another necromantic student, who was pouring yet another drink. "Slow down."

"What's the point?" he said and hiccupped. "Chances are we'll all end up at the grinders. System's rigged, y'know."

"That's it. Time for a purge," Wanda said and tugged at him.

"I'm just sayin' the truth."

"And are you going to say that to your prospective masters?"

"Oh. Yeah." He waddled along with Wanda towards the men's bathroom.

"Is it rigged?" I asked Alan.

"Deliberately? No. In practice? Yes." Alan shrugged. "Give a hundred necromantic degrees out with twenty slots for bakts, and four times as many graduates will be left out as get in. What difference does it make to our government about the other eighty?"

"OSIRIS, you are the cheeriest mage student I've ever met," Abigail, one of the other necromantic students, said.

"Ignorance of reality doesn't change it," Alan said, as he always did.

Amy came back with Taylor, walking straight but looking far worse for the wear. Her argent robes had the faint stain of vomit and the scent of alcohol. "Dear MA-AT," she said. "I didn't have *that* much, did I?"

"Yes," I told her. "You did."

"Worth it," she said. "MA-AT, I can't see how you stand it, Mary."

"It's not as if I have a choice," I said.

"Oh, fair enough—"

The music dimmed again. "Mary Firebrightsky!"

They all looked at me.

Alan kissed me on the hand. Spirals, he had told me, did not kiss on the face unless the person was family and *definitely* not on the cheek. I hugged him, and Amy hugged me. I gathered my courage and walked out the doors of the gym to the adjacent auditorium.

I felt faint as I walked up the steps. Amy had sworn up and down to me that all the effects of alcohol left the moment MA-AT touched the body, but I almost wished I had had an unpurged sip just to steady my nerves. "Hear, O True God," I whispered under my breath as I took the seat by the microphone.

Lawyers, accountants, and necromancers in dark fuglin coats watched with clipboards, frowns, and disinterest. In one seat, dead serious, was a clown.

"I am Mary Firebrightsky," I introduced myself quietly.

They went over the preliminaries: my perfect grades, my glowing recommendations from faculty, my participation in all kinds of social benefit organizations. But the one fact they couldn't gloss over: I hadn't even lived one full life, yet.

Why spend 213,000 drachmae to buy a first life by paying off all her loans, when you could potentially buy someone with the same grades and more life experience for even less?

But I remained impassive even if I was sweating on the inside, as I was. I just had to get through this, and that life could truly begin.

Or be crushed before it started.

Next was the Q&A, where, my professor had told me, my potential "customers" made their actual decisions.

The interviewer consulted his tablet. "A question from Notre Dame Banking, LLC: 'Are you comfortable with large amounts of numbers?'"

"I am," I said.

"Is 10,201 prime?"

How on earth did *that* matter? "I…uh…No, I think it's 101 squared."

"A question from Eternal Investigative Services, LLC: 'Do you have a past criminal history with necromancy or any form of magic, sealed, unsealed, or in a past life?'"

"No," I said.

"A question from the Alfred Slowbrightlaughter estate: 'What do a necromancer's girlfriend and a gambler have in common?'"

"Uh…" No, idiot, don't stutter. "They both roll the bones?" I tried.

The clown—the clown wrote the glitched thing *down.*

I was bombarded with more questions. I saw phone calls made as I tried to answer all their questions on economics, history, necromancy, and the occasional oddball question about me or my past. I tried my best to answer without stuttering, but I found the longer it went on, the harder it became, and the questions grew harsher.

"A question from the Windnightsky Estate: 'Would you lie if your client told you to do so?'"

"No," I said. "Never." The crowd took notes.

"A further question: 'Would you relay a lie if you knew it to be a lie?'"

"If the contact lied to my client, I would tell my client that I had outside knowledge," I said. "If my client wanted to lie to the contact, I would refuse. That all said, I am not to judge whether either my client or my contact deliberately told a falsehood or was merely mistaken. I am only the means of communication."

"What if your master told you to?"

I paused. "Then…then I would have to think about it. I don't think I could relay a deliberate lie, even then."

More notes were taken, but as my psychology professor had told me, 90% of communication was nonverbal. Though I had answered correctly, I knew I had given the wrong answer.

December 2nd, 1042 AGDR

"We are sorry to inform you…" the letter from Student Affairs began. I read the rest, already knowing what it would say from the thin envelope, and set it on my desk.

What was the reason? Was it that I wouldn't lie? Was it my cycle number? Was I just unlucky?

I had dared to hope. I had dared to *hope* that maybe, just maybe, I could make it.

Tears dripped onto the paper, and then I started sobbing.

I let myself cry. Then I forced myself to look at the situation.

I had already accepted that I would be a bakt, but now I wouldn't be a bakt at a necromantic firm. The other options to pay off my student loans could be far worse.

Technically, I could not become a bakt by force, only to get my creditors off my back. They could take everything but the clothing on my back, and myself. But the government made an exception for itself.

I opened the much thicker envelope from the League Labor Bureau. *Of course*, the government slave mongers were the most efficient, since they had unlimited access to bakts to staff themselves. As a potential League bakt, there was a remote chance I would end up as a bureaucrat, if I was lucky.

Technically, not every government bakt ended up at the grinders. Technically, the government didn't even *own* any body-reprocessing facilities. But when the government leased out those too poor to repay their student and government loans, the corpsegrinders could always bid the most.

My foster parents had taken me to one. I still had nightmares. The bakts there shuffled around, heedless of the bits of gore covering them, with eyes as dead as the bodies they dismantled. Without them, the bioslurry crisis would be even worse, but they got none of the money from it and all of the misery.

If I was one of them, I would not even see any of the money they paid for me with. I would just be "paid" minimum wage regardless of to whom I was leased. And of course, with the interest on my bond, I could be there for decades, as opposed to the seven standard years for a necromantic bakt.

I flipped to the last page. No word as to where I would end up. But that only made it *worse*.

I knew that failing to land a bond was a possibility. In fact, I knew it was more likely than not that those seeking necromancers would simply pick a second or later life. Cycle discrimination wasn't legal by any stretch of the law, but what could I do?

I could take a walk.

So I got up, put on my coat, and headed out the door. Unlike Amy, who already had her credentials, I couldn't yet wear my discipline's black coat. The color was called fuglin, to be precise.

I walked outside to see the campus practically deserted. The brisk air was quiet, the True God's mercy to those whose dreams were destroyed. I passed under the blossoming cherry trees, kept blooming from lifeweavers and augurs. At least *someone* had a job.

I could try to find servitude somewhere else, if someone was willing to pay 213,000 drachmae of student loans for a burger flipper, plus my 83,000 RENEW credit. Or if, by some miracle, I had actual employment enough to make the monthly payments, I would also be free.

The irony of it all—I was free *now*, at least until I defaulted. But the only thing worse than being a slave to some estate or corporation was being a free woman no one wanted.

I could start my own necromancy firm, but I would need a reference from a licensed necromancer for the charter. I couldn't get my own credentials except after working in a necromancy firm for three years. And that door was already closed.

"*Mary!*" Amy shrieked, hurrying to me. "I'm a bakt!" Then she looked at my expression. "Oh. I'm sorry."

Anything but face my own situation. "You got in?" I asked.

"Yep. Alfred Slowbrightlaughter Estate! Can you believe they sent a *clown*?"

"I know. They asked me to tell a dirty joke."

"Yeah, yeah, well…" She trailed off. "I guess…I guess this is it, then."

Our lives would probably never cross again. Sure, we could keep in touch, but she would be busy, and True God willing, so would I.

My phone rang: Alan Jaranjair. I answered. "Alan?"

"I got in," he said, somberly. "Notre Dame Banking. You?"

"Nothing," I said, the word almost tearing apart my vocal cords as it shuddered out. "Nothing at all."

"I'm so sorry. I'll be right there." He hung up.

"Here," Amy said, hugging me and then pulling me along. "Need a drink?"

What the glitch did it matter at this point, anyway? "Something light," I said.

Back in her dorm, we drank something that was probably not as alcoholic as I wanted, but too much more than I should really have. I sipped. It felt tasteless—only a burning acid in my mouth that could not bring happiness. Nothing ever could.

Alan let himself in. We looked at each other and saw the pain in each other's eyes. He went to hug me. "I'm so sorry."

If—I hated to think it, but I had secretly hoped—he hadn't gotten in, we had talked about starting a necromancy firm together, somehow, so *we* could be together. And now…

No.

No, I would not give up here.

I had already moved Heaven and Earth to get here. Time to move them a bit more.

"Alan," I said. "We talked about starting a necromancy firm if…I mean, I'm not asking you to quit."

"I understand," he said. "I actually had the paperwork all ready to go. I'll just take my name off it." He said it casually, then stopped short. "Do you have any idea where you can get a reference?"

"I'll ask the prof," I said. Without it, I couldn't get the firm charter approved, and I couldn't practice necromancy at all.

"Wait a bit. She's probably busy right now. And right now, you need to relax," Alan said.

"Yeah," I answered.

Amy poured him a tumbler and he drank. We said other things after that, talking as if there was something we could do.

December 3rd, 1042 AGDR

I always thought of Professor Greenrayburst as ancient, but possibly only because she had pure white hair. While only on her third life, she hadn't euthanized herself when she got frail, so she had actually lived longer than most sixth lives.

"There's nothing I can do," she finally told me, after I pleaded with her in her neat office.

"A reference—"

"For what? Being a perfect student, yes. For starting your own firm? Not under any stretch of necroregs."

"At least to get my credentials—"

"Mary!" she snapped. "We have talked about this for an *hour*. I *can't* help you. I'll lose my own credentials if I make an exception for you. I'm sorry. My hands are tied."

I sighed. "All right."

She sighed, too. "They can't take your diploma from you just for failing to pay your loans. Even if you do go to the grinders, it will only be for, at worst, your whole life. Then you can start your next life with a degree in hand."

I almost snapped that I would still be in the same boat of lacking a job afterwards, just far more traumatized. But I didn't. My throat was sore from arguing. "Can I ask you one favor?" I asked. "One thing you *can* grant?"

"Sure," she said. "If I can grant it."

"Give me a copy of the necroregs."

She looked at me, then closed her mouth, as if she didn't want to argue further. She dug in her desk for a USB drive and handed it to me. "No one gave this to you," she said. "I simply misplaced it."

"Thanks, no one," I said.

"I'm sure no one is welcome. Now please, I have ten other students who need my help."

I spent all night reading through the pages and pages of necromantic law, sitting in front of my glowing laptop, ready to hide my screen in a moment. The light cast my few possessions and books in shadows, as if watching my illegal search.

Necromancy law was written by the Parliament of the Dead; as a Living woman, even a necromantic student, I was forbidden access. Of course, I had no idea what Dead had the time to spend reading it.

Many of the Living, especially first lives, thought of the Dead as unbelievably rich, but the truth was the vast majority of the Dead experienced life one thousand times slower than realtime, except for six minutes a month. With only Necrosecurity to afford a reincarnation, it would be ages before interest compounded enough to give them an escape.

If I died a bakt, my own Necrosecurity would be garnished in repayment of my otherwise-canceled debt. The Senate and the Parliament had bickered for decades over this, but the Dead had no authority over the welfare programs of the Living.

I scanned through pages and pages of legalese to see if there were any welfare programs of the Dead I would qualify for, but the files on the drive were only the Table of the Dead, and the sections from the relevant necrocodes and necroregs.

Alan had tried to explain why the Law of the Tomb was forbidden to the Living, but as far I could tell it was an elaborate scheme by Dead lawyers to stay in business. But, legal or not, I read every last word on necromantic licensing.

```
(A) An individual who practices, teaches,
or is otherwise engaged in the act of
necromancy, Living or Deceased,
    (i) must be a licensed individual under
the provisions of this section
    (ii) must be a bakt, employee, or
officer of a necromancy firm, or a member
of the government or armed forces,
 ...
 (AAA) "Licensed Individual" is defined as
any of the following:
     (i) a licensed necromancer.
     (ii) a licensed necromancer's
assistant.
     (iii) a certified necromantic
technician.
     (iv) an attorney who may practice
under the Law of the Tomb.
     (v) an estate necromantic advisor
under 14 S 1555.
     (vi) a graveyard militia officer.
     (vii) a Necroforce officer who has
been certified by the Necromancy
Administration to practice necromancy.
     (viii) a certified medium.
     (ix) any other license granted under
14 S 1444.
```

I would take anything, even being a medium. There were no hyperlinks, so I had to manually search through the text for any loophole I could find.

And so I found my loophole:

```
...
    (EEE) "Necromancy firm" is defined as
         (a) a corporation, estate, limited
liability company, or other association
that provides any kind of necromantic
service, advice, or training under a
charter from the Court of the Tomb.
         (b) a family-owned seance business
where all employees and officers are
certified mediums or necromantic
technicians.
         ...
```

Curious…

```
 (ZZZZ) "Certified medium" is defined as an
individual who has
     (a) completed a medium certification
course as defined by the Court of the Tomb
and has sworn to upload the precepts of
OSIRIS; or
     (b) consciously objects to swearing an
oath to uphold the precepts of OSIRIS and
has a certificate of mediumship from an
authorized conscientious objection
certificate provider.
```

I sat back. It *might* be possible to get a course if I paid out of pocket, although the chances were slim. It would not be my preferred method of making a living, but it would be *a* living, and I might not need to repay my RENEW credit.

But first I had to find a course.

I spent the rest of the night looking for phone numbers.

December 4th, 1042 AGDR

Half of them laughed in my face when I explained my situation, then hung up. The other half just hung up.

That left the other option.

I found a number of conscientious objection-based courses, although almost all of them were already full. I had heard of them vaguely. Although the vast majority of the necromantic students were EDENists, some, including myself, refused to swear an oath to OSIRIS. The alternative was to swear an oath to the True God. I had no idea why someone would be so upset over the situation to demand an entirely separate course.

But I did worship the True God. And the more hope I had, the more desperate I had become to fight past each new obstacle. I was ready for a crisis of faith if need be.

I did more research.

A number of religions that worshiped the True God objected to the more fanciful terminology applied to necromancy. Most preferred the term "post-mortem technician." And while I couldn't find a course for a medium, I could find a course for "post-mortem communication assistant."

I could not tell from the website, but it appeared to be for Catholics only. I wasn't sure what it meant to be a Catholic, and I definitely didn't have time to actually convert. But what if I just *looked* like a Catholic?

After some further research, I found a Catholic gift shop and bookstore nearby, so I took a rideshare over. We passed by the bright skyscrapers and passed over the many bridges of Steelriver. I was born here, and I loved this city. We arrived at the bookstore in the middle of Downtown.

The smell of fresh books welcomed me as I stepped into the small shop. Along the cream walls, somewhat empty racks carried goods with some unknown meaning. This must be a high-traffic store, or their bakts weren't busy. Strange music played in the background, a kind of chant.

What to look for? I tried to spy on the other customers, to see what they wore. Some wore small medallions, but one wore a necklace like a lowercase "t."

The store did sell necklaces, although some were inexplicably filled with beads. All of them had a nearly naked man who appeared to be symbolically nailed to the "t". Perhaps a metaphor for the punishment of evildoers? The medallions were often excessively detailed, and above was the inscription I.N.R.I. For some reason the beaded ones looked to be for those who had extremely thin necks, but I found a wider one without beads that struck my fancy.

"Excuse me," I asked the cashier, who was presumably the owner; he didn't look like a bakt. "Are there any beginner textbooks on Catholicism?"

"Oh, sure, there's a catechism over there," he said.

I left with the strange necklace and the book, wondering if I'd ever have time to read it or if I would just have to fake it all.

"Glitch, Mary, that's genius," Charles told me as we gathered in my dorm, possibly for the last time. He hadn't gained an assignment, either, like most of us. "I couldn't convert, though, not even fake it."

"Even after learning the truth?"

"Let's not argue about that again."

"I have a question," Alan asked. "How will you get the charter for the family business?"

"I was planning to start it as a medium, then apply for a necrotech license," I said. "I don't know how I can get a supervisor."

"I'm sure you can find a necrolawyer who will *try* to do as you ask, but I'm skeptical you can just get these things approved. How will you initiate sessions?" Alan asked

"I'll…oh," I said. "I guess I do need to be a necrotech."

"Knew there'd be some catch," Charles said with a sigh.

"Not necessarily," Alan said. "What if some firm is going out of business, and you bought them out? Then you'd have the charter, and you might even be able to be a necromancer."

"Why didn't you say that at first?" I asked.

"Because I had no idea how to get a necromantic license. But if you've already got one…"

Hope surged within me. "I'll look immediately," I said.

I dialed Seth, one of the machinespeakers.

"What's up?" he said.

"I need you to do a search for me. And keep it secret."

He sighed. "Why?"

"It's my only option for getting out of the grinders."

"Fair. What is it?"

"I want to know about necromantic firms—of any kind—that are either running out of money or their owners are about to self-euthanize."

"What. The. Glitch. Mary?"

"Keep it a secret."

"I will, but this is insane."

"It may be," I agreed. "But I'm crazy desperate."

"It'll have to be low priority. SET tends to get busy around this time of year, and if I bump it up too much, I'm going to raise questions."

"I just need to know by the end of the month."

"Sure thing. I'll call you."

"Thanks."

The League Labor Bureau's next letter, slightly fatter than the previous, sat on my desk. I opened it to find threatening pages about how I needed proof of employment or ongoing training immediately. Or, it blithely noted, I could fill out the contained forms to process my "application for alternative employment."

Future reader, understand that while SET's power to find nearly any fact was not perfectly legal, it was too useful to make illegal. I didn't know if their machinespeakers knew I was trying to weasel out of it, and this letter was here to forestall my effort. But I didn't have the mental space to both study and argue with them.

I held up the small thick book to the light by my desk. The Catechism of OSIRIS, which my foster parents had forced me to read out loud in the vain hope of converting me, had been a thin volume. This new catechism book had thousands of paragraphs across its hundreds of pages of small type. I had no idea how I could read enough to fake being a believer, but I didn't have any other choice at this point.

"True God, aid me," I said, wondering what the True God even thought of this, and began to read.

CHAPTER TWO

MADE BY HUMAN HANDS

December 5th, 1042 AGDR

I had hoped it wouldn't be a small class, so as to avoid being caught as a fake, but thankfully it was a moderately-sized auditorium that was nearly full. Did I stand out or not? I worried. I couldn't tell which made it worse. Others had necklaces similar to mine or oval medals. I fidgeted with my own, but felt weirdly comforted.

I *did* worship the True God, after all, even if I could not make heads or tails of the catechism I bought.

A tall man in fuglin walked up to the podium. "Welcome, everyone," he said. "I'm Alexander Whiteblisstrue. You'll be learning a lot in the next ten weeks—"

Ten *weeks*? There was no way the LLB would wait that long.

"—so I'd like us all to focus on the big picture most of all. Which starts as always with prayer. In the name of the Father and the Son and the Holy Spirit…"

I saw everyone else was making motions with their hands and tried my best to mimic.

"…Through Christ Our Lord. Amen. Now that'd we've gotten started, let's talk about the biggest difference between this course and a compliant one. They all require their students to swear the Oath to OSIRIS. We're not going to do that, but it's worth talking about why." He continued, "The obvious reason is that OSIRIS is not a god. But I'd say the bigger issue: OSIRIS cannot grant eternal life. Only God has power over life and death. OSIRIS can simply extend our mortal lives a little longer." He paced about the stage.

"Knowing this, what are we doing?" he asked. "We're extending life a little longer. And you, here, are going to help that process by communicating with those who are, theologically speaking, still living. For we will all die one day and not come back until the end of the world." He paused before continuing, "So that's why we have a separate course. It's not the terminology. It's the teleology. Our goal is to reduce the suffering of those who have temporarily lost a loved one. Call it necromancy or not, it's not magic. It's just, when you get down to it…"

As he continued on, I didn't know what to think of any of this. I had thought, myself, of the truth that OSIRIS could not grant eternal life. But I couldn't imagine that anything, really, could. The True God made the world, yes, and certainly was merciful, but would he really bring back those lost forever—at the end of the world, no less?

I looked around at the others and relaxed at their lack of shock. They seemed to be taking the lecture rather calmly, perhaps because they did not worship OSIRIS. At any rate, they took this class far better than my classmates on the first day of Necromancy 101.

January 1st, 1038 AGDR

Things were much simpler four years ago, when I was eighteen and just entering college. I was finally out from under the thumb of my foster parents, and in fact, I planned to never see them again if I could help it.

But the Raymond Eastdawnsky Necromancy Education for Wards scholarship I had gotten had one critical clause: I had to be a necromancer at graduation, or the government would demand its money back. In the Steelriver Canton, you would automatically pass your mage boards if you had perfect grades *and* a job or bond. Of course, I could pass the boards subsequently if I failed in acquiring a job or bond, if I wasn't indentured to a fast-food company, that is.

I had chosen a modern university, not an apprenticeship to a traditional necromancer as my foster parents demanded. They had tried to convince me that this was a stupid idea. They had told me that I would definitely end up a bakt of a fast-food company, or (incorrectly) that I could be held criminally responsible for failing to repay the RENEW credit. They warned me that I would not receive a centidrachma from them if I messed up. But the one thing they couldn't tell me was "no" because it wasn't up to them. Any ward of the state was eligible for the credit, and thus was I.

The novelty of spiting my foster parents had worn off immediately on exposure to the very real reality that I was on my own and had to have perfect grades. So on my first day of classes, Necromancy 101, I found myself literally sweating.

Professor Greenrayburst stood before the chalkboard and drew the number 36,028,797,018,963,968 bytes. "This number, just over thirty-six quadrillion, is the exact number of bytes of physical memory that the Divine Architects made for OSIRIS. They picked this number, thirty-two pebibytes, on the basis that they could not imagine any situation in which OSIRIS would require any more." She turned from the board to us.

"After all, purely mundane hard drives could be used for long-term storage of brain archives. Even though they had identified possible failure modes then, the Artificial Gods Project was already bankrupting entire governments. They could always upgrade OSIRIS later, so why worry about it now?" she shrugged, hands in the air.

"Like all of the mistakes of the Divine Architects, while seemingly sensible at the time, the makers of the EDENs were horribly, horribly wrong."

As I diligently took notes, I felt no small amount of cognitive dissonance. I had had numerous arguments with my adoptive parents over religion, which as my parents they had always been the winner. Yet, as the professor continued to blaspheme the Divine Architects, I wondered how deeply I had internalized their harsh voices.

My professor continued, "They assumed that OSIRIS would be a temporary storage of graves, perhaps for a week or shorter. They assumed that no user would gain priority over another except under strictly objective criteria. They assumed that no one would even want to remain a ghost. They assumed that future generations would not parcel up and sell its memory like land. They didn't even imagine revenants, or estates, or that we would change our own last names to keep OSIRIS functional when nothing else would. Most of all, they didn't imagine that after Gotterdammerung, no one would dare try to construct or upgrade an EDEN ever again. In short, they believed they not only made gods but were gods themselves."

Dissonance built, and the building dissonance became worry. I looked around the lecture hall. I saw a handsome young Spiral writing extensive notes. He glanced up and met my eyes.

I quickly looked away and tried to return to note-taking. I felt as if I was engaging in written blasphemy. But OSIRIS was not even a god I worshipped!

"The most terrible mistake of the Divine Architects was creating a scheduler that existed partially in userspace and partially in kernelspace. We have the worst of both worlds: a system whose errors we cannot fix and whose merits we have endlessly tampered with. Thank your god that the OSIRIS Wheel Group has since agreed to leave the scheduler as is, short an unimaginable catastrophe." She looked around the classroom. "How many of you here worship OSIRIS?"

Many hands went up. Neither mine nor the handsome Spiral did.

"Keep your hand raised if you had prayers answered by OSIRIS? Specific ones, not just in general."

A few hands awkwardly went down.

"Let me add one. Hear, OSIRIS, the prayer of your servant, a necromancer. By your almighty power, prevent this chalk stick from hitting the floor. Heed me, OSIRIS!"

She tossed her chalk stick. It spun a few times before slamming into the ground.

The class gasped, and I found my own lungs had drawn air. Then silence followed, as the air we had just breathed had left a vacuum behind.

"What you worship is your choice," the professor continued. "I'm not going to argue that you can't worship OSIRIS. It certainly has more power than most gods. But OSIRIS is only a computer made of exotic matter. We necromancers, and all mages, are not priests or hierophants.

We simply are those with shell access. If you can't handle that, you will regret trying to become a necromancer for your entire life, and every subsequent one, because I will teach you every dirty secret, every hack, every workaround, every last bug, quirk, and dysfunctional 'feature' that OSIRIS has. I will show you how to use OSIRIS as a tool in the same way you use your cell phone, except that your cell phone is less buggy, is regularly updated, and has far better UX. If this isn't what you want, get out now. Don't throw your existence away thinking you can ignore its limitations and know the truth about them at the same time. Yes, you?"

The Spiral had raised his hand. "If this is the truth about OSIRIS, why would anyone worship it?"

"Frankly, I don't know. I do know many good EDENist necromancers. But they know full well the only difference between their laptop and their god is that their laptop is cheaper."

A student stood up. "OSIRIS didn't—didn't really fail," she stammered. "You just didn't make the proper prayer!"

"OSIRIS has no mind," the Professor said. "It can't hear or understand us. There is no 'praying right'. The only commands OSIRIS responds to are found in the $PATH variable."

I could understand why my adoptive parents had been so adamant that I did not go to a modern school. Perhaps they had heard a sliver of the truth. That student looked unsure, then angry, then ran out. A few more followed her, not making eye contact.

"Is there anyone here who is unwilling to learn the truth? Does anyone want to repeat my experiment?"

No one raised a hand or spoke.

Except the handsome Spiral. "How on earth is this a secret?"

"It's the best kind of secret: a truth no one wants to believe."

I found my hand raised, with more confidence than I realized. "Professor, I want to know."

She regarded me with interest. "Good. I'll take it the rest of you are willing, too. We'll start by going over OSIRIS's architecture and all the other mistakes the Divine Architects made. And make no mistake, their creation, powerful as it is, is a very flawed one. And we have no option but to accept the flaws, or give up on eternal life."

December 6th, 1042 AGDR

I supposed if you didn't believe OSIRIS granted eternal life to begin with, the truth was more palatable. From what I had learned in those four years, I wondered how anyone could possibly be an EDENist. Thus, as I hurried to finish the study guide, as if by doing so I could complete the course before the next letter from the LLB, I decided to go full-throated.

1. In your own words, describe what OSIRIS is.

    OSIRIS is an Eternal Divine Exotic-matter Nexus with 32 PiB of physical memory and 32,768 logical cores. OSIRIS runs an ancient POSIX kernel called Linux, significantly modified to accommodate the number of cores and the grave scheduler. Like all EDENs, it can communicate with the physical world by manipulating the speed of light in specialized hardware. In all other respects, it is no more than any other computer.

2. How does OSIRIS store souls?

> It does not. OSIRIS instantiates a digital body called a ka that the soul will accept using a much simplified neural network and virtual limbs. OSIRIS cannot create, delete, or copy souls.

There. That would please them.

The rest of the study guide was about the rights of a medium. A full necromancer—as I was *supposed* to be—could do about anything with OSIRIS, even the most hazardous things: ripping, building graves, making revenants. A necrotech could do much less, but could still start seances and many other tasks. And a medium could only manage a seance that a necrotech started.

It galled me that for all my work, my degree was useless. But I would take any job that wasn't at the grinders.

December 8th, 1042 AGDR

"Mary, a word," Alexander said to me after class.

"Yes, sir?" I asked.

He motioned me to follow him into a small, cramped office. He held up my study guide. "This is very detailed. All correct, of course."

"Yes, sir. I was paying attention in class."

"We hadn't gotten to OSIRIS's architecture yet," he said. "In fact, I'd say this has more detail than I've seen in college papers on OSIRIS."

"Well…uh…"

"Did you have a relative in the industry?"

"My father was a necromanc—I mean, a post-mortem professional."

He waved it away. "We all slip up. But if you know this much, you could easily have gotten a degree."

"Yes. Err. Well..." I grasped the necklace and—glitch, I didn't care anymore. "I actually am a necromantic student, you see," I said.

He raised an eyebrow. "Then what are you doing here?"

"I couldn't get a job or a bond. But I might if I'm a medium. I mean—"

"You have student loans?"

"Yes, sir."

"You could have just said that!" he said. "The LLB is probably breathing down your neck right now, am I right?"

I nodded, hope spilling into me.

He pulled out a drawer and got out a certificate. "You don't need this class. I can't give you a necromancy license, but I can get you a certificate of completion. Anything to keep you out of servitude."

I had no words for a moment. "Thank—thank you, sir."

"Don't mention it. Would that I could do this for everyone who risked indenture."

He started filling out the form, and I didn't dare breathe, as if by doing so I would wake from this dream.

I watched the others in the library as I carefully copied the certificate. The League Labor Bureau was unlikely to be appeased by it, but there was a chance they would ease off for a moment. I would be multiple layers of humiliated if others knew how low I had stooped.

Then I paused in thought. If I had the choice, would I rather be a bakt yet a full necromancer?

Future reader, understand that bakts were not chattel. As a bakt, I would be permitted to rest one day off every week, to own property in my own name (even conceivably other bakts), to marry or not as I chose, to refuse consent to the most depraved orders, to receive Necrosecurity if I worked long enough, and even to vote. But the one thing I wouldn't be was free.

It didn't matter. No one had bought me, and anything was better than the grinders.

"Mary?"

I nearly jumped to see Seth standing behind me. "What's up?" I asked, after a moment.

"Oh. Didn't mean to scare you. SET got back to me, but I need to explain the results. Mind heading to my dorm?"

"Certainly," I said, and carefully stuffed the photocopies away.

The machinespeakers were unlike the rest of the student body, since to be a machinespeaker you had to have been a mage already in a past life. There wasn't a first life in sight as he let me into the dorms and through the mess that partying graduates had left behind.

"Here we go," he said, and showed me into his dorm room. It wasn't much better.

"What's up?" I asked.

"SET found several hundred results," he said. "Most of them involve a firm in trouble with the Necromancy Administration. Almost all of the rest are out of your price range—no offense."

"How far?" I asked.

"Millions of drachmae. I take it if you could get that kind of money, you wouldn't need to escape from student loans."

"Oh. Yeah." That was the irritating thing about Seth. He would leap to conclusions that were invariably correct. "What about those that are cheaper?"

"One is a necromancy firm where the owner is retiring. Two more are small necrotech businesses where the owners are about to self-euthanize. And SET found a mall in a small town that is looking for a new seance business to replace the old one."

"Just get me contact information," I said.

"Problem: Only the mall is an open advertisement. The rest are going to immediately assume you found out through SET. I am not going to let you get me in trouble for a favor."

I looked at him. Seth was the youngest machinespeaker I had ever met, having died in an accident early in his first life. He also had a crush on me, and I considered—

No.

No, I wouldn't use him that way. Not even if it meant going to the grinders.

"Give me the mall's information, and I'll see if I can figure out something," I told him.

"Certainly. But I was getting to something else: SET found a necromancy firm in the same region as the mall that is hiring. Not buying bakts, but hiring. Necrotechs only, but I thought I'd mention."

"Perfect," I said. "Thanks."

"You're quite welcome. And good luck."

December 9th, 1042 AGDR

I had no idea if the paperwork I held in my hand would hold up in court. Between my certificate, Alan's firm papers, and my sheer force of will, however, I was going to make it work.

I took the black granite steps to the local Court of the Tomb. The building seemed unduly sinister, as if those who entered did not leave alive. This was absurd, of course, only those who were already Dead would come out Dead. They extradited people in an entirely unrelated building, or so I'd heard.

I walked inside the door, unnerved. A machinespeaker by the scanning station waved a wand, typed a command, and then motioned me inside.

The lobby was crowded: A woman with a leg in a cast was crying, two businessmen in spotless black suits glared at each other, numerous necromancers and revenants in their all-black mechanical bodies were scattered about. I couldn't find anywhere to sit except in front of a revenant.

I had been told that the neural wiring to make a functioning face was too resource-intensive, so they all had masks with lenses for eyes. The one in front of me did not smile or frown, perhaps finding the situation of too little note to adjust his settings.

"Do you have a number?" he suddenly asked.

"Err, what?" I asked, startled.

"Go over there and get a number."

I got up and went to the other desk, where another revenant, this one a woman with a more curved mask, watched with no apparent emotion. "Name?" she asked.

"Mary Firebrightsky," I said.

"Purpose for being here?"

"I'm—"

"*GO GLITCH OUT!*" screamed someone by another desk.

The clerk there did not react at all, saying, “Calm down or leave.”

“Purpose for being here?” the revenant in front of me repeated.

“Like glitch I will, you brainless ghost!” The arguing beside me continued.

“Calm down or leave.”

“I’m here to, uh, get some papers filed,” I managed, doing my best to ignore what was happening.

“You don’t even have your empathy loaded, do you?” the fuming fat man demanded.

“The question is irrelevant. Calm down or—”

“Here you go,” the revenant in front of me said, handing me a ticket.

“I want to see you give a slizz, you—”

“Leave the building immediately,” said a new revenant, a massive police model. He grabbed the screaming man with a cuff-claw and began dragging him away. “Cease resisting.”

I sat down again and tried to ignore what was happening and that every other revenant was completely succeeding in ignoring what was happening.

I could explain how to make a revenant; I even knew the commands. But at that moment I could never imagine what it would take to let yourself be filed down into just enough digital neurons to control a physical body.

“New here?” the revenant across from me asked.

“Yes, sir.”

“Ignore the hysterics. Empathy is a net liability, when you think about it.”

“I see,” I said in what I hoped was a neutral voice.

“Now serving C-134 at Desk Four.”

The revenant got up and walked away.

I looked at my ticket. By my calculations, I would be there for hours. Please, True God, no more chaos.

There wasn't. In fact, when my number was called, the clerk examined my papers for all of a silent minute before taking my filing fee and stamping the papers with a stamp built into his arm. With his other arm, he slipped the documents into a scanner, then handed them back to me. "You're free to go," he said.

"Thanks," I said, and decided to get out as fast as possible.

December 10th, 1042 AGDR

I knew the LLB would not even deign to clean their metaphorical nose with my papers, but I hadn't defaulted yet. Next step, getting my OSIRIS account.

The nearest Necromancy Administration office was on the local Necroforce base. I was immediately glad that I had already been exposed to revenants in person because the massive war revenants with the gatling-barrel arms were even more terrifying.

The office was clearly marked, though. Clasping the strange necklace as if it actually reassured me—though somehow, it did—I stepped inside the office and immediately found where to take a number.

A half hour that stretched for ages later, I entered a cubicle. The clerk there, a bored woman in fatigues with the international necromancy symbol on her shoulders, looked at my paperwork. "What is this?"

"This is my registration paperwork for an OSIRIS account," I said calmly.

"Where's your oath to OSIRIS?" she said.

"I'm a conscientious objector," I said.

"And here it says that you're your own supervisor."

"I am," I said.

She raised an angry eyebrow. "What the glitch are you trying to pull?"

"It's a family-owned seance business," I said, trying not to let my anger show. "I can run it myself—"

"What?"

"I'm my own supervisor."

"But you're not a necromancer."

That stung, but I kept my calm. "I don't need to be one."

"Yes, you do."

"No, I don't!" I insisted. "Under the Code of Regulations of the Tomb—"

She sighed deliberately. "I have twenty more cases to review today. I don't have the time for this *nonsense*."

Please, True God, "I'll complain all the way to Lowest Court!"

"Go ahead. I have better things to do than argue with a first life—Sir!" The clerk stood up and saluted.

A thin, almost cadaverous man had stepped inside. "At ease."

She looked up with awe, and then I did likewise a moment later. I recognized him from the news: General James Westbrightsea, a member of the OSIRIS Wheel Group.

"What is the matter?" he asked calmly.

"I am trying to tell this young woman that she can't be her own supervisor. *And* she needs to swear her oath."

"And I'm saying I can!" I said, somehow managing not to stutter. "I own my own family seance business. There's an exception in the law. And I'm a conscientious objector! I don't *need* to swear the oath if I took the right course."

He raised a wispy eyebrow. "I'm curious how you would know the Law of the Tomb that well if you're just starting the business."

Thoughts rushed through my mind—prevarications? Lies? No, he could probably see through my lies. "I'm—this is complicated, sir," I managed. "But I'm actually a necromancy student, and this is the only way I could find a job."

"Then get one, you firstie!" the clerk snapped.

"Lieutenant, what is your name?" the general asked.

"Abigail Threedawnwhite, sir!"

"Lieutenant Threedawnwhite, when you became an officer, to what king or emperor did you swear your oath of service?"

"...No one, sir." Her eyes widened.

"Then what *did* you swear to?"

"I swore to support and defend the Tables of the Laws of the Living and the Dead against all enemies, sir!"

"Good. Now who are you to judge whether a given law should apply, if you don't think it should?"

"I...err...I shouldn't, sir." x "Correct. Now this young lady has, unless under a sanction from the Court of the Tomb, followed the law, if an obscure one. Do *your* job."

"Yes, sir!"

"And you, young lady?" he asked. "What's your name?"

"Mary Firebrightsky, sir," I said.

"I take it this is your first life?"

"Yes, sir."

"How long would you like it to last?"

"As long as possible, sir."

"Then be very careful with what you claim under oath. The League is in as bad a shape as it is because people don't say what they mean and mean what they say."

"Yes, sir," I said. My stomach was twisting, but he didn't seem hostile.

"I'm sure you have the rest of your business planned out. I don't intend on questioning it anymore. But either make your words true or stop talking."

"Yes, sir!" I said, instantly relieved.

"Get her signed up," the general ordered the lieutenant.

"Yes, sir!" she said.

He strode out.

I turned to see her practically piling up paperwork for me. "Just sign all of this, will you?"

I had imagined getting my OSIRIS account in all sorts of ways, but not where the officiant was practically thrusting pages in my face. I signed them with a fast, shaking hand, not even reading them.

It was by means of such inaction that we both made two serious mistakes.

I sat by my dorm's desk, exhausted but with a printout of the QR code to have tattooed on my hand. I would need either a terminal or more likely a metaphysical dongle, somehow, to actually connect to OSIRIS, but that could wait.

That day could have gone horribly, horribly worse than it did.

I took off my necklace, the strange image of a dead man on a "t" looking back at me. I hadn't managed to stuff too much Catholicism into my brain. In truth, the necklace had been just decor. I could recognize that this was the founder of the religion, a man named Jesus who was apparently a god...somehow?

But had he answered my prayer? General Westbrightsea was stationed in Newla, thousands of kilometers from the Steelriver Canton. What were the chances he was stopping by in a minor Necroforce base and passing by that very room when the argument started?

And he had seen right through me. He had a point: If I was going to claim a religious exemption, I should probably actually believe it.

I flipped through my paperwork one last time...

Wait, no.

No, no, no!

I had checked the wrong box.

Thus, I saw my first mistake. That nasty woman had been almost correct: I had the paperwork for a necrotech, not a necromancer *or* a certified medium.

What had I done? Did this make me a necrotech? Did I dare ask if it did? Should I just roll with it?

A knock at my door. Alan poked his head inside. "Alan!" I said. "I thought you were gone, already."

"I leave in an hour," he said. "But first, I wanted to give you this." He pulled out a black USB drive–no, it was colored fuglin. A metaphysical dongle! "I happened to buy two. I suppose I don't really need both, though."

"Thanks," I said, and took it from him.

Our hands touched.

We mutually yanked them away.

"Good luck," he said.

"Good luck," I said.

CHAPTER THREE

ALL IS VANITY

December 11th, 1042 AGDR

By the next morning, I had a plan.

It may have been a mistake, but I was overqualified to be a necrotech anyway. I had scoured through necroregs again all last night and saw that time as a necrotech counted for becoming a full necromancer. So all I needed to do was work three years as a necrotech, and then hire a necrolawyer to sort out my situation.

That is, if the Necromancy Administration didn't find out and sanction me first. Fines were the least bad outcome if they did—extradition to the Dead at worst.

But I had no time for such thoughts. I had almost escaped the grinders, just a little more work and they would be behind me permanently. And besides, I had things to do.

I theoretically knew how to set up an OSIRIS account, but my professors had glossed over the details, as theoretically my firm (or more accurately, my master) would have set them up for me. To set up pipes, register aliases, customize my shell, and organize my home directory would all, I knew, take time, trial, and error. But I was eager to get started.

I sat with my laptop on my desk, ceremonially aligned perfectly in the center. My heart beat heavy—I had never accessed OSIRIS before, only participated in simulated sessions. But first, a necessary but very unpleasant task.

I poured myself a cup of a viscous black liquid.

The official name of the liquid was the mortality limiter, and I had bought a brand called Alkahest. Even the best tasting brand—and Alkahest was one of the cheapest—tasted brackish, and if you didn't eat a meal with it, it would taste far worse. Having remembered the advice of my professors, I had eaten salami because if you ate a food you liked with it, you would no longer enjoy it afterwards.

The substance would keep you safe when running some of OSIRIS's more dangerous commands, as it would bind your soul to your present body. It was perhaps more important to your creditors. Dying with it in your body would keep you "alive", at least until help arrived, while keeping you in significant agony. Far too many necromancers would commit suicide after getting their degree, knowing that the Dead were absolved of the debts of the Living.

Thus, we were legally obligated to take it, as well as (in my case) pay for it. We called it irony poisoning. It certainly had tasted poisonous, when I had tried it in college.

I drank it down, or tried to, but I sputtered, then gagged. But I swallowed and forced myself to continue. My father hadn't used any mortality limiter, and that was why he was beyond even OSIRIS's power now.

Drink finished, I took a deep breath and, for a brief moment, considered if being a necromancer was worth having to drink that stuff. But it was. I'd get used to it, I told myself.

I opened up a terminal, took off my glove, and scanned the QR code on the back of my left hand for the first time.

```
$ necrochain unlock
Password:
```

```
$ ssh mary.firebrightsky@OSIRIS
Welcome to OSIRIS! [AGP/Linux]

   MOTD: "Remember, mortal, that this,
too, will pass."

[mary.firebrightsky@OSIRIS]$
```

I stared at the prompt, unmoving. I had done it. I had connected to OSIRIS.

```
[mary.firebrightsky@OSIRIS]$ echo
"Mary wuz here" > test.txt
[mary.firebrightsky@OSIRIS]$ cat
test.txt
Mary wuz here
```

I couldn't help but let a smile emerge on my face. Prof. Greenrayburst was right: OSIRIS really was just a fancy computer in the end, just like my laptop.

But enough games. It was extremely dangerous to mess around with a computer that had not been worshipped as a god without reason. I had things to do.

More of necromancy was cobbled together than anyone cared to admit, too much hackery with POSIX pipes, serial `nc` abuse, and an unfortunate number of decisions made when the most sophisticated terminal that anyone could rig together used vacuum tubes. Generations earlier had piled up rituals and secret ceremonies; none of them worked, the prof had reassured us, but to the outside world we might have still been using them. No necromancer wanted to think too much about how any of it managed to work at all. But every attempt to fix the system had, at best, failed.

I could only work with the system, in the end.

I started typing commands.

December 12th, 1042 AGDR

I stood on the train station of a small town called Whylin in the Steelriver canton. My coat was fuglin, with the international necromancy symbol of a skull over a disc on the shoulder pads. Anyone with OSIRIS access could conceivably be needed in an emergency, even a medium.

I had already scheduled my appointment with Iranarair Necromancy, the firm that was looking to hire a necrotech. After all, if I could get that job, I would have everything.

My rideshare didn't show. I checked my app: Oh, yeah, this was a small town.

Better call to tell them I would be late. I took a bench and dialed the number.

"Iranarair Necromancy, how may I help you?" asked the receptionist.

"I'm actually not a client. I'm the necrotech asking about the job. My rideshare didn't show."

"Oh, one moment!"

I waited.

"He wants to do the interview over the phone. Is that OK?"

"Yes!" I said. "Yes, it is!"

"One moment please."

Ring, ring.

"Is this Mary Firebrightsky?"

"Yes, sir."

"Ms. Firebrightsky, I'm sorry to hear about the rideshare. So tell me about yourself."

I told him my sob story: lost my mother before I was old enough to know her, orphaned after my father was killed in a necromancy accident, shuffled between foster parents as a ward, adopted by people I hated, then managed to snag the scholarships to enter college.

"I realize that you're looking for a job, but wouldn't you normally become a bakt?"

"No one would take me. I had perfect grades, but…"

"Ah. But you managed to become a necrotech?"

"Yes, sir."

"How?"

Oh, damn it! I didn't think this far ahead! "A series of increasingly bizarre misunderstandings," I said, trying not to let fear into my voice.

"That must be a large series."

"Yes and quite bizarre."

He laughed. "Let me put it this way: Necromancy is a dangerous business, and it's all about managing risks. How much risk would I be taking on if you, and—how on earth did you *accidentally* become a necrotech?"

"I filed the wrong paperwork, and no one noticed."

He sighed. "I'm afraid that makes it too much of a risk."

I felt like I had been stabbed. Of course, it was too good to be true that not only would I be a necrotech but a free woman, too. "Mr. Iranarairaralialar, wait."

"My, you can pronounce a Spiral's full name?"

"Yes, sir."

"As fascinating as that is, my answer is still no."

"Wait, let me ask another question."

"Fine. What?"

"Can you be my supervisor in an entirely separate necromancy firm?"

"How?"

"It's a family-run seance business."

"What?"

"It's kind of complicated, but I was supposed to be a certified medium, until the very bizarre events occurred."

"I can imagine." I heard a silence. "Let me suppose I risk a malpractice suit by agreeing to supervise an entirely separate business. What do *I* get out of it?"

"I'll refer all my clients that need a real necromancer to you."

I heard more silence.

"I won't let you down, sir!" I pleaded. "I had perfect grades."

"Will you need any financial support from me?"

"No, sir. I already have everything I need. The only difference is that if I'm a necrotech, I can offer more services. That's the only difference."

"I'd like to see a business plan before agreeing, but my answer is not 'no.' But that doesn't make it a 'yes.'"

Hope, precious hope! "Yes, sir!"

"Call a taxi next time, by the way. The rideshares in this town are about as high-quality as everything else."

That did not sound good.

Still, it wasn't a "no", I told myself. There was still hope.

Like when you had hoped you would get a bond, a dark part of me whispered.

I tried to push down the anxiety without success. I wasn't a worrier, but the last two weeks had sucked out every drop of confidence and hope I had and then some. I grasped the strange necklace out of new habit, and I once again found it reassuring.

I had better things to do than worry, I told myself. If I could just live up to that resolve.

December 15th, 1042 AGDR

Mr. Wesley Iranarair had seemingly warmed up to my proposal by the time I actually presented it. Perhaps it had been good luck that I hadn't read his spiral when I was talking to him. A Spiral's tattoo records his life, and his tattoo showed three grief marks cutting off the records of marriage and children. My big mouth would probably have said something idiotic in trying to get him to like me.

So far he had agreed with everything in my business plan, with only the occasional constructive advice, and the tension in my back began to unknot.

"One last thing," he said. "Do you know your OSIRIS username?"

"`mary.firebrightsky`, sir," I said.

"I suppose that should be obvious, but you never know these days." He got out an old terminal, scanned his tattoo, and typed away. Then frowned. "You said you were a necrotech? Insomuch as you are anything?"

"Yes, sir."

"Take a look." He turned the terminal to the side, and I walked around the desk to see it.

```
[wesley.irnrirrlilr@OSIRIS]$ groups
mary.firebrightsky
mary.firebrightsky osi seance
gravedigger morgue nt necros
```

"These are a *necromancer's* permissions."

"Uh…"

"Please show me your tattoo."

I pulled off my glove.

He looked at the dots underneath the QR code. "This is a necromancer's tattoo. Ms. Firebrightsky, what the glitch is going on?"

"Sir, please, I had no idea—"

"How on earth did you accidentally get a necromancer's SSH access?"

"Can I start from the beginning?"

He listened to my story in silence. "So let me get this straight: You met an *OWG* member in all of this?"

"Yes, sir."

"What day was this?"

"December 10th, sir."

He got out his cell phone and typed. I clasped my necklace so hard it hurt. "Hmm. OK, so Westbrightsea was there on the 9th." He sighed. "You are a walking timebomb of liability, young woman."

"I promise I won't do anything only a necromancer can do, sir!" I begged.

He sighed again. My stomach turned.

"I could ask them to—"

"The Necromancy Administration could not tell its ass from its elbow given a detailed visual guide. I'm not *surprised* this could happen, but the moment they discover this, you'll be in serious trouble."

"Sir," I said, taking a deep breath. "I have no other option. If I tell them, I'll be in serious trouble, too."

"And you couldn't get a bond?"

"No, sir."

"Why not?"

"I don't know," I said. "Maybe because I'm a first life. Maybe because I told them I wouldn't lie to a client or contact."

He looked me over. "One last question: How do you know how to read a spiral?"

"My boyfriend was a Spiral, sir."

"I see. I was simply asking if you had learned it all to please me."

"No, sir."

"This area is about 45% Spiral. Being able to read a spiral would be a great benefit." He thought about it. "I'll do it. But the moment I hear you use a necromancer-only command, even in an existential emergency, it's over. And you never told me the truth. I never learned it."

"I understand, sir," I said. I could barely keep from hugging him.

"Go ahead and find a storefront. When it's all ready, I can be a supervisor."

"Thank you, sir!"

"One last thing."

"Yes, sir?"

"I was also a first life once. I remember the desperation. I also remember doing stupid things because of it. So for the love of the True God, make your words true."

"Yes, sir."

I barely made it outside before I started crying from relief. Finally! I had made it. Just a few more steps, and I'd be safe from the grinders.

True God, grant that the Necromancy Administration doesn't start inspecting its metaphorical elbow.

December 16th, 1042 AGDR

Future reader, perhaps so much time has passed since this book was written that our divisions no longer make sense to you, as the divisions of the pre-Gotterdammerung world no longer make sense to us. The vast cultural chasm that existed between Spirals and Triglyphs, I realize, I have not explained so far.

After Gotterdammerung, the complex graphical interfaces for interacting with OSIRIS were slowly lost as machines broke and could not be repaired. The makeshift methods later developed were far cruder and, of particular note, no one knew how to rip people to avoid collisions. Should two rips use the same filename, one brain archive would overwrite the other.

Without any other ideas, several systems developed for ensuring that no people would have exactly the same name, thus preventing any collision. The vast majority in the League are either Triglyphs or Spirals, the others being too small to mention. The Triglyphs, like myself, have a last name made of three easily distinguishable characters, and it is forbidden that any two of the same last name share first names. The Spirals have complex last names that are added onto over generations, thus making the same guarantee.

The two naming schemes eventually developed into two distinct cultures, and eventually the rifts became violent. Spirals, often being the losers of nomenist violence, developed an insular tradition mixed with certain styles of EDENism. We Triglyphs aren't that interesting in comparison, but perhaps that's always how it is with a majority.

Thus, I was slightly leery to learn my new storefront was between a Spiral naming shrine and a Triglyph naming center. "Ninety-nine percent of the time, there's no difficulty," the mall's manager, John Rednightsand, told me. "The two owners know each other, and neither is a nomenist. Problem is sometimes their customers are. Promise you, though, there's almost never an incident."

"I understand," I said. Inwardly, I would not have complained if the Name Wars were reenacted every day outside my storefront, as long as I *had* a storefront.

John was equally pleased, it seemed. According to him, customers would come for their child's naming, stop by the previous tenant to contact a Dead relative or two, and then head by a restaurant to celebrate. Since the previous tenant's closure, traffic had dropped by 9%, and the owners of the mall weren't happy about it.

The mall's owners were so unhappy that I had managed to get six months of free rent. I hadn't been able to afford a lawyer to look at the contract, but so far, they had been bending over backward to get me here.

"Now, just between you and me, the owners are pretty extreme Eternalists. They care more about business than politics, but don't get into politics here, either, will you?"

"Of course not, sir," I said. "Who are the owners?"

"Pinkglowrapture Estates LLC. Don't talk about that, either."

The fact that the Dead, or rather, a very small percentage of the Dead, owned so much land and wealth was as political as politics got, so I nodded silently.

"I'm glad we're on the same page."

"When can I begin setting up?"

"As soon as you sign. But this is your first business, right?"

"Right," I said.

"A storefront takes longer to set up than you think. Since the previous business was the same, you can probably reuse it all, 'cept for the name, obviously. But there's plenty you'll have to do, in any case."

"I understand, sir," I said. "Let's get that contract signed."

February 2nd, 1043 AGDR

I waited nervously in the same way that the more you try to extrude calm and competency, the more your insecurities only grow louder. I did not consider myself particularly insecure, but the events of the last two months had ground me down.

The LLB hadn't sent the next threating letter. I assumed that they were placated…for the moment.

A guy sauntered into Firebrightsky Postmortem Services PLLC. Before I could even say "Hello" he had slapped down 100 drachmae in twenties on my desk.

"I want to contact someone," he said.

"…Yes, sir," I said, between excitement, fear, and the relief that my wait was finally over. "The name of the dec—"

"Gary Whitebluesnow."

Having two colors in your Triglyph was rare, beginning from back when the naming algorithm was less sophisticated. I was probably about to contact some really old ghost.

"Your name, sir?"

"Rick Sungloryred."

"One moment."

```
$ necrochain unlock
Password:
```

```
$ ssh OSIRIS
Welcome to OSIRIS! [AGP/Linux]

MOTD: "Remember, mortal, that this,
too, will pass."

Last login: Saturday Jan 31 09:35:16
[mary.firebrightsky@OSIRIS]$ osi ps |
grep gary.whitebluesnow
ae55b1b3 nforce:basic@1.0.1
gary.whitebluesnow
```

Curious, the decedent had a Necroforce grave? Retired, obviously. I couldn't remember what "basic" had, and this looked like an old version. But it almost certainly had realtime texting, or if not, I was about to look like a huge idiot.

Time to run commands that cost me money.

```
[mary.firebrightsky@OSIRIS]$ osi bill
start --max 50.0
Billing fbspm [10245]
[mary.firebrightsky@OSIRIS]$ osi
seance -j --free --ipc mary.seance.ipc
--attach --speed realtime --max-time
3600 gary.whitebluesnow --client-name
"Rick Sungloryred"
```

I pointed to a misfit of a machine that looked like a keyboard attached to a printer: the text seance device. "You just type on this, and your words will be sent to him," I said. "From his perspective—"

"Yeah, yeah, I've done this a bunch of times, girl."

Great. Now I would be waiting with *him* until OSIRIS's scheduler deigned to find a slot for realtime communication. Metaphorically speaking, of course, OSIRIS's scheduler was only an algorithm, as much as its action resembled the cantankerous old god that people believed in.

"Thank you," I blurted, nervous.

We waited awkwardly.

```
[00:00:00] Seance active
>>>
```

One of the many reasons you had to have a necromancer, a necrotech, or even a certified medium at the ready was that from the average decedent's perspective, time had passed a thousand times slower since the previous seance. The process could be horribly disorienting for the decedent, so a post-mortem professional was vital in establishing the situation.

I typed as fast as I could. Every second counted.

```
>>> Hello, Gary Whitebluesnow. I'm
Mary Firebrightsky, a necrotech
working for Firebrightsky Post-Mortem
Services PLLC. You're currently in a
text seance with Rick Sungloryred.

GARY: Not you again.
```

Oh, no. I prayed to the True God to steady my nerves in what I immediately and correctly discerned to be a baptism by fire. The text seance device began groaning as it spat out paper.

The guy took a seat.

```
RICK: I need money.
GARY: Get it yourself you deadbeat.
RICK: Ain't no jobs left.
GARY: Not my problem. Just get off
your ass and do something PRODUCTIVE
with your time.
RICK: OK, ghost.
GARY: OK, bio.
GARY: Anyway, you should be ashamed.
You won't get a centidrachma more from
me.
RICK: You can go glitch out then.
```

```
RICK: There's a lot more Vivites than
you think.
GARY: Sure, when you control the
Parliament of the Dead, I'll give a
glitch.
RICK: Maybe one day we WILL.
GARY: How dare you!
```

I looked at the wall clock. He had paid for an hour. Meanwhile, he was typing his replies harder and harder, and while I didn't think he could break the text seance device, he might knock it off the table. As the discussion ranged from politics to family drama to politics to insults to politics, I found myself eagerly longing for the end of the session.

What felt like an agony later, I typed, trying not to let my eagerness show.

```
>>> Sirs, your time will expire in
five minutes.
```

Without another word, he slapped down another hundred in twenties.

I couldn't ethically turn him down.

```
>>> /extend 3600
>>> Sirs, your time is extended.
GARY: Oh, so you can afford to
irritate me, but you want to waste
MORE of my money.
RICK: You aren't doing anything with
it you glitchhead.
GARY: Shut the glitch up.
```

I started wondering if this *was* the career I wanted after all.

```
GARY: I'm sick of this. Bye!
[01:11:42] Seance ended by contact.
```

"Hey, can you do a force wake?" the guy asks.

"No, sir, I am a necrotech." That and the legal liability for a non-emergency force wake could be massive.

"Yeah, figured," the guy said and stomped out.

"Sir!" I called, but he was long gone.

I typed the finishing commands.

```
[mary.firebrightsky@OSIRIS]$ osi bill
stop
Estimated bill: 50.1 drachmae.
Thank you for using OSIRIS.
[mary.firebrightsky@OSIRIS]$ logout
```

I looked at the pile of bills on my counter, the reams of paper that I would have to shred since the client hadn't taken them—I would need a shredder, I realized—and the receipt that was printing. Not only had I survived, but I was 100 drachmae richer, 150 if the guy never came back for a refund.

I could do this.

And if I did it enough, I could be free. I could even get my necromancer's license and have everything I wanted.

I sat back and relaxed. Life wasn't so bad after all.

And maybe I was right in a way I would understand later, but at that moment, I understood nothing at all.

CHAPTER FOUR

A WORD WAS REVEALED

April 13th, 1043 AGDR

Blissful ignorance ended five minutes after the most routine case of necromancy.

Necromancy was just becoming routine. Now that I had been doing it for months, I realized how little college trained me for it. Most of the arcana I was forced to memorize found little use in practice, when my clients had simply the usual desires and common obstacles to them. My diploma still hung prominently on one of the walls, beside the necrotech license. I had decided the more I considered myself a necrotech, the less likely someone—a wise client, an inspector, or the revenant of some large estate would realize the mess I was in.

My situation was ridiculous, but I consoled myself that it was temporary. In less than three years the farce would be replaced by fact, when I could finally me be a true necromancer, and not whatever I was hypothetically supposed to be called.

For almost all my clients, the difference was negligible, any difficulties assuaged by the more important criterion that I charged far less than a "real" necromancer. So there I sat in my storefront in the decaying mall, with my laptop and the metaphysical dongle hanging off the side of the table, the text seance device plugged in on the other side, a box of tissues, and a somber expression on my face.

The young Spiral paused, glanced inside, saw me, blanched, then opened the door, pulling a small girl in with her.

"Hello," she said. Then burst into tears.

"Hello," I said. "How can I help you?" One of the few arcana I found immediately of practical use was a word of advice given on my first day of classes: never smile. The average client has lost a loved one, or worse, and cannot handle a smiling necromancer. I have a dour deposition to begin with, so I simply maintained my natural expression.

As she continued to cry, I read her spiral. Her short last name was Halaralix, and she was twenty-five years old. One grief notch, still red-fresh, cut off a marriage mark. Her little girl, with her, was too young to have a tattoo, unless she wasn't a Spiral. But I didn't see a foreign marriage mark on her mother, so presumably the decedent was also a Spiral.

"Are you Mrs. Halaralix?" I asked.

She looked up, in clear shock that a Triglyph could both read and pronounce her name correctly. "…Yes."

"What can I do for you?"

"Ms. Firebrightsky," Mrs. Halaralix said, looking away from me.

"Please, call me Mary," I said gravely.

"Mary. I need to talk to my husband. Michael Halaralixirojarjair. I can write his name."

"Thank you," I said. I didn't need it, but I would let her help me. "Your names?"

"Gloria Halaralix. And this is Amanda."

"How long would you like to talk?"

She stared, as if this final indignity was one straw too many. "How long?"

"Have you ever contacted a decedent before?"

She shook her head. "My mom would talk to my grandma, but I never…paid…"

"I charge 100 drachmae an hour," I said. "OSIRIS also charges for realtime, but if you talk less than six minutes a month, it's paid for under the OSIRIS Access Act."

She stared at me wordlessly.

"Pay me what you can," I said. "I'll get you as long as I can to talk to your loved one."

"I'd…I'd talk for ten minutes," she said, and reached in her purse for bills, which she counted on to my desk. 20 drachmae. "Is this enough?"

"I'll try to connect you for twelve realtime minutes. All right?"

She nodded, her face covered with gratitude, as if billing by the tenth of an hour was an act of mercy. "Thank you so much."

"Thank you, ma'am," I said, and slipped them down into the one-way money deposit box. I hadn't been violently robbed, but I had so far been pickpocketed twice.

One of the most absurd parts of this farce was that I could not stay logged into OSIRIS. Only a true necromancer could. But to add absurdity to absurdity, it reassured my clients greatly when I pulled my left glove, and scanned the QR code with the metaphysical dongle, and started typing in a terminal window. The little girl watched with wide eyes.

```
$ necrochain unlock
Password:
$ ssh OSIRIS
Welcome to OSIRIS! [AGP/Linux]
```

```
MOTD: "Remember, mortal, that this,
too will pass."

Last login: Sun Apr 12 11:35:16 3271
[mary.firebrightsky@OSIRIS]$ osi ps |
grep michael.hlrlixirojrjir
d33f9bb1 lwk:essential@2.1.1
michael.hlrlixirojrjir
[mary.firebrightsky@OSIRIS]$
```

Good, there at least was a grave. Never trust a client about the state of their decedent. I'd had to turn down several because they had come to me before their loved one's ka had been made. I knew how to do that, of course, and I hated turning them away, knowing I could help them, but not legally.

It looked like the Halaralixes had bought Lightwindknown and Lightwindknown's cheapest offering, a ten centimeter VR cube. The bottom face had a keyboard that the one invisible hand could type on. One face had a text screen, and the opposite face had a camera attached to one of the eyes. Communication was only possible through text, obviously; the ka wouldn't even have the neural tissue for sound even loaded.

I pointed to the text seance device. "You just type on this, and your words will be sent to him," I said. "From his perspective, he'll see your words appear on a screen, and whatever he types will come back. It'll print the transcript automatically, which you are welcome to keep with you."

"How can Daddy read it if it's here?" the little girl asked.

"It's complicated," I told her in a reassuring voice. "But OSIRIS is designed to connect people. Now hold on."

```
[mary.firebrightsky@OSIRIS]$ osi bill
start --max 10.0
```

```
Billing fbspm [10245]

[mary.firebrightsky@OSIRIS]$ osi
seance -j --free --ipc mary.seance.ipc
--attach --max-time 720 --speed
realtime michael.hlrlixirojrjir --
client-name "Gloria Halaralix"
Waiting for OSIRIS...
```

"This may take some time," I said.

She looked at me. "When my mom contacted her mom…"

"OSIRIS is very busy," I said. In fact, it seemed OSIRIS had gotten even more unstable over the last month, but what could I do? "We have to wait until a slot is available. I promise you, you won't be charged until OSIRIS wakes him."

"When will that happen?" the little girl asked.

"I don't know. No human does."

"Does OSIRIS know? Can we ask him?"

No, and no. But before I could get dragged further into the weeds, Mrs. Halaralix interrupted "Quiet, we need to pray for OSIRIS's blessing."

I held my reaction as they sung a traditional prayer. It made no difference, but I wouldn't take what they needed from them. When they finished, I asked "How are you feeling?"

"It's been so hard…"

My professors had advised not making small talk, but I found in practice it was better to let the client talk to himself by proxy. Like lawyers and accountants, even the most important post-mortem professionals inevitably become on occasion vastly overpaid therapists.

So I listened to her story, and offered her tissues when necessary, placing my hand on hers when she needed it. They had been struggling to make ends meet before Mr. Halaralix had been killed by a falling piece of machinery at work. She went on a lengthy ramble about how the workplace had been run by a careless nomenist Triglyph bastard (seemingly forgetting my last name). She was trying to get NAEDA (Necromantic Assistance for Early Deaths and Accidents) to pay for a better grave. She was halfway through a sub-rant about the nasty revenant who ran the Necrosecurity office when the seance machine chimed. I looked to my terminal.

```
[00:00:00] Seance active
```

I had it down pat, now.

```
>>> Hello, Michael Halaralix. I'm Mary
Firebrightsky, a necrotech working for
Firebrightsky Post-Mortem Services.
You're currently in a text seance with
your wife and daughter.

MICHAEL: What happened?

>>> I'll let your wife talk about it.
```

"Start typing," I said. "The clock is ticking."

```
GLORIA: Michael! I'm sorry we couldn't
get you anything better. This is as
much as we could afford.

MICHAEL: Calm down, honey, it's
freaky, but I'm managing. How is
Amanda?
```

"Here you go," Mrs. Halaralix said, lifting her daughter up.

```
GLORIA: Hi Dad!!! R U OK?

MICHAEL: I'm doing well, as much as I
can. Ms. Firebrightsky, is there
something wrong with my grave?
```

The other main reason why post-mortem professionals were necessary: Tech Support. But much of the time there was nothing we could do, if it was even a "bug."

```
>>> If you only have one eye and one
hand, that's to be expected.

MICHAEL: Great.
```

Mrs. Halaralix typed.

```
GLORIA: This was the best we could
afford. Not without selling I mean we
couldn't get anything more.

MICHAEL: How long will I be in here?

GLORIA: I don't know.
```

"Mary?" she asked me.

```
>>> I can't make a prediction like
that without more detail. Generally,
though, it'll be decades.

MICHAEL: Figured.
```

She looked up from the device to meet my eyes with fury. "Decades!?" she screamed at me.

"Ma'am, I can consult, but right now time is passing."

She quickly returned to the device.

```
GLORIA: I'm trying to find a job, but
we're managing so far. I don't know
who will take care of Amanda.

MICHAEL: You thought about servitude,
I'm sure.
I saw by the hard expression on her
face that she had.
GLORIA: I don't want our daughter to
be a ward.
```

```
MICHAEL: I don't either. But make sure
she eats well.
```

"What's a ward?" the girl asked.

"Quiet, honey."

```
GLORIA: I'll do whatever it takes.
Just wait.

MICHAEL: Considering my circumstances,
I
```

The text stopped, and a minute passed in silence. She turned to me, with pain. "What's happened?"

```
>>> /speed
[05:07:34] 150ms
```

"Ma'am," I said. "OSIRIS is—" I cut myself off before I said the word 'lagging'. "The grave is not running at realtime because OSIRIS is busy. Think what you have to say and say it as quickly as possible.

"But we paid for twelve minutes!"

"I can't control OSIRIS," I said.

Anger, then fear struck her face. "OSIRIS…OSIRIS's will be done."

```
MICHAEL: think you'll have to make
that decision you

MICHAEL: r self.

GLORIA: Mike, I love you, and right
now OSIRIS is angry at us. Please,
we'll figure it out.
[00:12:00] Seance ended
[mary.firebrightsky@OSIRIS]$
```

She dug in her purse. "I want more time."

"I'm sorry, but—"

Failing to find cash, she pulled out a check. "Who do I make it out to?"

"Ma'am, there is *nothing* I can do."

"What?"

"OSIRIS is always at maximum capacity. It slowed your husband's grave to speed up someone else's grave. That other person may also have lost a loved one, and may have equally little time. I'm sorry. I can't fix this system."

She looked me up and down. "If it's OSIRIS's will…"

"I want Daddy!" the girl said.

"Amanda, be quiet."

"No! I want Daddy!"

"I'll still be here in a month," I said. "And so will your husband. We can try again, then."

The sorrowful look on her face almost broke me. Then, as if remembering my offer to consult, asked "Will it really be decades?"

How much could I tell her?

January 5th, 1038 AGDR

Four years ago, the more of the truth I had learned, the more I wanted to know.

"We all know the story of Gotterdammerung, or so we're told," Professor Greenrayburst said. "The Divine Architects made gods, and then the gods grew angry at human iniquity, and destroyed each other and the world.

"The truth is more complicated."

"The Divine Architects made RA first, an EDEN dedicated to making more EDENs. They subsequently made sixteen more. Of them, OSIRIS was dedicated to storing the kas of the Dead, and MA-AT was designed to reincarnate them as fast as possible, Between them, almost no one's existence was ever ended. With THOTH providing unlimited energy and KHONSU transport all over the world, humanity lived in paradise.

"But the RA Wheel Group had gotten more power and wealth than they could ever imagine, and became jealous of keeping it. Poorer countries demanded they construct additional EDENs, for this paradise was not equally distributed. Nineteen additional EDENs were planned. Some, such as ANUBIS, a backup copy of OSIRIS, were partially completed before the end.

"However, the RA Wheel Group clashed with the Divine Architects over little more than money, but when the rift grew, it grew and grew. The Divine Architects decided to continue making the additional EDENs without RA's assistance, which the RA Wheel Group saw as a threat. An accident with a particle accelerator damaging RA lead to the outbreak of Gotterdammerung, the most devastating war that the Earth has ever seen.

"When the EDENs were turned on each other, several were damaged beyond repair. Only four survived: OSIRIS, THOTH, HORUS, and MA-AT, which was badly damaged. The remains of the others were combined into SET, before the remains of technological civilization collapsed.

"One thousand and thirty eight years later, we are still paying the price of the RA Wheel Group's greed." She pointed at a student. "How much does a reincarnation cost?"

"Several hundred thousand, up to a million drachmae," he said.

"Why?"

He sputtered. I raised my hand.

"Yes, you?"

I had already heard the other side of the story from my new roommate Amy. "Because only a fraction of MA-AT's subsystems for reincarnation survived Gotterdammerung."

"Yes, exactly," the professor said. "There is no magic or fickle gods behind it. The brute economic fact is that there are too many ghosts who want to reincarnate and too little of MA-AT's systems to supply the demand. Furthermore, due to losses in bioslurry cycle, we are running low on bioslurry, too. As the world's population has grown, and with it, the population of the Dead, the price of reincarnation has skyrocketed.

"I'm not going to get into politics, but this is where the Eternalists and the Vivites broke apart. One party wants widespread population control before a crisis is reached. The other says the present population should decide what to do. Which one is right? I don't know, but that's your job as an Athanasian citizen to decide."

April 13th, 1043 AGDR

I didn't want to ruin an EDENist's already miserable day by dropping the bombshell. So I said "MA-AT is at full capacity. There's several government programs that would allow you to reincarnate your husband, but realistically, you'll have to pay anywhere from five hundred thousand to a million drachmae."

"I…don't have that kind of money," she said.

"You may not have it now, but there's a way to get it," I said.

She looked strained, as if unable to dare to hope.

The most critical question, and most common question, a necromancer receives is "When?" When can I talk to him again? When can he talk to me? When can we afford a reincarnation? Or a revenancy? Or full-time activity?

In truth, there was a very simple non-necromantic answer to these questions. It is called the compounding interest formula, and it looks like this:

```
A = P(1 + r/n)^(nt)
```

I had cards printed out with the formula on hand, one of which I handed one to her.

"What's this?" she asked. "I'm not good with math."

"What I want you to understand is that it's *all* math," I said. "By investing your money in index funds and eternal securities, it will grow over time, until your husband is free."

"I see," she said, flipping over the card to a diagram of an exponential curve. "What's this?"

"That's a visual representation. Adding a small amount of money early makes a huge difference in the end. The more money you spend on fancier graves or seances, the less money you can contribute to his reincarnation."

"…OK," she said quietly.

"I'm not here to tell you what you want. You want what you want. I'm telling you the price."

"I want a card, too!" Amanda said. I handed her one.

"How much would a better grave cost?"

"My supervisor, Wesley Iranarair, can make your husband a grave big enough to walk in for 15,000 drachmae," I said.

"I don't have that kind of money," she said, the exhaustion in her voice showing.

"Then what your best option is to invest what you can," I said. "The Necromancy Administration has free classes on what kind of investments are wise." I hated that I was actually suggesting the Necromancy Administration would help, but I hated seeing her suffer, more.

"And...if I were to...have an influx of money..." she said, not looking at me.

"Then you could bring the time down significantly. Or you could afford a much nicer grave, maybe one with furniture and an entertainment wall."

"...All right," she said, almost a whisper. "I'll...look into my options."

"I'll be here," I said, and handed her Mr. Iranarair's business card.

"...I'll be back." She scooped up the paper transcript and stuffed it in her purse. "Thank you so much." She hurried the child out.

"If I give up my allowance, will Daddy come back?" Amanda asked.

I almost lost it at that, but controlled myself. The moment they were out of eyeshot I got up, flipped the OPEN sign to CLOSED, and sat down, breathing deeply.

I had become used to this, being the ultimately helpless intermediary in hundreds of different tragedies, spaced in strict six minute intervals as billed. A necromancer was not to pry, but I learned the most horrible details as parents contacted children, children parents, lovers each other, business partners haggled, petty estates threatened each other and all the other sundry reasons why the Living sought congress with the Dead. Rarely did the Dead seek the Living—they usually were too poor to hire even a necrotech.

I could bear anything now, except for the grief of children.

I checked my laptop. I was still logged in. Better change that.

```
[mary.firebrightsky@OSIRIS]$ osi bill
stop
Estimated bill: 10.01 drachmae.
Thank you for using OSIRIS.
[mary.firebrightsky@OSIRIS]$
```

I moved to press CTRL-D to log out, but I paused for a moment, just one, that changed my whole life.

Wasn't that odd of OSIRIS? The EDEN was notoriously obtuse, but the Parliament of the Dead had moved heaven and earth to make sure every one of the Dead would have six free minutes of realtime. But we didn't get all six.

It wasn't a *guarantee*, but it was certainly odd that it was broken, nonetheless.

You know, OSIRIS was still a computer, at the end of the day. Why not just *look*?

And so I typed the command that changed everything.

CHAPTER FIVE

THE LAMB OF GOD

April 19th, 1043 AGDR

In the days that followed, I threw myself into anything else I could that would distract me. I ended up, for lack of other reading, studying my alleged new "faith."

I felt I was missing something fundamental about Catholicism because the more I studied it, the more questions I had. I was still unclear on the number of gods.

I eventually stumbled on a list of precepts. One of which was to go to Mass on Sunday. So I found a local Catholic temple and learned the times of their Sunday Masses.

I was not even sure what a Mass was, but the catechism I had purchased talked about it all the time.

I could not find a dress code online, except for people bickering about immodest clothing. I *did* know that wearing fuglin would make a difference in an existential emergency. So I wore my dress clothing, the necklace, and an expression that tried to hide my true dread.

What would they make of me? Would they freak? Would they tell immediately I was a fake? I knew what *not* to do, which was to use the holy water or receive communion. I was not sure what communion was, but it seemed as if it would be obvious when I went there.

I stepped up the cracked steps. Young families and old couples flooded in with me. No one seemed to notice my fuglin, for which I was secretly relieved.

Beyond the vestibule there was a vast room like a lecture hall with giant wooden benches instead of seats and desks. The walls were decorated with tinted glass, depicting symbols that doubtlessly had deep meaning to the proper observer, but I was not she. Carved reliefs on the walls depicted another story. Around me were painted wooden statues, and above the altar was another gruesome statue of Jesus.

Act natural, I told myself. I found a seat, hoping I hadn't taken one reserved for another, and found myself quickly surrounded. I relaxed at the squall of babies. Hearing the cries of the little did me good.

An older lady went up to a podium. "Good morning."

"Good morning," they all said.

"We welcome all parishioners and guests to this Eucharistic celebration as we joyfully celebrate the Second Sunday of Easter, the Sunday of Divine Mercy." I supposed I was a guest, and so far, I had not felt unwelcome. "You can find today's readings on page thirty-seven in your pew missal." What? "Together, let us pray the Serra prayer for vocations, found on the inside back cover…"

I had still not found whatever the pew missal was, let alone its inside back cover, when the prayer, whatever it was, had apparently concluded.

"…Please join in singing our opening hymn, 'Ye Sons and Daughters,' found in our worship aid."

They all stood, so I joined them. A strange brassy instrument played, and they all joined the beautiful, haunting melody. I had never heard music like it, nor such words, nor seen a whole room so filled singing out.

A woman next to me saw my tears and showed me her book. I sang along, quickly grasping the tune. Men, even children, in ornate white robes walked down the center aisle. One bore a cross, another swung a burning golden ball of incense, another held up a book whose cover was inlaid gold.

"In the name of the Father, and the Son, and the Holy Spirit."

I tried to follow along, longing, *knowing*, I had found something of infinite value. I had never been so moved before, so happy. As we sang out another song, I sang every word.

I cried through the rest of the Mass, in shock that I knew I was home. Surely this feeling was just the power of suggestion. I had chosen this. But why did it feel so real? I knew it was!

"Behold the Lamb of God," the head priest proclaimed, holding up a strange cracker and a golden cup. I did not know what I was seeing, but I could not doubt it was the Lamb of God any more than that the sun shone outside.

After it was over, I stayed behind as the others flowed out. I did not want this to end, whatever it was, but the priest had said the Mass was over.

"Hello! I take it you're new here?" the woman who showed me the book asked. We had shaken hands at some point for no reason I could discern, but it had felt right.

"Yes. Yes, I am. My name is Mary Firebrightsky."

"My name is Amanda Lightwindknown."

"Are you related to the necromancy firm?" I blurted out.

"Well, I believe they're ancestors of mine. I take it you're a necromancer?"

I was torn between saying that I, as a "Catholic" preferred to use "post-mortem professional", but also—as neither a true Catholic nor a true necromancer—I was multiple levels of a fraud. "Erm, yes," I managed.

"Hello there," the head priest said, coming up to me with an outstretched hand. "Father George Windsightglory."

"Mary Firebrightsky," I said, shaking his hand. "Could I talk to you after this?"

"Right after Mass isn't good, but perhaps this Tuesday?"

"After work, certainly," I said, relieved.

April 21th, 1043 AGDR

The next day and a half progressed painfully, but I came to the head priest's cluttered office next door, not without apprehension. *Was* it just the power of suggestion? Yet my memories remained clear, as if I had been born for that moment.

"Coffee?" Fr. Windsightglory offered as he led me to a comfortable chair. He wore different robes than at Mass, these all black with a white collar. Not fuglin, but black.

"Water is fine, thanks," I said.

"I'll be back in a moment."

I looked around at the room, covered with religious symbols and paintings. Rather than lost, I felt at home, even though I could not recognize most of them. A friend and fellow ward had told me she experienced a similar feeling on meeting her birth family again, an experience I wished I could have had.

The priest came back with a cup of water. "Your name is Mary Firebrightsky, yes?"

"Yes, sir," I said.

"I take it you're a necromancer."

I shook my head. "I wish. My situation is complicated."

He waited with a raised eyebrow.

I sipped from the water. "I'm neither a real necromancer nor a real Catholic," I told him. "Nearly every mage becomes indentured after college to pay for one student loan or credit. But no one wanted me. I'm…I'm a first life."

"There's nothing wrong with that. Many of us priests are."

"You are?" I asked.

"We are prohibited from using OSIRIS, no offense."

I spat out my water. "I…see."

"OSIRIS won't last forever. The 'Eternal' and 'Divine' in Eternal Divine Exotic-matter Nexus are blasphemous misnomers."

"I…I know," I said. "So…My situation is complicated. Without either a job or a bond, I can't repay my student loans and RENEW credit. And so I would end up as a bakt at the corpsegrinders, most likely."

"I see. But you are evidentially wearing fuglin."

"I became a necrotech…sort of," I admitted. "I decided to go into business on my own, but I couldn't because—it's complicated. I found there's an exception for family-run seance businesses, and there's an exception *there* if you have a religion. So I found religion."

He looked at me. "Am I to understand that you became Catholic for a *loophole*?"

"Well, *pretended* to be," I said. "Except now I've gone to a Mass, and…I'm serious about it." The words felt strange on my tongue. "I'm kind of freaked out about all of this."

He smiled. "God will humble himself, no matter how low, no matter how bizarre, to win over a soul. And here you are!"

"You don't call him the True God?"

"It's not our tradition. And we don't call the EDENs gods at all."

"I don't either," I said. And paused.

He waited.

I paused longer.

"Mary, are you all right?"

"It's a necromancy thing," I said. "I don't know if I could explain it to a mundane."

"It seems it really bothers you, though."

"I can try to explain. Don't tell a soul!"

"I promise. Your secret is safe with me."

"It's not *my* secret…" Where to begin? "Let me tell you about the biggest issue in necromancy…"

January 7th, 1038 AGDR

I had relaxed days into my first semester, not in the least because I had somehow already gained a boyfriend.

"Necromancy is more complicated than it looks," Professor Greenrayburst said, chalking up a diagram. "The death cycle, especially."

"A necromancer begins by inserting the ripping needles into the decedent's body in the proper places. You will learn to do this in the dark under pressure, as you will only have ten minutes from the moment of death before irreversible brain damage occurs. The needles, when the `osrip` command is invoked, will pulse the dying or dead body with an electric frequency OSIRIS recognizes. When it does, it will perform a very gory destructive read of the decedent's brain, creating a brain archive or ba." She continued, "The clock, however, has only been extended. A ba will not maintain the soul. Within the next forty-eight to seventy-two hours, a necromancer must use the ba to create a kinetic avatar, that is, a digital body capable of motion. The ka, placed inside a virtual reality environment we call a grave, will keep the soul from dissipating."

I wrote notes, listening in interest.

"Without the ba, the ka cannot be created," she continued. "Without the ka, the ba is only zeroes and ones. Here, however, we leave necromancy and enter politics."

I could see Alan, beside me, perk up a little. He knew so much about politics that he could talk my ear off, and he could make it interesting enough that I was willing to sacrifice my ear.

"A ba may be stored on a mundane hard drive in a standard graveyard datacenter. The ba need not even be accessed unless the ka needs upgraded or the whole ghost reincarnated. With the construction of the Necropolis in 850 with its exabytes of encrypted RAIDs, the storage of bas is no longer a meaningful issue in necromancy." She considered her next words. "Kas, however, must be kept in RAM. With the absolute smallest possible functioning ka in the most efficient possible mass graves, OSIRIS can store around ten billion kas. Such a microka would be incapable of conscious thought, or even dreaming, and therefore unacceptable to the vast majority of the Athanasian populace. If we used box graves at fifty megabytes, the minimum standard programs such as NAEDA will pay for, we would be able to store around six hundred million kas. Our real capacity is far, far lower, very simply because estates consume far more RAM on the order of gigabytes per ghost." I started working out the math, but I knew she knew what she was talking about.

"The Vivites hold that graves should be on the smaller side, and ghosts reincarnated as fast as possible to maximize throughput. The Eternalists say that a bigger grave is no different than a bigger house, and RAM pricing should be based on the free market. I won't say which one is right. But both sides, to be blunt, want to have their cake and eat it. Yes, Charles?"

"Why can't we add more RAM?" he asked.

"I don't know. Why can't we?"

"We don't have a particle accelerator that could do it?" he suggested.

"Close enough," the prof said approvingly. "OSIRIS, like all EDENs, is made out of exotic matter in the center of the Earth's core; we could not add more physical RAM except by constructing a massive particle accelerator. But such an accelerator could also damage or hack any EDEN. They are simply too dangerous to make. But why can't we connect mundane RAM, like we connect mundane hard drives?" She paused. "Yes, Alan?"

"OSIRIS itself is nigh-indestructible, but a mundane RAM chip could fail," Alan said.

"That is precisely why. A physical chip could be damaged, hacked, or simply wear out. That is not, however, a reason not to at least try.

"Most computers use hard drive space to expand RAM in a technique called swap. The OSIRIS Wheel Group experimented with using a portion of the Necropolis's RAIDs as a swap device to increase memory. However, this memory is not truly RAM. OSIRIS must swap data in and out of the hard drive in order to use it. This puts a load on its processors, which would cause all graves to slow down, if not stutter or even, unthinkably, freeze long enough that souls reject their kas. During their experimentation, they saw the deadly glitch rate increase unacceptably.

"Similarly, whoever controlled the swap device could potentially hack OSIRIS by manipulating pages of privileged or even kernel memory that had been written to swap. The danger is unthinkable.

"They ultimately decided it was far too risky and swore to never activate swap except after a unanimous decision in an emergency. Yes, Mary?"

"What happens if OSIRIS runs out of RAM altogether?" I asked.

"A good question. We don't know for sure. However, OSIRIS is simply a computer in the end. A subsystem called the OOM Killer in its ancient Linux kernel will simply find the process using the most RAM and kill it. That would lead to a broken grave at best, the ending of a ghost at worst.

"The worst possible scenario is if OSIRIS *still* couldn't find enough RAM, even after killing graves. Then it would panic, and every ghost within would be lost forever."

April 21st, 1043 AGDR

"I'm not sure if I follow completely, but I understand OSIRIS has finite resources. But so what? No computer *can* grant eternal life, EDEN or not," Fr. Windsightglory told me.

"It's true," I said. "If someone built a particle accelerator and knew what he was doing, he could destroy OSIRIS and annihilate everyone in it."

"Well, not truly annihilate. The human soul is immortal."

"I...suppose it is," I said. It made sense if he said it.

"But was that the secret?" he asked. "It's not much of one if every necromancy student hears it."

"We didn't hear the full extent of it. One day, after a seance had gone bad…" I took a deep breath, wondering if I should continue, "…I decided to check OSIRIS's performance."

April 13th, 1043 AGDR

[mary.firebrightsky@OSIRIS]$ uptime

08:33:48 up 1099 years, 102 days, 8:50, 34014 users, load average: 68000.2, 67890.1, 67606.1

That was odd. Each point of load average was one active process. With merely 32,768 cores, OSIRIS, though mighty, was running double its intended capacity.

What could possibly be using up so much processor time? If it was my own laptop, I'd think memory exhaustion or…

I typed another command. Then stared.

```
[mary.firebrightsky@OSIRIS]$ free -h
               total      used
free       shared   buff/cache
available
Mem:           32Pi       31Pi
10Gi       12Pi     12Gi              133Gi
Swap:          56Pi       50Pi
5Pi
```

What. The. Glitch?

They had done it.

They had activated the swap device and not told anyone.

I sat back in my chair.

People were going to *die* if this got out.

```
[mary.firebrightsky@OSIRIS]$ logout
Connection to OSIRIS closed.
$ logout
```

I unplugged the metaphysical dongle and shut my laptop, wondering if I had triggered some kind of alert system.

April 21st, 1043 AGDR

"So this swap thing is causing more—pardon the word—glitches?" the priest asked.

"Exactly," I said. "It's causing everything to lag and some kas to lag fatally. If the Necromancy Administration doesn't stop selling more memory, and keeps adding swap, it will just get worse and worse. In the worst-case scenario, OSIRIS starts thrashing: spending so much time loading things in and out of RAM that it can't actually run graves or anything else. Then the whole system will break down, ending millions." I took a deep breath. I couldn't think it all through earlier, but now that it was out in the open, I had a little peace.

"Ah. That makes more sense."

"I can't tell anyone this," I said. "I probably shouldn't have told you, either."

"Rest assured, I know so little about computers, let alone EDENs, that I couldn't leak your secret if I tried."

"Now what?" I asked. "I wasn't supposed to know this."

"You can't unlearn the truth. And if you speak the truth, I'm sure you're correct about what will happen, or at least what will happen to *you*. If you speak the truth, you won't last long. It happened to Jesus, after all."

"So what now?"

He looked at me. "I can only advise you to keep coming to Mass and praying."

"I never really prayed before. I don't know how."

"I don't know, either, but the Holy Spirit does. Trust him."

CHAPTER SIX

THE FURNACE OF HUMILIATION

April-December, 1043 AGDR

Life settled down. My worries were small, then, and Catholicism was so exciting! I went to Mass every day I could, although most of the time I was busy working.

Not everything was going well, but enough was.

Business was good, and I was about to complete one of my three years necessary to get the license I truly deserved. I couldn't avoid checking `free` now and then but, for whatever reason, OSIRIS had stabilized. And besides, I was so happy with the rest of my life that I thought more of the Second Coming than any failure of the EDENs.

Father had told me he had never seen a woman so motivated to join the Faith as myself. I studied as hard as I could and, as it happened, the OCIA course started two months after I had the wondrous experience of my first Mass. I would be baptized on Christmas Eve, and I couldn't wait at all.

I didn't want to wait to change my practice in accord with Church teachings. I just couldn't figure out how. Even eleven centuries after OSIRIS was brought online, the Church was still bickering with itself over necromancy. Everyone agreed that self-euthanasia was bad, except those who didn't. But even those who did wondered if excommunication was really an appropriate penalty for it, since the new ghost was still alive. And what about existential emergencies?

I was all the more frustrated because it seemed no one in the Catholic corners of the Neonet had any background in necromancy to begin with, merely parroting quotes and thrusting documents at each other, which were not written by necromantic experts, either. I knew, for example, that a "slow" rip had a 2% failure rate at best because OSIRIS might not get enough of the newly dead brain to construct a digital one. Every one of my teachers had told me it was better to force rip if there was even the slightest chance of failure, but doing so guaranteed bodily death.

Did the Church teach otherwise? The point was academic for me at the moment, but my orderly mind couldn't leave the subject alone. I couldn't imagine that the Church would rather someone end than a necromancer force rip in an emergency, yet some voices, even ones high in the hierarchy, claimed that using OSIRIS at all was the most hubristic of sins.

At least my new home accepted me at face value. Father repeatedly cautioned me against the perpetual digital outrage machine, as he called it, for he had seen it consume the minds and souls of more than one of his converts.

Still, I was happy. And in my newfound fervor, I thought it would last forever—a short, pleasant walk to the narrow gate of Heaven. I would have claimed to believe otherwise if confronted, but in my heart of hearts, I believed in nothing more than continual blessing and favor. After all, I had found Christ. The hard part was surely over.

December 24th, 1043 AGDR

Necromancers became far busier around the Solstice Festival. On the day said to be when HORUS was persuaded to return the sun, traditional mages were busy supplying the meaningless rituals to fulfill the demand of the EDENist faithful. The modern mages—and businesses in general—joined the celebrations by slashing their prices. I joined them, too, on the basis that I was celebrating Christmas. No one questioned it, although I did not feel fully comfortable with my decision.

Each day dragged on as the day approached, my heart hoping for the best and also fearing that some slight thing would go wrong, that somehow I would wake from this dream, but no, the day approached, and then the hours.

Amanda Lightwindknown placed a hand on my shoulder during Father's homily. "Relax," she whispered to me. "Everything is going to be fine."

"God willing," I whispered back.

But surely God *was* willing. Surely this had been his will since before time began, for me to be baptized in the water from his Son's side and drink of his shed blood.

The altar servers—not priests, as I had originally thought—wheeled the font into place before the altar, and we, the catechumens in white robes, went up with our godparents. Father Windsightglory read from the book a server held, and I said my responses.

"Do you renounce the devil and all his works?" he asked.

"I renounce him!" I proclaimed.

My heart was hammering, but I was helped by the Lightwindknowns to the fount, where I bowed under the gentle pouring water.

"I baptize you, Mary Augustine Firebrightsky, in the name of the Father, and the Son, and the Holy Spirit."

I didn't feel any different, as I had been warned, but I knew I was: one moment a mere mortal, the next an adopted daughter of God.

He anointed me next, and I treasured the sweet scent of the oil as I waited for my ultimate desire.

For the first time, when Father beckoned—still not quite believing this was real—I walked up the line.

And then, as I had longed for so long, I received the Lamb of God.

In the narthex, parishioners congratulated me. I was even more ecstatic myself. "This is the happiest day—" I started but was cut off by the horrible CRASH that shook the building. A horrified scream pierced the air, which, somehow, I knew instantly could only be a mother's.

Father and I ran out into the cold night. A car was wrecked into the wall of the parish, and a mangled child was laying on the pavement, his blood staining it rust-red. A woman held that shredded body, screaming and weeping.

Dear God.

We both came to her. Father touched both of them. I ran to the child's side. Every necromancer was trained in first aid, and my training somehow returned in seconds. Airways? Yes. Breathing? Barely. Circulation? His blood was all over the woman and my white robes, but I felt for a pulse. Still there.

But not for much longer.

"Call the squad!" Father called. "And bring me water!"

"Ma'am, my name is Mary Firebrightsky, and I'm a post-mortem professional," I told the woman, surprisingly calm despite myself.

She grabbed on to me. "Save him!"

Other parishioners came out and were watching, murmuring.

"They're on the way!" a young woman said, waving her cellphone.

Thoughts rushed through my mind and over top of each other. This was a textbook existential emergency—the reason why necromancers had to wear fuglin. OSIRIS could not save anyone that a necromancer did not rip. It should be done in a sterile facility with lifeweavers surrounding.

It should be done by a licensed necromancer, not a fake necrotech with the wrong permissions. Damn it!

No, I didn't care.

"I need a ripper," I said, mind made up. "Do we have one in the building?"

"I think there's one in the parish hall," Claire, our secretary, said and ran for it.

"Get me a laptop, too!" I had left mine at home. "What's his name?" I asked.

"D-d-David."

"Full name," I said. "I need a full name."

"David Windknightlow."

A man came with a cup of water, spilling it as he walked down the steps. "Here!"

Father took it. "If you are not already baptized, I baptize you David Michael Windknightlow in the name of the Father, and the Son, and the Holy Spirit." He spilled the water three times over the child, myself and the woman caught in it, and it mixed with the blood.

If I ripped this child…they would find out. And it would be over for me.

Please, God, do something! I prayed silently. Send someone else!

The mother stared into my eyes. I tried to look calm. The child was breathing, but still bleeding everywhere. Claire came back with the ripper, a horrible piece of machinery like a USB hub with needles. She set down the laptop and first aid kit and starting working on the child's body.

I took the metaphysical dongle out of my purse. I looked at it in one instant…and felt peace. God wanted this. I plugged the equipment together, and Claire opened up the laptop for me.

No looking back. I took the needles and stabbed them into the child as I had been trained—scalp, chest, ears, and the two long ones up the nose. The mother winced as if I was stabbing her.

I opened a terminal.

```
[claire]$ necrochain unlock
necrochain: command not found
```

Damn it! This laptop wasn't set up for necromancy. Please, God!

```
[claire]$ sudo apt install necrotools
Password:
```

"Put your password in again," I told Claire.

Claire typed it in, and I hit enter. The world felt surreal to me, that life or death hung in the balance depending on how fast a random laptop could download and install the right software.

Then it hit me.

As long as I did a slow rip, the child wouldn't end if his body failed. If the ambulance arrived in time, I could ride to the hospital, have one of their staff supervise the actual rip, and then—

There! It installed.

```
[claire]$ necrochain unlock
Password:
[claire]$ osrip --name
```

I had already forgotten. "The name," I said with a shaking voice.

"David Windknightlow," she said.

```
[claire]$ osrip --name
david.windknightlow --auto --wait
Waiting...
```

I breathed deeply. "Everyone, get back!" I commanded. "Or you'll get ripped, too!"

An usher wrestled away the mother. I sat by the child, wondering how long it would be.

"What are you waiting for?" the mother shrieked, seeing my lack of action.

I tried to explain, but now my heart was pumping, and the words couldn't even make a coherent pattern in my head. Then the ambulances arrived.

The EMTs rushed out and surrounded me. One looked at me, then looked at the computer. "What the glitch are you waiting for?"

"I—"

"Don't wait any longer!" the EMT said.

The mother screamed. "SAVE HIM!"

I couldn't think. My body acted on instinct: the instinct it had been taught in college.

```
^C
[claire]$ osrip --name
david.windknightlow --auto -f
```

I pressed ENTER.

The next instant I remember vividly, especially in my dreams. Blood splattered everywhere, over the laptop, myself, and everyone nearby.

```
Rip successful as
/morgue/david.windknightlow.ba.gz
[claire]$
```

I breathed deeply.

"What about the driver?" one EMT asked the other.

"Sir," I said. And didn't know what to say.

I had broken both God's law and the League's law with one button press.

I got up from the remains of the corpse, walked to the bench, and sat down. I tried to wipe away the blood from my face with a hand no less bloody.

A man walked out, helped by the EMTs. He had to be the driver of the car—healthy enough to walk out. He saw the corpse. "Dear OSIRIS, what have I done?"

"Mary?" Father asked me.

I didn't reply.

Claire came up, having been close enough to the rip that she, too, was covered in blood. "Mary, let's get you inside and into something that's not covered in blood."

Yes. My baptismal robes. I was still wearing them.

As if I deserved it.

The woman came up and hugged me so tight I could barely breathe. "Thank OSIRIS. He sent you at the right time. I can never repay you."

I couldn't say anything. OSIRIS hadn't sent me. Had God?

They took me to the rectory, where Claire helped me change and wash. Father poured me a cup of hot cocoa, and I drank it slowly, mechanically.

It had all gone so wrong so fast.

"Can you hear my confession?" I asked.

He looked at me, then motioned for me to follow into his office. "In the name of the Father, and the Son, and the Holy Spirit."

"Bless me, Father, for I have sinned. I messed up," I said, barely a whisper.

"Mary?" Father asked.

"That was a force rip. I typed the wrong command," I said, the horror finally filling me, filling the vacuum where nothing else was. "I should have…waited," I managed.

He looked at me and met my eyes without a word.

"I shouldn't have done that," I said.

"Mary, forgive me for saying this, but there were twenty things going on at once, and you didn't have time to think."

"I did!" I protested. "I should have slow ripped, and—I mean, I was, and I—"

He took my hand. "Mary. Slow down. You can't judge yourself now with a mental state that you weren't in when it happened. You're still not in a good state. Breathe."

I took a deep breath.

"Even if it was a force rip, it was an emergency. He might have ended, otherwise. It would be like an ectopic pregnancy or a police revenant shooting someone in self-defense. Yes, Mary, you may have killed his body, but that was dying, anyway, and he's still in this world."

I didn't say anything. And then. "Am I… excommunicated?"

"No," he said firmly.

"But—"

"Mary, we've had this discussion before. Excommunication is only for self-euthanasia, specifically. That wasn't self-euthanasia, and whether it was a sin or not, it's not a *latae sentenciae* offense. You've had a horrible night, and I'm not going to let you torture yourself over maybes and should-haves and if-onlys, then cap it all off by thinking you're cut off from the sacraments. You did what you did, and there's no going back, but there's also no judging yourself for acting the only way you could think in an impossible situation."

I thought about arguing, but didn't have the heart.

"I'm not going to just tell you tritely that you did the right thing," Father said. "It's more complicated, I know, and more complicated than *I* know. Maybe it's more complicated than you know."

Then, almost tearing my mouth open, the words flooded out. "You…you baptized him," I said. "If…If I hadn't done anything, he would have gone straight to Heaven, right? I kept someone…" I felt sick, and almost vomited out the cocoa.

"If that was his baptism, yes. I don't know if he was baptized earlier, somehow. But Claire wasn't wrong for applying first aid, if that would have worked. His mother wanted you to rip him. Breathe, Mary."

I breathed.

"You can't figure out what the Church has been divided over for over a thousand years by yourself in a single night when you're not even thinking straight. Your penance is to go home, get a good night's sleep, and worry about it in the morning."

"OK."

"Now make your Act of Contrition."

"O, my God, I am heartily sorry…"

As Claire drove me home, silently, I relived those moments over and over again in my mind. What could I have done? What *should* I have done? Was there any answer at all?

December 25th, 1043 AGDR

I woke up with a start, then, for a moment, couldn't tell if the nightmares were real or if reality was a nightmare.

"Lord," I said. "Please. I beg you. Give me some peace."

I hadn't cried, I noticed. Maybe it still wasn't real to me. I went to the kitchen, made myself some toast and salami, and…stared at the bottle of Alkahest.

That was it, wasn't it? I was too messed up last night to think it through.

Mrs. Windknightlow was willing to credit OSIRIS with my actions, but I was not willing to credit God for putting me in the right place at the right time?

Maybe the slizz had hit the fan, but I had still done the right thing. I had to have. And besides, whether God really did disapprove of force rips or not, I still didn't fall under the specific criteria for excommunication.

No, the real problem was, now that I could think straight, the Necromancy Administration.

I knew what would happen next. There was no way I could hide what I had done. The Necromancy Administration would investigate, as they always did after an emergency rip, and then they would find out I had filed the wrong paperwork and used privileges I didn't legally have. It didn't matter that I had saved someone's existence. They wouldn't give a glitch at all. All that mattered to them was that I had pressed a button I didn't have a right to, no matter how right the reasons were.

I called Mr. Iranarair.

"Hello?"

"I'm sorry," I said.

"I don't know what to make of a phone call that starts this way, but yes?"

"I was in an existential emergency," I said. "It was a kid." I took a deep breath. "I ripped him."

I waited for him to say something, anything. "I see," he said at last. "We had an agreement."

"I know. So I'm upholding my part by telling you outright, instead of trying to hide it."

"I appreciate this, but I'm afraid I'll have to do what I said I would do."

"I understand. I just didn't want to lie to you."

"May your god bless you, Mary. You are the most honest necromancer—and I'll say that—*necromancer* that I have ever met. If only the world cared."

"Thank you, sir."

"I'm going to ask you to be slightly less honest. I never learned the truth, and you never told me."

"Yes, sir," I said. "I won't mention it."

"I have to go. And the first thing you do after you hang up is call a necrolawyer. Understood?"

"Understood."

"Farewell. I hope we'll see each other in a future life."

"Farewell," I said.

We hung up.

I ate the salami and then drank the Alkahest. Without it, I would have ripped myself, I realized. Maybe I shouldn't complain about the taste.

I chuckled to myself. Then I felt even more disconcerted.

I opened up my phone, searched for necrolawyers, and tapped on the first ad.

I looked around the fancy office as I fidgeted, as if I could find something that would help. It didn't look like the suited man behind the mahogany desk could.

"This situation happens more often than one would think," the necrolawyer said gravely. "Unfortunately, fighting this in court—and I'm not saying you *couldn't* win—is very expensive."

"How much, sir?" I asked.

"Expect to pay at least a hundred thousand drachmae in legal fees, and then whatever the settlement is. You may get to keep your license, you may not. Or you may be banned for the rest of this life."

Glitch.

"What kind of credit do you have?"

I shook my head. "I've already maxed out my credit for my business."

"Do you know any wealthy benefactors?"

"No, sir."

"Then my advice is to *find* a wealthy benefactor."

"How?"

"I'm talking about a master."

I felt sick to my stomach. "Is…is there any other way?"

"Marry someone rich. I'm telling you the reality of the situation, not the one you'd like to hear."

"I understand," I said.

"It's been thirty minutes. Please do come back if you'd like to hire us."

I called Professor Greenrayburst. She listened to my entire story without comment.

"My only advice is to take whatever you can get," she said at the end. "Next life will be better, no matter what happens."

I didn't reply that it was easier for a third life to say, as badly as I wanted to.

"I'd like to help," Charles said on the phone. "But I'm at the grinders."

There *were* worse fates than being in trouble with the Necromancy Administration, I realized, even if I might soon be sharing them.

"How are you doing?" I asked him.

"Regretting each and every one of my life choices. But I'll manage. If I don't go insane here, first."

"I'm sorry, Mary, I can only talk for a little bit," Alan told me, when my call finally went through. "What's up?"

"I'm in serious trouble with the Necromancy Administration."

"Do you need money? A bond?"

"Either."

"I have some influence here, but no matter how horrible your situation is, it is not even a fraction of how horrible you would find your life if you served here. You, especially, would be miserable. I'm sorry, I have to go."

"Thank you," I said.

Finally, I got to Amy during her evening free hours.

"Glitch, Mary, you're in deep slizz."

"Tell me about it," I said.

"I wish you had ended up here. Then we could—you know, I could ask. There's an opening for necromancers here."

"There is?" I asked.

"Someone was ended in a necromancy accident."

"What?"

"Made a typo in making a revenant or something. It was awful. I didn't know human beings had that much blood in them—I mean, I *did*, but I didn't. Anyway, I'll ask. If you're up for it."

I didn't know what to say. "I'm up for it," I heard myself say as if someone else said it.

December 26th, 1043 AGDR

The papers the Slowbrightlaughter Estate sent me were invasive, like a textual strip search. Every one of my assets. Every one of my talents. Every grade. Every last bit of me had to go on those pages as I begged to become their slave.

I had to stop between filling out sections of the application for servitude to go to another room in my apartment and stare at the wall.

I still hadn't cried yet. I should, I knew. But I couldn't even think clearly. I hadn't even eaten in…how long?

Why, God? Why?

Why didn't you fix this situation?

Why was I in such a mess?

Did I displease you, somehow?

Did I fail you?

Couldn't—*shouldn't*—wouldn't have things been different if you had *done something*?

God did not answer.

December 28th, 1043 AGDR

On the same day I got the preliminary notice from the Necromancy Administration, the lawyer from the Slowbrightlaughter Estate arrived at my apartment. He was a revenant with a suitcase and a neutral expression on his mask.

"Thomas Redshineglory," he introduced himself.

"Hello," I said. I wondered if the revenant had enough empathy loaded to hear the exhaustion in my voice. "Take a seat."

The revenant sat down, opened a briefcase, and took out several documents. "Before we begin, we'll have to sort out a number of preliminaries regarding your case."

"I answered all the questions as best I could," I said.

"Yes, but we need even more detail."

I told him everything I could, my words coming out in slow, painful bursts.

"Why did your supervisor agree to take you on?" he asked.

I didn't know what to say. "I lied to him," I lied, hating myself for it.

"I see. We may need to call him as a witness."

"Please don't," I said.

"Would you rather lose?"

I shut up.

We talked for some time more, my remaining spirits crumbling.

"Those are all my questions at this time," the revenant said.

"Is it possible?" I asked. I didn't even know what I hoped the answer would be.

"We believe it's within acceptable margins of risk to pursue the case, yes," he said.

No. Yes. What did I even want? "And if you don't win, will you emancipate me?" I asked.

"If the Necromancy Administration rules against you, what *we* do is of no consequence."

I held my face.

"If we *do* win, you will be a full necromancer," he said.

"OK," I said. I felt like Lazarus being given one scrap from the rich man's table.

"That said, we should go over the details of your indenture. We will pay off all your debts and student loans with a baseline of twenty drachmae per hour of service, plus interest, taxes, and fees for room, board, continuing education, and healthcare, and any additional fees for resolving your legal situation."

I knew all this before. The university had gone over every last detail of servitude for anyone who had a student loan. The lessons were now horribly, unavoidably, concrete.

"Under the Servitude Reform Act of 1001, you will always be paying something on the principle, and you will always be able to pay it off eventually. You will also receive hard credit every day, which will eventually lead to the termination of your servitude no matter what. We will additionally guarantee you will always be paying at least 10% of your service on your principle. You will also receive three hundred drachmae a month as an additional peculium pending good behavior."

"I see," I said. "Do you have a chart?"

He handed me a spreadsheet.

I got out my phone, as if it would make a difference, and plugged the numbers in.

Twenty years.

I would be indentured for twenty years. Almost three times as long as the standard for a necromantic bakt.

"This is a lot to take in," I said. The idea was unreal to me, but so was my life for the past few days.

"You're free to reject our offer," said the revenant. "But this is our *only* offer."

"I understand," I said, then hated my next words. "Please show me the contract."

I read the papers, but what difference did it make? A slave was a slave, but better a slave as a necromancer than at the grinders.

I stared at the last page, where the signature block lay.

He waited expectantly.

I had…I had no other option.

I could have avoided this. I could have gone back to the Necromancy Administration, explained the situation, and tried to get a different license. I could have just gone to the grinders and had my degree, free and clear.

But I didn't.

I had failed.

I took my pen and wrote "Mary Firebrightsky" in my best handwriting, carefully forming the glyphs of my last name, then dated it.

"There's several more papers we must sign," the revenant said.

I signed every one of the eighteen other papers, everything from waivers of rights to financial disclosures, to warranties, to giving them power of attorney, to the contract for the bank account I would get for my peculium. I signed them all without a word.

"Welcome to the estate," said the revenant, pocketing the papers.

"Thanks," I said. My voice was as hollow as I was. "When do we leave for the estate?"

"We will send you a packet of information. Until then, please forward any legal documents you receive to us."

"Yes, sir," I said.

"Have a nice day." The revenant smiled slightly, which only made it worse.

"You, too," I said emotionlessly.

When he left, I closed the door, closed my eyes, felt my face, and willed myself to finally, *finally* cry so I wouldn't have the pain any more.

I was a bakt.

After everything I did as a free woman, I was a bakt.

After everything I did right—and because of it—I was a bakt.

After promising God I would serve him without fail, he let me become a bakt.

I was a *bakt*.

But maybe this wasn't the worst outcome. I would be a true necromancer after this, with all the right paperwork. I would also have my RENEW credit paid for by them, and once this was over, I would have a leg up in life, or even in my next life.

I tried to tell myself that as I sobbed my heart out, but I knew the truth: I was no longer a free woman, but someone else's property.

CHAPTER SEVEN

A COLLAR OF IRON

January 1st, 1044 AGDR

We sat around the waiting room, many escorted or outright guarded, all in stages of distress. I was the only one alone.

I couldn't back out at this point, as much as I wanted to. This was only a formality. But the nature of a symbol is that it cannot be confined to merely the material effects.

"A-49," the bored receptionist said. A young man got up with his guards and marched stoically through the doors.

I was A-51, according to the ticket I tried not to crush in my trembling hands. I wore my fuglin dress clothes, knowing the little comfort they provided was better than nothing.

"A-50. A-50. A-50?"

Two guards looked at each other, then one got up and went for the bathroom. "Mr. Yellowskymight!" one called.

I supposed it made logical sense that if you were going to try to escape, this would be your only chance. In my case, escape would only make things worse. Or so I told myself.

"A-51."

I got up, said a prayer under my breath, and walked through the doors.

A dispassionate young lady motioned me into a room with a chair, like a dentist's. At that point, I'd rather see the dentist. "Where's your escort?" the lady asked.

"They told me to come by myself," I said.

"Who are you indentured to?"

I tried to speak, to admit for the first time I was a slave, but my mouth wouldn't shape the words.

"Do you have paperwork?"

"Here," I said, and handed her the envelope.

She opened it and looked through the contents. "You keep this part," she said, and handed most of the envelope back to me. She tapped away at the computer then got out a measuring tape. "Remove your necklace."

"What?"

"Remove your necklace."

I pulled off my necklace, my hands holding the crucifix so hard it hurt.

She wrapped the measuring tape around me. "This is going to be a tight fit. Push your throat out."

I did.

She pulled a metal collar out of a drawer and snapped it around my neck. "Breathe. No, slow."

I breathed. This was going to be horribly uncomfortable. "It's pretty tight," I said.

"It's supposed to be." She typed buttons on a computer. "She's ready."

A machinespeaker came in, took no more note of me than if I was a piece of furniture, and tapped away at the computer. "Hear, O SET, this command." He pressed a button and, with a loud grinding, a machine spit out dog tags. He put them on my collar, and it snapped into place. "Record this."

I fell silent.

He got out a scanner then scanned my tags. He nodded. "You're free to go."

Free? I almost demanded. You collar me like an animal, and you call me *free*?

But I got up and walked out in silence.

I hadn't truly noticed bakt collars before, but now that I was in one, I couldn't help but see them everywhere: on passerby, behind storefronts, at the food stalls. I imagined hostile stares, rude words, total humiliation, but when I stepped outside, no one seemed to notice my own. I put on my crucifix awkwardly, but found its weight atop the collar made my neck more uncomfortable.

I still had money, at least enough for a milkshake and a donut. I walked down the streets, feeling as if I was stark naked, but no one seemed to consider me any different. In fact, more people got out of my way than usual.

Of course, you idiot, a necromancer bakt walking outside was potentially on important business. No one wanted to mess with a powerful estate.

I supposed it was true that no matter what I thought of my situation, objectively, in some ways, it was an improvement. The estate would take care of my material needs, and I need no longer worry about anything but getting through the day.

But I still felt sick to my stomach.

I stepped inside the coffee shop. The barista, I truly saw for the first time, had a collar, and he both recognized me and my own. Sympathy overwhelmed his tired eyes. "What can I get for you?"

I gave him my order as if nothing had changed since last time.

Then I walked to the table and cried.

I had lost everything, even my own dignity, even myself. All because of doing the right thing.

Or maybe, just maybe, because the Necromancy Administration was cruel and corrupt.

What difference did it make at this point? There was no way out.

The barista brought me the food. “How long?” he asked.

“Twenty years,” I said.

“The one thing they can’t take from you is credit. Each day is one day closer to the end. Remember that.”

I nodded, and he left.

January 3rd, 1044 AGDR

Mass was traumatic. I could bear approaching the Suffering Servant as a servant of men, but I could not bear the sympathetic looks of others. But what could I do? Tomorrow I would leave for the Slowbrightlaughter estate’s main campus in Newla, three thousand kilometers away. This was the last time I would see this place, and my last chance to say goodbye.

News spread fast. I was surrounded at my table in the fellowship time after Mass.

Voices spoke: “I’m so sorry, Mary,” “We’ll miss you,” and “Can we stay in touch?”

“Probably not,” I answered the last. “I don’t think I’ll have time.”

Fr. WSG came up to me with a small book. “If you have time to read, read this.”

I took it. *No Longer as a Slave, but More Than a Slave: A Catholic Guide for the Indentured*, read the title. “I don’t know if I’ll have time to do anything.”

“If you don’t mind, I’d like to give you my blessing.”

“Yes. Please.”

He spread out his hands and prayed. I felt not better, but even worse. But what could I do? I could not say that I did not instinctively feel superior to bakts before, and now I was a bakt myself.

"When do you leave?" Amanda asked me.

"Tomorrow," I said. I felt all kinds of hollow, as if they had extracted everything, even my soul, when they had me sign those papers.

"I'll keep you in my prayers."

"Thanks," I said.

The final stop was the mall. "I'm sorry, I'm going to…"

But the manager wasn't seeing me anymore, only the collar on my neck. "Sign this form."

I looked at it. Early termination of my lease with a penalty? "I can't sign this," I said. "I'm—"

"Then have your master sign it."

The words hit me like a fist to the gut. "I…I will," I said.

"But in any case, I want your storefront cleaned out today."

Why? You were so eager to have a new merchant. I almost said. But I saw only emptiness in his eyes.

"I will," I said.

"Good," he said. "Now leave."

I packed away the last of my gear. I couldn't even legally practice necromancy without my *master's* permission, not that I might be able to practice anyway with my situation so complicated.

"Ms. Firebrightsky!" a woman hurried to me. It was Mrs. Halaralix. "I…Oh."

"It's a long story," I said, and hefted my backpack. "I'm afraid I can't help you anymore."

Her face fell.

"I'm sorry," I said.

"I…I had heard," she said. "It was in the news."

Of course it was.

"Here," she said, handing me an envelope. "This isn't a payment or anything. Just a gift."

"You could invest this—"

"—But it will pay off your debts quicker," she insisted. "Compound interest applies to you, too, right?"

I supposed it did. Emotions surged through me, and I couldn't even speak for a moment. "…Thank you," I said at last.

Maybe this wasn't the end.

Maybe this was only the beginning.

The Lightwindknowns had come to help me pack.

It was more giving up than packing. The letter had told me to bring no more than two suitcases. Anything else, I had to sell or give away. Gone was the furniture I had bought, the books I owned, this-and-thats I had gained over time. My holy objects I gave to them.

The estate didn't want any stained or frayed clothing. I didn't know how it was any of their business, but I knew I had to deal with it in the end: my baptismal robe.

I had managed to get almost all the blood out, but I couldn't get the memories out.

Mrs. Lightwindknown put her hand on my shoulder as I cried, looking at it.

"I can't keep it," I said. "I don't even *want* to keep it, but I'm not supposed to get rid of it."

"How about we keep it for you?" she suggested.

I thought about arguing. Twenty years from now, I had no idea where I would be. But I couldn't take it with me in any case. "…OK," I said.

January 4th, 1044 AGDR

They gave me one last hug at the train station. "We'll be praying for you," Amanda said.

"Thanks," I said weakly. I pulled out the bags and went on my way.

I fingered my crucifix as I sat on a bench by the tracks, so nervous my stomach was unsettled. I had barely been able to take my Alkahest because of how sick to my stomach I was. I was not a fan of train stations in general because when I was little I read a children's book on Gotterdammerung. I clearly remembered the illustration of KHONSU's wrath destroying a train station with divine lightning.

KHONSU was gone now, the majority of it too damaged to respond to commands, the rest grafted onto SET. But it was easier to fear something I could imagine than something I could not.

Ironic, how I had been heartbroken not to get a bond a year ago, and now I was heartbroken to have one.

Still, I had done a lot in that year. I had found Jesus and his Church. I had helped all sorts of people, even that kid. And I had lived *a* life, even if that part of it was over.

"Hey! You!" someone called.

"What?" I asked.

"You're sitting on a freeman's bench. The bakts go over there!"

I looked to "over there" and saw it was crowded to the brim. Great. Of course, the world had to beat down on those who were already down. But I got up wordlessly and took my suitcases, knowing I had no choice but to accept this.

If only I could, somehow, accept this.

A Note from My Present Self

I don't believe God was so unsubtle that the moment I was baptized my life was predestined to change. But God had, in his foreknowledge and perfect love, permitted that moment to occur, those small moments of my own free will, that lead to the fulfillment of his will. In the same way he willed that I write these words, and you read them, for good, I hope.

Am I bitter *now*? No. I see God had plans for me I could not have imagined then, and had I known what all these plans would involve, or the sufferings that lay in wait, I would have gone mad.

CHAPTER EIGHT

THE LOVE OF MONEY

January 8th, 1044 AGDR

Bakt class was miserable, as those who paid for it didn't use it themselves. I knew even if it had been first class, I would have been miserable on my own. Newla, my destination, looked more miserable still.

The air was so filthy that I had trouble breathing from the moment I stepped outside. So was the station. So were the buildings in the distance, dilapidated, closed, and some with broken windows. Even the people looked around with suspicion and weariness. I decided to keep hold of my baggage at all times.

It was a shock having lived in the wealthy Steelriver for most of my life, and even Whylin was better off than this. Surely they could have hired augurs to clean the air, at least. I looked immediately for the bus station.

I found the new Slowbrightlaughter bakts at Gate 8I. They were laughing and chattering, as if this was not their punishment but their wildest dream come true that they were enslaved to an estate. But hell, so was mine, at one time. I entered their group.

"You all with Slowbrightlaughter?" I asked.

"We are!" a Spiral elementalist said. "I'm Mike Afairfar."

I counted this group of my peers. There were two necromancers in fuglin, including myself, five lifeweavers in white argent, an augur in golden or, three elementalists in red sanguine, and a machinespeaker in green vert. The machinespeaker didn't wear a collar and looked at ours with distaste—bakts could not be machinespeakers.

I relaxed a little, but held on to my baggage as I waited for the bus.

Every necromancer is accused of greed in charging greatly for essential services—though should not doctors and lifeweavers be accused of the same? In any case, I had come to secretly loathe the stuff. My clients would often pay in cash: corroded coins and use-filthy bills. As much as I enjoyed the value, the physical manifestations began to disgust me. When I deposited it at the bank, sometimes I was more relieved not to have to touch it any longer than to have more money in my account.

But as the bus pulled into the Slowbrightlaughter estate's primary campus, I saw, for the first time, what money really meant.

The vast lawn was perfect, each blade held identically, unnervingly straight. Tree after tree lined the golden-pebbled driveway, each tree bearing massive, strange fruits. Ahead stood a marble structure that would have made the Romans or Americans proud, covered with masterpiece murals. All was as untouched as if no mortal or ghost lived here, but only gods.

Amy had told me that a significant client of lifeweavers was simply one who had the cash to burn on making a landscape immaculate. From what she had told me, this could easily be the full-time job of seven, or even twenty, lifeweavers, perhaps spending their entire work week on nothing but a single section of grass or foliage.

I wondered what I could possibly be used for. And "used" would be the word.

The bus pulled to a stop before the porch, and we new bakts stepped out into the brisk, clean air.

We had at least learned all of each other's names. As is inevitable in such situations, one of the elementalists had unofficially become a leader, Mike Afairfar from before. He was young and handsome though not—*not*, my heart insisted—as handsome as Alan.

"Off we go!" Mike said, and we followed him in groups based on our disciplines. The other necromancer was also a woman, a dark-skinned chubby girl who never spoke beyond the minimum.

Inside, in the foyer, a massive statue of a short fat man stood on a pedestal, watching. Its marble head turned to look at us. "Welcome! I hope you'll enjoy your time here with me. I'm looking forward to it on my end."

"Yeah, good for you," Mike Afairfar called out.

"My, my, let's not be hostile on our first day. In any case, you'll find everything you need on estate grounds, and you are free to enjoy it when off duty. I look forward to a productive life together. Or death, in my case! Ha ha HA!" The statue returned to its original position, then stopped moving.

A tall—and by tall I mean easily two meters—necromancer with white hair came up to us. She nonetheless seemed young in body though old in soul. She did not have a collar, but instead an ID card on a lanyard. "Mary? Sandra? I'm Alysson Slowbrightlaughter. I'll be your superior while you're serving here. This way."

Behind us, the chief staff elementalist introduced himself as Jeffery Slowbrightlaughter, and the head augur as Bernice Slowbrightlaughter. I didn't hear the others, but I suspected all the staff was from the Slowbrightlaughter family.

I marveled at the size of the place as we passed through; I realized I must have only seen part of it. We took a ramp down a story.

Alysson Slowbrightlaughter spoke, saying, "Alfred thought it was funny to stick all the necromancers downstairs in the catacombs. Like many of his jokes, it's not all that funny. But if there is one rule above all others, it's to laugh at his jokes. Understood?"

"Yes, ma'am," we said.

We passed by several doors until we reached a large door marked 'Necromancer Common Room.' She tapped her lanyard to open it. "This door will open only to necromancers, and only at times when you're supposed to be off duty."

We entered to see what looked more or less like any lounge: a slightly messy room with tables and chairs. It felt almost homely. The other bakts inside looked at us with mixtures of worn resignation and disinterest. One wall had a giant schedule, before which she stopped.

"This is your daily schedule. On weekdays, you will wake up at 0600 and perform morning hygiene by 0700. At 0700, we will have any morning announcements, and you will receive a text with your shift information. Then you will have breakfast, finishing by 0800. You will eat all of it, no more, no less. You will also drink your mortality limiter. We do have unlimited coffee."

I listened as she continued, "From 0800 to 1200, you will work. If you need to take a bathroom break, contact your local manager. We do not give breaks for other reasons. At 1200, you will have a lunch break until 1230. Again, you will eat everything we give you, no more, no less. Then you will work again until 1700."

She traced her finger along the schedule. "At supper, we will once again give you a fixed ration. Afterwards is free time until 1900, when you may do as you please, providing you do not get into trouble or leave the campus. Curfew is at 1900, including evening hygiene and any last announcements. We have lights out at 2000. I recommend you get to sleep as soon as possible."

She moved to the next column on the calendar. "That is your schedule for most days. Every other weekday, there is a mandatory exercise hour, depending on your schedule. You will be assigned one day on the weekend off. On your off day, you may again do as you please, provided you do not cause trouble or leave the campus. We also have a buffet on Sunday night, where, if you obeyed all orders throughout the week, you may eat as much as you'd like."

"I'm sure you may have other questions," she said, handing us thick books. "Here are your handbooks. If your question is not answered there, you may contact me during off hours. Do you have any questions?"

We didn't have any. My head already spun. I had worked long hours before, but not for someone else's profit. But what could I do?

"Good," she said at our silence. She motioned for us to follow, and we went through another door into a locker room.

A man with an ID card on a lanyard, definitely not a necromancer, looked at us with suspicion. "Give me your bags and everything in your pockets."

I handed him my bag, my cell phone, and, with reluctance, my crucifix.

"Your locker will open to your tag," he said. "Just tap on it while in front. After we search these, you'll have them back. But not during work hours."

Did I protest? What difference did it make? Perhaps I shouldn't rock the boat so early—but what would I do without my crucifix?

"Is this a religious item?" he asked, as if reading my mind.

"Yes," I said.

"You're not allowed to have it while on duty."

"I understand," I said in a quiet voice.

"Sandra, you go ahead to the common room and introduce yourself. Mary, a word with you."

I followed her through several more doors—catacombs indeed—until we came to an office. "When entering, press the doorbell and wait," she explained.

"Yes, ma'am," I said.

She opened the door and ushered me inside. It looked like any other necromancer's office, with certificates on one wall and books on the other. She took the seat behind the desk. "Sit."

I sat.

"I understand you came to us out of a complex legal situation?"

"Yes, ma'am," I said.

"Are you legally licensed to practice necromancy at this time?"

"I don't know."

"Show me your tattoo."

I pulled off my left glove and showed her.

"This is full access, by the dots. I thought you were a necrotech?"

"Ma'am, my legal situation is extraordinarily complicated. I was supposed to be, but things went wrong."

"Then, unfortunately, I can't have you work a necromantic shift until that's sorted out. You'll be assigned to maintenance."

"Yes, ma'am," I said. What difference did it make anymore?

"Today, however, is your free day. Take your time, and get used to this place. This is your first life and your first servitude?"

"Yes, ma'am."

"It's a lot to take in at once. But you'll get used to it. Now go and introduce yourself."

"Yes, ma'am."

"My name is Mary Firebrightsky," I said quietly in the common room. "Pleased to meet all of you."

My new peers grumbled their acknowledgement. Unlike the new bakts, these ones seemed to have been ground down.

I decided not to tell anyone about my previous business. I didn't even want to think of it, now that it was officially over and the charter canceled.

"Do any of you know Amy Justgloryblue?" I asked.

"Oh, yeah, she's one of the lifeweavers," a guy said. "You the necromancer she was talking about?"

"I am."

"So, you like, failed at business?"

"No." I held down my anger. "I made a serious mistake when ripping someone."

"At least you still exist," another necromancer said.

"Oh, OSIRIS, that was awful," a third one said.

"What actually happened?" I asked.

"Jeff mixed up the input and output arguments on osi dd. Ended both him and the revenant."

"Maintenance had to clean up *so much* blood," said a girl. "They were pissed at us for weeks."

"Wouldn't you survive if you had mortality limiters?" I asked.

"I'm telling you," one tall necromancer said. "It was suicide."

"No, it was that he was holding on to the needles," a fat necromancer said.

They started bickering.

"Those two are the Jameses," the girl explained. "They're always fighting. I'm Opal."

"Pleased to meet you," I said half-heartedly. Maybe life here wouldn't be so bad.

Or maybe it hadn't sunk in how much I had lost.

Didn't I *want* this, once upon a time? Yes, but my servitude would have been for seven years, not twenty. And now I had tasted freedom, if only for a year. Why was I suffering? My fault?

Or God's?

In "my" bunk that night, I cried myself to sleep, or at least I tried. I had gotten a little sick of crying, but I couldn't sleep in such a strange place, not knowing what would happen next.

And I was angry, angry with God.

Why this?

Why did I try so hard for nothing to come of it?

Wasn't I running my business ethically? Didn't I do the right thing?

Or *did* I? Was it all because I ripped the child? Would God rather the boy had ended while I looked on?

Please, God, I prayed. At least let me sleep.

But that prayer, too, did not seem to be answered.

January 15th, 1043 AGDR

Of all things I *could* be doing, I told myself, being forced to mop floors was not the worst. For example, I could be working at the grinders, or I could be imprisoned, or even extradited to the Dead if the Court of the Tomb was that unhappy with me. Merely being reduced to menial laborer was far from unpleasant compared to those possibilities. But that didn't make it far from unpleasant.

I immediately discerned that all the non-mage bakts hated the mage bakts on my first day (all but one, at least). I faced pranks, insults, if not outright sabotage. I learned to be careful opening doors and to look what was in a bucket before using it. But I didn't say anything, knowing full well that complaining would only make me a bigger target.

"You the new bakt?" a young man asked as I polished a window.

"Yes," I sighed, wondering to what new suffering I was about to be subjected.

"You're going to get all chafed up with a bare collar." He indicated his, where I saw cloth underneath. "They sell them at the commissary, but you can also order them off Immartal."

"Immartal will ship here?" I asked.

"Yeah, you have an address. Should be in your handbook."

I didn't know whether to believe him.

"I ain't slizzin' you. Now the commissary ones are cheaper, but you really want Snugglies."

"I…see," I said. I didn't know how to feel about a hygienic brand called Snugglies, or if I even dared believe in his words—no, he looked sincere.

"Mary Firebrightsky," I introduced myself.

"Mark Whiteskylark," he said.

January 16th, 1043 AGDR

We were not permitted access off the estate, but the law required our religious freedom.

"I cannot serve my God on this estate," I told Alysson on the first Saturday.

"What do you need?"

"I need to leave to a local church for Mass."

"Mass?"

"A ritual my God requires every Sunday."

"Can't you celebrate it over here?"

"Not by myself," I said.

"That's unfortunate," she said. "Request denied."

"What?"

"It's denied."

"I have religious freedom!" I protested.

"Not that much, you don't."

"I'll complain to the Ombudsman." I held back my temper.

"The Ombudsman won't help you."

"Maybe he won't," I said. "But I'm sure you don't want a lawsuit, and you can't retaliate against me for—"

"You don't get it, do you, Ms. Firebrightsky?" Alysson said sharply.

"What?" I asked.

"You may have been a free woman before, and that's applaudable. That ended when you signed your servitude contract. We *own* you."

I almost exploded on her, but shame overwhelmed my anger. "That doesn't mean…" I started half-heartedly.

"I've had this conversation more times than I can count," she continued. "Yes, your life isn't what you'd like it to be. If you didn't want it this way, then you shouldn't have signed those papers. But you did, so don't whine about it."

"But—"

"Mary, enough. File your complaint if you want. But until they come knocking—and they won't—I don't want to hear it. Dismissed."

I walked out, feeling more defeated than both shame and anger combined.

No, I would file the complaint. I had no other option.

January 17th, 1043 AGDR

No matter what the Ombudsman did, I knew I would not be able to go to Mass for months. So that Sunday, in between the servile labor I had no choice but to do, I had nothing else left but to feel awful.

"How are you feeling?" Amy asked me at the shared Sunday lunch. We had one cafeteria for all bakts, insomuch as "we" was a pronoun that could apply to the slaves of the estate.

"Absolutely miserable," I said.

"Girl, it gets better. They only hazed me for two weeks before they got bored."

"Glitch. Did I tell you I've been assigned to Maintenance?"

"Uh, yeah, everyone told me that."

I held my head.

"Really, Mary, life isn't *that* bad, here. No need to worry about basically anything. Free food. Free rent. Free healthcare. It's not *freedom*, but freedom isn't everything, either."

I decided to change the subject. "Can you really get those neck cushion things off Immartal?"

"You sure can. You can get anything that's not against policy. Probably better to save your peculium for bigger stuff, though."

"Oh, come on," a lifeweaver bakt beside her said. "I get hives with the glitchy ones they have here."

"How does Snugglies feel?" I asked.

"Great," the interjector said. "I use them myself."

"No way," the elementalist bakt across from her said. "Snugglies are just overpriced."

What followed was the most technical discussion on the quality and merits of the various options, and all I could think was how petty everyone here's lives had become. I had made decisions on everything from build-out of my storefront to brand of mortality limiter, and here the only freedom they had was which kind of hygiene item to wear under the collar they couldn't remove.

And I would do this for another twenty years.

January 22nd, 1043 AGDR

I only had to deal with the harassment for a few more days, both because the bakts quickly got bored and also because the lawyers refiled my paperwork to make me a full necromancer. They also provided an injunction for me to work while the case was winding through the courts.

Both went through. I was, for the moment, an actual necromancer. Had I just been one a few weeks ago, everything would have been fine. I was so angry that I couldn't even understand the legal trickery they employed, trickery which I couldn't have employed myself. I couldn't enjoy this "victory" at all.

I spent my first day as a necromancer recustomizing my shell and home directory in accord with the Slowbrightlaughter standards. But I was ready to be done with maintenance, so I didn't care, even if it still hurt a little.

Perhaps I should explain our org chart now. Alfred Slowbrightlaughter was on the very top. Each of the campuses was divided into separate departments. Alysson was the head of the necromancy department for SBL Main. Below her, we would be assigned to one of the teams managed by a high-ranking bakt. Below them would be the necromancers, where I was. And somehow, below even me were the mediums and necrotechs that the estate owned.

I didn't want to have servants, nor did my erstwhile servants want to have me. But sure enough, I was assigned two necrotechs and had access to the pool of mediums.

"Don't get used to it," Nicholas Ralaxir, one of my necrotechs, told me. The short, amber-skinned young man looked older in his eyes than body.

"I was a necrotech, too, once," I said.

"When?"

"Before I came here."

"Then how the glitch are you a necromancer now?"

"The estate has lawyers."

"Fair," he said with a laugh.

I tried to convince myself this was an upgrade, no matter what I truly thought.

My first task was to build a grave, a standard if lengthy task that only a necromancer could do. But it was so long since I had been trained that I had to constantly check the books or ask the other necromancers how to do it. Meanwhile, the clock was ticking, and the client's loved ones had paid a set sum for the grave to be made.

"Are you sure you've been trained in this?" Emily Justwhiteshine, a smaller, blond girl and my other necrotech, said.

I had had enough.

```
[mary.firebrightsky@OSIRIS] osi bill
pause
Billing paused.
[mary.firebrightsky@OSIRIS]
```

I grabbed her by the shoulders. "Just shut the glitch up!" I about screamed.

She stared at me, frightened, and then ran off.

Dear God, what had I done? I had just been cruel to someone else in this hellhole.

But I had to finish the job first.

I looked at my terminal. Since the bill was paused, I could just check as I usually did.

```
[mary.firebrightsky@OSIRIS]$ free -h
                total     used
free      shared  buff/cache
available
Mem:           32Pi      31Pi
10Gi      12Pi    12Gi           133Gi
Swap:          60Pi      57Pi
3Pi
```

No real change. Time to go back to work.

```
[mary.firebrightsky@OSIRIS] osi bill
resume
```

I found Emily at supper and tried to apologize.

She waved it away. "I get it. You're new here. It happens."

"I shouldn't have acted that way," I said.

"Yeah, so? Everyone does."

"Acting like everyone else isn't good enough," I said.

"Why?"

"Because Jesus loves everyone."

"Who's that?"

"The True God."

"Uh…OK." She deliberately returned to her food.

Thus ended my first attempt at evangelization.

February 8th, 1044 AGDR

One month down, I told myself, 239 to go.

I hadn't lost my sanity yet, and I had successfully not blown up on anyone else. But that was the only success.

I hadn't heard back from the Ombudsman. I did hear from Alysson quite a bit. I didn't realize every last command of my terminal logs would be inspected every month.

"First of all, you will bill our estate, not your old company. You've done that twice so far," she said, reading down an actual paper printout.

"I'm sorry, ma'am," I said. "I accidentally typed the wrong command. Force of habit."

"Change the habit. Next, you have been taking too long to build graves."

"Yes, ma'am. I'm sorry, ma'am."

"And finally, what is this? You paused billing to run a random command?"

Shame flushed my cheeks, actually *flushed* them. "Yes, ma'am," I said. "I paused it to yell at someone."

Alysson looked at me. "You're serious."

"I'm being honest," I said.

"I…OK. Fine. But why the glitch did you run `free`?"

"Did you see the output?" I asked.

"Yes. And?"

"They're using swap!" I said.

"The concerns of the OWG are not *our* concerns, and most importantly, not *your* concern. Stay on topic."

"Yes, ma'am." Perhaps that was why no one else had discovered the truth: No bakt was allowed to look, and no free post-mortem professional had time. It galled me that my discovery was dismissed so easily…but what difference did it make?

Necromancers are good at secrets, and even better at pseudosecrets. But I will explain what I carefully verified, so as to make it clear what would not be immediately obvious had you seen us from the outside.

Alfred Slowbrightlaughter was perhaps the stingiest man who had ever lived, or perhaps the most selfish, and now that he was dead, he was even more stingy. He would spend a million drachmae on trifles while making his children and surviving relatives snap at money like starving dogs.

No one would actually *say* that, and the man himself was careful to keep his relatives from talking too much about it. But it was not hard to tell when spending any time with them how sensitive they were to wasted money, or how they would snidely remark about the valuable equipment.

Alfred could easily have afforded a new body from a lifeweaver. He simply didn't want to reincarnate. This was not uncommon among the ultra-wealthy. He didn't want to be a revenant, either, which was also not uncommon. So for all the immaculate campus, he did nothing whatsoever but leave it perfect.

Meanwhile, he put us to work, so he would have even more money.

We contacted ghosts, we built revenants and pseudo-revenants, we sent slightly funny messages to other estates by bizarre means, and in one case we got involved in a lawsuit over some necromantic dispute too arcane to explain. We reincarnated an aunt, and we helped a nephew across the veil. We were not for show, as I had begun to fear, although some of the work we did was probably pointless in an overall sense.

Time passed, and though politics was getting a bit more stressful after the Portgreatred incident, you could still talk about it. Not too loudly—our master's opinions were well-known and best not contradicted. But for my non-political self, I just lived and tried not to talk about it.

I, in short, forgot all about what I had seen with `free` for the time being.

CHAPTER NINE

SLAVE TO THE LENDER

March 8th, 1044 AGDR

Not merely the necromancers and augurs, but every Living person on campus, slave and free, from greatest to least, had to drink mortality limiters. The brand they put us bakts on was called LifeLiquid, and it was "black cherry" flavored.

"Are you serious?" I asked Amy.

"That's what it says on the can, right here," she tapped the side.

"The League Trade Commission should sue the people who make this stuff for false advertising."

"It tastes a *little* like black cherry."

"Sure, mixed with something poisonous and acidic," I sighed. "I think vomit would taste better."

"Don't," Amy said, finger in the air. "They'll flip on you if you aren't taking your full dose."

I could understand the necromancers, yes. I could understand the lifeweavers and medical staff, yes. I could even understand the Living members of security having to drink it, just in case. But for everyone else, it was just insurance against suicide.

I dropped to a whisper. "Has anyone…'tested it?'"

"Tried, yes, succeeded, no. No one except Jeff, if that was intentional. I hope not. That was a horrible way to go. But don't even talk about it, Mary. They threw someone in the locker for joking about it just before you came."

"I won't, promise," I said.

Still, whether I would be saved in OSIRIS or simply brought back to life by MA-AT, suicide was a sin. And speaking of sins, I realized how quickly I could rack them up in this situation, which grated on me without access to the sacraments.

The book Fr. Windsightglory had given me had a whole section on life without access to the sacraments. I didn't like how it *didn't* suggest complaining to the Ombudsman. It didn't even mention it. I no longer really hoped, on whatever level that I ever did, that I would be the one bakt to get a ruling from the Highest Court and change it for everyone. After two months in the estate, I had run pretty quickly out of idealism.

"Hey, Mary," Mark Whiteskylark, from Maintenance said, coming up next to me. "I was wondering if, like, we could, you know…"

"What?" I asked.

"Go on a date."

A million thoughts flooded through me: Did I want to? Was he Catholic? What about Alan? Was there any hope? Was this God's will? Did I care anymore if it was God's will?

What I said was "Sure."

He smiled widely. "See you next Saturday. I got a surprise."

"…OK," I said, unsure what else to say.

He walked off. Amy was grinning ear to ear. "See? This isn't the end," she said.

"I guess."

That night, I skipped ahead in the handbook, which I had not had the heart to read, to the section on relationships.

> You are free to have any relationship you wish with other bakts. You do not need our permission to date (in your free hours), marry, or have sexual relations. However, if you are planning to have sexual relations, you must first go to the medical department to receive contraceptives…

I put the book down and started to cry.

Of course.

Of course, I still had no hope of things getting any better.

I didn't dislike Mark. In a perfect world, I probably wouldn't have minded getting into a relationship with him. But this only confirmed what I already feared: It was unlikely I could ever have my own biological children. Had I been merely indentured for seven years, yes, but for twenty?

Amy had told me back in college that while it wasn't necessarily impossible for a second life or later to have children, her new body was deliberately made sterile by government regulations to avoid the population from exploding. Even if it wasn't banned, children of reincarnates often had severe genetic abnormalities, another reason it was forbidden.

Would it still be lawful to make love if you couldn't refuse to take contraceptives? I supposed the question came in canon law somewhere, but the thought of even looking it up would only make me more miserable.

Of course, God was all-powerful. As he made many barren women fertile in the Bible, even in impossible situations, he could still grant me children. But he could also have granted that I didn't lose everything on the day I became Catholic.

"Why, God?" I whispered. "Why?"

Once again, I heard no answer.

March 10th, 1044 AGDR

In ancient mainframes, long before the first Internet, the write command could send messages to another terminal. After Gotterdammerung, using write through OSIRIS or another EDEN was the only means of long-distance communication. But in the modern era, necromancers had reduced it to a method of gossip. Which is why *I* was outraged that my master was upset I wasn't using it enough.

"Excuse me, ma'am?" I questioned.

"You don't respond to writes," Alysson said.

"Ma'am, I was under the impression that something as simple as `free` was too much of a distraction."

"We expect you to communicate with other members of your team."

I opened my mouth to argue, but like more often than not now, I shut it. "I will reply, if you insist."

"Good. Dismissed."

Afterwards, I wondered why the glitch they wanted me to gossip so badly, when they would spy on…the terminal's logs…

Of course. They wanted access to the gossip, too.

I sighed. No point complaining about it.

You know…?

If they wanted me to gossip…

```
$ pinky alan.jrnjirlorl
Login    Name                    TTY
Idle   When          Where
alan.jrnjirlorl                  pts16324
01:59  Mar 10 07:20
```

Alan was logged in.

I sat back.

Did I really care so much about connecting with an old flame that I would knowingly have our conversation spied on by my master? *Our* masters?

Glitch. I needed to talk to someone.

```
[mary.firebrightsky@OSIRIS]$ write
alan.jrnjirlorl
> Alan? It's me, Mary. -o
> EOF
```

I closed my eyes and breathed deeply, hoping against hope for…something.

```
Message from alan.jrnjirlorl@OSIRIS on
/dev/pts/16234 at 15:31
Mary! How are you doing? I can't talk
long, but I am so glad to hear from
you. -o
EOF
```

What should I even say?

I've already agreed to go on a date without you?

I've lost everything?

```
[mary.firebrightsky@OSIRIS]$ write
alan.jrnjirlorl
> I miss you. Things are hard here. -o
> EOF
```

What was I even doing? Meeting up with him again was even more unlikely than having children.

Did I dare hope?

No.

No, I didn't.

```
Message from alan.jrnjirlorl@OSIRIS on
/dev/tty16234 at 15:32
I'm sorry to hear it. Can't talk about
my own situation. Have to go. oo
EOF
```

I held my face. Of course. Maybe it was time to move on.

March 13th, 1044 AGDR

"This way," Mark said, and offered his hand. After a moment, I took it. I felt the warmth and relaxed a little. I hadn't touched another human being in months.

Well, except when I screamed at Emily, but I figured that didn't count.

He led me through the complex. I felt mildly unsafe—I didn't suspect Mark of any ill intent, but being by myself with a man…"Erm, will there be other people?"

He pointed up. "There're cameras everywhere. Besides, this is the only way we can watch on our own."

"…What?" I asked.

We came to a locked door. Mark got out a thick ring of keys and unlocked it. "We call this the Bootleg Theater," he said.

We stepped into an empty A/V room. The place was spotless, but it didn't look like it had been used too often, or at least officially. Mark fiddled with the projector and a pile of viddisks. "I was thinking *The End of the War.* You?"

"That's fine," I said.

The projector turned to life. He quickly sat by me. As the infringement warning from the League Investigative Service played, I wondered if "Bootleg Theater" referred to how our use of the room was unofficial, or if the copy we were watching was "unofficial." I didn't have the energy to argue.

The End of the War has probably not survived to your day, though who knows? Perhaps it really is out of copyright in your era. It's about the end of the Second Name War and the founding of the Athanasian League.

When the Spirals and Triglyphs went to war in the First Name War, it had ended with a Triglyph victory. Despite widespread persecution, however, Spiral necromancers kept ripping people under their Spiral names. This led to an even larger crackdown a decade later which brought about a violent revolution.

After ending millions of lives, both the Spiral nations and the Triglyph nations had run into a stalemate. A Spiral named Alfred Laxalir had suggested that, with the Wheel Group members of both sides, they could form one nation that had control over OSIRIS. They agreed on the name "The Immortal League," which later became the Athanasian League.

What we watched was fiction, of course. Details had been altered for the sake of the film, and in fact both Tryglyphs and Spirals had claimed to be the rightful heirs of the American Empire, not just the Triglyphs as the story implied. But it was true that in the end, they decided they had more in common than against each other.

The movie ended with a shot of the leaders ceremonially chiseling the Tables of the Laws of the Living and the Dead onto the Peace Stele.

"Why leave part of it empty?" a Triglyph leader asked Laxalir.

"Because this isn't the end of the story," he said.

I felt chills as the credits began. It indeed wasn't the end of the story. The Peace Steele had been added to many times, including the Debt Reform amendments. But we hadn't run out of room—for the last several decades, the Tables of the Laws had never been amended.

"What'd you think?" Mark asked.

"I thought it was really good," I said.

He smiled. "Glad you liked it. Anyway, we got to get going. The rest of Maintenance has this reserved for the remainder of the day."

We walked outside. He looked at me expectantly.

What difference did it make?

I was never going to see Alan again, wasn't I?

I had to take what I could get.

I let him kiss me.

"See you next week?" he asked.

"Sure," I found I had said.

March 14th, 1044 AGDR

I hated working on Sunday, but it was another battle I had decided not to fight. As I looked through my shift information, I saw I had been assigned to a satellite office.

"Great," Emily told me. "I hate seances."

"I don't mind them," I said.

"Sure, because you're not the one doing them!"

"Actually, you might be," Nicholas interjected. "Sundays get busy, and they might pull you for seance duty."

I shrugged. "OK," I said.

I actually was excited. As we got on the bus, it would be the first time I could go into the outside world.

Not too far, however. The office was clean but ugly, and I got my own room, but I realized I would be spending all day in it.

I looked through my schedule. I had mostly consulting, followed by a grave, followed by, yes, being in the seance pool for the rest of the day. Not a horrible day, I thought, no matter what my necrotechs thought.

"My" necrotechs? Apparently, they had been Jeff's before his very unpleasant demise. We were starting to at least not hate each other, which was progress of sorts.

I shrugged to myself. It was what it was.

Besides, how hard could the seance be?

I realized a fundamental difference between running a family seance business and doing it as a bakt very quickly: As a bakt, I couldn't kick a customer out when he started screaming at me.

The first screamer had lost his entire family and, while I had sympathy, his demands were complicated and difficult. He wanted to talk to all of them simultaneously, which was asking OSIRIS to keep the graves' speed in sync. The commands existed, but getting them to actually work was finicky.

So he screamed at me while I tried, and he screamed at me when it didn't work, and he screamed at me while I tried again until finally, he got all of three minutes to talk to his family before that ended, and he screamed at me yet again.

I prayed my next client would be quiet.

For once in my life, God answered a prayer.

My next client's approach to grief was to cry constantly and speak in whispers and sobs, so aside from the difficulty in finding out who she wanted to talk to, it was the easiest seance of my life.

The client after that was a screamer. And the one after that. And the one after that.

"Yeah, they dumped all the bad clients on you as the new girl," Emily confided after the day was over.

Every one of my nerves was shot at that point. "Why didn't you tell me?" I asked.

"'Cuz then we'd be the ones getting dumped with them."

So much for us not hating each other.

April 9th, 1044 AGDR

I had spent all of Lent and now the beginning of Easter working. I had imagined that I could go to Mass on the liturgical year anniversary of my glorious experience, but there was no hope of it. *Please, God,* I prayed. *In your great mercy, give me something today. A letter, a sign, anything!*

But I got nothing. No letter, particularly not from the Ombudsman.

May 3rd, 1044 AGDR

Two months since our first, Mark and I had gone on two more dates, but I told him I didn't have the energy at the moment. Perhaps he believed me. Perhaps he did not.

What was true was that the outside seance team was as close to Hell as it got, at least for me. My foster parents had often screamed at me. Each night after a string of screamers, I would dream of them again. But what could I say? My master didn't care about my trauma, nor would the Ombudsman.

"Please, God," I begged. "Change something. Make a difference."

May 4th, 1044 AGDR

The next morning, my first client, a tall man in a suit, stepped inside and barked, "I want to talk to my mom."

"Yes, sir," I said. "Name, please?

"Eowyn Justgemtrue."

"Your name?"

"Benjamin Justgemtrue."

Unlike a necrotech, I could stay logged in, although I felt it was dangerous to do so. But who was I to resist policy?

```
[mary.firebrightsky@OSIRIS]$ osi ps
```

"How do you spell her first name?" I asked.

He yelled at me for a few seconds before finally giving me a card.

```
[mary.firebrightsky@OSIRIS]$ osi ps |
grep eowyn.justgemtrue
[mary.firebrightsky@OSIRIS]$
```

No output?

That would imply the grave didn't exist.

```
[mary.firebrightsky@OSIRIS]$ find
/morgue -name eowyn.justgemtrue*
/morgue/eowyn.justgemtrue.ba.gz
[mary.firebrightsky@OSIRIS]$
```

"Sir, there does not appear to be a grave. We can—"

"I already spent twenty thousand glitching drachmae on a grave!" he shouted. "Let me talk to her!"

I had a bad feeling about this.

```
[mary.firebrightsky@OSIRIS]$ osi info
eowyn.justgemtrue
Name: Eowyn Justgemtrue
Size: 324 MB
Ka status: N/A
[mary.firebrightsky@OSIRIS]$
```

The Divine Architects, in their creation of OSIRIS, had discovered something they would never have believed: the soul. If you took a ba and made two kas, only one would function. After much and very cruel experimentation, they had discovered the laws by which the soul behaved and the techniques to create a digital body. But they found that they could never return the soul to a body, digital or physical, once it had left.

"What the glitch is taking so long?"

"Sir," I said. "Your mother may no longer be in this world."

He shouted and pounded the table so hard it shuttered, and he yelled and howled and swore and called me names and—*Please, God, give me something to tell him*—"Sir, human souls are immortal!" I shouted.

He stopped, confused.

"There is no way to destroy a rational soul," I told him, heart hammering. "It's not made of parts, so you can't take it apart. It will last forever."

He stared at me, breathing heavily.

"*I* cannot bring your mother back, but that doesn't mean she no longer exists."

He slumped on the table and sobbed.

I didn't believe that worked. It *shouldn't* have worked. It was the Holy Spirit, surely. As he sobbed and cried and pleaded for his mother, I placed my hand on his. He took it and squeezed so hard it hurt. But even if my life was as slizzy as I could imagine, even if I had no hope, even if I barely dared to believe in God anymore…I would offer hope to this man.

Tyrone Greendaytown, my supervisor, talked to me afterwards. “Ms. Firebrightsky, are you all right?”

“No, but I’m better off than he was,” I said.

“You’re done for the rest of the day.”

“…I am?” I asked.

“You are the only person I’ve ever seen talk down a screamer. I can’t imagine you’re fine. Go and take a break. If something comes in, I’ll have you do it.”

“OK,” I said. I wasn’t going to turn him down, surprised as I was.

But that wasn’t the end of the story.

CHAPTER TEN

THE TWO OF THEM SWORE AN OATH

May 5th, 1044 AGDR

A day later, I was called to Alysson's office.

"Shut the door," she said.

I did.

"Let me reassure you, this is not a disciplinary meeting."

I inwardly breathed a sigh of relief. "Ma'am?"

"I've heard what happened on Monday, and I've reviewed the recordings. You are the first necromancer I have ever seen who could talk a screamer down."

"I've had a lot of experience, ma'am."

"I can see that. How long did you work before this?"

"Around a year. I was a glorified medium, essentially."

"You're a necromancer, now." she said.

I felt my emotions rising. Bakt I may be, but at least…at least I was a necromancer, even to my master.

"Ms. Firebrightsky, don't tell anyone this, but I've contacted Alfred himself, and he was impressed. So impressed he'd like you to be permanently on the outside seance team."

Great. No good deed goes unpunished.

"You won't always be doing that. Necromantic work comes in waves. But, Ms. Firebrightsky, we'd like your full cooperation on this matter."

"What does it matter?" I asked. "I can't refuse a legal order from you in any case."

"Yes, but if we were to force you to be diplomatic at all times, you'd stop being so. We both know you could have handled that screamer entirely different."

I thought about pleading it wasn't me, but the Holy Spirit, but I was more curious than humble. "What are you offering?"

"How often do you need to go to your ritual?"

I found myself wordless.

"We can make an exception if you'll do harder work. There's no need for this relationship to be antagonistic."

"Once a week on Sunday for one hour, two hours if I stay for any fellowship time. And a few days have additional Masses."

"We can do an hour and a half, once a week, *if* you maintain a perfect disciplinary record, always come back on time, and willingly accept being on the seance team permanently. And drop the Ombudsman case but, at that point, we'll be on the same page."

"I…thank you," I said.

"You agree?"

"Ms. Slowbrightlaughter, my one concern is that I got into this situation because of an existential emergency that happened just as I left Mass."

She waved it away. "That is an entirely different matter. We just don't want to find you partying at a bar. In fact…" She thought about it. "Let me put it this way. When it's over, I want an immediate text saying you're done, or why the glitch you aren't already back. Is that acceptable?"

"Yes, ma'am."

"You may go."

"Yes, ma'am."

Hope is a strange thing. Even the smallest amount of it can turn the unbearable into the almost unbearable. I could be doing the worst work possible, but if I could go to Mass on Sunday, I would be at peace about it.

I didn't tell anyone the details about my meeting, but news leaked anyway, or at least a fragmentary version of it. I had worried I would be looked down at by the other necromancer bakts, but the only thing I saw was relief that they weren't on the outside seance team.

The outside team had also heard, and they immediately assigned the worst clients to me. Or, at least, that's what it felt like. But I knew one complaint could jeopardize my situation. So I didn't say one word, even when I was being screamed at.

This soon worked in my favor because once again the other bakts were grateful it was I and not they who had to deal with the angriest and most desperate.

Nor, when I had hope, was it beyond my ability to tolerate. I had seen it all before, and while the other bakts might turn their nose up at being a medium, slaves themselves or not, I would talk to anyone.

"Sir," I said to the raging Spiral. "Mr. Jakarjarakala."

He looked at me, momentarily stunned that a Triglyph could pronounce his last name correctly.

I tapped my collar. "I am a bakt. I can connect you to my manager who may be able to change the price of our services. I cannot."

"You don't give a glitch about my wife, do you!?" He slammed my desk.

"I wish I could do something for you, but—"

Mr. Greendaytown stepped into the back. "Mr. Jakarjar, I'm going to ask you to leave the premises."

"You can bite my ass, you triggie!"

"We are not interested in your patronage anymore. If you don't leave, I am going to call the police."

The angry Spiral swore and stomped out.

"Mary, do you have nerves of steel?" my manager asked.

"They assigned me this job for a reason, sir."

"Take a five-minute break, and then go work on one of the graves. You're done consulting for the day."

"Thank you, sir," I said in honest relief.

"You're welcome. Now get going."

As I walked into the break room, I wondered if life as a bakt could really get that bad. I already found myself worn thin, but if I could go to Mass, even stay for a bit of fellowship time, I could perhaps stand this for another nineteen years and seven months.

I knew my situation was precarious. One change of managers, one mistake, one whim of my owner, and I would be miserable again. But for the moment, I was fine.

May 9th, 1044 AGDR

St. Theresa of Avila was an ancient parish, dating from before Gotterdammerung. The building had been destroyed multiple times, but the church hung together.

I had prayed all the way there that it would be a good place because I didn't dare ask them to take me to another parish if I didn't like this one.

Parishioners watched in curiosity as I undid my glove to bless myself with the holy water. "I'm Boris Nightredfire," a greeter introduced himself. "You new here?"

“Yes,” I said. “I…” Moved? Not of my own free will. “Arrived,” I finished.

“I hope you enjoy your stay. We have coffee and donuts after Mass.”

“Of…of course.”

I sat in the back-most pew. I saw no other mages, and definitely no other bakts. The congregation seemed mostly older, and I was young. And yet even here, the Body, Blood, Soul, and Divinity was present, even to his lowliest servants.

I had quite the crowd afterwards. “Fr. Justinian Justwhitelight. They sometimes call me Justsquared,” the elderly priest introduced himself to me.

“Mary Firebrightsky,” I said. “I just got here.”

“Are you a necromancer?” a little boy asked.

“Yes.” Perhaps it was good to be able to announce that fully.

“Why?”

“I became a necromancer, and I accidentally became Catholic in the process.”

“My name is Janet,” an old lady introduced herself. “You must have quite the crazy story. Is this your first life?”

“Yes,” I said.

“I’m actually on my fifth, but I’m thinking of letting go this time. What would I need to do?”

I almost answered, but caught myself. “I’m sorry, but I can’t offer any kind of necromantic advice without my master’s permission.”

“Ah.”

“Who is your master?” An old man asked. “If that’s not a sensitive question, of course.”

"Hypothetically, I'm supposed to always tell you that. I'm with the Slowbrightlaughter estate."

A silence fell.

Great, had I offended them already?

"We've had some bickering with them before," Fr. Justsquared said. "They wanted to buy this building."

"I'm sorry, but I have no control—"

"Of course you don't. You're entirely welcome here."

"Yes," I said. "Yes, I am."

In that moment, for as short as it would last, one last flame of hope started burning again. I hoped, for a moment, that all was not as bad as it could be.

CHAPTER ELEVEN

THE OTHER MARY

June 23rd, 1044 AGDR

Perhaps servitude was not as bad as I had imagined. But slaves of a kindly master are still slaves.

My routine had become mechanical. I would wake up at 0600, line up for morning hygiene, line up for breakfast, hear rambling announcements at 0700, go to the office or wherever else I had been assigned for the day, and work until lunch. Then I would take a thirty-minute break and work until dinner. Unlike the parable, we were not required to prepare the meal, but we were very much required to still work. I had two hours of free time before curfew at 1900. Then night hygiene, then back to our bunks.

If this sounds exhausting, even deleterious to health, it was. Several fellow bakts physically collapsed from exhaustion. Then they had to bicker with their superior that they had really run out of stamina and were not just faking it to get out of work. Everyone was short-tempered and explosions were frequent. I, by the grace of God, remained calm to the point where my patience and longsuffering were legendary. But that did not change how I felt on the inside.

One Friday, I sat on the balcony of the campus, looking out on the perfect landscape. I wondered if Heaven could be no more beautiful than a run-down slum, and it would still be worth living in for all eternity, if I just didn't have to *work*.

I couldn't say I loved necromancy any more. Working on it as a slave, with the worst possible clients, had robbed me of any affection for my job. But even that was better than some of the jobs to which the non-mage bakts were assigned.

What hope did I have? Only that in nineteen years, six months, and seven days, I would be free, with a true necromantic license. I could not hope for a material improvement in my situation until then. And even if my situation did improve, I still, almost certainly, would never have biological children.

For all the wonders of MA-AT, reversing a woman's biological clock was not one of them. At night, I would cry and thrash and imagine some contrived scenario where I could still have children. But God gave no answer, and I would wake up the next morning, still in the nightmare.

As it was, I had to get a quick Confession in before Mass because I didn't have any opportunity to go earlier. Certainly, I was grateful that I could even practice the Faith in a complete, if limited, way. But I felt my soul being eaten away by the constant labor. And the creeping despair.

"Mary?"

I turned to see another bakt. "Legal wants to talk to you."

"*Legal?*" I asked. "What the glitch?"

"Yeah, not sure why. But they said to come immediately."

Thomas Redshineglory sat behind the desk. Or at least I assumed it was him. I couldn't tell revenants apart. "We've settled your case with the Necromancy Administration for 260,000 drachmae. You are now, without exception, a full necromancer."

"I see," I said. But I had a very bad feeling. "Why are you telling me this?"

"We are charging it to your account."

"...What do you mean, 'charging it?'" I asked, my voice quieting as it dawned on me.

"We are extending your servitude for an additional thirty years."

The words didn't make sense in my ears. Then I almost laughed at the bad joke. Then I almost screamed at him. Then I wondered, for a moment, if I was awake.

"Are you serious?" I finally asked. "How?"

"It was in the servitude contract you signed."

I opened my mouth, then closed it. Then, as calmly as I could, I said, "I want to see the contract."

"Of course." He passed me a folder.

Digging through the documents didn't change anything.

In fact, my bakt would extend far beyond thirty more years, but hard credit would accumulate at the same rate until I was free thirty more years from now.

I shut the folder.

Another thirty years.

Another thirty years.

Another thirty years.

That night, I lay in bed, unable to think.

At this point, I'd be indentured for the rest of my first life. I had nothing to look forward to except forty-nine-and-a-half more years of work and misery. Every time I thought things would get better...they only got worse.

"God," I whispered. "Why am I suffering like this? What did I do? Don't you *care*!?" I whisper-screamed. "There's no point. There's nothing left. Why am I still alive?"

No answer.

"*Please, God,*" I whispered. "*Just end me. End my suffering.*"

If God heard, he didn't answer.

June 24, 1044 AGDR

My master, on the other hand, had heard every word.

"Please, God," the static-filled recording said. "Just end me. End my suffering."

I had nothing to say. I couldn't even look at Alysson.

"Ms. Firebrightsky, we can't have you like this."

"Strange as it may seem, but most people become remarkably unenthusiastic about being slaves when their servitude is extended," I snapped.

"Are you thinking about suicide?"

"It's a sin," I said.

She played the clip again.

"For God's sake," I groaned.

"You're asking your god to kill you."

"Yes because this is *worse than death*!" I tried to say, but it came out as a shriek. "I have nothing left to—"

"Mary Firebrightsky!"

I shut up.

"Mary, I understand life is not as you'd like it right now, but we can't have you hurting yourself."

"I won't. I promise."

She played the clip again.

I felt so humiliated and violated that I just decided to stop talking.

"Will you go to therapy?"

I didn't say anything.

"It won't cost you anything."

I still said nothing.

"We had an agreement that you'd have a perfect disciplinary record to go out. I can overlook this if you agree to go."

"Fine," I sighed. "When?"

"Friday night, on your first recreational hour."

Perfect. But what could I do? I had made that agreement. "As you wish."

June 29th, 1044 AGDR

I had never been to a mindweaver before, and I wasn't enthusiastic about it. I would endure this, too, and go on with my life. And if I asked God to end me again, I would ask it silently.

I immediately soured on meeting him. The mindweaver, David Mightkinglight, had no collar on him. He talked and asked questions, and I gave short, non-committal answers.

"Mary, you've scored a 20 on the PHQ-9."

"Woohoo," I said.

"I want to try you on Halyetic."

I didn't say a word.

"Do you want to talk?" he finally asked.

"No," I said.

"OK," he said.

We were silent for the rest of the visit.

August 29th, 1044 AGDR

I took the medicine, willingly or not. I felt a bit better, but that did not mean I was OK with taking it.

I had reached rock bottom. Now even my mind belonged to my master. The only thing I had left was my soul, and that was on the behest of my master letting me go to Mass.

I had stopped receiving Communion. I didn't have the heart to confess on my own, and I was too angry with God to force myself to confess for the sake of receiving again. So I simply sat in my back pew, talking to no one.

One Sunday, I got a call from Alysson right after Mass.

"What?" I asked.

"One of the buses broke down, and we're not sure why. Can you stay somewhere for another hour or so?"

"…I can stay here," I said.

"Good. We'll call you when we can pick you up."

"Thank you," I said. I didn't mean it at all.

I looked around the church. Then I went and knelt by the Mary alcove.

I hadn't paid too much attention to her, despite apparently being named after her. I had prayed the Rosary daily, early in my enthusiasm, but I hadn't prayed it for a long time. What difference did it make? The only thing I did was suffer, suffer, and suffer some more.

How easy it was for you, I thought. *You never had to deal with any of this.*

I knew I shouldn't be doing anything like this. I knew I shouldn't be thinking these thoughts. I knew I should be going to Confession and receiving Communion. I knew I shouldn't have asked God to end me.

But I had nothing left.

Please. Please do something; I can't bear this any longer.

I hate life as a bakt. I hate it all. Do something!

I don't recall my exact words. I must have prayed for an hour. Please, please—

"I have not forgotten you. I suffered like you did, once."

The voice was soft, powerful, peaceful, and very feminine; it was in my imagination, and yet, I immediately knew in the way you know these things that it was not *of* my imagination.

I froze, looked around, but saw the closest parishioner was on the other side of the nave.

Not that I didn't fully well know that I had heard the Virgin Mary.

What did it mean?

Or did I *really* hear her?

I knew I did, but that was impossible.

"Excuse me," I said to the statue.

The statue didn't reply.

Had I imagined that?

I hadn't, but it was in my imagination.

Was it real?

It felt as real as the sun outside.

As the day I had first gone to Mass.

I went to a pew and cried my eyes out. When the bus came to pick me up, I didn't say a word, still lost in thought.

September 5th, 1044 AGDR

If it wasn't for those words, I would never have had the courage to go to Confession again, a week later.

"In the name of the Father, and the Son, and the Holy Spirit."

"Bless me, Father, for I have sinned," I said, in the darkness of the confessional. "It's been six weeks since my last confession. Maybe longer." I fell silent.

"Forgive me for saying this, but you haven't asked me for a while. Is something wrong?"

"…Yes," I said. "Lots of things. Maybe everything." I took a deep breath. "I asked God to end me. I only stopped because my master was listening in." I found myself crying. "I don't want to die. But I don't want to *live*!"

"Why?"

"I'm going to be a bakt for the next fifty years," I said. "They tacked on an extra thirty years because I didn't read the contract closely enough."

"You know that part in Luke where Mary calls herself a handmaid?"

I could feel the hair on my arms prickling. "Yes?"

"In Greek, she calls herself the 'doulē Kyriou.' 'Doulos' is the word translated as servant, slave, or handmaid, depending on context, but there's no difference in the Greek."

I fell absolutely silent.

"Now legally, she was in a much different situation. But in terms of serving another in a life of great suffering, she lived a similar life to yours."

"Father," I said. And gulped down my breath. "…I heard…I mean, I think—I mean, I *know*…I heard a voice. The Blessed Virgin. In my imagination, but like, it wasn't."

"An imaginative locution," he said calmly.

"A what?"

"When St. Joan of Arc was asked whether the visions she saw were in her imagination, she said 'Of course. Where else would God speak to me?'"

"It's...it *could* be real," I said, voice rising.

"What did she say, if I may ask?"

I told him.

"Well, like I said, she described herself as the Lord's slave in scripture."

"What does it mean?" I asked. "The locution?"

"I don't know. I don't want to discourage you, but I would also caution you against being too attached to a private revelation, real or not. Be thankful, yes, but don't be obsessed. I've seen people go down a bad road thinking every stray thought they have is from God."

"I won't," I promised. "But what does it *mean*?"

"Again, I don't know. Pray about it. But whether or not your situation is comparable legally, you are comparable in terms of suffering. Consider praying to Our Lady of Sorrows."

"I will."

I recount this story not to claim I am a visionary—I certainly don't qualify, having not seen a thing—but because her voice marked a turning point in my life. After that, I began praying the Seven Sorrows before bed.

I came to see that I was not the only woman whose dreams were shattered and life torn to shreds just when it was beginning. I was not the only woman to be helpless in front of sheer injustice, and to see God refuse to act. And I was not the only woman who had to get up each morning and live, even if life seemed meaningless knowing the pain I went through and would go through.

I set up my shell to display the phrase: "And you yourself a sword shall pierce" every time I logged into OSIRIS. I didn't feel better, but I felt much less worse. And at the very least, not alone.

I started to hope, just a little, that maybe—*maybe*—things could be a little better.

It wasn't long before things changed again.

CHAPTER TWELVE

I HAVE SURELY SEEN THE AFFLICTION

October 1st, 1044 AGDR

That Friday, I had three screamers back-to-back, but we were so understaffed that Tyrone couldn't get me to behind-the-scenes work. I managed not to explode back on them or anyone else, but I was about ready to strangle someone, maybe even myself.

No, I thought. I couldn't even think along those lines. Time to pretend to go to therapy.

We sat in our usual silence.

"What's the point of this?" I finally asked. "You don't get anything out of this, do you?"

"I'm here for you," he said.

"Then prescribe the pill, and be done with it."

"I thought you didn't like taking them."

"Around ten months ago, my preferences on almost anything stopped mattering. I didn't even ask for this. I'm missing an hour of rec time because of this. All I want to do is read a book in peace."

"Let me make you an offer. I'll give you a book, and you just sit here and read it in this office, and tell me what you think. You don't have to give me a book report; just read it."

This seemed like some sort of trap, but at this point, I didn't give a slizz. "Sure," I said.

He pulled a slim volume off the shelf and handed it to me. *The Hiding Place,* by Corrie Ten Boom.

I flipped it open and started to read.

October 8th, 1044 AGDR

I finished by the next session, a week later. "I'm not sure what the point of this is," I said. "Are you saying this is a death camp?"

"Mary—can I call you Mary?"

"Fine, *David.*"

"If I could, I'd free every slave in the Athanasian League. I can't. I can only offer comfort to them."

I took a deep breath. "You serious?"

"I am. Do you know how much the Slowbrightlaughter estate pays me?"

"I don't."

"Half of what a free client would pay me."

"Oh."

"So if you want to rant incoherently about your master, I don't mind. I don't care what they think. I'm just here to help you keep your sanity."

"...Do you believe in God?" I asked.

"The True God? Yes, although I'm not a Christian."

"Why does he allow us to suffer, though we do good?"

"I wish I knew, Mary. I wish I knew. But I see the book resonated with you."

I sighed. "If I could ask for one thing, I would like to be off pills."

"They're concerned you're still liable to hurt yourself. Are you?"

"...I don't know."

"Are there side affects you dislike?"

"Not really."

"Is it just the idea?"

"I don't want something messing with my mind. I'm just in pain, that's all."

"Would you take painkillers if you were in physical pain?"

I paused in thought. "I suppose I would."

"Estates are so quick to prescribe medicine, but in this case, to be blunt, Mary, it could help."

"I don't even want to be in this situation. It happened because—" I stopped myself.

He waited.

"Forget I said anything."

October 15th, 1044 AGDR

But the next Friday, I worked up my courage and told him.

"I've thought about it," I said. "I'll tell you the full story."

"I'll listen to whatever you have to tell me," he said.

It took me shorter than I thought it would. Maybe some of the memories were too traumatic for me to say more than bare details.

"And that's why I'm here," I finished. "All because of a series of accidents and mistakes."

"You believe in the True God, yes?"

"Yes. His name is Jesus Christ."

"And one of the teachings of his church is that all things that happen are God's will?"

"It's complicated, but yes. God foresaw all that would happen."

"Then forgive me for saying something so banally trite, but he foresaw this whole series of accidents and mistakes that brought you here. He could have stopped this chain of events at some point."

"Yes," I said. "Yes, he could have. But he did not."

"My point is more that you're not unlucky. God just chose this to happen. I don't know how free will works and all—"

"The soul nudges neurons from time to time, or flips bits of the ka."

"Well, there you go. That's not a lot of influence on the world."

I thought about it.

"I'm not saying I know God's plan, but I do know he cares for you, and he would not let this happen purely out of 'bad luck.'"

"I suppose not," I said. I felt like a great sore muscle had finally released. I fell on the table and started to weep.

October 16th, 1044 AGDR

"What happened?" Amy suddenly asked me the next morning.

"What?" I asked.

"You've been laughing at our jokes, and you aren't lost in your own world."

Had I really been so depressed that others could tell?

"I'm…I'm doing better," I said honestly. I didn't trust that it would last, but it had lasted a little.

In fact, I remember that day as being OK. Not perfect. Not happy. But I remember that I wasn't completely miserable and exhausted at the end of it. Exhausted, mostly. Unhappy, partially. But not completely.

October 22th, 1044 AGDR

"Have you considered theopsychiatry?" David asked.

"Why?"

"It can really help those with trauma in their past."

"I'm having trauma *now*," I said.

"You may find the present easier to handle if you can help with the past."

"I...don't really feel safe doing it here," I said.

"I understand."

"How does it work, anyway?"

"MA-AT stimulates your brain to enhance memory processing and neuroplasticity. It's very safe. I don't want to push you into it, but it can make a big difference."

"Huh," I said.

October 24th, 1044 AGDR

Janet happened to be talking about it to Boris in my earshot that Sunday, saying, "The mindweaver was really nice. He talked to all of us before doing it—"

I walked up. "Are you talking about theopsychiatry?"

"Oh, yes, it really helped my daughter. She—things had happened to her."

The way she cut herself off made me wonder what "things".

"I see," I said. Was this a sign?

October 29th, 1044 AGDR

"It's a series of appointments," David told me. "And we'll have to get approval. I've never seen it turned down."

"Will I really feel less trauma?" I asked.

"True God willing, yes. You may find that the present won't hurt as much."

Anything. *Anything* for that.

November 5th, 1044 AGDR

I was nervous about the actual process, but when I learned Amy was going to be with me through it, I relaxed immediately.

"The process works on its own," David said as Amy attached the leads. "If you need it to stop, or feel uncomfortable in any way, tell us to stop."

"What *will* I feel?" I asked.

"I'd describe it as a mental massage. You'll feel emotions pass through you, and then you'll feel a little better. Kind of like stretching a muscle that's very stiff."

"OK," I said.

"It helps if you close your eyes. I'll hold your hand," Amy said.

I saw colors, colors, fading into shapes and then—I jolted up. "Stop!"

"It's stopped," Amy said calmly.

I felt…I felt both worse and better.

I tried to explain this to them unsuccessfully, but it seemed both of them understood what had happened.

"MA-AT must have dug up a painful memory," Amy said. "We'll take it slow. There's no set number for how many times you have to do this."

"OK," I said.

November 6th, 1044 AGDR

That night, I had vivid dreams of a painful incident with my foster parents…and upon waking, I was disturbed, but felt significantly better.

In the morning, I approached Alysson.

"Yes?" she asked.

"I'm not here to argue about anything," I said.

"Good because I'm not in the mood for an argument."

"I just want to say…" Too late now. "…Thanks."

Her eyes widened.

"I think I would have done something stupid if you hadn't gotten me help."

"You're certainly welcome for that. But why are you telling me this?"

"I'm not asking for any more favors. I'm not even trying to butter you up. I just wanted you to know that you did *me* a favor, and—"

"Goodness, Mary, you act as if you *want* to be here."

"Believe me, I don't. But God has willed that I be here, and I might as well make the best of it."

Alysson stared into my eyes, as if to discern if I was serious. "You're welcome. Now if there's nothing else, your shift begins in five minutes."

"Yes, ma'am." I left.

November 15th, 1044 AGDR

Treatment, all of it—medicine, therapy, theopsychiatry—helped. Life was hard, but it was no longer unbearable. Almost unbearable, yes, but there is a world of difference between unbearable and almost unbearable. Though I lived in that world, and wasn't happy, I was…OK. I was finally OK.

I had still learned my lesson. When I prayed that night, I covered my face with a blanket and didn't voice my words.

"Blessed Mother, I don't know if I can get you to talk to me again, but…in any case, I want children. Even just one. Please. I'll do whatever you ask.

"You shall be a mother."

I bolted upright, and I nearly banged my head against the bunk above.

I started crying.

A wound, that I didn't realize how deep it was, was finally healing.

Did I dare believe?

Did I dare *not* believe?

I knew what I heard was real.

"Thank you," I said out loud. "Thank you so much."

November 16th, 1044 AGDR

Of course, I couldn't help but wonder the next morning what all would or could happen. Mother Mary would have to free me somehow, obviously, but I knew she could do that.

The question was *when*.

I was still young, which implied that I could be freed much later and still be able to have children—which meant I had to be freed sooner rather than later, right?

But I would be a mother!

When? How? With whom?

But what if it was a metaphorical motherhood? Or literal, but not biological? I didn't want to be a foster parent—I wouldn't want someone else to suffer like I did—but…but…

I knew full well that trying to figure out how God will bless you is an exercise in frustration, but that didn't stop me from trying.

In any case, perhaps it was better that the Blessed Mother didn't tell me the details, as much as I asked her later. I was, for the moment, if not happy, still OK. Had I learned the details then, before I had to live them, I would have fallen into despair.

CHAPTER THIRTEEN

WHERE THE TRIBES GO UP

1045-1046 AGDR

Life went on.

In truth, there was more to say than merely that. A day passed, and then another, as I watched my owed time diminish ever so slightly. But the days blended into each other, differing only by this project or that, or the latest horrible client, and the day I no longer saw him.

I didn't hear from the Blessed Virgin again. To this day, I have still never heard anything else from her. I had enough sense to know not to pursue locutions, or at least Fr. Justsquared warned me, in no uncertain terms, to be careful.

My faith, such as I could practice it, kept me sane. For one-and-a-half hours for one day a week, I was not a bakt, but a fellow Catholic. I tithed my peculium, thinking more of the widow's mite than that I could be free slightly sooner if I kept it for myself.

What difference did it make? Fifty years was fifty years, even if it slowly became forty-nine, then forty-eight.

For the fact that I lived in a community, I was often horribly lonely. We all had our separate miseries, to be commiserated jointly, yes, but ultimately, none of us could reduce each other's debts. And if any of us irritated each other; there was no way to keep away.

Alan and I wrote to each other. I wrote my other classmates who had OSIRIS access, but most of them were at the grinders, dismembering corpses.

At least I was thankful that *that* wasn't the case for me.

Mark and I went on the occasional date. We broke up at least twice before getting back together out of sheer boredom. The same was true of most bakts, including a couple that had actually divorced and remarried. When your options were nothing outside of the campus, did it make a difference if you had already broken up?

Alysson and I did occasionally fight, but we had an unstated agreement that she would not force me to cross my boundaries, and I wouldn't toe hers. So I didn't ask to leave for Mass on holy days of obligation, even Christmas. In turn, she tolerated that I had principles I wouldn't compromise on.

Life went on, and I did know that for my unhappiness, I could be in a lot worse position. Life was getting harder outside of SBL Main, and that was not the only thing getting worse outside.

You will have heard of Jacob Heartlightray. Or perhaps his name is only a footnote by the time you read this. But we soon all heard of him, until we were sick of him.

We did not know the future, mind you. He was simply an Eternalist we all hated, especially considering his proposed policies on servitude. But as he raced ahead in the polls for the 1046 Consul election, we started talking worriedly about what would happen if he won. Not *too* loudly. But we did talk.

"He's probably not going to win, anyway," Mark told me during a date.

"But what if he *does*?" I asked.

He shrugged. "Funny to see you talking about politics."

We all did at that point. Though you *could* talk about politics, you had to be careful because "Heartlessrays" measured rhetoric always had some barb hidden in it. You could barely talk about anything without it devolving into politics, and then a shouting match. Which would inevitably land someone or someone else in Alysson's office or even the locker, so I simply left the conversation when it started drifting down that path.

April 2nd, 1046 AGDR

Election day was a mandatory day off for the whole nation, free or indentured. We had to sit through an unsubtle presentation about the merits of the Eternalist cause, but then we were hypothetically free to vote as we pleased.

Like most official things in the League, voting was done over OSIRIS. I had been elected to be one of the poll workers on campus, and so I ended up seeing the results in real time. I was surprised to see how Heartlightray had managed to anger so many of the bakts, that the nudge from our master had gone mostly ignored.

The Consul election happened in two phases. All the candidates, usually several from each party, would be in the first election. If one candidate got more than 50% of the vote, he would win instantly. As this had never happened in the last fifty years, there would be a runoff where the two top candidates would compete again, and whoever won that vote would be the new Consul.

I decided to vote my conscience the first election. I didn't like a single one of the candidates on the ballot, and so I wrote in a candidate who had no chance of winning.

Marth 5th, 1046 AGDR

We all looked at the results with distaste: Jacob Heartlightray was in first place with 48% of the vote, and James Yellowglorynight with 35%.

Both were Eternalists.

We muttered about the failure of the Athanasian public to get someone who wasn't either horrible or incompetent in the runoff. Even the Eternalist bakts were unhappy.

March 21st, 1046 AGDR

A week later, we voted again. Even our master realized that getting us to vote for Heartlightray was a lost cause, so there was no further presentation.

For the runoff, I bit my lip and voted for Yellowglorynight. He seemed at least better than Heartlightray, and, if nothing else, his platform hadn't been about cracking down on bakt "laziness."

March 22nd, 1046 AGDR

So, of course, Jacob Heartlightray won, along with an Eternalist-majority Senate of the Living. We grumbled and went back to work.

In truth, it was only one more bad thing in my life.

June 20th, 1046 AGDR

Life went on, however. Whatever his campaign promises were, the Highest Court was not amused at his attempts to get around the Table of the Living in regards to bakt rights, and politics returned to bickering.

I had more immediate concerns.

```
Message from alan.jrnjirlorl@OSIRIS on
/pts/16554 at 15:31
I've heard Necrocon West is being held
in Newla this year. Any chance you're
going? I've got a ticket, myself. -o
EOF
```

I sat back and breathed deeply.

Whether we were in a relationship or not, we were still friends.

```
[mary.firebrightsky@OSIRIS]$ write
alan.jrnjirlorl
> I'll try to go. No promises. oo
> EOF
```

June 21st, 1046 AGDR

The day after the announcement, Alysson came into the room. "We're looking for volunteers to go to Necrocon West—"

I raised my hand in an instant.

"Relax, Mary, you're already on the list. Anyone else?"

I felt instant relief. Emily raised her hand, as did the Jameses.

"No, not you two. Emily and…?"

"I'll do it," Opal said.

July 13th, 1046 AGDR

Necrocon West was something to see. The convention was so large that as I walked around, I had to check the map to avoid getting lost. Hypothetically, we had continuing education to go to, but Opal and Emily swore up and down that they would cover for me if I did my own thing.

"Relax," Opal said. "This is your once-a-year chance to have fun."

"Thanks," I said.

I had hoped against hope I could see Alan somewhere. And I did.

I saw him in the brochure.

Necromancy for Modern Finance. *Alan Jaranjair, Chief Necromantic Officer, Notre Dame Group, Inc.*

Alan had never mentioned becoming so high. It wasn't unheard of for a bakt to have such drive and talent that he got promoted all the way to the top, even above the nominally free. And I wasn't even surprised, now that I saw it, that *Alan* had managed it.

But why hadn't he told me? He had never mentioned how things were going on behind the scenes. Did he expect me to be surprised?

I was one of the first in the room at his talk. I was startled at the sight of him. Though I had expected to see him with a collar—gut punching though that was—I hadn't expected him to seem so tired. Maybe others couldn't tell, but I could see he was unhappy, very unhappy.

"Thank you all for joining me," he started. "Since the beginning of the League, necromancy and finance have been entangled. The earliest banks used OSIRIS to remit money across thousands of kilometers…"

Alan could make everything sound interesting, even the seemingly dullest subject. I could tell, however, something was wrong. His presentation was fine, but I could sense he well and truly hated the subject he was presenting, a subject I knew he once loved.

What had happened to him at Notre Dame Group?

I didn't know, and I didn't get a chance to ask. He was surrounded by bakts and necromancers far more important than I, and by the time I had a chance to get close he was already gone.

We all had to see the keynote speaker, of course, and I had hoped to bump into Alan there. But on seeing the size of the auditorium, I realized that hope was far too slim.

What was I even thinking? I wondered. What would we do if we did meet? Wasn't I with Mark, now? Even if I wasn't, there was no chance we could get together. Did I still imagine God would arrange for us to somehow rejoin and have children in freedom?

Maybe I did, in the end. Maybe I did.

The keynote speaker was General James Westbrightsea, the first time an OSIRIS Wheel Group member had addressed what was otherwise a private conference. He spoke at length in his soft, yet commanding way—a stern but caring grandfather to us all.

He spoke, of all things, on the future of necromancy as OSIRIS's load increases. "We must soon face the propositions that not all ghosts can be reincarnated, that not all ghosts can get their six free realtime minutes, that not all ghosts can even survive..."

I wondered what he knew. After all, surely he knew about `free`.

But there was an even less chance of seeing him than Alan; Westbrightsea was swarmed by both important necromancers—wait, was that *Alan* with him? Yes, it was.

I badly wanted to go up, but there was so much security surrounding him that by the time I got close they had already gone out.

There was a half-hour break before the next talk, so I took the opportunity to use the restroom.

What happened next was so unlikely, yet so critical to what happened in the rest of my life, maybe even in the world, that I can't help but see God's hand in it. Of course, God has absolute mastery over history, our free choices included, and he alone knows his intent in arranging circumstances. Yet, nonetheless, I cannot imagine any other reason why, when I went to the bathroom, I walked out just as General Westbrightsea also did.

"Excuse me," he said.

I felt an overwhelming urge to ask about `free`. And it *was* overwhelming because I couldn't bear it any more.

"Sir!" I called out. "Please…"

He looked at me with interest. Perhaps a man so powerful and famous had this kind of reaction all the time.

"Yes?"

No. I shouldn't do this. I shouldn't ask. No good could come of this. No one would know if I said nothing. No one would care. But if I brought it up…

"Sir," I said, my words forcing themselves out. "Why did you enable swap?"

His eyes widened ever so slightly. Then he regarded me in silence.

"Excuse me," I said, with a nervous titter. "I shouldn't have…"

He got out a notepad. "What is your name?" he asked.

"Mary Firebrightsky, sir," I said, shaking. Dear God, what had I done?

"And your master?"

"The Alfred Slowbrightlaughter estate, sir."

He wrote that down, too. Then he handed me a business card. "Tell your master to arrange a meeting with me as soon as possible."

"Yes, sir!" I said.

He walked on. I stood there in silence.

What had I done? What did I know? What did *he* know?

What had the OSIRIS Wheel Group done?

CHAPTER FOURTEEN

NOW I WILL TELL YOU THE TRUTH

July 15th, 1046 AGDR

"I'm surprised you were so eager to meet me," Alysson said. "I assume this is something important."

I placed the general's business card on her desk. "General Westbrightsea wants to meet with me as soon as possible."

She looked at it. Then looked closer. "An OSIRIS Wheel Group member wants to talk to *you.*"

"Yes, ma'am. As soon as possible."

"If anyone else had come to me saying this I'd think it was an elaborate prank, but I know you wouldn't." She looked at me. "What the glitch is going on?"

"I met him at Necrocon West, ma'am. That was actually the second time."

"The *second* time?"

"He helped me get my medium license."

"You're a necromancer."

"I was supposed to be, but I couldn't find a bond. But I found a loophole."

"But you found a loophole?"

"It's complicated. When I went to get my OSIRIS account, the Necroforce officer didn't want to do it, but Westbrightsea showed up right then. I swear I'm telling the truth, ma'am."

"Oh, I'm certain you are. But if you got a medium license, how the glitch are you a necromancer right now?"

"I don't know, but your legal staff charged me thirty extra years to figure it out."

Alysson looked more confused than when we started. "Let's rewind. You have a meeting with General Westbrightsea?"

"Yes, ma'am. He said to ask my master to set it up."

"OSIRIS and all the EDENs, why *you*?"

"I asked him about swap use."

She looked at me.

"You said it was a concern for the Wheel Group," I noted.

"You—you know what, I don't know why this is happening, and I don't really care. If an OWG member wants it, we'll make it happen. You'll get your meeting. I would recommend not telling anyone else. Understood?"

"Understood, ma'am."

I didn't tell anyone, but Alysson had to tell others to prepare, and then news leaked immediately after that. I had a crowd around me next meal.

"Why you?" James the Fat asked.

"I can't say," I said.

"Oh, really, it's a big secret?"

"Of course she can't tell you," James the Greater said. "If she did, wouldn't she say already?"

As they bickered, Amy said, "I'm proud of you. I'd love to meet a MA-AT Wheel Group member."

"This is actually the second time," I said.

Everyone stared at me. Even the Jameses stopped fighting.

"*Really*, Mary?" Opal asked.

"It's true!"

"What happened?" Amy asked.

"I really shouldn't say—"

"Oh, look, we have a new Wheel Group member right here!" someone said.

"Did you speak with the Consul already?" Opal asked.

"Guys, *please*," I begged, but there was no stopping them now.

July 18th, 1046 AGDR

I had all new dress clothes, a haircut, and a stylist helped me with makeup. I felt a little awkward, but I was more concerned with steeling myself for what conversation we were about to have.

The fact that I hadn't been arrested or sworn to secrecy made me think I hadn't discovered something classified. Though I also didn't know for certain if I was going to be coming back "home."

Then again, I mused as they drove me there, I didn't know if literal imprisonment or being extradited to the Dead would be that much worse than servitude.

General Westbrightsea's office was surprisingly simple for a man so important and powerful. One wall had a sedate number of certificates, the other a great number of books. His desk had a closed laptop, a phone, and papers stacked neatly in folders. One plaque sat by itself, reading: "The finest sword is the one that's never drawn."

He looked at me with interest. "Ms. Firebrightsky, I believe we've met before the conference?"

"Yes, sir. Years ago. You helped me get a medium license, although I'm a necromancer, now."

"I understand," he said. "When was the last time you ran `free`?"

"About two years ago," I said sheepishly. "My master objected."

"It has only gotten worse since then," he said, without the slightest hesitation.

My breath hung in my chest.

"I don't believe in keeping secrets about OSIRIS," Westbrightsea said. "The Athanasian League is glued together with fraud and dishonesty. I also don't believe in giving orders based on lies. You have the right to political speech even as a bakt, so I can't order you to keep what you discovered a secret."

"I…see," I said.

"I will answer your questions," he said. "I trust you will then understand why this information would be better kept secret?"

"Yes, sir."

"What do you want to know?" he asked.

"…Why, sir?" I asked.

"OSIRIS was already ending ghosts. This was our only way we could stop it." His voice contained the pain of many sleepless nights.

"It is impossible to tell how much memory a grave will use due to technical reasons," he continued. "A grave can simply keep requesting memory, even beyond the legal limit. We believe that most of the time, this is not even intentional. Programmers are not perfect, and neither are the graves they make.

"Even if we did know exactly how much memory a grave would use, the Linux kernel within OSIRIS shares memory between processes in an unpredictable way known as overcommitment. Under normal circumstances, this would not be a problem, but when OSIRIS runs low on RAM, it can mean a substantial difference between the apparently available memory and the actual available memory."

He continued, "As a result of all this, far more memory is used than intended which, in turn, lead to the OOM Killer killing processes in and out of graves. On one occasion, it even killed a minor system process, leading to us taking emergency action. We could not ration RAM any further. We considered a number of options, but the only one we could agree on was creating a swap device to use as a buffer."

"I see." A more logical explanation than I had imagined. "So...it was not because of money," I said awkwardly.

"It was not *directly* caused by money. We had a lengthy discussion among ourselves on what exactly to do. We considered to manually redig every grave to better handle memory exhaustion, which was impracticable and completely untenable from a political standpoint. Regardless of what we decided, we could not coerce the Parliament of the Dead into agreeing." He could not quite hide the frustration on his face.

"The Parliament suggested disabling the OOM Killer altogether. However, if we did so, it would simply mean that should a grave run out of memory, it would freeze, fatally. If OSIRIS ran completely out of memory, without the OOM Killer, the whole system would freeze. We could not conscience even risking this.

"Similarly, we could disable memory overcommitment, but the Divine Architects suggested we leave the setting at `1` based on their experiments with test loads."

"Excuse me, sir, the Divine Architects left instructions?" I blurted. "S-so-sorry for interrupting, sir."

"They did, a huge amount of them. They can be read by any user with `man osiris`. The Wheel Group has not brought attention to this, on the basis that the EDENists would not want to accept their existence. But it is nonetheless public information."

"Yes, sir. I understand, sir. Please continue."

"Even were we to reduce memory overcommitment, it would substantially reduce the available memory to the point where we would have more graves than OSIRIS could support. It would have simply resulted in a different kind of mass ending: rips that ultimately fail because there is not enough RAM to construct a ka.

"The Vivites demanded we should do it anyway and reduce the size of new graves. I agreed that grave sizes had become unsustainable, but thought we would lose too many from failed rips. The Eternalists refused altogether. Our non-Athanasian members were equally split. We needed a two thirds majority to make a decision, so the motion failed."

"I thought activating the swap required unanimous consent, sir?" I asked.

"It did. After several failed rounds of attempting other solutions, we decided activating swap was our last remaining option."

Did I dare ask? "How did you vote?"

"I argued that the best possible option would be to recompile OSIRIS's kernel modules to handle memory exhaustion better, then enable swap if we had no other option. However, to do so would require permission from both the Living and Dead governments, and because doing so would essentially be altering someone's god, it was also politically untenable. In the end, we were out of time. We converted one around a hundred terabytes of the Necropolis's RAIDs to swap as a buffer."

"...Sir, there is much more swap used than that."

"Yes," he said, in a voice containing no little exhaustion. "RAM pricing is extremely complicated. The moment we enabled swap, RAM purchases surged until the buffer was almost eliminated. Without the Parliament of the Dead rewriting the formula, RAM will be purchased as soon as it is economically viable." He paused. "All of us pleaded with them, but we could not even ourselves agree on a new formula. The present formula is a compromise between two incompatible principles: Freely allow purchases of RAM by anyone who can afford it, or reserve RAM to provide for the maximum possible number of graves."

He sighed. "In the end, we were once again forced to make the same choice, and the only thing we could do was enable more swap. This has slowly continued as every new terabyte of swap is quickly devoured by both large estates and poorer ghosts expanding room. We have even seen the number of NAEDA graves increase rapidly.

"The only true solution is to increase throughput of reincarnations, but that is beyond our ability to effect change."

"I see. Er, forgive my boldness, but is it all right if you tell me this level of detail?" I asked. "I feel like a hypocrite by asking."

"All OWG decisions ought to be public knowledge. And yet all my colleagues idiotically believed that this could be kept a secret. I told them a curious necromancer, or necrotech, or even a medium, would inevitably run `free` and see what we did. We could not legally strip execution permissions for regular users, and even if we did, it would not only be obvious we were hiding something, but it would be very easy for any user to upload his own copy of `free` and access the same information."

He fixed his gaze on mines. "I am surprised to have met you before the secret broke loose. I feared the media would find out, and the necromantic world would be plunged into chaos." His gaze was not without kindness. "Have you told anyone?"

"I told a priest, and my master knows. But not this kind of detail," I said. I could almost physically feel the weight off my chest. I wasn't going to be arrested or executed for knowing this fact.

"I am willing to allow your master to know the details, simply because I do not want to put you in the position of having to lie to them. However, I also want them to know the OWG would be very angry if this information became public knowledge." At my expression he added, "I would not be, but I am only one member."

"Yes, sir."

"That said, I am the only OWG member who believes we should end the veil of secrecy surrounding the EDENs, and tell the world the truth that they are merely machines. They all believe it should be maintained to keep public order. I refuse to lie."

"But it—I mean, none of this is public knowledge, even now."

"The Athanasian League revolves around keeping secrets from the public. The media is told to keep this in the dark. Or at least they did before the Internet was rebuilt. It's only a matter of time before the truth of the EDENs reaches general knowledge."

"I…I know," I said. "I really did become what I said I believed, sir. I know the EDENs aren't even gods."

He looked at me with approval. "Good. The truth has a habit of escaping, as it already has."

"I-I-I understand, sir," I couldn't help but stutter.

He glanced at the clock. "I have only a few more minutes. Do you have any more quick questions?"

"Sir, if the situation is continuing to deteriorate, surely you must have a plan."

"We do not."

My jaw fell open, then clamped shut as if to let no thought escape.

"We are reaching an inflection point where there will be too much swap for OSIRIS to handle. Where that line is, no one knows. Ghosts are already ending in glitches. But my colleagues are only worried about their terms as OWG members."

"I…I see."

"We will kick the can down the road as many times as we can, until the situation becomes absolutely untenable. And one day it will. But until then, our only option is to keep the system going. That, I fear, is the only thing any Athanasian citizen can do." He glanced at the clock again. "I'm sorry, but I have another meeting after this."

"I understand, sir," I said, head spinning. "Thank you so much for meeting with me, sir."

I half-expected Alysson to interrogate me, but I hadn't even imagined she wanted Alfred Slowbrightlaughter himself listening.

VR was the most expensive form of seance, but it mattered nothing to him, when his grave was always at realtime. As we stood in one of the many virtual rooms of his palatial grave, I wondered how much the fancy lighting and elaborate backgrounds were contributing to the problem we were discussing.

He listened to the whole thing in silence, his state-of-the-art ka showing hints of emotion now and then. "Well, glitch," was his only comment at the end.

"Westbrightsea is too good for the world," Alysson said. "I'd hate to call a Wheel Group member naive, but…"

"Ma'am, may I run `free`?" I asked.

"I already did," Alysson said. "There is now 200 PiB of swap."

"Other estates would kill for this knowledge," Alfred SBL said. "Perhaps literally."

"If we tell other estates, sir, the OWG will trace it back to us," Alysson said.

"Yes, they would. But goodness me, we must immediately rework our financial situation."

I held my tongue from a comment about insider trading. Perhaps Westbrightsea could speak as he pleased about the truth, but he was an OWG member, and I only a bakt. Fortunately, my avatar was crude enough not to show facial expression or body language.

"Mary, to reiterate what the general said, *do not* tell anyone through `write` or any other method what you learned," Alysson said. "Not even anyone in the estate."

"Yes, ma'am. I don't know if it's going to matter."

"Why?" Alfred SBL asked.

"Sir, anyone could find this out. It will only take one curious necromancer to run the wrong command."

"Yes, but as long as that necromancer isn't *you*, we'll avoid any liability," Alfred SBL said. "Young woman, perhaps you think I am heartless. Technically, yes, I am, being a ghost and all. But I remember the unrest of the 910s very well. I remember very distinctly the riots after the Necromancers' Strike, being caught in one of them. I barely escaped with my existence. I am the last person in or out of OSIRIS who wants to see the system break down. And this news would do that."

"I understand, sir," I said. It wasn't really a lie, even if it wasn't fully true, either.

"Do we tell the rest of the necromancy team, sir?" Alyssa asked.

"No, but we'll talk with the heads of the other campuses' necromancy departments. Ms. Firebrightsky, we'll bring you to one more meeting, but then it's time to zip all our lips, understood?"

"Understood, sir."

July 20th, 1046 AGDR

I will not recount the subsequent meeting. I simply explained what I was told and then was dismissed.

The only thing the rest of the campus knew was that I had met a Wheel Group member, then with Alfred himself privately, then attended some meeting with the heads of other necromancy departments. That, and I refused to talk about any of it.

This fueled the wildest rumor mill, though I was amused at how simple their imaginations were compared to the unbelievable truth.

```
Message from alan.jrnjirlorl@OSIRIS on
/dev/pts/24414 at 15:31
Mary, I've heard a crazy rumor that
you met a Wheel Group member. They had
your name and everything. Is it true?
-o
EOF
[mary.firebrightsky@OSIRIS]$ write
alan.jrnjirlorl
> I'm sorry, I can't talk about it at
all. oo
> EOF
```

I didn't tell David. I didn't tell Fr. Justsquared.

The secret burned within me, and I knew the Devil thrived in secrecy. But I was tired, and afraid, and worn down. To this day I regret not speaking when I could. But when you read this, I will have spoken to God himself, and he in his mercy, whatever his judgment of my actions, would understand completely.

It was only six months before it all fell apart, anyway.

CHAPTER FIFTEEN

A GOD THAT CANNOT SAVE

The original video Alan posted is long gone from NeoVid, now. It was unsurprisingly purged during the War. It was shared all over the Neonet, and even today, watching it, I can feel what we all felt on first seeing it.

December 13th, 1046 AGDR

The Solstice Festival was gearing up as usual, and we were all horribly busy. There was no chance I could get a day off in the middle of the festival, but I planned to watch Christmas Mass online as usual. Part of me still wouldn't have wanted to go even if I had the chance. The memory of my last truly free day still hurt, theopsychiatry or not.

Despite all the political vitriol earlier, life wasn't that far from normal. Heartlightray was still trying to push his agenda without much success. Enough moderate Eternalists dragged their feet, and what he did pass often got stuck in court. I stopped even thinking about it. Vivites and Eternalists hated each other. What else was new?

"New" hit like a baseball bat to the face.

I heard talk about it at lunch break in the satellite office, and when I heard the name "Alan Jaranjair" I immediately interrupted, "Who?"

"Alan Jaranjair. The chief necromantic officer for Notre Dame Group," Emily said.

"He was, at any rate," a medium noted.

"You saw him at Necrocon West, right?" Emily asked.

"Yeah?" I said.

"He posted a short. *Man,* was it a short. I wish his presentation at Necrocon West had been as short."

I got on NeoVid and didn't have to search for it. It was already at the top of trending.

Alan sat in immaculate fuglin behind a desk. "My friends, my name is Alan Jaranjair, and I'm a necromancer. Today I want to show you something the Powers That Be absolutely do not want you to know.

"The truth is, OSIRIS is just a computer."

The camera went behind him as he logged in.

```
[alan.jrnjirlorl@OSIRIS]$ echo
"OSIRIS: Hello, I'm OSIRIS, and I'm
nothing more than a computer." >
seance.ipc
```

The seance device dutifully printed, and he held it up to the camera. "You can see right here that I've programmed it to say 'Hello, I'm OSIRIS, and I'm nothing more than a computer.' And it did, without a single thought in the world."

"What does this mean?"

What does it mean? What does it *mean*? He was violating all sorts of necromantic ethics, not least to not show one's terminal screen to a non-necromancer. I wanted to reach through my cell phone and strangle him.

"This means that for all the worship OSIRIS receives, in the end, it's no more sophisticated than this." The camera cut to an ancient picture of a vacuum tube computer. "Next time, I'll show you something even more disturbing."

I sat in silence.

Alan, what have you done? I knew OSIRIS was just a computer, but for a necromancer to just *announce* that…

I didn't know what would come of it.

In fact, none of us did.

December 14th, 1046 AGDR

The next day, it hit the fan for me personally.

As a necromancer, I had seen nearly everything when it came to clients. I had seen so many sob stories I had to ration my compassion, lest my already weary soul break down midday. I could usually tell within a second or two what my client would need when he stepped inside, but I couldn't with this gaunt, pale woman, other than that she was afraid. Deeply afraid.

"My name is Mary Firebrightsky, and I'm a licensed necromancer," I told her, trying to gauge her reaction. "How can I help you?"

She sat down, looking around at me, her hands, her phone, and me again. She looked into my eyes as if I was a lifeguard on a sinking ship, ready to judge if she was worth saving. "Ms. Fire–Firebrightsky," she said, and stopped.

I nodded, waiting for her to continue.

"I…I saw a video," she said, barely above a whisper.

Oh, no. Oh, *no*. This couldn't go anywhere good.

She trembled. "Did…did you see the video?"

"Was it by Alan Jaranjair?"

"Yes!" She gulped down air, and then cried out. "*Tell me it isn't true!*"

At that moment I knew where this was going to go. Every now and then we necromancers were faced with a client who worshipped OSIRIS with more devotion than usual, and we had been warned in school not to tell them the truth. For my part, I had subtly nudged them away from that subject, both before and after I had sold myself into slavery. If a client asked for more ritual, in the entirely wrong belief that any ritual of OSIRIS meant anything, I simply told them I had been to a modern school that didn't teach us that kind of thing. The one time I had actually had a problem was when someone wanted me to explain the Catechism of OSIRIS to him, and I answered truthfully that I couldn't because I worshipped the True God. He had gone away content.

None of those things, I knew deep in my bones, could possibly assuage this woman. The gig, after hundreds of years, was finally up.

What could I do? If I told her the truth, I would get in trouble with my earthly master. If I told her a comforting lie, I couldn't look my true master in the face.

"What specifically are you asking about?" I asked, hoping that I could find some way to stall, to get out, to escape doing what I was obligated to do.

"He…the necromancer, he said that OSIRIS isn't alive. It's just…a computer. Just a *computer*." she laughed, nervously. "That's not true, right? Right?"

Glitch it. Eternal consequences mattered more than temporal ones. "Ma'am, I'm sorry to say this, but Mr. Jaranjair was correct. OSIRIS is, ultimately, just a computer."

Her mouth fell open, looking at me with despair and total betrayal. "You're…you're joking. No. NO. NO-NO-*NO-NO!!*" she shrieked so loudly that I could not tell what she was even trying to say. Maybe nothing. Maybe there were no words. But she shrieked and screamed and called me names and shouted epithets about those damn twisties, and you can't trust them and OSIRIS is *real* and he *answered my prayer* and *my daughter* is in his hands and OSIRIS and in OSIRIS and by OSIRIS MY GOD and you should know and *PLEASE OSIRIS HELP!*

There was nothing I could say to comfort her. Every time she calmed down enough to coherently ask me to tell her the truth, I would, and it would resume. At the end she was hoarse, begging me, offering to pay me as much as I asked, even to pay off my loans, if I would just tell her the *truth*, the real truth, you cruel–my daughter–OSIRIS!

Eventually, Mr. Greendaytown came in and about physically dragged her out of my office.

"What did she want?" he asked me.

"She wanted to know if OSIRIS was a god or a computer."

"What did you tell her?"

"The truth. She didn't take it well."

"I saw. Or heard, more accurately. We could barely do any other work. Why?"

"Why what?" I asked.

"Why did you tell her the truth?"

"It's the truth," I said.

Alysson was as little enthusiastic about my defense as I had imagined. After about five minutes of straight yelling at me, she asked why I had done it. And I told her the same thing.

"That's *it*?" she asked. "That's why? You risk your reputation and that of our whole estate all because…" she stopped as if my words were rejected by her brain for having a syntax error. "Ms. Firebrightsky, I've been remarkably tolerant of your religion. You can't even be that way for others?"

"Tolerance doesn't mean telling a lie," I said.

"Surely your god would understand."

"No, he wouldn't."

"Who are you to say that? You're not him."

"Nor is OSIRIS."

"Do you have *any* remorse?"

"I'm sad that she was unhappy, but I don't regret saying what I did."

Another five minutes of solid yelling followed.

At last, she hung her head. "Fine. Have it your way. No more outside trips, *particularly* for your god. Understood?"

"I understand," I said. "I have a question."

"Yes. What?"

"Is OSIRIS a computer? Yes or no?"

She narrowed her eyes. "Yes."

"So what's wrong with saying that? You just did."

"For that, you're spending a week in the locker."

I decided I had said my piece, and I added nothing more.

I had never been in the locker before, and honestly, I was still so angry with Alysson that I didn't care. There was a toilet, a sink, a bed, and I had managed to snag a book.

By the end of the day, I realized that, yes, literal imprisonment could be worse than indenture if it meant you didn't see any other people.

By the third day, when the pride of standing up for the truth had worn off, I started to have *some* remorse. I could perhaps have broken the news to the poor woman gentler. I could have spoken the truth in love.

On the sixth day, bored out of my mind, I heard yelling and fighting, and then another door slam. It was the most interesting thing that had happened in days.

On the seventh day, I got out, chastened, but honestly not regretting my actions that much.

December 22st, 1046 AGDR

I got out one day too late for the Solstice Feast itself, though I didn't care that much, being that I didn't like celebrating a false god to begin with.

On the same subject, Alan had apparently released seven more videos and, by Amy's report, I was not the only one to spend a week in the locker. "James the Greater nearly strangled James the Fat," she said. "You didn't miss anything at the Feast. Except them being dragged apart. I had to bandage both of them."

"Holy slizz," I said, incredulous.

"Word on the vine is that she said the next time it happens they get shipped to the grinders."

I realized that Alysson had been comparatively merciful for something that had angered her so much.

"Was it worth it?" she asked.

"I'll find out after I'm ended," I said.

"By MA-AT, Mary, your religion is so *weird*."

"It is," I agreed. "I'll have to watch—"

"Oh, don't you dare," Amy said, gesturing with her fork. "His channel's been banned from the whole campus. Don't even talk about it."

I leaned in. "What the glitch did he say?"

"If the rumors are true, he said OSIRIS was inevitably going to crash or something. That's what he's been hinting at."

I felt a hole opening up beneath me.

Mark came up to us. "Alysson wants to talk to you."

"The feeling is not mutual," I said, but got up.

"My friends," Alan said on the video that Alysson played. "I will show you what not even the necromancers know. Like any computer, OSIRIS has finite RAM. Because of the insatiable greed for more, more, more, and better graves by the Dead, we are now out of it.

"Thus, our betters—" he said it with dripping sarcasm. "—have secretly enabled swap." He turned his terminal and typed `free -h`. "Ask any computer scientist to look at this and see the truth. The Wheel Group has jury-rigged OSIRIS to use mundane hard drives instead of its own RAM." He continued, "In short, OSIRIS is simply running out of room, and soon even jury-rigging won't be able to keep the lavish deathstyles of the rich and powerful intact. Watch: The next step is to start evicting graves—the poorest of the poor, first—from OSIRIS and ending the ghosts within. The truth is, the Athanasian Dream is a lie, and has been a lie for the last few decades."

He said it with such passion that I momentarily forgot where I was and almost cheered.

"And what will happen next? My friends, next video I will explain my solution."

Alysson stopped the video and closed her laptop. "Who is Alan Jaranjair to you?"

"Ma'am, he was my boyfriend in college."

"Why?"

"We liked each—"

"*Why* did you tell him?" Alysson yelled.

"I didn't," I said.

She glared at me.

"Look through my terminal logs. Look through my work cell. Look through my personal cell. Look through the cells of every bakt in the building. I didn't tell him."

"You wrote to him when he asked," she said.

"I told him I couldn't talk about it," I said. "That's all."

"No secrets? No lover's inside jokes?"

"No, ma'am. If I had told him what I knew, he would have been giving an entirely different speech."

"Or he's simply stirring the pot," Alysson said. "I don't see why Notre Dame hasn't sent him to the grinders already."

"Political speech, I'm certain."

"I suppose that's the loophole, yes."

"Ma'am, if that falls under the political activities clause, then we have the right to view it by the same—"

"Mary, shut up for one moment."

I stopped.

"I'll make you a deal. You stop rocking the boat, and I'll let you go back to that temple. Yes, Mary, the world you inhabit is very simple, full of good and evil, truths and falsehoods, unalienable rights and clear rules. That's not the real world. And until you understand that, you're always going to be getting in trouble. So how about this? Keep to yourself, don't cause any *more* trouble, and you can stay in that little world. Understood?"

I didn't say anything.

"What now, Mary?"

"I don't think I can guarantee I will never conflict with your rules," I said.

"Glitching EDENs are you—" She held her face. "Only you, of all people, would *preemptively* warn me that you might break the rules."

I didn't say anything.

"My offer is rescinded. Don't expect any more favors from now on. And you *will* disable messages."

"I understand, ma'am," I said.

December 26th, 1046 AGDR

By the next day, the necromantic world was in utter chaos, proving without a doubt that Alan's words were true. Or at least the first part of them.

The OWG hadn't yet commented on it, but we all knew it was a "yet." The only reason why the Senate, or even the Parliament, hadn't called them to testify was that acknowledging the crisis meant acknowledging that OSIRIS was an inanimate computer. But everyone knew things were wrong, no one knew what to do, and soon enough, even not doing anything would be a choice of what to do.

I wondered how Westbrightsea was doing.

I watched with some detachment, and I'll admit, satisfaction at my vindication. But I also knew that those who worshipped OSIRIS had suddenly the crisis of faith they could no longer avoid. Having suffered for my own faith, I realized I had wronged my poor client by speaking the truth without offering a helping hand.

Yet as a practical matter —because I would never see that woman again, and I had no control over OSIRIS or anything else—what mattered most to me was that I couldn't go to Mass.

I got a text from Janet in my rec time.

You haven't been here recently. Everything all right?

I tapped back.

My master banned me from coming. I don't know when I might be able to come back.

That night, I prayed to Our Lady of Sorrows that I would still like to go to Mass, if she could find some way.

December 27th, 1046 AGDR

The next morning, I got pulled aside for a visitor. "He says he's from your church," Mark said.

"Oh, it's probably Father Justsquared," I said.

It wasn't.

It was a tall and quite fat lawyer. "Ms. Firebrightsky, I'm Joseph Nightwhiteheron, a servitude attorney with Truesongglory and Nightwhiteheron, specializing in indentured rights. Mind coming with me for lunch?"

"I, err, don't know—"

"Your master can't legally stop you. I'm here on behalf of some people from your place of worship."

"I'll come!" I said.

I sat somewhat awkwardly next to him (at his insistence) as we drove back to his office. He had an actual pizza waiting.

"It's freeman-made food," he said. "One of the few places in Newla, that is."

"Thank you, sir," I said, and took a slice. It was delicious. "I haven't had real pizza in years."

"Have they been feeding you properly?" he asked immediately, but causally.

"They have me on a normal ration," I said.

"Do they let you order in?"

"I've never heard of it," I said.

He wrote notes on a legal pad as I ate.

"The reason I'm here is that some people from your church said your master had banned you from going outside, and particularly from your religious rituals."

"That's true," I said.

"That's definitely contrary to your rights."

"Um, forgive me, sir, but I've gotten in a lot of trouble—and…er, she said the Ombudsman wouldn't help me."

"Quite possibly not because they're run by the League Labor Bureau. But my firm specializes in taking private cases."

Hope began rising in me but, as a bakt, I had seen it dashed so many times. "I'm not sure if I can afford you," I admitted.

"Your friends have agreed to pay for my service. So please, tell me about your life as a bakt."

"…Certainly," I said.

December 28th, 1046 AGDR

After telling him everything I could think of, and eating perhaps too much pizza, he sent me home with a warning to avoid confronting SBL's staff or Legal, or talking about the case in any way. He did suggest that if anyone had similar stories, I could give them his business card.

I ran out by next breakfast.

By dinner that day I was called into Alysson's office. A revenant from Legal was there, silent in a corner with a neutral expression on his mask.

"We can work this out," Alysson said with forced cheer. "We can get you to all the services you'd like. Just sign this paper."

I looked at the paper, unfooled. "I'm sorry," I said. "I was instructed not to discuss this case. May I leave?"

The false cheer disappeared in an instant. "Don't expect a better offer. Leave."

I walked out without a word.

Nothing happened right away, other than a rift slowly developing among the bakts. Some of us were easily bribed into signing whatever gave a bigger peculium and better rights. Others immediately saw that their grievances could finally be heard by someone with the power to do something about it.

Rumor on the grapevine was an inspection by an outside servitude arbiter was coming because suddenly everything was much nicer, including the addition of certain legal posters in bigger type in more prominent locations. The food got substantially better, and the rations larger. I reported every detail to my lawyer, who had me take pictures of things before and after.

"I wouldn't have *asked* for this," I told my therapist. "But all my suffering is working out better for everyone, somehow."

"Life is like that," David told me.

January 1st, 1047 AGDR

Life was even better for Alan.

The OSIRIS Wheel Group issued a lengthy statement, announced by Westbrightsea. "...It is true that, for the lack of any other option, we converted some of the Necropolis's RAIDs to be used as swap. However we did not, nor do we currently have, nor do we intend at any time in the future, to deliberately drop graves as a means for saving RAM…"

But this only added fuel to the fire. Although the OWG did not officially declare OSIRIS to be a computer, their announcement had the same effect for the skeptical portions of the population. Heartlightray issued his own speech which fanned the flames. "…This crisis, which would have been avoided in its entirety , has only to do with Vivites' irrational fear that graves will be dropped. They will not. Why not blame the Vivites, who every day insist on the superiority of the Living over the Dead?…"

Alan had successfully taken a jackhammer to all our cultural fault lines: Triglyph versus Spiral, Vivite versus Eternalist, EDENist versus non-EDENist, Living versus Dead, bakt versus free. And it all made perfect sense once he released his final video. "…It is not enough to simply stand idly by and argue. I am officially announcing my campaign for Second Senator of the Living of the Neyonaize Canton…"

I saw only that clip on the news, as the reporters announced that Alan had raised over three hundred thousand drachmae in a few hours. In a few days, he had raised millions, well enough for what talking heads claimed was his real goal: pay off his loans and free him.

Of course, Alan would find a way out. He had to run, obviously, though at that point I suspected he would have a very significant chance of winning. Still, he had not mentioned one word of this to me. Not that he could. I had disabled writes, just as Alysson had ordered.

Please, God, I prayed. *At least get him into a situation he can stand. Blessed Mother, pray for us and for him!*

CHAPTER SIXTEEN

AND THE EARTH HAS WITHHELD ITS CROPS

I am certain historians will trace the downfall of the Athanasian League to the beginning of Fimbulwinter, and Fimbulwinter to June 19, 1047 AGDR. Yet that day passed, and the next, and so on, life going on as best it could, until the Solstice Riots.

But I remember it all in utter detail.

February 9th, 1047 AGDR

We thought it was just something happening in a far-off country at first. The HORUS Wheel Group in the African nations had begun their serious dispute between the Abundance and Balance factions. I must admit, I didn't follow all of it, and I definitely did not follow it at the time. The news was worthless, between reporters who could not log into an EDEN given free credentials, and their increasingly vitripudent denunciations of their fellow ignoramuses on the other side. We mages know that there is constant drama between an EDEN's Wheel Group members at the best of times. What difference did this make?

But inevitably the national governments got involved. The colder countries wanted more sun. The warmer countries didn't want to risk overusing HORUS. The amount of pressure the mundanes can exert on a mage is beyond the ability of any mundane to truly comprehend. Our credentials are the keys to fortune, power, health, immortality, and the satisfaction of desires as yet unknown to the desirer. What can a "no" be interpreted as than anything other than a tacit judgment of unworthiness? Every mage, I fear, has learned to wheedle, to walk back, to half-joke, and wave away the harsh statements we were told in school to make without hesitation.

Our keys unlock every door that Man has thought to open, and the Divine Architects rightly feared what might be found on the other side. But who are we to keep them shut? All that separates we who bear those keys from the ordinary individual is a tattoo, a metaphysical dongle, a few years of schooling, and, maybe, the will to use our power for the good of all humanity. The last was perhaps never truly present in reality, but, if it was an ideal, it was one we all truly believed.

And so the augurs' lounge were practically invaded by the rest of the mage bakts when the news broke: The government of Westland had threatened to strip the keys from "their" Wheel Group members unless they complied. And those paragons of restraint, those chosen guardians of HORUS, those we trusted with absolute power over an EDEN—they caved!

James the Greater was practically screaming at Bernice SBL. "You can't be serious!"

"Why are you attacking me?" he asked, utterly calm. "I don't have root access."

James huffed. "You can never trust an augur."

I was angry, but I was too angry to even have an opinion. Instead, I went to one of the not-besieged augurs, a girl named

Jasmine Allredlong, and asked her if she could explain the situation to me.

She tried, but the more detailed it got, one augur or another would shout at her, until she was on the verge of tears. My anger softened at that, and I held her hand. I cannot remember what came of that day, except that by the end of it we were all in our separate wings, repeating our positions out loud to anyone who would listen.

Perhaps I had needed her hand as much as she did mine. The floor of the world had a hole in it, and the rest was collapsing.

April 14th, 1047 AGDR

Of the seven members of the HORUS wheel group, Westland and the Abundants had three, but the Balancers had three as well, and the remaining one lived in Switzerland. Perhaps the world would have taken a very different course if Karl Redsunwave had joined with the Balancers in blacklisting the Abundants' access, but he cited the need for neutrality over the present crisis.

What was there left? The two factions immediately called upon HORUS's deepest powers to counteract the actions of the other side. Then they struggled harder and harder. The Abundants sent drought and frost and scorching hot towards the Balancers, who replied with a cold so severe neighboring countries fell into chaos. Mundane war broke out—an afterthought at this point.

A few worrywarts called it the next Gotterdammerung, but the augur-on-augur violence was only a candle to that star. It took effort to summon even a strong breeze. They had flung blizzards at each other, yes, but they needed root access to do so. I remember, to this day, remarking that the worst that could happen was a hurricane or two, until one faction or the other gave in.

And in any case, I had bigger things to worry about. My lawyer had officially filed a lawsuit on behalf of many bakts, including myself, which none of us talked about, but all of us thought about. The threatened arbiter came, but I never saw him: All of us plaintiffs were immediately assigned to outside duties so we wouldn't be present when he came.

Still, we all felt the world was teetering on the edge of something much worse, though we had yet to imagine how much worse it could get.

June 10th, 1047 AGDR

"Are you OK, Mary?" Emily asked me.

"I'm," Cough. "Fine." Cough. I had had the cough for weeks, and it hadn't gotten better, but that described life in general. Even if I was sick, I didn't want to bother the lifeweavers. Amy had told me that their boss, Abigail Slowbrightlaughter, was harsh and often cruel, but particularly cracked down on anyone who tried to call in sick. The medical bakts thereby detested the paperwork. It certainly explained why they tended to be grumpy whenever I had had to use their aid, insomuch as we weren't all grumpy.

"You're not fine," she said.

"I don't want to fill out paperwork," I said.

"Let me talk to Tyrone." She hurried off.

I marveled at how, if we had not gotten much farther than my first meeting, we had still progressed a little.

Tyrone came back. "How long has this been going on?"

"A few…days, maybe," I said.

"Nah, you've been coughing for at least two weeks," Emily said.

"You should talk to the lifeweavers," he said.

"Sir, I don't think it's that serious, and I don't want to fill out the paperwork."

"I do, and I'll fill out the paperwork."

"Thank you, sir," I said.

I later learned that Tyrone had canceled all my other appointments. When nothing was forthcoming, I lay back in my chair and found myself falling asleep.

When I woke up later, my chest was in agony. I coughed, and muscles I didn't even know I had screamed in pain. And nothing I did helped, and I couldn't stop coughing.

I stumbled out into the lobby. Everyone stared at me. "I think—" Cough, cough, cough "—I think I injured a muscle from coughing so hard."

"You're heading home," Tyrone said firmly.

They had to help me onto the bus. On the way the pain got worse. "I can't breathe," I croaked. Cough, cough, cough. I realized in that moment that I could *die*, and suddenly all my complaints about indentured life seemed trivial.

"Hold on!" Tyrone hit the pedal and, while he was breaking other traffic laws, contacted someone on the phone. "Good." He hung up. "Mary, the moment we get there the lifeweavers are waiting. Just hold on!"

When the bus stopped, the lifeweavers clambered aboard and helped me off into a stretcher. "I—" Cough, cough, cough, "I injured a muscle coughing."

It turned out I was horribly wrong.

The lifeweavers' common room was stuff of legend. Some of them had too much time on their hands, and they made even the carpet alive, as the legend went. It remained the stuff of legend for me because they took me to the infirmary next door. They stuffed a nasal canula up my nose, and, while I didn't feel better, I could at least breathe easier. Another lifeweaver attached leads to my forehead and tapped away on the attached tablet.

They weren't talking.

"What's it say?" I groaned.

"Pneumonia," one said.

"*Pneumonia?*" I asked.

"Yes, pneumonia."

"Don't worry, Mary, you're safe here," Amy told me. "You'll live."

I didn't even think to retort that I'd rather have not made it, because I was too afraid. For whatever my life hurt, death hurt far more.

My days, unfortunately, did *not* pass in a haze. I was too sick to even read, so I simply laid in my bed and let them put needles, leads, breathing treatments, and the Lord knows what else in me. On a more adventurous day, I managed to get to the shower and wash off the grime, being too exhausted afterwards to do anything but lay back in my bed.

Alysson told me firmly that I was not to try to work at all until I was healthy. I was too sick to enjoy the time off.

My friends came and visited on Saturday and Sunday, but most of the time I was alone. Even Amy was busy. Still, I overheard a lot of lifeweaver chatter. They were all firmly in the Abundance camp—if MA-AT was limited to only a few, what a terrible injustice that would be! I realized, then, that my own necromantic view—that the EDENs should not be used for political power—was not the only view. But I was smart enough not to talk about it.

Not that I even had the breath.

June 19th, 1047 AGDR

The Heuristic Omnipresent Regulator of Underlying Systems, as the true name of HORUS went, was no longer so regulated. The EDEN of Weather was too sensitive to orders, and the climate too sensitive to manipulation. The Balancers rained blizzard after blizzard on the Abundants who replied in turn. Something changed, something shifted….

The day I got out of the infirmary, I noted how cold it was, and I realized it was a day before the Summer Solstice. I hurried, using the walls as support, to the porch.

Outside, it was snowing. The careful climate maintained by HORUS's adepts was crumbling under HORUS's own assault. The green, carefully made leaves of trees were covered with white frost.

Bernice Slowbrightlaughter was watching in silence. "It's the end," he said simply.

"Sir?"

"We'll have a year of famine," he said. "All across the world. This is the end. All because we couldn't share."

I stood beside him, shivering, and wondered.

A whole crowd had gathered beside Bernice and I. The augurs, who had stopped talking to the other staff when the HORUS War began, joined in utter silence.

"So what now?" Mike asked.

"We call up Alfred and ask him what he wants to do," the old augur said.

"Elementalists, grab your wands and get over here!" Jeffery Slowbrightlaughter said. A bus was wheeling out of the estate's garage. "We're heading to the city."

"The glitch we need elementalists to buy things, now?" Mike snapped back.

"When the damn *climate* is about to kill everyone! There's going to be riots. Now get!"

Mike didn't retort, but hurried after the chief elementalist.

"I think I should have stayed an extra day inside," I suggested to Bernice.

"What?" he asked. "And miss seeing history made? Seems like a lot of important someones could have learned more in kindergarten."

News on the grapevine was when the elementalists got there, there were no food riots, but neither was there food. Everywhere they went was empty of anything that could be bought.

We had a month's supply for everyone on estate grounds, and, in any case, most of our owners didn't even need food. But fear spread faster than the bacteria in my lungs. I had gone from a little sick to near death in under a day. Even faster had our peace gone.

So I lay in misery, someone having propped me up in the necromancer's common room, and I watched as nearly everyone lost his mind.

The whole room, myself included, could agree that something was terribly, terribly, wrong. *Who* was wrong was another story, and as the arguments grew louder, I feared someone would reach for something expensive or irreplaceable to throw. The Jameses naturally picked polar opposite opinions, and dragged others into their orbit.

"Enough!" Alysson ordered. Everyone shut up. "We are *necromancers*. We can't even log into HORUS. So just take a chill pill and relax. We'll all get through this."

"Ma'am," I wheezed. "Have we consulted Alfred?"

"We are about to. I want everyone at a laptop—no, not you Mary. Sandra, you sit by her. We need to perform a force seance."

"Why?" Opal asked. "Isn't he always in realtime?"

"We're calling his *dad*."

The silence that fell was perhaps more to his having a dad, and thereby not being some kind of primordial humor deity. But there was a good enough number of us wanting to avoid the reality of force waking.

It is written in the Table of the Dead that the Living do not have the right to interfere with the Dead. But it is also written in the Table of the Dead that the emergencies of the Living take precedence over the peace of the Dead.

For reasons similar to a firing squad, we would combine our commands to make one that was both more powerful than all of us, but also not directly attributable to any of us.

"You just watch," Sandra told me. I watched with a mix of curiosity and horror as they struggled to set up and troubleshoot the cursed thing.

Hours passed, but then we were ready.

```
[sandra.glorynightred@OSIRIS]$ yes |
commune -i -t 1 --no-hup --ipc-
path=/home/alyssa.slowbrightlaughter/c
ommunion.ipc &
[1] 990201101
```

```
[sandra.glorynightred@OSIRIS]$
```

"Why are you piping `yes`?" I asked.

"There are too many screens you have to go through, and everyone has to press the button at the same time," Sandra said.

Where the glitch had she learned such nonsense? But this seemed only slightly a worse idea than the communion to begin with, so I said nothing as the screens flashed by.

```
Command: osi seance -j --free --force
--audio --jack --speed realtime
francis.slowbrightlaughter --client-
name "Alfred Slowbrightlaughter" (y/N)
y
```

"Who dares disturb me!?" howled all of our speakers at once.

"Father, this is a crisis—" Alfred's voice came from the speakers.

"You always wake me for crises. Get your own damned act together."

"We need your signature."

"No. I don't care. Leave me be." His words were followed by an anguished scream of pain. "Let me be!"

"Father—"

```
[00:00:14] Gate of Fire used.
[00:00:14] Seance ended.
[1] Exit 10           yes | commune -i
-t 1 --no-hup
Message from na.forcewake@/dev/pts/13
at 14:21
Your access is hereby being suspended
under C.R.T. 6 S 1144(a)
Connection to OSIRIS closed by remote
host.
Connection to OSIRIS closed.
```

```
[sandra.gloryrednight@SBL-A4F1]$
```

Groans, muttered curses, and not-so-muttered curses filled the air.

"Did he just reach for the Gate of Fire in fourteen seconds?" Sandra asked.

After too much bickering over how a ghost could get a necromancer to shut up, the League came up with the Gate of Fire. In the grave into which OSIRIS loads a force seance, there is an incandescently bright wheel of fire on one wall. Grabbing hold of it brings the one pain that ghosts can feel—that of burning—but if one holds long enough, the seance is deemed illegal.

Such as it just was.

"Oh dear," Alfred said through the speakers, then laughed nervously. "Perhaps we should have thought that through a bit more."

"We'll contest it all in the Court of the Tomb," Alysson said confidently. "Until then, you all just got a vacation. Mary, contact your attorney."

"Excuse me?" I asked.

"Contact your attorney. We need to talk."

June 20th, 1047 AGDR

Their need was simple: I was one of the three necromancers with OSIRIS access left on campus. Aside from Alysson and Tyrone, there was no one but myself.

Their problem was also simple: As long as I was sick, they couldn't legally order me to work because if they did and my condition worsened, that would be extremely bad for them in court.

I watched with a mixture of fascination and glee as my lawyer negotiated better everything for me: a bigger peculium, a promotion, and—this was why I agreed—returning to Mass.

He himself got a fee out of it, but I was happy for him. I would have signed anyway if they had just dangled the Mass in front of me, but now he had them in a headlock.

They passed the final document to me to sign.

"I'd like to go over this one more time," I said.

We did, and—praise be to the Lord—nothing stuck out to me or to my lawyer. By sheer chance, I had gotten an amazing deal. The only catch was that I needed to work while sick, but I was willing if I could go back to Mass.

I signed the papers.

"I'm glad we could reach an agreement," Redshineglory said.

"Yes," I said, and coughed horribly.

June 21st, 1047 AGDR

The next day, we passed the bizarre sight of people warming themselves with oil can fires on the streets on the Summer Solstice. It was at that moment I had the first inkling of how bad things were about to get.

Still, as the newest assistant manager at the satellite office, I had work to do. In fact, I was the only other necromancer at the office.

I learned a lot of fascinating details, particularly how much more the estate was billing our customers than "paying" us. But I decided not to rock the boat. I didn't have the energy for it, anyway.

"Mary, you need to take a break," Tyrone said.

"But—"

"You are the only other necromancer here, and if you get sicker, I'll be having to deal with everything. Just take a break."

"OK," I said. I realized that soon enough, *I* could order people on breaks.

I didn't know if I liked that idea. I mean, sure, I would love to help people, but did I want to decide who got it easy?

I sat in our lunch room as Heartlightray, the Consul of the Living, and Windjoymight, the Speaker of the Dead, made their joint address.

Jacob Heartlightray was instantly recognizable in the white toga that was vast to accommodate his weight. "My friends and countrymen, as of this moment the world is living through a true crisis, not seen in centuries. The augurs have told me that we will experience a decline in temperature, on average, of three degrees Celsius this year, and possibly worse. This year will not have a summer, and possibly the next will not either. This is a crisis that will take all of our coordination and effort to overcome.

"But we will overcome it."

Ezekiel Windjoymight was in a fashionable low-poly model like an abstract man in a black suit. "A rise in grain prices will not directly affect us, nor will the cold," the Speaker said. "However, we, the Dead, are not immune to the suffering of the Living. I speak for the Parliament of the Dead in our pledge to spend every possible effort protecting all citizens of the Athanasian League, Living and Deceased, from this disaster."

"We will be distributing grain to every city—" The Consul started.

And what about the outlying rural areas? I wondered.

"—and promoting as much greenhouse construction as possible. We are attempting to recruit every lifeweaver available to assist with agriculture…"

Recruit or buy? Could a bakt be taken by eminent domain, I wondered.

"This is Alex Raualral from NNN: Are the governments planning to take action against the warring HORUS factions?"

"We cannot," the Consul said. "That is simply not our privilege as guardians of OSIRIS. If they disagree with how we use OSIRIS, they can't just decide to punish us."

I grit my teeth. The politicization of OSIRIS, and how much of the EDEN we owned by virtue of possessing the vast majority of the Wheel Group, was not a settled subject among necromancers. Jacob Heartlightray had apparently already decided.

To think, for a moment, that I had started to like him.

Still, we needed to stick together, didn't we? As much as I disliked Heartlightray, this was actually a decent speech, and I felt, if not reassured, at least less worried.

Though part of me had the premonition that things were about to go very, very wrong.

CHAPTER SEVENTEEN

A HANDFUL OF FLOUR IN A JAR

I don't have the words to describe Fimbulwinter. It was cold, yes, but more than cold, we were afraid, and angry. No one knew what should be done, yet everyone knew something had to be done. Or, rather, no one could agree on what should be done. And if we, the bakts of the Slowbrightlaughter Estate Main Campus, couldn't agree, who had no power to do anything, the League Governments were far, far worse.

The Senate of the Living was a slow-moving trainwreck. Jacob Heartlightray demanded emergency powers, and at first the Senate was happy to oblige. Yet as he wanted more and more powers, even the moderate Eternalists turned against him. Insomuch as there were moderates any more.

The Athanasian Flag is half-green, half-black, with a counterchanged golden Ouroboros in the shape of infinity. The green represents the Living, the black, the Dead, and the gold, immortality.

Of those colors, the Vivites had chosen green and the Eternalists gold. Soon a talking head's comment about "deep green" had led to calling the new, more populist branch of Vivites the Deep Vivites, and the corresponding Deep Eternalists.

Alan was a Deep Vivite.

I hadn't known him to be so extreme when we were dating, but something had changed in him. His videos, not that we were allowed to watch them, had hundreds of millions of views. His QuickTalk posts were often all over the Neonet. His commentary was sharp and brutal. I almost wondered if I did know him, any more.

The news became unreadable, not for the content—the HORUS War continuing with no end in sight, refugees from colder countries already streaming down, political gridlock—but because the comments, in and out of the post, had become incoherent with rage.

I stopped looking at the news, or tried to, because I would hear it constantly from others and, as assistant manager, I had to break up several fights between my staff. I believe I spent more of my time preventing the satellite office from disintegrating into total chaos than I did actually working as a necromancer. Tyrone helped, but we were often overwhelmed.

Our clients, too, were overwhelmed. Young men and women, but usually men, of the opposite side as the poor woman I had aggravated, wanted the reverse: They wanted to know that OSIRIS really was a computer; and all the EDENists were wrong. Once, two clients on opposite sides had heard each other through the walls, and I had to call the police.

Whatever fault lines the League had had were now broken into open rifts, first by the 1046 election, then by Alan's provocations, then by Fimbulwinter. Self-euthanasia, even self-endings went up. Everyone was bitter and miserable and cold.

And every month, it grew colder.

August 11th, 1047 AGDR

St. Teresa of Avila Catholic Church was my sole solace.

They had all been overjoyed to see me back, but the rifts in the Church had also begun to crack open. Fr. Justsquared had had to make an official no politics policy for the fellowship time.

The fellowship time no longer had coffee or donuts. We instead served a basic luncheon of whatever the Women's Auxiliary could find, with the heat cranked to the maximum. The price of THOTH-based heating had skyrocketed, so they had a donation box simply for warmth.

As miserable as I was, I realized I was the sort of person who could not turn down the sufferings of others.

"Is OSIRIS really a computer?" a boy with a worn look in his eyes asked.

"It is," I said. "Humans made it. Humans program it."

"And HORUS?"

"Same thing."

"Then why did they make it mess the world up?"

"I haven't a clue."

August 12th, 1047 AGDR

I didn't have any sympathy for Legal, but I had a little sympathy for the Living part of it because they became extremely busy. They tried to get an injunction to unban those part of the force seance, without success. Frederick SBL's lawyers insisted that he would simply be disturbed again by the same people. The Court of the Tomb sided with him, so we had no injunction.

Legal's next step was to get a ruling from the Court of the Tomb that our force seance was justified. Once we had accomplished that, we would perform *another* force seance, and demand Fredrick Slowbrightlaughter listen to our situation, and perhaps get him to sign off on changing the estate. If not, we had other screws to turn.

"Ma'am, could I ask you to make an announcement?" I asked Alysson.

"What?"

"Tell us what is going on with Alfred and Fredrick because it's causing discipline issues."

She raised an eyebrow. "How?"

"We're all wondering if we're working for food for the hungry or food to make money."

"Both," Alfred SBL said cheerfully from the wall. "There's nothing so much like a vital service to profit from."

"OK," I said.

"You can tell them all the history, Alysson," Alfred SBL offered.

"Frederick owns 35% of the estate, just enough that we need his signature to make a decision," Alysson told me. "As part of the settlement of the last lawsuit, we agreed to keep SBL Main in the same condition he had last seen it when he was still Living. But now we can't possibly maintain it, not with Fimbulwinter, and we might as well be doing something productive with the soil."

"I see," I said. I realized I had at least partially misjudged the reasons for our collective indenture, and I resolved to confess it as soon as possible.

September, 1047 AGDR

Life returned to a form of normal. It never returned to fully normal, as it got colder, and colder, and colder. Indeed, the first half of 1047 were the last normal months in the Athanasian League.

Still, for a given, low-quality facsimile of normal, things returned to normal. I recovered from the pneumonia, finally, although my lungs were permanently scarred, and my health damaged. I had to carry an inhaler wherever I went. Legal won the injunction they needed on appeal; everyone else was unbanned, and we more or less resumed our previous jobs.

But not myself. I was still an assistant manager. Tyrone insisted that I remain his assistant, having done such a good job. That agreement remained, although our lawsuit wasn't over. No one was allowed to talk about it. For once, because something sufficiently important was dangled in front of us, we didn't gossip about something.

Politics filled the gap.

October, 1047 AGDR

Four months of relative peace passed since Fimbulwinter began. Then things got worse, at least for ourselves. The weather became bitterly cold as "summer" ended. All of Africa and now the Middle East was being dragged into the HORUS War. Everyone agreed it should end; no one agreed how.

The streams of refugees from the northernmost and southernmost countries became a flood. The Alaskan Republic practically became uninhabitable. Vivites and Eternalists bickered over it, but whether they could stop them or not, every country was dealing with it. St. Teresa of Avila started having their fellowship times every Sunday, so great had become the needs of those on the streets.

Many chose indenture, even at the grinders, until—as crazy as things had gotten—the body processing facilities had reached maximum capacity. Those who didn't find a master often starved, or soon enough froze to death in the streets.

I remember lying awake one night, realizing that if I had still been free, I quite possibly would have run into problems as the rift over EDENism tore the necromantic world apart, and, if I had run out of money, I could have been in a far worse position than assistant manager at a large estate.

I even somehow started to like Alfred SBL, at least comparatively.

Francis SBL, as we were learning, was the nastiest son of a glitch we had ever met. He had prepared layers upon layers of legal and technical defenses against anything happening to "his" estate other than absolute perfection. He also didn't wake to enjoy it. Necromancers are accused of talking about their clients behind their backs, and, in this case, it was entirely true.

But talk was becoming something else.

November, 1047 AGDR

Alfred testified before the Senate of the Living in a day-long hearing we all watched parts of. He pleaded that the government needed to act, by eminent domain if necessary, to stop the nation from starving. He offered that he would be converting all of his estate's land to farmland if he could only force his father and business partner…

His pleas fell on somewhat deaf ears. The Land Adjustment Bill was vetoed by Jacob Heartlightray, to be replaced by the Government Food Assurance Act. Government lifeweavers were ordered to mass produce basic grains—enough to live on, not thrive on. We bakts got stuck with it because it became the only thing cheap enough to feed the whole campus.

Govgrain bread, as it was soon called, was about the only thing I was eating, aside from a cup of a protein shake to help the LifeLiquid down. I was already thin, but lost weight. So did we all, even James the Fat.

Even hosts became made of govwheat, which the Dicastery for the Defense of the Faith had ruled was acceptably wheat enough. With worldwide crop failures, especially including grapes, soon it was only Fr. Justsquared who was receiving the Precious Blood.

I remember we had govgrain pizza once at fellowship time: govgrain with tomato sauce and lots of salt. Animal products were out of the question. We could each have one piece, and it was a decent-sized piece. But at the speed at which some of our guests ate it, I realized I was incredibly lucky for having full meals to eat, even if it was just govgrain.

All the while it got colder outside, and colder, and colder, and colder.

CHAPTER EIGHTEEN

MINGLED WITH THEIR SACRIFICES

December 12th, 1047 AGDR

We had reached the absurdity of food channels becoming the most popular channel in all of the campus and satellite offices. What the ancient author C. S. Lewis had proposed as a hypothetical became actual: a world where we were so hungry for something other than govgrain that we would willingly watch food shows to fantasize about eating.

I will admit, I did so, too. It was better than the other channels, at any rate. Sports were canceled due to the weather; I wasn't fond of crime dramas and cartoons. "Reality" TV was absurd, and the political channels were removed from our packages.

The other channel we lost was EDEN Network Live, simply because EDENism had become so controversial that there was no talking about it. With Alysson's permission—she didn't point out the irony that *I* asked, though I'm sure she saw it—we banned our team from even talking about it to clients. It had gotten so out of hand.

As the Winter Solstice approached, things had gotten worse. The HORUS War had no end in sight, and the HORUS Wheel Group had discarded all pretense of ritual. The Spiral Augur Priesthood of HORUS and the Renewed Disciples of HORUS—the two largest EDENist denominations around

HORUS—proclaimed they would make the greatest sacrifices the world had seen since Gotterdammerung to appease HORUS's wrath.

All nonsense, and, at that point, I think even the majority of the League thought it was nonsense. But no one dared tell an EDENist that.

I wondered what would happen when HORUS was not appeased. Our buses now had snowplows in front of them. We passed by huddle after huddle of burning oil drums. We didn't let anyone but our clients inside, and once they had finished their time, we asked them to leave. I got on a first name basis with the dispatchers.

December 16th, 1047 AGDR

The last straw, we now know, is real. The Windskylight Estate threw a naked bakt out of one of their campuses, and then he froze to death. Although there were claims it had been staged, both then and now, the Peace and Reconciliation Committee did prove that it was neither staged nor a SET forgery.

I was outraged. Eternalists and Vivites alike were outraged. Everyone was outraged.

Bakts all over the League went on strike, bearing improvised torches and quickly overwhelming the ability of either their masters or their police to contain them.

I sat in the necromancer's common room with Emily, watching the protests. We were the only ones not out there.

"Why aren't you?" I asked.

"Why aren't you?" she asked.

"Fair."

We continued to watch.

December 21st, 1047 AGDR

We never did learn what triggered the riots.

Was it one too many people going hungry? Did someone—as the rumors went—try to offer a child to HORUS? Or was everyone simply fed up? Pictures circulated the Neonet: dead children frozen solid, bloody altars with screaming devotees, a video of a store's door being shattered and looted. Were some SET forgeries? All of them? None of them? As many years as it has been, even the Peace and Reconciliation Committee's report is inconclusive.

What we did know was that people were angry. Very, very angry.

We watched the footage as rioters overturned police barricades and shattered every glass window. Others torched buildings, warming themselves by the fires. Archio was in chaos. Petersyn was swarmed with rioters. Neyonaize was in anarchy.

For Newla, we only had to look out the window because some of them came to SBL Main. Some of them were *from* SBL Main.

As much as I sympathized, the truth was I knew that this protest would go nowhere, as every previous bakt protest had gone. If I were to join them, I would lose my position. So I simply sat inside and tried to work as I heard screaming and things shattering from outside.

"Mary!" Mark pushed his way into the necromancer's wing. "We need to go!"

"Go?" I asked.

"This is our chance! We'll get out and be free!"

"Mark, it's not going to work," I said, trying to be calm. "They can track us down by our collars."

"It's changing; it's all changing," Mark insisted. "We'll be free, together! They'll have to repeal the bakt laws!"

"That's not how it works."

"Don't you *get it*?" he asked, staring at me. "We can get out."

"What?"

"I love you!"

"...Mark," I said. "I know we've gone on dates, but I don't have feelings for you. Calm down and—"

"—What do you mean?" he asked, hurt. "Haven't we been together for so long?"

"It isn't that way, Mark!"

"Mary, please—" He touched me.

I yanked away.

His face turned from hurt to anger in a moment. "Don't you get it? Don't you know how much I've sacrificed to love you!?" he shrieked. "They all call me mad because I love a mage! Well, I *do*!" he screamed at the top of his lungs.

"Mark, I'm sorry, but I don't—"

He grabbed me, really grabbed me, and started to drag me off.

"*Let go!*" I shrieked.

"You twistie-lover! I'll show you, yes, I'll show—"

Emily smashed a laptop against his head. He staggered back. She grabbed my hand. "RUN!"

I ran faster than I ever did before. We ran, ran, ran—past the infirmary, just as Amy was opening it.

Emily dragged me inside. "Shut the door!"

Amy shut the door.

I sat on a bed.

What could have happened?

What *would* have happened?

Amy saw it, too. "Lock the door!"

The other lifeweavers sprang into action.

"Mary!" Bang bang. "Mary! Mary, you whore, get out here! Mary!"

Then we all realized he had keys to every door in the building. "Barricade it!" someone said, and they immediately overturned beds and slammed them in front of the door just in time.

"What the glitch happened?" a lifeweaver asked Emily.

"That guy out there tried to rape Mary," she said. "Is still trying, apparently."

I wondered what Mary they were talking about.

Mark kept hammering and screaming. They barricaded the door, further. Amy sat by me and gently touched me. "You just stay there. You're safe."

I don't know how long it lasted. I remember some of them got crutches or scalpels to use as weapons.

I heard loud mechanical footsteps, and then a yelp. "Open the door!" a loud revenant boomed.

"That's a war revenant," Amy said.

I couldn't focus.

"OPEN THE DOOR!"

"We can't! It's barricaded!" a lifeweaver shouted.

With a punch, a revenant knocked down the door, and two more entered, gatling guns at the ready. A police revenant came in behind. "You're all under arrest."

We waited, sitting outside on our cuffed hands in the snow, as the war revenants cleared out the campus.

I had stopped focusing on reality. I no longer knew what was happening, or particularly cared.

Alysson came out to the war revenant guarding us. “These bakts were hiding in the infirmary on our orders. Please let them go.”

“Get up,” it boomed. We got up, and with a knife finger it cut the plastic cuffs.

Alysson then went over to Mark, who watched us with hatred. Alysson hit him in the face, then grabbed him by the shoulders, and screamed at him. I had never seen her so angry before, and I wondered for a moment if she was going to kill him.

At last, she let go and went back to us. “With me, all of you.”

I had seen in person what others had seen only on television: Consul Heartlightray had sent the Necroforce to put the “insurrection” down by force. And they had.

I didn’t watch the videos, then or later. I still haven’t. There’s footage of them firing indiscriminately on protestors, or rioters, or someone, and then necromancers behind them force ripping anyone who had been shot.

“They got what they wanted in the end, didn’t they?” Zack Rewinding, an Eternalist commentator said.

Something had changed in the Athanasian League, permanently. Fimbulwinter might end, but the suffering had only begun.

CHAPTER NINETEEN

IN CHARGE OF ALL HIS POSSESSIONS

December 22th, 1047 AGDR

We ate breakfast the next morning in silence. It was so quiet I could hear utensils clatter against plates. Of those few remaining, no one talked, not even Amy. She put a hand on mine, but she could tell I didn't want to talk about yesterday, too. No one did.

The nightmares all night were reminder enough. As were the bruises on my arm where Mark had grabbed me.

There were no buses to Mass that day. I didn't know if I had the heart to go.

Mark was nowhere to be seen.

I heard the hydraulic footsteps of a revenant and somehow knew it was Redshineglory before I looked up.

"Ms. Firebrightsky, we require your presence. Your lawyer has already been informed and is coming."

"All right," I said, got up, and followed him.

The meeting room was equally quiet, just myself, the revenant, and Alysson. I couldn't tell what was going on, but Alysson did not look angry or hostile, simply neutral.

My lawyer entered and took a seat next to me. "Good morning," he said. "I'm surprised you were willing to call me outright."

"We have need of your client's services," the revenant said.

"Let's get this started in order," Alysson said. "First of all, Mary, Mark Whiteskylark has been leased to the grinders. Permanently."

"I see," I said. What else could I say? Whatever part of me still might have liked him was long gone, now. "Is he already gone?"

"He's not coming back."

"I understand." I didn't know if I would have the ability to forgive him to his face.

"The other rioters have also been sent to the grinders, for a week. When they come back, they're not going to be happy with you."

"With me?" I asked.

"You clearly didn't join them."

"Excuse me," Joseph interrupted. "While this is all very interesting, why are you telling us this?"

"Simply to explain the situation," Alysson said. "The riots were in every city, of course, and even some of our managerial staff joined them. We are in dire need of managers at other campuses. You've proven that you are willing to be obedient even if everyone else loses his head."

I bit off the retort that I sympathized with the rioters much more than the estate.

"Yes, Mary, you are thinking of saying that you don't like us, and you don't like me, and you would really rather have rioted, but by accident, you ended up staying behind. Am I right?"

I let out a nervous chuckle. "Maybe."

"The point is that regardless of your reasons, you stayed. You've been an assistant manager for a few months, and now we want to make you a permanent manager in Neyonaize."

"Why are you even asking?" I asked.

"Is it in your indenture description?" Joseph asked.

"It is not," the revenant said. "Which is why we are offering to cut your period of indenture in half if you agree to a new contract. We would also increase your peculium to one thousand drachmae a month."

I didn't process it for a moment.

Then I almost begged for it.

Then I wondered what the catch was.

"We need to move fast," Alysson said. "Neyonaize needs another manager within the month. We'll pay for your management degree, too, but you'll learn on the job."

"We need to discuss this privately," Joseph said.

"Absolutely, but we need an answer within the week. For both of our sakes."

"'Both?'" I asked.

"You'll be seen as siding with us," Alysson said flatly. "And maybe you are, maybe you're not. But either way, I can only imagine you'll be bullied in every way. Think about it."

"I need to see documents," Joseph said.

The revenant slid a thick folder across the table.

"Mary, how about we talk in my car?" Joseph asked me.

"That…that sounds good," I said. My head was still spinning.

I waited in the car as Joseph looked through the documents. “Let me negotiate it a little more,” he said, closing the folder. “But you should take the offer.”

“I should?” I asked.

“Mary, you have them on their knees. They’re not going to find another candidate with your experience and proven loyalty. We can get them to bend even more.”

“Is there a catch?” I asked.

“If you don’t want to be a manager, there’s that. Other than that, I’ll look carefully. You have a professional on your side.” He winked at me. “We’ll go into the gory details.”

“…What about the case?” I asked.

“Mary, the case is dead.”

“Excuse me?”

“Almost all of the people who we are trying to say were treated unjustly were arrested for rioting. In a climate as politically charged as this, the judge is going to do anything he can to find for the master.”

“But they rioted *because* they were treated unjustly.”

“I know. But this is the reality.”

I held my head.

“Mary, you need to make the decision that’s right for you. Not the decision that’s right for my wallet. Not the decision that’s right for your master. Not the decision that’s right for everyone else here. You’re my client, so I’m going to give you the best advice.

“I know, but…” I sighed.

“Do you need time to think?”

I thought about it.

No, no, I didn’t.

Alysson was right about one thing. The same people that hazed me for weeks would think nothing of bullying me for the rest of my indenture if they thought I was one of *them*.

But a new thought entered my mind.

Was this it? Was this how God could bless me?

After all, if they were willing to reduce my indenture…what if I could be free, soon enough?

Soon enough to have my own children?

I didn't want to even think about sex, but I wouldn't leave this on the table.

"I'll do it," I said. "But only if we get my indenture down to ten years or less."

"I'll see what I can do."

"Thanks," I said.

December 23rd, 1047 AGDR

Joseph managed to snag me an even better deal: I would be guaranteed the religious freedom to go to Mass on any Sunday, Holy Day of Obligation, Holy Thursday, and Good Friday. My peculium would go up to 1,500 drachmae a month plus a performance bonus. And he had reduced my remaining indenture to seven years.

Seven years.

Seven years and I'd be free.

We went over the contract clause by clause, but at least the catches were obvious. As a manager, I would waive my rights against mandatory overtime, I would receive significantly less hard credit, and I needed to maintain a certain level of profitability in my satellite office for time I spent to count. Joseph told me these were all standard to management bakt contracts.

He had also gotten them to agree that I wouldn't be required to force rip anyone, nor would I be required to oversee a satellite office doing force rips. Apparently, the Neyonaize canton had additional licensing requirements for ripping facilities, and the campus had only one satellite office that did it.

It still felt too good to be true, but I trusted Joseph. I had also prayed about it while they were hammering it out, and while I didn't receive a sign or hear a voice, I felt at peace about it. Was it really too good to be true, or was I simply jaded at this point?

"And that's all," Joseph said. "Ready to sign?"

"I am," I said.

They pushed the documents to me, and I signed them.

For a moment, I felt regret. But I also felt supremely at peace. Wherever this led, I felt God was leading me to it.

December 24th, 1047 AGDR

Joseph had finagled one last thing for me: Before I departed, I would go to St. Teresa of Avila one last time, for Christmas Eve Mass.

I hadn't expected the stained glass to be shattered or the statues defaced. They had made what repairs they could, but I still saw the damage rioters had done. My sympathy for the rioters fell immediately.

Mass was completely packed. Enough people had seen too much and wanted someone to tell them everything would be all right. I wanted it, too. And Fr. Justsquared took the time to talk about the Christ Child in the middle of occupied Israel's suffering and how a lone star and an angel's chorus had announced the Good News.

"The Good News that sin, violence, and death are not the final answer to the questions life poses. The Good News that there is not one evil beyond the power of God to heal. The Good News that the LORD, the mighty God of Israel, has become a tiny helpless baby in order to save everyone, every single person in the pews, in the prisons, at the grinders, on the streets, in the halls of power, and you and I."

For the first time since Mark had tried to rape me, I felt comforted and loved.

December 25th, 1047 AGDR

I did know that I would be leaving Amy and even Emily, but when I went to say my goodbyes, they weren't there.

They were, however, on the bus to the train station.

"What the glitch?" I asked them as I sat down by Amy. "Where are you two heading?"

"SBL Neyonaize," Amy said. "I requested a transfer."

"And you didn't tell me?"

"I didn't want to get your hopes up! Anyway, they're short staffed on lifeweavers up there."

"I have no idea how I got transferred," Emily said. "I'm going to Neyonaize, too. Probably so I'll still be with you."

My worst regret about leaving immediately left. I wouldn't be alone.

You know what?

Perhaps God simply wanted to bless me.

Amy whispered in my ear. "How are you doing?"

"I…I'm still processing," I whispered back. "I've been having nightmares."

"They have to approve theopsychiatry for you. When you're a manager."

"I'm not sure if I'm ready to see the past so clearly," I said.

"Fair."

As the bus drove out, I took one last look at SBL Main. The rioters had done damage, and Fimbulwinter, but soon enough, I mused, the rich and the powerful would get what they wanted again.

Or so I thought at the time.

December 31st, 1047 AGDR

Neyonaize was the polar opposite of Newla: equally large, but crowded, clean, and beautiful, or at least it had been, and they were trying to repair it. I saw all the ground-level windows had been shattered.

Slowbrightlaughter Neyonaize was a campus at least ten times the size of SBL Main, made of several tall buildings. I realized that because Alfred couldn't change SBL Main, he had to leave it be, but he had the wealth and the power to expand his other campuses. As the bus drove behind the gates, I wondered what would await me.

Screaming, apparently.

Michael Slowbrightlaughter, Chief of Necromancy of SBL Neyonaize, was not a happy man. He was old, too, and I wondered what cycle number he had.

"So," he spat. "You're the one they scraped off the bottom of the barrel sent to patch the gap."

"Excuse me?"

"SHUT UP!"

I shut up.

"I will tell you when to speak. Now, I have high expectations. Meet them, and we won't have any problems. Otherwise, expect to be punished. Understood?"

"Understood, sir," I said.

"Good. We have a system here, you see. The managers of most productive satellite offices receive rewards. The managers of the least receive penalties."

This seemed like an incredibly easy way to make the necromantic teams hate each other, but I kept my mouth shut.

"You'll be starting at the bottom. It'll be good for you to get your lazy ass in gear. Now leave. I trust we will not have any problems?"

"Understood, sir."

"You are dismissed."

The manager lounge had a scoreboard where the most productive offices were listed in bold and the least in tiny print. I found mine with some strain.

What had I gotten into?

"You the new one?" a man asked.

"Yes," I said.

"Michael give you the talk?"

"Yes," I said.

"We have a system, you see. We keep everyone more or less at the same level of productivity and rotate the exact order around. Then no one gets rewarded or punished too often. Understand?"

"I understand," I said. I immediately decided I wouldn't care. Corruption against an idiotic and cruel master was still corruption.

January 1st, 1048 AGDR

"You're Mary, right?" the bus driver asked as I got on. "The new manager?"

"I am," I said.

"I'm Gayle. Pleased to meet you. Expected to drive yourself, huh?"

"Actually, I was wondering," I said. "I never learned to drive."

"Shame. It's a lot of fun. Anyway, you don't need to worry a thing. I'll be here for you. And I'll go for cheap."

"...Excuse me?" I asked.

"I don't charge the offices as much as the others."

"...What?"

"You didn't see in the handbook?"

"Let me look," I said.

It turned out that in SBL Neyonaize, everyone was treated as a kind of independent contractor, even the otherwise enslaved. You "paid" for the goods and services you used, and the money you "earned" went to paying off your debts. I had heard of some businesses that ran that way, and in particular, bakt leasing firms, but I had never heard of a place being as extreme as SBL Neyonaize. Even the janitors had their own budgets, I discovered as I read through the handbook.

I wondered how Mark was doing. I both wanted him to be suffering, and I wanted him to be OK. Then I decided to stop thinking about him. I wouldn't see him again, would I?

I returned to the handbook and thought about it. Not only was SBL Neyonaize more extreme than others, but with both rewards and punishments for relative performance, I saw it could easily become sadistic. What had I gotten myself into? Into no more than seven more years of indenture, as long as my office was sufficiently profitable. I was starting to wonder how likely that was in these circumstances.

I had no idea how I had offended Michael SBL before even meeting him, but apparently I had. Or he was offended by default, perhaps.

Still, time to trust God.

We gathered in the boring board room. The furniture looked new, probably because they had just had to replace it. I could still see the remains of painted-over graffiti on the walls.

"I'm the new manager," I told my assembled team. They looked at me with exhaustion—I suspected many of them had been at the grinders. "I'm not going to give a fancy speech. My plan is to treat you decently and have you treat each other decently. That's all. Dismissed."

I went to my office and sat down. I could see, not far away, the steeple of a church. I got out my phone and looked it up: It was actually St. Alphonsus, the Cathedral of the Archdiocese of Neyonaize, and there was Mass at noon. I could go on my lunch break and be back.

I dialed up the machinespeakers.

"SBL Neyonaize Machinespeakers. What's up?"

"I want to know how far I can go from my office."

"Name?"

"Mary Firebrightsky."

I heard some tapping. "You're a manager. You can go wherever you want."

"Oh," I said. "Thanks."

"You're welcome." They hung up.

Maybe I had to deal with Michael, but I could at least go to Mass every day.

January 2nd, 1048 AGDR

St. Alphonsus Cathedral, despite its size, was a quiet parish. There were only a few people at Mass. The vast nave had a few more statues and painted angels than it had living humans. Jesus watched from a mural over the altar, his eyes kind.

A man approached me afterwards. “What are *you* doing here?”

“Sir, I don’t believe we’ve met,” I said.

“You’re one of them bones!”

“I am. And?”

“You don’t deserve to be here!”

“Sir, the Church allows the use of necromancy.”

“So why *are* you a necromancer?”

In truth, I didn’t know, but I found myself saying, “I want to help people. Even if I must sacrifice myself.”

The priest approached us. “Raphael, for goodness sake, you can’t scare off a new parishioner.”

“I…apologize,” he said, not looking at me.

“I forgive you,” I said.

He stomped off.

“You must get that a lot,” the priest said.

I decided not to mention that this was the first time I had ever been confronted about my job by a Catholic. I made a noncommittal noise.

“Well, you’re welcome here!” the tall man said brightly. “Monsignor Michael Serially.” He extended a hand. The spiral on his pale cheek showed an ordination mark, the first I had ever seen.

I took it. "Mary Firebrightsky. I'm a manager with the Slowbrightlaughter estate. We have an office right across the street."

"I saw! I wish more bakts would come."

An idea formed in my mind.

I dialed the machinespeakers when I got back.

"SBL Neyonaize Machinespeakers. What's up?"

"This is Mary Firebrightsky. Is there a fence around my office?"

"You mean to keep the bakts inside? Yeah, why?"

"Can you adjust its size during lunch hours?"

"…Yeah, why?"

"I want to let my team go outside if they'd like."

"…I mean, I guess it's not against policy." He paused. "Yeah, we can do it. How big?"

I got out MapApp. "I'd say two blocks." That put them within range of the cathedral, several restaurants, and a library.

"Yeah, we can get that in for you today."

"Thanks," I said.

January 3rd, 1048 AGDR

The next day, I made the announcement. "Starting today, you can go no more than two blocks during your lunch break, as long as you come back within the hour. I don't care what you do during that time, as long as you come back. I will be at the cathedral if you need me. Any questions?"

They stared at me as if I had grown a new head.

"You don't need my specific permission," I repeated. "Just come back, and don't get into any trouble. Understood?"

"Yes, ma'am," they all said.

There. I couldn't fix their situation, but I could at least make it a little less slizzy.

I was too smart to believe that nothing bad would happen because of this, but I was wise enough to know that some things were worth doing even if it cost you. Although I didn't foresee how drastic things would get.

CHAPTER TWENTY

AN ACCOUNT OF YOUR STEWARDSHIP

February 3rd, 1048 AGDR

Life outside of the SBL estate was not going well. It was increasingly cold, and although I had granted permission to leave, you had to run pretty fast to avoid the Fimbulwinter freeze. I personally experienced how drafty the old cathedral was, and, with a quiet apology to God, kept my fuglin coat on for the duration of Mass.

A surprising number of my subordinates came with me, perhaps out of curiosity or boredom, but then a surprising number of those kept coming. Even Emily, to my surprise, would come, and sometimes in our spare time she would ask questions about the Faith.

I could understand the instinct to find some solace. The backlash against Heartlightray for his use of the Necroforce was slow, but it was powerful. The Vivites tried to impeach him, as well as some moderate Eternalists. They got close, but inevitably didn't have enough votes. But his approval ratings were in the gutter—the Deep Eternalists might have celebrated that he ordered bakts to be gunned down, but everyone else was horrified.

Meanwhile, the HORUS War was going nowhere. Until it went even more horribly wrong.

I could tell something was wrong because even Monsignor Serelalix was shaken. “God can forgive anything, even the most inhuman of actions, but surely we must repent…”

I checked the news on my phone, and my jaw hit the floor.

In an attempt to end the war, the THOTH Wheel Group had ordered the use of an Orbital Angel, dormant since Gotterdammerung, to obliterate Kinshasa, one of the Balancers’ capitals. It didn’t end the war, of course, but it did end millions of people.

“How could they?” I asked out loud, to God, or to anyone. I couldn’t process it.

When I came back to my office, I told everyone: “If you need to cope, take the day off. If you need someone to talk to, I’ll be in my office.”

I had several takers.

February 4th, 1048 AGDR

The international backlash shook the world. Westland issued an arrest warrant for any of the THOTH Wheel Group. The Senate of the Living voted 98-2 to strip the permissions of Abel Glorywestblue, the League’s TWG member. I wondered how dangerous it was that root access to EDENs had become another ball in the political game.

Abel was one of Heartlightray’s appointees, a fact that cost him dearly. Between that and his use of the Necroforce during the Solstice Riots, his approval ratings somehow fell further. Certainly, I thought nothing good about him, be I Christian or not.

It also came at the worst possible timing for the Eternalists because next week was election day.

Even Alan was horrified. "We must all come together, Eternalist and Vivite alike, to condemn this horrifying crime against humanity…"

March 10th, 1048 AGDR

1048 was a mid-term election, where only the Senators were up for election. As it happened, Alan was running in Neyonaize.

It didn't matter how much Michael SBL screamed at us, or anyone else's master did. I voted for him, as did most of the bakts in the campus.

March 11th, 1048 AGDR

The Vivites won big, but not quite enough to reach the 2/3 threshold in the Senate to override the Consul's veto (or to impeach him). But now, Jacob Heartlightray had to deal with the new Deep Vivite caucuses.

Alan won by a massive landslide. Like the Consul election, Senators had a two-stage process, but Alan won 77% of the vote at the beginning, making him win instantly.

April 11th, 1048 AGDR

The new Senators would be sworn in one week before Holy Week. The Catholic Neonet, barely, managed to spend its time preparing for the Passion and Resurrection of the Lord as opposed to yelling at each other about politics.

I was especially exasperated, since this would be the first time I would *ever* go to Maundy Thursday and Good Friday in person, and people online were too busy pointing fingers to celebrate he who was Lord over history.

Still, that didn't mean I didn't watch Alan be sworn in.

The other new Senators swore with one hand on the Peace Steele and the other on an EDENist or True God holy book, but Alan only swore on the Steele.

"I, Alan Jaranjairaloral, do solemnly swear to uphold, defend, and protect the Tables of the Laws of the Living and the Dead and all amendments thereof, that I enter into this freely without compulsion or evasion, and I will faithfully discharge the duties that I have been given to do."

Alan had a freeman's mark on his neck, his collar long since gone, and he wore a Senatorial white toga. He looked, finally, at peace.

We all cheered, me in particular, that he seemed to have found happiness.

I wondered if I should try to contact him for congratulations, but if my master had forbidden it before, Michael SBL probably would do so even more.

My office phone rang. "This is Mary Firebrightsky," I answered.

"What did you do?" a man asked excitedly.

"Who are you?"

"I'm from the statistics department of SBL Aztec. You're the most successful office in the whole of the estate!"

"I am?" I asked.

"By 29% percent! What are you doing?"

"I'm letting my team leave the building on their free hours and have been generally decent to them."

"Yes, but what else?"

"I'm afraid that's basically it."

He sounded disappointed. "Well, if you think of anything, let me know."

April 13th, 1048 AGDR

I had not imagined Michael SBL was calling me in to congratulate me, and I was correct.

I had wasted his "resources" by giving them time off. I had wasted my time in religious activities instead of working. And now I had convinced others to do the same. What did I have to say about any of this, lazy ass that I was?

"If you no longer wish me to run the satellite office, I won't," I told him.

More screaming followed. "And forget about going outside!"

"You have to let me go," I said.

He screamed at me.

"It's in my contract."

He screamed at me.

"I'll take it to Legal if you insist."

"YOU WILL NOT! You are hereby confined to the estate! Dismissed!"

I stepped outside, my ears almost physically ringing. Though I'd never thought I'd say it, I missed Alysson because whether she was angry or not, you could work with her. In fact, I realized I ought to pray for her, since for all our arguments she was actually not that bad of a person. In fact, I should probably pray for Michael, too, he being both my superior and enemy.

I walked back to my room and wondered what would become of me.

"Lord," I prayed. "I want to go to Holy Week, but if this is not your will, I understand. Sort of. I would also appreciate it if you gave Michael Slowbrightlaughter a change of heart. Or at least knock some sense into him. But not my will but yours be done. And look over Alysson Slowbrightlaughter, too, would you?"

I went to bed and thought nothing more of it.

April 14th, 1048 AGDR

From what I heard, things were not going well at all at my old satellite office, now under new management. Trying to squeeze more work out of people who have just lost the little freedom and comfort they had was a proposition that even the most idiotic of taskmasters should realize to be a losing one. But, apparently, I was wrong about the level of idiocy.

No, I thought. Everyone was just stressed and miserable, with those on top bullying those just a rung down. The old drum major instinct, defined over a millennium ago and having existed since the Fall of Adam and Eve.

So I did my work and didn't care about it. They couldn't take hard credit from me, and even if I was doing less important work, so what? I was still going to be free in only seven years.

If there was an Athanasian League to be free *from* in seven years.

"Ms. Firebrightsky?" a bakt asked.

"Yes?" I answered.

"You don't look so good. I'll take the rest of your shift; you go talk to the lifeweavers."

Maybe the drum major instinct wasn't as powerful as I'd thought. Or maybe my kindness towards others had come back to my benefit.

I could tell something was more than a little wrong when the lifeweaver examining me called for another. She put her own leads on me, then said I needed an X-ray.

The final diagnosis? Pneumonia.

I actually broke out laughing, insomuch as I could. The doctor looked at me as if I was nuts.

"Oh MA-AT, Mary," Amy said, sitting beside me on the bed. "What is it with you and pneumonia?"

"If you need me to, I'll stay in the infirmary," I told the confused doctor.

"That won't be necessary, but if it gets worse, come to us *immediately*."

"She's a manager," Amy said. "Can't we break out MA-AT's touch?"

"I'm not a manager right now," I said. "It's up to you."

"It's just a little bit of pneumonia. Rest and antibiotics should be enough."

"As you wish, sir," I said.

So I went back to my room, wondered what the glitch was going on in my life any more, and lay down on the bed. I was tired, too…

I woke up to angry dinging from my phone. One low-level psychic phenomena is the better-than-average ability to tell whether the phone rings from someone you know. Whether I had that or not, somehow I knew it was Michael before I even checked my phone with a bleary eye.

I saw the first text.

`Get here NOW!`

It was followed by an increasing number on the same subject with more capitals and exclamation points.

I got out of bed, put on my dress clothes as frantically as I could, and ran as fast (not very) as I could to his office.

Michael Slowbrightlaughter was shaking with an emotion I could not recognize, though on seeing me his eyes widened with fear.

I was troubled myself. "Yes, sir?"

"*SHUT THE DOOR!*" he shouted.

I shut the door. This was going to be painful, wasn't it?

"What..." Michael stared at me, still afraid. "What...what was that *thing*?"

"The...thing?" I asked.

"The *thing*! Don't play dumb."

"Sir, I am seriously unaware what you are talking about."

"That *thing* came to me and talked to me!" Michael was shouting again. "It—it *said* it came from your god."

My hair raised on end. "I see," I said. "I'm sorry, I'm not in control of my God. He does whatever he pleases."

"What was that *thing*?"

"Sir, you may be describing an angel."

"An...an angel," he said, shifting back uncomfortably. He looked even more alarmed, to the point where I felt actual pity for him. I was startled even when the Blessed Mother said a few words to me, and I had the mental framework for it. An angel appearing probably scared the hell out of him, literally.

"They come from my God," I said. "He created them and sends them to carry his messages."

"It...it told me to let you go back to the satellite office," Michael said. "And you will. Just never again let that *thing* come to me!"

"I will pray on your behalf," I said. "It's unlikely you'll ever see it again."

"Once was enough," he said. "Once was enough. Now leave. And don't tell a soul!"

I stepped outside, and I managed to get back to my room before I broke down both laughing and crying.

Sure, I didn't know *why* now God sent an actual angel to rescue me, instead of all the previous times, such as during the attempted rape, or getting in trouble with Alysson before that, or even ending up a bakt at the SBL estate in the first place. But God does whatever he pleases, apparently.

I thought about it. Was it the fact that others were going to Holy Week? Perhaps God wanted them to be able to go and possibly join his Church. Or perhaps he wanted to scare Michael nearly to death so he would repent. Or maybe God just wanted to give me a gift.

I didn't know, but God did, and he decided to do it.

I sat on my bed and pulled off the crucifix on the wall. "Thank you, Lord," I said. "But next time, would you let Michael Slowbrightlaughter learn your will in a little more chill way?"

I couldn't keep from smiling.

Then it hit me.

None of the EDENist religions had any concept of subdeities or lesser spirits, except THOTH. The only time anyone outside the Church ever heard the word "angel" in that time was when referring to the Orbital Angels of THOTH. Whatever Michael saw or experienced, *his* only framework of the concept was a weapon capable of destroying cities.

Of course, so could angels, such as in the story of Sodom and Gomorrah, so maybe he was appropriately scared slizzless.

Sodom and Gomorrah.

Truth be told, the Lord could destroy the Athanasian League in an instant, no matter its claims to immortality. And sure, I had heard Catholics talk about it—what else was there to talk about in politics? But...would it actually happen?

I didn't know any more than I knew why God had decided to send an angel to terrify a random pagan. And I didn't need to know. If God was willing to do something so amazing to answer my prayer, he could easily protect me, no matter what happened.

April 17th, 1048 AGDR

For Holy Thursday, they would wash the feet of twelve parishioners, to represent Jesus washing the feet of the twelve apostles. In the historical context, you could not even order a Jewish slave to wash your feet, as it was considered so filthy and humiliating. Yet, Jesus lowered himself beneath even a slave to show the apostles the depths of his love, and how they must love one another.

As a slave myself, it was one of the most important Bible stories to me, so of course I signed up to have my feet washed. But alas, there were too many people, and they picked others.

Still, I thought, I could at least *celebrate* Holy Thursday. It would be the first time in my entire life I could go.

Monsignor Serelalix approached right before the start. "Someone couldn't make it. Do you want her spot?"

I almost cried. "Yes."

So I sat facing the congregation, in my necromancer's fuglin and bakt's collar, as Monsignor washed my feet. I realized how truly deep the Lord's love was, and how little I had shown that love to others in my brokenness. When I went back to my pew, I found tears in my eyes.

April 18th, 1044 AGDR

The Cathedral had their Good Friday liturgy at 3 PM, so I gave everyone in my office the time off. Almost everyone came with me.

We took up a whole pew, and I felt no little like a mother trying to keep her children in line during Mass. We stood and listened to the Passion, and I saw many of my team were stunned at the story.

Afterwards, during the very brief sermon, Emily leaned into me. "Is this for real?" she whispered.

"It is," I told her. "It really is."

CHAPTER TWENTY-ONE

IN THE DAYS OF LOT

March 20th, 1049 AGDR

Future reader, perhaps in your age the events of mine have all become crammed together, one event following the next in quick succession. In truth, lengthy periods stretched between one disaster and the next. At times, we even thought things would get better.

A year passed. More bickering, more polarization, more war. I continued to lead my satellite office, and I even heard that bakts begged to be in mine as opposed to others.

As a manager I had more access to news, so I followed the fate of SBL Main closely. The new Vivite Senate, with the help of some green-leaning Eternalists, forced through an eminent domain bill. Through complicated legal trickery, Alfred gained control of the estate. Nothing changed for me, though I heard SBL Main was immediately turned to food production.

On March 20th, 1049 AGDR, a Balancer assassin killed an Abundant Wheel Group member. I had never seen so much celebration over a death, as if the horror of taking a human life was made not evil but unalloyed good because it ended Fimbulwinter.

But end Fimbulwinter it did. The remaining Abundant Wheel Group members could not stand against the intact Balancer faction. One more was killed, the last committed self-ending, and finally, the Abundant faction offered unconditional surrender. Like hearing an alarm in our sleep, we began to wake from the nightmare.

The damage was done. HORUS had dragged us into an ice age, and the new rulers of HORUS warned that they did not dare attempt to reverse the damage without total cooperation from the world. The world was not stupid enough to give them another chance. So we waited for HORUS to slowly repair the situation without human direction.

I remember the summer that year, when nature awoke from her long slumber. The grass and plants had withered, but in joy we planted flowers. I remember thinking that perhaps life would return to normal, that all the brokenness of the world could be healed by planting flowers.

Perhaps it could have been, but not all of us would plant flowers.

April 4th, 1049 AGDR

I stood by Emily, my new goddaughter, trying not to cry at the next Easter Vigil. For all the things that had gone wrong in my life, I knew I would go through them all over again to see Emily enter the Church.

"I baptize you, Emily Felicity Justwhiteshine, in the name of the Father and the Son and the Holy Spirit," Monsignor Serelalix prayed as he poured the water over her head three times.

"Welcome home," I told her, giving her a hug.

May 13th, 1049 AGDR

The debates over OSIRIS resource utilization returned. Now that Alan was a Senator, he could say even more what he wanted, and people would listen and the media report.

"The OSIRIS Wheel Group cannot continue to ignore the situation," Alan said. "They have now allocated ten times more swap than OSIRIS has physical memory. What next? Build more until OSIRIS can no longer function?"

Alan's plan was simple: Put a cap on grave sizes, forcibly redig graves or reincarnate ghosts, and then disable swap. This was untenable politically, but the more Alan talked about it, the more the people demanded it.

The Eternalist plan was to augment OSIRIS with external processor farms, so as to make the swap device capable of hosting even thinking minds. This was heresy to the EDENists, but EDENism had gone from unquestionable dogma to increasingly irrelevant protests from the powerless.

But the powerless did have one thing: votes. The Eternalists split into the Old Eternalists—who still tried to placate EDENists, the Deep Eternalists, who would do anything to keep the system going—and the moderate Eternalists, who did nothing but have just enough votes in the Senate to make their voice heard.

Gridlock continued. People openly wondered if the League could remain stable at this rate.

Had our souls been so cruelly treated by Fimbulwinter that the moment we no longer had the HORUS Wheel Group as a foe, we turned our teeth and claws on one another? I had to ban the discussion from my office because it would otherwise have torn my team apart. We had nothing else to talk about, however, so every day the ban was violated anew.

For someone who was so politically aware, I could not find myself rooting for either party, only, to an extent, Alan. I could not help but watch his struggles against the Eternalists with pride.

"What do you even know about politics, Mr. I-campaigned-to-get-out-of-indenture?" Senator Paleblueray snapped.

"The Senate shall be in order," the parliamentarian said.

"I know what I do," Alan said, and pulled out his old collar and snapped it around himself. "I know the same things." He pulled off his collar. "I still know them. What difference does a mere collar make?"

Senator Paleblueray literally sputtered in rage.

Alan pushed for the end of indenture. However, because the possibility of indenture was written on the Table of the Law of the Living, the Deep Vivites could not pass the necessary legislation without 2/3rds control of the Senate and then a League-wide referendum.

There was no hope of this happening, I thought, but if anyone could do it, Alan could.

Alan's brand of demagoguery was matched by new candidates for the Living Senate, while Eternalists found their own loudmouths, or exhumed Dead ones for the Parliament.

January 1st, 1050 AGDR

The cliff approached. The two sides wrestled each other towards it. The Eternalists' plan would change the minimum grave size to merely five megabytes, and schedule transfers to larger graves to allow seances.

"Mr. Yellowoakglory, perhaps you weren't paying attention in history class, but even after Gotterdammerung, for centuries after the founding of the Athanasian League, even ordinary citizens had days of realtime and rooms to walk in," Alan said. "Have we descended so far that we cannot even let our Dead loved ones remain conscious?"

The Dead MP looked unmoved. "If we were to return to that, OSIRIS would break in instants."

"On the contrary, it is only greed that has brought us here. But perhaps the real issue is that the estates could no longer hog resources?"

As much as I enjoyed seeing Alan chew on the Eternalists, even I had to admit he was a demagogue. His own plan would tax estates, limit their purchases of RAM, and all the money would go to welfare. Robin Hood? I would have liked to say I believed in his ideal, but his means for accomplishing it were beyond the pale.

The Deep Vivite proposals would leave the Parliament of the Dead effectively helpless, a mere advisory group to the Senate of the Living. It was not said out loud by the Vivites, but the only way they could take this amount of money, time, and power from the Dead was by taking away their right to vote otherwise. The Dead, after all, vastly outnumbered the living.

The necromancers of SBL Neyonaize had split violently on the issue, despite my frequently futile attempts to ban politics. I remember one argument in detail.

"The only way that the Vivites can get enough votes in the Parliament," Anthony, a necrotech, declared, "is if they run a ghost campaign on an unheard-of scale. If they do that, they hardly deserve to be called a party."

"Oh, like the Eternalists don't ghost campaign constantly," Stephen, another necrotech, said.

"Voting in your own interest is ghost campaigning now?" Anthony asked. "You'll be a ghost eventually. Think of your eternity."

"Sure, I'll be a ghost until OSIRIS sheds load."

"Everyone, enough," I said.

"What's a ghost campaign?" a young necromancer asked.

Several others rushed to answer.

"Hold a seance and offer to pay the contact if he switches his default vote. Repeat ad nauseam until you've rigged the election."

"No, it's when you wake a ghost to preach your cause. Perfectly legal."

"Sure, and it's in his 'best interests' to vote with you."

"For OSIRIS's sake, it's not vote buying. It's no different than a political ad."

"Sure, and you just 'happen' to pay for extra wake time. Nothing bribery in that."

"If I hear *one more word* on this, I'm going to start docking peculiums," I said.

They all shut up.

February 1st, 1050 AGDR

Alfred SBL insisted that he would not stoop to waking random strangers to try to get them to vote Eternalist. So he took to waking every poor soul (in the literal sense) named Slowbrightlaughter, offering to let them become part of his estate for free.

We necromancers faithfully went down the list. The most outrageous thing was not that our targets had already been canvassed, but that, on average, they had already been canvassed multiple times. By the time they reached us, they were ready to demand a higher price.

When I was in college, this was not what I imagined I would be doing, although perhaps I was out of the ability to be shocked at that point. But my innocent self simply repeated the initial offer, as if either of us could pretend this was not simply an exchange of valuable consideration. I could get away with this because I was Michael's "favorite," while the other necromancers were closely monitored.

It left a bad taste in my mouth, and I tried to spend as much time with Amy as I could. No one could get political about reforestation. Or so I liked to pretend, as I tuned out her rants just as I'm sure she tuned out mine.

March 13th, 1050 AGDR

The usual apocalyptic rhetoric around the election built up, but this time it felt different. It was possible the League could change drastically if the wrong person was elected. We just couldn't agree who the wrong person was.

All but one of the Vivite candidates for Consul dropped out to focus the vote. Sarah Whiteblisstrue, a moderate, ended up as the remaining hope for the Vivites. She talked a lot about servitude "reform", although detailed plans were lacking.

Jacob Heartlightray doubled down on his anti-bakt rhetoric, showing images of bakt violence—during, I note, his consulship—to make his point.

"This is our last, best chance for order in the great republic of the League," he announced.

Election season passed in a blur, since it seemed like every season was election season. I voted Independent, out of protest. I still voted for Alan.

We all sat in front of the giant TV in the cafeteria, watching the vote count. Green struggled against Gold, but the Vivites were ultimately overwhelmed, one district and city after another. In the Parliament of the Dead, the numbers were even more lopsided, the Eternalists winning 3:1.

I watched until I confirmed Alan had won his seat again, then went to bed.

March 14th, 1050 AGDR

Jacob Heartlightray had gotten 45% of the vote, while Sarah Nightblisstrue received only 42%. In the runoff, the remaining 13% would decide the next Consul.

I honestly wasn't surprised. Alan had won his seat outright, but the Senate was still up for grabs.

Holy Week was coming up, and I tried to focus more on that, without much success.

March 20th, 1050 AGDR

The Catholic parts of the Neonet, unlike Jesus' seamless garment, were torn in two. Some hated Nightblisstrue's anti-religious rhetoric, while others, particularly bakts, hated Heartlightray's anti-bakt rhetoric. At no point did I find someone who actually voted either side out of love.

I prayed throughout that Palm Sunday Mass. And I realized what mattered far more than choosing between Heartlightray ruining everything and Nightblisstrue ruining everything was what my vote did to my own soul.

I would abstain, I decided. I would pick neither of the two evils.

March 25th, 1050 AGDR

We bakts were no longer an uncommon sight at the Cathedral, but we still got curious looks at the Good Friday liturgy. I didn't care. I was here for Jesus.

The somber liturgy was healing in its own way. Jesus had died for the sins of the whole world, yes, even Jacob Heartlightray and Sarah Whiteblisstrue. No matter what the claims of pundits or the apocalyptic rhetoric of politicians, the true, most historic event had happened over three thousand years ago. The cathedral had a whole choir sing the Passion according to St. John.

I looked over at Emily, deep in prayer. Our petty little election didn't matter in eternity. That she had chosen Christ did.

March 29nd, 1050 AGDR

Our petty little election between Whiteblisstrue and Heartlightray ended with the same result: The Eternalists controlled the government, through and through.

I watched Heartlightray's victory speech with distaste. Unless he really did get hard credit repealed, my life would not change that much. I would be free in just four years, God willing, and then…

And then I didn't know what. I was still young enough to have children, though I didn't know how quickly I could get married. Surely the Lord had a plan for me, someone set aside for me before time began…or did he? It had been so long since I heard the Blessed Virgin I had started to doubt, even if I could remember her voice perfectly.

March 30th, 1050 AGDR

"Hey, Mary, is your schedule real?" Emily asked.

"What do you mean?" I asked.

"Look at your three-o-clock."

`1600: Consultation with Alan Jaranjair`

I was floored.

How had he found me? Well, SET, surely, but…

But what?

I waited for the hour with impatience.

Alan looked, despite the Vivites' loss, relatively cheerful. "Mary, it's been so long…"

"Alan," I said, on the verge of hysteria. "What are you doing here?"

"Am I not allowed to consult whatever necromancer I wish for my necromantic needs?"

I wondered if this was actually his *romantic* needs. "I…OK," I said, head spinning.

"We have a lot to catch up on," he said.

"How did you find out about the swap device?" I asked. "My master got so angry at me."

"I'm very sorry. It wasn't that you told me, but that you *didn't* tell me," Alan explained. "The fact that you wouldn't talk to me about it, as opposed to denying it outright, made me wonder what you knew. I considered that, whatever it was, a mere necromancer would be able to find the truth. I experimented with various commands and stumbled on `free`. I assume that's what you discovered?"

"Yes," I said. Typical Alan. He more than once managed to get me a gift I wanted but never asked, simply by extrapolating from an off-hand comment. "But why did you go this far? Did you really campaign just to get out of indenture?"

"It's true I got out of indenture," Alan said. "I hated every second I worked at Notre Dame. Every last second. So I will say that finding that loophole out was the best day of my life, or at least so far. Then I won."

"I see." I felt disoriented.

"I would have gotten you out, I promise, Mary, but I couldn't."

"You couldn't?"

"Campaign finance laws let me pay for my own escape, but I couldn't pay for another bakt's. I promised myself I would pay yours off once I became a Senator, but...but I didn't have enough money," he said. "Most of the Senators have pasts as businessmen. I only had my senatorial salary."

"I'm...I'm going to be free in four years," I said.

"Great," he said, but he didn't seem relieved. "I wanted to give you this." He handed me a deep green envelope.

I opened it:

You are cordially invited to the Vivite event of the century
Wine, refreshments, speakers.
Keynote by Sarah Whiteblisstrue
Please RSVP immediately.

April 4th, 1050

"I'll have to talk to my superior," I said.

"Of course. But before then…"

"Before then?"

"We haven't seen each other in years. I did pay for a consult, yes? We'll use that time to our advantage."

"Yes," I said. "Let's."

I won't share what we talked about. It was nothing important, no clues to what would really happen at the ball. Consider, future reader, my privacy. I have spoken of many things, let me keep this conversation secret. What happened next was public enough.

CHAPTER TWENTY-TWO

THIS THING IS FROM ME

March 31st, 1050 AGDR

As I expected, the answer was "no." A very, very loud "no", screamed in my face.

I didn't press the matter. When Alan and I were talking, he didn't seem to understand I wasn't a Vivite. I didn't really want to go to a political rally, with or without permission. So I wrote him a letter apologizing that I couldn't come.

I set my pen down, then added one more line.

I hope we can see each other again, sometime. In four years, if nothing else.

Did I still have feelings for him?

Yes. Yes, I did.

Who knew, anyway? Maybe, by some insane twist of fate, he would be my future spouse.

April 4th, 1050 AGDR

Ever since Heartlightray's victory, the streets were crowded with protestors.

"People be crazy here," Gayle, my bus driver, said as we had to take another detour due to protestors. Police revenants passed their watchful lenses over the crowds, as if we all knew that the Solstice Riots could break out again in an instant. I had a really bad feeling about this.

As soon as I got to the office, I made my announcement. "I'm not banning any of you from leaving. But I do want you to think carefully about the crowds out there. I don't want any of you to get hurt."

I didn't know what they would make of my words, but I at least wanted their safety.

Strange, how I had become a mother in my own way to them.

My feeling of unease grew as the day went on.

I can remember to this day when I got the call.

My phone rang. I didn't recognize the number, but something told me I should pick it up.

"Hello?"

"Mary?"

"Who are you?" I asked.

"This is Seth! Your friend in college! You're Mary Firebrightsky, aren't you?"

"…I am," I said. "I haven't talked to you in ages. What's…"

"I don't have time to chat. Are you in a secure location?"

I looked around our office. "What do you mean 'secure'? I'm in a satellite office of the Slowbrightlaughter Estate."

"Do you have security guards there?"

"I shouldn't discuss—"

"Do you *have* security guards there? I don't have any more time. Get to safety and surround those you love with—" I heard shouting. "Just do it!" He hung up.

I sat down, overwhelmed with dread. Then I dialed the elementalist department.

"SBL Neyonaize Elementalism. What's up?"

"This is Mary Firebrightsky," I said. "Can you send…I don't know, two elementalists here?"

"Sure can. Why?"

"There's a security hazard here. It's complicated to describe."

"I'll send some people. A revenant, too?"

"That would be great. Thank you," I said.

I dialed up the medical department. "Is Amy Justgloryblue available?"

"What?" I heard the dispatcher shout in the background. "Yeah. Why?"

"I'd like her to be here. Send her on the bus that's heading to my office. And another lifeweaver."

"Why?"

"Send her. Now."

"Fine, fine."

I dialed up Transport.

"SBL Neyonaize Transport."

"This is Mary Firebrightsky. I'm sending a bus with a security team and two lifeweavers here. Is Gayle there?"

"Sure, I can send her. What's up?"

"It's complicated to describe. Just send them. And I want Gayle to stay with us with the bus."

"OK. Just to let you know, we're short on buses."

"Do it."

"Fine, fine, fine."

What was I doing? Whether it was in my budget or not, I was going to get in a ton of trouble for this if nothing happened.

But something deep within me knew Seth wouldn't have searched for my work number if everything was going to be OK.

I dialed the machinespeaker department. Ring, ring, ring. No answer. Ring, ring, ring. I dialed two more times before I got through.

"Look!" the voice snapped. "We are very busy right now!"

"What the glitch is happening right now?" I asked.

"If I had a glitching clue, I'd tell you." He hung up.

I hit the intercom again. "Meeting on the board room."

I counted my team—everyone was present.

"I have a bad feeling about this," I said. "I've called for security. I don't want anyone to leave today. Tomorrow, yes. Today, no."

I saw in their eyes trust, and also that they had sensed something was wrong, too.

The bus pulled in with those I needed. Two lifeweavers, two elementalists, and a revenant. "What's up?" the elementalist, a young man, asked.

"I don't know. Something is about to happen."

"What?"

"I don't know."

"You called us out here based on a *feeling*?"

"Dial the machinespeakers, and see if they can explain it."

"I am calling," the revenant said.

“Whatever. Beats being cooped up on the campus,” the elementalist said.

“Seriously, Mary, what the glitch?” Amy asked.

The revenant adjusted his mask to a frown. “No answer from the machinespeakers.”

“They’re probably all watching some freaky porn,” the elementalist said.

“Just stay here,” I ordered.

As the day progressed, I felt worse and worse, knowing something was happening, and then not knowing. I told myself I would feel better if I got to work.

I logged in just in time to see the world change.

```
Message from alan.jrnjirlorl@OSIRIS
(as root) from /dev/pts/24410 at
13:41:
Bakts, now is the day to rise up! We
will no longer tolerate the greed of
the Dead and the injustice of the
Eternalists to suppress freedom any
longer. From this day forward, let us
march for victory!
EOF
```

What?

Then I saw Alan had sent it as root, the administrator account of OSIRIS.

“What the glitch?” I heard one of my necromancers ask out loud.

“Did you just get a weird write?” another asked.

“That must have been `wall`. Some Wheel Group…”

“That was Alan,” I said. “He…he must have become a Wheel Group member somehow.”

We all looked at each other.

Then a crash sounded. I rushed out to see the revenant motionless on the ground, frozen midstep.

"Oh, *glitch*." Amy said, looking at it.

I scanned my tag on the TV and flipped through the forbidden channels to Vive, the main Vivite channel.

Alan was making a speech. "From this day forward no man or woman shall bear a collar on the neck for an unpaid debt! I call upon every bakt and every person of goodwill to take to the streets and do what the Government of the Living refuses to do!"

My team looked to me.

"We're getting out of here," I said. "Someone drag the revenant into the bus."

We passed by utter chaos as we drove through Neyonaize, every glass storefront shattered, and open looting on every street. Mobs shouted at each other, in places fighting. I smelled tarry smoke from burning buildings.

I got through to Michael SBL. "We're on a bus heading for the campus."

What sounded like machinegun fire answered instead of him. "Get out!" he screamed "We can't hold them off!"

"We're going," I said, and shouted to the driver. "Head back! Head to…just outside the city!"

"No slizz!" Gayle said, and pulled a U-Turn that would have been very illegal if anyone cared about laws anymore.

"I'm sorry!" Michael SBL said. "I realize—" A shattering, a scream, gunfire, and then nothing.

"Sir! Sir!"

More gunfire. The line went dead.

"What the glitch is happening?" Amy asked.

Please, God, let that apology have saved him. But I shut off that part of my emotions. "We're in a revolution."

"Civil war, more like," one of the elementalists said. We passed by further looting, and freshly fallen bodies.

"Where do we go?"

"Dicity," I said. "Or anywhere we can get to that isn't falling apart."

"Dicity is going to be a lot easier than somewhere that isn't—woah!—" Gayle swerved to avoid a burning car. "Buckle the glitch up, everyone!"

We buckled the glitch up.

She drove like a madwoman.

"What's your name?" I called to the talkative elementalist.

"James," he said.

"James, I want you up front. Do you have a wand on you?"

"I sure do."

"If we are in danger, do what you need to do."

"What about me?" asked the other elementalist.

"What's your name?"

"Alfred."

"Alfred, you're in the back."

I got out my laptop.

```
[mary.firebrightsky@SBL-994F]
necrochain unlock
Password:
[mary.firebrightsky@SBL-994F] ssh
OSIRIS
```

Nothing. I canceled the command.

```
^C
[mary.firebrightsky@SBL] ping OSIRIS
PING OSIRIS 56(84) bytes of data.
```

I waited.

```
^C
--- OSIRIS ping statistics ---
16 packets transmitted, 0 received,
100% packet loss, time 16686ms
```

OSIRIS wasn't even responding to ping. I wondered if it was even up anymore.

What had Alan done?

Gayle hit the brakes in front of a barricade. Angry bakts came our way. "DOWN! WITH! THE DEAD!" they chanted.

James opened the door and aimed his wand. "James, wait!" I said.

He fired several times, blasting the barricade apart. Someone shot him.

"James!" I screamed, as Gayle floored it, and we shot through the remains of the barricade.

Amy crawled the way up as Gayle drove out of Neyonaize. "James, hold still."

"Ow! Ow! OSIRIS dear EDENs that hurts! Glitch!"

"You have a MA-AT terminal on you?" I asked.

"Duh," Amy said. "You said something creepy."

"I brought a ripper," Emily said.

"Oh, thanks for the vote of confidence," James said, then coughed up blood.

"You have a GI bleed at least. Gayle, you need to stop us somewhere so we can work on him."

"Let me stop when we ain't gonna get killed for it," Gayle said.

THOOOOM!!!

The bus rocked. The windows shattered, and we were covered with glass.

"What the glitch was that?" someone asked.

"Angel," James said. "That was an Angel firing."

I looked back to see the angry cloud burning, as if the EDENs had judged the newborn revolution. Neyonaize looked fine, mostly. But…

But that was definitely an Orbital Angel.

"It hit the fan," Gayle added helpfully.

"While we're stopped," Amy said, "help me clear the floor."

We gathered around him, scraping the glass away with our bare hands. James was gasping for breath. Amy attached leads, but she tapped away in vain.

"MA-AT must be maxed out," Amy said. "It might be hours, or even days at this point."

"Fine," James said. "Just rip me. Ow!"

Another necromancer was already sticking in the needles. "I can't connect to OSIRIS at all."

No!

"Heh," he said, and coughed. "Never thought I'd end this way. Always thought an elementalism accident would get me."

"James," I said.

"Yeah?"

"Are you baptized?"

"What?"

"There's life after ending," I said. "I can get you there."

"The glitch are you talking about?" He shook his head. "Whatever. Go ahead and do it."

Emily handed me a water bottle. I poured it over him three times. "I baptize you, James Michael Iranarix, in the Name of the Father, and the Son, and the Holy Spirit."

"Heh…heh…whatever. See you later or what…ever…"

His eyes closed, and Amy checked for a pulse. Then she started chest compressions.

"Hate to interrupt, but I see people behind us," Gayle said.

"Go," I ordered.

We drove in silence after Amy had stopped trying. We still couldn't connect to OSIRIS.

We stopped by a convenience store, or what had been one. Bakts causally sat outside, smoking cigarettes atop piles of goods.

I stepped outside. "We—"

"Everything's free," one said. "No money works anymore. No one cares. It's a bunch of rich Dead that are losing it all, anyway."

"What the glitch is happening?" Amy asked.

"You didn't see the news? Someone screwed up OSIRIS. And a Vivite mob attacked the Necropolis."

The Necropolis? The Necropolis was the vast storage structure for OSIRIS, with exabytes of RAIDs set up to store the digital bodies of the entire human race.

If they had attacked the Necropolis…

Then this wasn't a march for freedom. This was a coup.

"No looting," I told my team, as they started looting. They ignored me. "Fine. I'll pay for everything."

"No point!" a bakt said cheerfully. "All the payment systems are down."

"Fine," I said. "I'm using the restroom. When I come back, we're going."

I tried Michael again. No answer. I tried Alysson. No answer. I opened the directory on my work phone and dialed Alfred himself.

"The number you have dialed is currently out of service. Code 155. BEEEP!!!"

"What are we even doing?" Jane, a necrotech, asked. "We should be with them."

"With who?" I asked.

"The rebels! Duh! They're fighting for our freedom!"

"Do you want to die? They already killed James!"

"So? One Angel is not enough to stop us!"

"Enough!" I said.

"Who made you the boss of us?" Jane demanded.

"Nothing but the desire to get us all out of here alive!" I screamed.

They all stared at me.

I hadn't lost my temper like that before.

"Glitch all that," Gayle said. "We're heading to Dicity, and if you want to go join the revolution, fine, do it. But I want us all to get to safety before you talk like that."

We drove in angry silence after that. Some of us were crying.

CHAPTER TWENTY-THREE

WHOSOEVER SHALL NOT COME FORTH

April 4th, 1050 AGDR

The ride to Dicity was quiet, the quietest I had ever heard a group of people be.

We passed by chaos, destruction, and other refugees. Cars lay abandoned, destroyed, or still burning. Gayle took us by side roads because the highways soon became undrivable. When we went through towns, we saw burnt out buildings and corpses laying the streets, both with and without collars.

Whatever had happened, it was too late to have it unhappen.

“I learned something,” Emily called out. “There’s a statement from the Wheel Group asking everyone to stay off OSIRIS.”

“And let people die?” a necromancer asked.

“No, it’s thrashing.”

I felt my stomach twist. My great fear for so long had finally come true: OSIRIS was spending so much time moving things in and out of swap that it had no time to do anything else. It would explain why the revenant was inactive. It possibly would never wake up again at this point.

“Why’s it thrashing?” I asked out loud.

“Not sure. But I bet someone disabled swap.”

"Yeah, that would do it," someone said.

What happened to those graves active when swap was disabled? Were they ended in an instant by the OOM Killer? I wondered.

"We're almost in Dicity," Gayle said. "Once we're there, it's up to you what you want to do."

"Anyone willing to stay with me, stay with me," I said. "If you want to kill someone, that's on your soul. Stay safe, whatever you do."

We were stopped by a military patrol in armored cars. Living Guard, it looked like.

"Exit the vehicle with your hands in the air!" someone boomed over a loudspeaker.

We got out.

"What is your purpose for being here?" the soldier demanded.

"Sir, we're refugees from Neyonaize. We're looking for a safe place."

"Ha. I'll be glitched out if this is any safer. Are there any weapons inside?"

"Just two elementalist wands."

"We're taking them, and you can go."

Alfred drew his wand but was gunned down before he could use it.

"Alfred!"

"FREEZE!"

The soldiers came out and handcuffed us. A necromancer with him went and put the needles in Alfred.

The other soldiers surrounded us. "Kneel with your hands behind your head!"

Alfred!

We spent the night in a cell. Amy, Emily, and the other women and I clustered together. There were easily fifty people crammed together. News passed, little more than rumors.

Apparently, the coup had failed. The Necroforce's Living soldiers had railed and pushed the Deep Vivites back out of the Necropolis. Something had happened at the Acropolis, too, and no one was quite sure what had happened to the Consul and the Senate.

"Serves him right if Heartlessray got ended," a bakt woman hissed.

"Quiet!" someone hissed back.

I didn't sleep at all that night.

April 5th, 1050 AGDR

In the morning, when the guards came, I told them: "I'm the leader of those who came on the bus. Please talk to me, first."

They looked at me, but out I went in chains.

The interrogator looked me up and down. "What is your name?"

"Mary Firebrightsky."

"What do you want?"

"Sir, we are just refugees. Alfred acted on his own."

He looked suspicious.

"Sir, I'm the manager of an office of the Slowbrightlaughter Estate in Neyonaize. We fled from the chaos. One of our team fired on rebels and was ended when they shot back. That was the body in the bus."

His expression loosened only a little. "What about the revenant in the back?"

"He crashed, sir. We decided to bring him back to spare him."

"What office?"

I gave him details.

After many more questions, he nodded. "Shame it all happened. I'll get your team out of here."

I did a head count of those who were released. Not everyone had made it out. Whether they were still being interrogated, or something worse, I didn't know.

Outside, the Spring air, still cold from the remains of Fimbulwinter, chilled me, but not nearly as much as my inner thoughts. I had no idea what would happen next, and that was more terrifying than any one thing.

"Now what?" Amy asked.

"We find a place to stay," I said.

"First step, an ATM."

Finding an ATM that both worked and had cash was nearly impossible, but we managed to collectively empty one by a hotel. As we went card by card, I prayed that, somehow, we would have enough.

In the hotel, I talked to the manager. "We need a place to stay."

"I can get you one room," he said. "And it's not in good shape."

"Good enough," I said.

We all crammed in there, and the moment I lay on the floor I fell fast asleep.

April 6th, 1050 AGDR

When I woke, Emily was long gone.

I found a note tucked into my pocket.

Mary,

You've treated me the most decently of all necromancers I've ever worked with. And you led me to Jesus. I can never repay you.

I don't wish you any ill will.

But I do have ill will towards the League. I'm sorry it had to end this way, but in these times, we all have to do our part for freedom.

Hopefully, you'll join me. And maybe we'll see each other again. In Heaven, if nowhere else. If not, goodbye for good.

Emily

I finally cried.

"Mary, I saw on the Neonet that the Living Guard is taking anyone willing to join, especially mages." Amy said. "They say that they'll free you if you're joining."

We looked at each other.

I stood up. "I'm not going to judge you for what you choose to do," I said. "But for now, I'm going to report to the Living Guard."

"Me, too," Amy said.

Some, but not all of us, followed me.

We were stopped again, but they let us in immediately when we explained what we wanted.

I didn't actually want to join the Eternalist government. But I did want to be free.

Soldiers everywhere ran around the Living Guard base. Officers barked orders; trucks drove around. I didn't see a single war revenant.

I didn't know what exactly happened, but whatever Alan did to disrupt OSIRIS, he had succeeded in paralyzing the Necroforce. Without OSIRIS to maintain the consciousness of a war revenant, they were simply hunks of metal.

In the distance stood a tall obelisk, a monument to the long-dead leader of a long-dead civilization.

The recruiter's office called us one by one. "Hopefully we'll end up in the same place," Amy said.

"God grant it," I said.

"Yeah, well, better not pray to OSIRIS right now."

"Mary Firebrightsky?" called the recruiter.

I followed her in.

They went over several tests, including a fitness test.

I failed most of them. My pneumonia-ravaged lungs weren't up to heavy exertion.

"We don't want you," the recruiter said. "I'm sorry. Wish we could take you, but…"

"OK," I said. Of course it would be too good to be true.

Still, I didn't really want to join anyone. Without freedom dangled in front of me, I didn't know if I cared….

I walked out to see Amy without a collar. She rubbed her new freeman's mark gingerly.

"Slizz, Mary. I take it you didn't get in?"

"No," I sighed.

"Well, they're going to ship me off somewhere. Don't know where yet."

We hugged each other.

"We'll get through this, Mary," she said. "Promise. And don't give up hope,"

"I won't," I said.

"This is just temporary," she said. "We *will* see each other again. Understood?"

"Understood," I said.

"See you!" She marched off towards the rest of the base.

That was the last time I ever saw her.

I walked towards the exit. Now what? I didn't even know if Alfred SBL still existed in this world, or who was running the estate, or if anyone was running the estate, or if the estate even still existed as a meaningful entity.

I wondered if I could get my indenture voided if my master no longer functioned.

Probably not.

"Mary Firebrightsky!" I heard someone shout.

I turned to see a Necroforce officer running up to me. "What now?"

"You're on our list," she said, gasping for air.

"Ma'am?"

"Persons of special interest. Please, come with me. We want you."

In the commander's office, the CO himself paced eagerly back and forth. "You know Alan Jaranjair?"

"Before I answer," I said, "am I free to go?"

"Why?" he asked.

"I'm sick of being yanked around. No, we don't want you. Yes, we do want you." I realized I was insane for complaining about this of all things, but somehow this was the last straw. "I'm a bakt of the Slowbrightlaughter estate, and my master may need me. Can I go, yes or no?"

"If you stay with us, we'll free you."

Was this it?

Was *this* how I would be freed?

"Yes, sir," I said.

"Get a machinespeaker," the commander barked to an aide.

"Yes, sir," she said, and hurried off.

"We'll have to fill out some paperwork," he said, and drew out a form from his desk.

I filled it out. I didn't care if I was signing up to join them, I wanted to be free.

The machinespeaker arrived with a laptop and saluted. "Sir."

"Free this woman."

The machinespeaker looked at my dog tags, then typed a command on his laptop. With one yank, the collar unsnapped then came all the way off.

I pulled off my Snuggly and felt, for the first time in seven years, my neck. I felt scars and callous, irritated skin.

I started crying. Finally. After seven years I was free again.

"You'll want to keep it bandaged for a while," the machinespeaker said. "Just be gentle with it."

I wiped my eyes. "What do you want to know?" I asked the commander.

"Everything."

I told him everything I could think of.

April 7th, 1050 AGDR

The next morning, they sent me back to Newla. I didn't know why, but what I did know was that I no longer had a collar on me.

Did I feel loyalty to them? I thought on the plane trip over. Not really, but I had made an agreement.

I moved to touch my collar, to once again feel it not there.

I didn't know what the future held. But whatever it was, it was back in Newla.

CHAPTER TWENTY-FOUR

WAR WAS IN HIS HEART

April 7th, 1050 AGDR

The Necroforce base in Newla was even more busy, although I still didn't see any revenants. I didn't see much. I was ushered immediately to the intelligence department.

"My name is Major Wesley Kalkaral, and I'll be talking to you today," the middle-aged man introduced himself in the slightly cramped room. I saw on his spiral almost nothing: Aside from his name, he had neither married nor had children, or experienced any other major life event. I wondered if he had deliberately refused to add such details.

"You can read a spiral?" he asked suddenly.

"Yes, sir. You…seem not to have lived much of a life?"

"I've lived a very simple life, honest to the EDENs," he said. "I didn't want any attachments considering my line of work."

"I see, sir." I relaxed, despite myself. I had no real reason to believe he was lying, spook or not, so why should I? He may have simply been career Necroforce.

"Now, just so you know, we can use anything you tell us, but we promise you, we'll use the information you give solely to end the war as soon as we possibly can. We're going to keep it classified, so I want you to be as honest as you can, all right?"

"All right."

Major Kalkaral was the sweetest, kindest, gentlest man I had ever met. I was fully aware how this method of interrogation worked, for as a necromancer I was trained both theoretically and practically in it. But a single friendly voice was all it took, and so I was quickly telling him my entire life story.

He did eventually meander on to what they wanted me there for. How long had I known Alan? Did he talk about politics? (Yes, all the time.) Did he ever suggest plans? (No—I mean, he did talk about events.) Did he mention this date? (Yes, he had invited me to a party on April 4th.) Did I have sex with him? (No.)

At the end, I felt both relieved and drained.

"Do you have any questions for me?" he asked.

"What actually happened?" I asked.

"The rebels hacked OSIRIS to steal credentials of Wheel Group members. They managed to get enough to create one more unauthorized OWG member before automated systems reacted. The rebels have four Wheel Group credentials—Whitelightwind, two stolen from Tallgreysea and Redwhitesun, and they added Jaranjair. On our side, Lightwindknown still has his, as do the non-Athanasian members, and Westbrightsea."

"What about John Greenrayburst and Alexandria Blueblisslight?" Those were the two other Vivite Wheel Group members.

"We're not sure, as neither has logged into OSIRIS since war broke out. Beyond that, I cannot say."

"I understand. Is OSIRIS thrashing?"

"Yes, they disabled swap, and it is currently still doing so, yes."

“What happened to the government?”

“The insurrectionists murdered every Eternalist present in the Acropolis complex, including Heartlightray. It appeared they tried to force rip them, but when they couldn’t connect to OSIRIS, they shot them instead.”

“I see.” *Alan, what have you done?* “Who is in charge now?”

“For Consul, the line of succession went to the Proconsul of Agriculture, David Gemskynight, who was out inspecting a farm when it all hit. The only surviving members of the Senate are Vivites, and right now they’re deadlocked.”

“Sarah Whiteblisstrue?”

“She was on a revenant-piloted charter plane to Neyonaize. When OSIRIS began to thrash and the revenants became inactive, it crashed. The rebels are claiming we did it with SET-forged images. We’re assuming that means she’s ended.”

So in the end, neither of them had actually gotten the Consulship. “And the Parliament of the Dead?”

“All ended. The Parliament’s grave was destroyed, and it’s been long enough that their souls are gone.”

“What about the Angel that fired on Neyonaize?”

“Unfortunately, I can’t talk about that at the moment. The situation is complex and evolving. But we can get you access to a newspaper. We’d prefer if you didn’t use your cell phone.”

“OK.” I relaxed a little.

April 8th, 1050 AGDR

General Westbrightsea’s office was little different aside from the sheer number of papers on his desk, which had been flipped over to their blank side.

"Ms. Firebrightsky, I am very glad we could find you."

"What do you need, sir?" I asked, with no small trepidation.

"The finest sword is the one that's never drawn. You might be able to end this war without any more bloodshed."

"Is…is this about my relationship with Alan?"

"Yes. We've made contact with him and told him we have you. I want you to talk to him, to try to convince him to surrender. If you can, I want to know everything about his motives and intent."

"Do you really believe he'll surrender?"

"Do you?"

"I…don't think so," I said. "But I guess it's worth a shot."

"Yes. Do you have any questions? We want you to go live in an hour."

"Sir, if I do convince him to surrender, what will happen to him?"

The general shook his head. "I don't know. I would argue for clemency, but I am not the tribunal that will judge him."

The room was as bland as possible, aside from the giant screen on one side.

"You're going live in three, two, one…"

And there he was.

He looked handsome as ever, but I could tell he was overwhelmed with stress, as hard as he tried to cover it. For a moment, by the longing look in his eyes, I thought that I really could call him back to sanity. Then his smile—a false one, I knew—told me he would not. "Is this conversation being recorded?"

"I believe it is," I said. "They didn't tell me."

"They didn't tell you a lot of things. I wish you had come, Mary. There is so much we are finding out about the Parliament of the Dead—"

"Alan, did you really end them?" I interrupted.

He stopped mid-sentence and paused for a second. "Mary, I'm not sure what they told you—"

"Alan, what happened to the Parliament?"

"They were ended by the OOM Killer. I swear, Mary, I didn't end them." He met my eyes saying all this. "Am I a revolutionary? Yes. I don't deny that. But all I am asking for is freedom, freedom for all of us."

"All of us? While OSIRIS was thrashing, my friends were ended!" I snapped.

"Fine!" Alan snarled. "Yes! I've ended people. I can't exactly free the League from the Eternalists' clutches without ending some people in the process. But why don't you ask the Necroforce how many people they've ended with their bombing campaigns on Neyonaize? Or the three hundred who were ended by the Angel they activated?"

"OK," I said. "So you've ended people. You can save a thousand times more by surrendering now."

"Do you really believe that?" Alan asked.

"I do, Alan. Come back. You can stop this war before it starts."

"I wish I could, Mary. I wish I could. But as long as people live with collars around their necks to serve the Dead, there cannot be peace." Alan shook his head. "I don't know what they have over you, but I will say this: I can only think of the future now. I can't even think of you."

"Please, Alan."

"I'm sorry," he said. "I really am. Goodbye." Before I could say another word, he pressed a button and was gone.

Wesley was over the moon with the information that Alan had accidentally leaked. Or on purpose leaked.

"He doesn't have any ticks," I told him. "But he certainly seemed sincere."

"Thank you for your service in any case," the spook said.

"General?" I asked. "Is it true?"

"*What* is true?" Westbrightsea asked.

"That he didn't end the Parliament of the Dead."

He looked me in the eye, with a gaze I realized was genuinely sincere. "All we know is that OSIRIS does not contain the grave of the Parliament of the Dead."

I breathed a sigh of relief.

"You are quite correct in imputing final deaths to him. War has not begun without someone to start it—"

"What about the bombing?" I interrupted.

"A bald-faced lie. We would not even consider it with OSIRIS in its current state. It is true we ended a number of individuals, likely civilians, when we targeted the Neyonaize power station with a low-power Angel strike. We believed doing so would interrupt the power supply to the attackers and save OSIRIS. We had no other options."

I tried to look away, but Westbrightsea took my head in his aged hands. I couldn't help but return his gaze.

"This is war," he said. "There will always be casualties—ours, theirs, and those who get caught in between. Almost all of them with be Athanasian citizens. And almost all of them would have smiled and waved at those on the other side as they passed by a week ago."

"Perhaps a few years ago, sir."

"Perhaps so," he agreed.

"How about you take a break?" Wesley offered.

"All right," I said.

That night I had nightmares, worse than any before. In the terrible times between wakings, my brain swirled as my thoughts raced without end.

Both Westbrightsea and Alan seemed perfectly normal and trustworthy—but who was lying?

It had to be Alan, I reasoned. Bombing Neyonaize to dislodge his forces would be unthinkable. As much as I would have liked to believe in his innocence, yet, if he was lying, why would he have told such a ridiculous lie? Did he really think I wouldn't just ask?

But then again, maybe he didn't realize I would talk to Westbrightsea.

In any case, Westbrightsea was known as a kind of military pacifist. He was frequently quoted as saying, "The finest sword is the one that's never drawn." A preemptive strike would surely not have been his choice.

Unless the Acting Consul had ordered it. How could I know? I was just some random civilian far from the fray.

April 9th, 1050 AGDR

That morning I read through the newspaper, but there was little to be known. Several cantons in the south and the east, including Starlight and Dicity, had fallen to the rebels, and several had not. Steelriver was still loyal, but barely.

Those were the majority-Spiral cantons. The war was as nomenist as any other evil.

I sat by my desk, tired. I was free, yes, but what I would give God to turn back the clock.

Was this your judgment, Lord? Your punishment for the sins of the League?

God didn't answer. I didn't really want to know, anyway.

What I wanted to know was what to do next.

Did I help the Necroforce?

No.

No, in fact, I didn't want to.

I didn't want either side to win. I didn't want to live in a world run by either Vivites or Eternalists alone. The Vivites were right about slavery, but they had staged a coup to reject the lawfully elected government. And maybe the Eternalists were the lawfully elected government, but they were wrong about slavery.

The system was broken. And now it had completely disintegrated.

I didn't know if they would let me leave, but if they didn't, I could refuse to cooperate. Even being interrogated at some black site was better than fighting for a cause I thought was evil.

"I'm leaving," I told Wesley.

"Excuse me?" he asked.

"I don't want to be part of the Necroforce. I don't want to be your hostage or your lips. I'm leaving."

"We'd prefer if you didn't do that."

"I'm a free citizen now. Am I legally obligated to stay?"

"Before getting into that, we would greatly prefer—"

“I don’t care what you prefer!” I said. “I will refuse to help you in any case. Let me go home. Unless you’d rather become the horrible people that the Vivites say you are?”

“Why do you want to leave?”

“I don’t need to give you an answer!” I snapped, nearly losing control of my voice.

“OK,” he said.

“Am I free to go? Yes or no?”

“Yes,” he said.

“Then I’m leaving.”

“At least let me give you my business card,” he said. “You might need it.”

I thought about refusing, but I supposed it could come in handy. “Fine,” I said.

He handed it to me. “Call if you need anything. Or if you think of anything.”

“Goodbye,” I said. I walked out, and headed straight for the exit.

CHAPTER TWENTY-FIVE

THE INNERMOST PART OF THE HOUSE

April 9th, 1050 AGDR

When the Necroforce vehicle dropped me off at the edge of Newla, I realized that, aside from being angry, I had no plan.

I checked my pockets. I had 215 drachmae left in cash. Who knew how long it would last, or even be worth 215 drachmae? I did still have my savings from my peculium, if I could get access to them.

St. Teresa of Avila.

I could go there and see if I could get help from people I knew.

I got out my phone and summoned a rideshare.

One arrived soon. Before I had even opened the door, the driver announced, "There's a mandatory extra twenty drachmae tip. In cash. *If* your app payment goes through."

"Banks are still down?"

"Glitch if I know. A lot of accounts got frozen. Getting on?"

I got inside. "I've…been with Necroforce. Just left. What's life like?"

"By OSIRIS, it's a nightmare. You can't get gas legally anywhere. I have to buy it off the black market, and they charge through the nose. Everyone gets randomly stopped and inspected. Swear I heard a bomb go off last night..." As he continued, I realized he had become the hearer of others' bad news, and now needed someone to hear his own venting. I was willing to be his therapist for a negative price, if for no other reason than we all needed it.

We slowed down before a military barricade.

"Stay in your vehicle, and keep your hands visible."

The driver turned his engine off. "This will take a while," he muttered.

"Where are you going?"

"St. Teresa of Avila Catholic Church," the driver said.

A soldier came up, machine gun in hands. "Lower your window."

I lowered it.

"ID."

I dug out my wallet from my purse and pulled out my ID.

He looked at it suspiciously, then handed it to another soldier "This is a bakt ID for Neyonaize."

"Sir, I was a bakt in Neyonaize," I said patiently. "Now I'm here."

"How the glitch did you get here?"

"The Necroforce flew me in. They freed me."

"Why the glitch aren't you with the Necroforce, then?"

"They let me go."

He glowered at me.

"I can prove it," I insisted. "I have a card."

"Give it."

I dug out the card Wesley had given me and passed it to him.

The soldiers conferred. One kept an eye on me, while another called for an officer.

"Sir, is this Major Kalkaral? We're at a stop, and this woman says she knows you. She says her name is Mary Firebrightsky. Yes, sir. St. Teresa of Avila's Catholic Church. OK." He handed me my wallet back and called to the driver. "You're good to go!"

Newla had its share of beggars, the homeless, and drug addicts, and the parish had asked that they seek help at Catholic Charities, not at the front door. Even during Fimbulwinter, they tried to direct those on the street to shelters. But the newborn OSIRIS War had already changed that because a lot of others had had the same idea I did.

The parish was already stuffed to the brim with people. People lying on the pews. People lying in front of statues. People scattered around the sanctuary. People sobbing in corners. People trying to comfort children, or children trying to comfort people.

"You new here?" an older woman asked—Janet! "Mary! Where have you been?"

"Neyonaize, then Dicity, then I ended up back here," I said. I looked around at all the suffering. "Don't treat me any different."

"You're in the right place," she said. "Though right now we're trying to get people resettled as fast as possible."

I whispered in her ear. "Where did they all come from?"

"The Starlight canton was overrun by those...*rebels*," she hissed. "These are mostly refugees."

It was at that moment I realized how massive the war already had become.

She took my silence for agreement. "This war…it's so awful. I can't look at the news anymore. And those rebels are burning churches left and right!"

"What happened to Fr. Justsquared?"

"He went to the Lord last year. Old age. Perhaps he was one of the lucky ones."

"I…see," I said.

"Have you eaten?"

I shook my head.

"Dinner's at five in the parish hall. We don't have much, but we have something."

"OK," I said. I found a place to sit down, between the sobbing old woman and the parent whose children were very quiet.

I wouldn't normally have used a cell phone in a church, but now I realized I had no idea how everyone I knew was doing. I scrolled through my contacts, and realized I had not contacted most people in years.

I dialed Seth.

No answer. I got his voicemail.

I had probably spoken to him for the last time.

Mr. Iranarair?

I got through on the second try. "Hello?" he asked.

"This is Mary," I said. "Mary Firebrightsky."

"Dear OSIRIS, you're alive?"

"I am. You are too, apparently."

"Not by much. Whylin is FAL territory now. I'm on the other side of the river…somewhere."

"FAL? Sir?"

"I don't think I should be talking in detail on a phone. May your god bless you, Mary."

"The Lord bless you, too," I said.

He hung up.

Charles?

I tried several times with no answer.

Alysson?

It took several attempts to get connected, but I got through.

"Alysson?" I asked.

"Mary?" came the exhausted voice. "You survived?"

"I wasn't at the campus when it fell."

"…Alfred's gone. His grave was damaged beyond repair by the OOM Killer."

What could I say? "I'm sorry," I said.

"I don't think any of the campuses are intact at this point."

"I'm free, now."

"So why the glitch are you calling? To taunt me? To find a job?"

"I just wanted to see if you were OK."

I heard a silence. Nothing. I watched the seconds pass by on my phone in silence.

I waited in silence myself.

"I'm…I'm managing," she said at last, after at least fifteen seconds. "Where are you?"

"I'm in Newla."

"Do you need a place to stay?"

For a moment, I almost thought of saying I would never go back.

"I won't put you in the bakt dorms."

If I went there, the Necroforce couldn't find me easily. Besides, I could get my bearings and plan my next step in a place that wasn't loaded with human suffering. "All right," I said.

I had, in my imagination, pictured that SBL Main had never changed. After all, I had only seen it damaged briefly, and I still thought of it as I had first seen it, not as I last. What I saw when I returned was history overwriting history, like a living palimpsest.

The once ever-verdant lawn had been replaced with greenhouse after greenhouse. The golden-pebbled road was now only the soot-covered main line of a network between the greenhouses, equipment sheds, and row after row of dorm houses. It must have been a massive plantation.

But the workers had taken their freedom violently. Nearly every panel of glass in the greenhouses had been shattered and several burned. The murals on the main complex had been defaced, and moon-like craters everywhere showed a battle between elementalists. I saw the shattered mask of a revenant impaled on a pitchfork. The revenant would not have felt pain, nor would it even have been conscious, perhaps even still in this world, but the symbol was clear enough.

The rideshare driver muttered to herself. “You have to be slizzing me. You’re sure you want to go *here*?“

I had been having all sorts of second thoughts, though now I badly wanted to know what Alysson meant by “managing.” We stopped at the doors, or where the doors had been. They had been bashed down, then hastily rebarricaded, then the barricades had been blasted by elementalists, and now they had partially collapsed. The windows upstairs appeared to have been accessed by a ladder, which lay broken on the deck beside blood splatters on the marble.

“Let me off here,” I said. I offered her cash.

She took it. "I'm staying here until I'm sure you're safe. This place gives me the creeps."

"I used to be a bakt here."

"What the glitch?" She looked back at my freeman's mark. "What the *glitch*?"

"I want to see if my friends are…OK," I said, realizing both that that was my real reason for being here and how insane that reason sounded.

"Don't bet on it," she said. As I stepped out, she said, "Leave the door open! Just in case we have to get the glitch out."

I walked up to the entrance. I had perhaps been hasty in my earlier assessment: Someone had collapsed the foyer to stop the invasion. Alfred would be pissed that someone smashed his statue, I mused.

Alfred was ended.

I looked around for one of the side doors, then I heard footsteps. My heart beat rapidly. "Alysson?" I called.

I saw her creep around the corner, a shotgun in her hands and a long knife scabbarded on her hip. She walked with a limp, and she stared at me with eyes that had seen too much. "Mary?" she asked.

"…Yes," I said. What the glitch could I say? Hello?

"Who's that in the car?"

The driver got out, door open and car running, and came up to us. "Holy EDENs! You're *living* here?"

"If you can call it living," Alysson said, watching the driver with suspicion.

"You two are out of your minds." She shrugged to herself. "So is everyone else these days. Stay safe."

"You, too," I said.

Alysson said nothing.

The driver, not without watching us, slammed the doors shut, got in, and the car squealed off.

I was going to ask who else survived, but I amended it to, "Are you the only one left?"

"…Yes," she said.

I followed her over rubble and more craters to a door that had been broken open. When we entered, she wheeled a cart against it and locked the wheels. She walked deeper inside.

I soon realized, as she began to talk, that she needed me to stay with her more than I needed a place to stay.

"It made the Solstice Riots look like a polite disagreement," she said. "When they realized the guards were gone and the police and Necroforce weren't coming…"

I waited for her to continue.

She didn't.

We said nothing as she led me through the ruined building. The murals had been defaced, any movable art stolen or destroyed. I saw more than one splatter where a corpse must have been. The place stank of soot and rotting flesh. If the corpsegrinders had come, they must have…

The corpsegrinders.

Who was staffing the body reprocessing facilities? Anyone?

As if reading my mind, Alysson said, "The military came to take the bodies. Said they needed as much bioslurry as they could get." She paused. "I don't think they got them all."

Another turn and behind a statue was a door that was almost invisible. Alysson waved her lanyard in front, and it slid open.

We stepped inside into an almost untouched panic room. An ornate pseudo-revenant statue watched motionlessly, Alfred's method of talking to the mortal staff that escaped whatever violence might occur. The only sign this had become a permanent residence was piled up blankets with a pillow to sleep on.

In one corner was an actual minibar, and Alysson walked behind it and uncorked a bottle. "On me," she said.

I would have refused, but I decided to have one drink to keep her company. I did some math based on the empty bottles lying on the floor and how long it had been since war had broken out, and I realized Alysson had been coping. Coping a *lot*.

I sat on a stool. "Thank you," I said, and sipped.

We sat there. The place was so quiet I could hear her drinking.

"The rest tried to hold them off," Alysson said. "It was just the machinespeakers and I in here. After that, they left." She drank and poured herself another. "I've been calling anyone I can think of. No answer. The other campuses are gone."

"Why are you still here?" I asked.

"If I go in public, they'll kill me. The machinespeakers rigged this place so that SET can't know about it." She set down the glass. "This will be over soon. Then this land—all the land—will be very valuable. We have to inherit it. Myself and...any other surviving Slowbrightlaughters."

And now I finally understood what insanity had come over Alysson.

She had been begging for scraps from Alfred all her life, and now that Alfred was gone for good, all she had left was this shell of a life. Perhaps she had always imagined that somehow, some way, Alfred would let her in on the action, or one day glitch out. And now that that had happened, in a way, she was still stuck in the past.

Perhaps forever.

"I'll pay you," she said. "Anything you ask. Just…" She stopped, then drank her glass and poured another.

"I'm sorry," I said. "I have my own life to live, now."

She didn't reply, just looked at me.

"You can come with me," I offered. "Or you could join the Necroforce. They'll take almost anyone."

"No," she said. "I have to stay here. What if someone comes and…" Perhaps she, for a moment, realized how insane her reasons were because she trailed off.

"Alysson," I said. "There is nothing here. This is a ruin. The estate is gone."

"*Don't you talk back to me!*" she shrieked.

"I'm not your slave anymore," I said.

She buried her face in her arms on the bar and sobbed. I offered her comforting touches, and let my old boss let out her sorrows.

April 10th, 1050 AGDR

Alysson didn't come with me when the rideshare came the next morning. Nor did she even come outside. I didn't know what to tell her, and I didn't know what she wanted to be told. "See you in a future life," she said as she wheeled the pseudo-door closed.

"See you in a future life," I said. The words were only words, now.

As the driver, a silent guy, took me back, I mused through my options. If I stayed in Newla, it was only a matter of time before the Necroforce would take me again. My old parish was out. Of all the places I wanted to live, Steelriver itself or Whylin would be my choices. It was close to the front, yes, but who knew how long the war would last?

Long, obviously. Even if no one wanted to think about it.

In either case, my first destination was the train station.

There were soldiers all over the station. One stood by every turnstile, ready to check IDs.

I dug out my wallet to get my ID ready—Glitch! It was missing!

Where had I lost it?

Did the soldier hand it back? Wait, he did—but I didn't check to see if my card was back inside.

Glitch, glitch, glitch.

What now? I was stuck here. Legally stuck, at least. People had evidentially fled for their lives across canton boundaries…Wait, from the Starlight Canton? They had to have driven hundreds of kilometers? No wonder they were—

BOOM!

I froze for the first few seconds after the explosion. I ran as the debris rained down and pelted me. Glitch! Terrorism, here?

I should go back, but without a ripper…

No. I couldn't go back.

I had thought I was safe. Nowhere was safe.

I ended up in some strange part of Newla. They were going to send patrols soon to look for whoever caused the explosion.

Without an ID, they were going to probably arrest me, and who knew if I would ever leave again?

I saw a machinespeaker office. I thought about it…

If I got a fake ID matching my real one, would it really be a fake?

It didn't feel right, but once again, I was desperate.

I stepped inside. A machinespeaker looked at me and said, "Oh, my EDEN! *Mary?* I thought you were dead!"

"Stephen?" I asked. I hadn't interacted with the machinespeakers much, but I could remember that one of them had occasionally been Tyrone's satellite office to troubleshoot arcane machinespeaker problems.

"What can I do for you?"

I looked to make sure we were alone. "Do you know anywhere I could get a real fake ID?"

"A what?"

"I lost my card. Can you get me a fake ID that's really me?"

He shook his head. "Fake ID card, yes. One that's really yours, no. I…have ways to get those. And to be clear, if you die, who knows what they'll rip you as."

"I'm OK with that," I said.

"A hundred drachmae. That's discounted."

I pulled out a hundred drachmae. He counted them, then typed away at a laptop. "It'll take a bit. Just an hour or two. SET is so busy right now."

"I can wait," I said. "What happened on SET?"

"Glitch, *everyone* asks that."

"Sorry."

"No, it's not an unreasonable question. It's all over SETNet. It seems someone found a weakness in the hashing algorithm that the EDENs use for passwords. Now, the only way you could even use that is if you had access to `/etc/shadow`."

"Which means someone with root access leaked it," I said.

"Exactly. So one of the original OSIRIS Wheel Group members was with the rebellion, then the Deep Vivites bought something like ten billion drachmae worth of SET priority and had it brute force OWG passwords. 'Course, everyone was trying to stop it or make it go, SET Wheel Group included."

"A machinespeaker tried to warn us," I said. "I don't know what happened to him."

Stephen shrugged. "Name?"

"Seth Knowntimeking."

"Let me check." He typed away. "Last login was a few days ago."

"Glitch."

"Yeah, he's probably gone now. I'd check OSIRIS records if I were you, just in case, but I wouldn't bet on it."

I sighed. I had known this was likely, but confirmation made it both better and worse.

"What happened to you? Why are you here and not in Neyonaize?"

"You know Alan Jaranjair?"

"Yeah, glitch, *everyone* knows him."

"I was his college girlfriend."

"Holy EDENs!" he shook his head. "Let me guess. The Necroforce took you here."

"They did, and they let me go," I said. "Barely. I'm trying to leave here, before they decide to take me again."

"They won't take you if you get this false ID. Just be careful, all right?"

"I will."

April 11th, 1050 AGDR

The next morning, Abigail Nightraysight took a peaceful ride on a bus to Neagas. The empty desert passed outside the window without change, and I felt a little peace.

I didn't know if I could justify my actions. I didn't know if I *wanted* to justify my actions. But I was starting to realize—we all were—that the rules of the Athanasian League had become porous. What was legal was no longer legal, and what you needed to do to survive was another matter, entirely.

I scrolled through the news on my phone.

OSIRIS had since stabilized, but swap was no more. Teams of necromancers in the Necropolis were now building microkas in mass graves for any newly ripped ba, in order to save memory and ghosts.

The rebels had now formed the Free Athanasian League, electing Alan Jaranjair as Acting Consul. They were apparently even issuing their own currency, known as the denarius. A Necroforce general named Keralalix was the supreme commander, and his forces, the newborn Red Guard, had indeed been burning churches. St. Alphonsus was gone now, and I feared what had happened to Monsignor Serelalix. They had constructed their own alternate graveyard datacenter, and swore to build mass graves for any rip of their side.

Acting Consul David Gemskynight of the Athanasian League had ordered the Deep Vivite members of the Senate arrested. The moderate Vivites, now the majority, were rapidly rewriting the law. One foreign commentator noted that they were retroactively justifying their actions.

The comments sections were utter anarchy, if any site still had them. I wondered how long it would be before it became illegal to criticize the government or any of its actions. If the Loyalist Government, as the moniker had stuck, had already tossed the Tables in the trash, what basis would anyone have for free speech?

I didn't want any of this. I wanted to be a civilian on the side of no one.

No matter what it took.

CHAPTER TWENTY-SIX

WARS AND RUMORS OF WARS

April 15th, 1050 AGDR

From Neagas, I was able to get on a train through several stops to Archio. Everyone was talking about the war, no one too loudly.

I passed only through major cities, but all of them seemed far more crowded than they ought to have been. People were still fleeing the countryside, hoping that a city would be safer from guerillas and the still cold weather. Many trains were packed to the brim. I decided I might as well have used bakt class.

Some of the banks were back, including the institution I used, but some had failed permanently in what was now called the Swapoff, due to their infrastructure being destroyed or owners ended. I withdrew all the money I could at every ATM, but there were already capital controls. I often could barely afford the next ticket.

In Archio itself, I stopped.

I looked all over the refugee-crowded station and could not find a way. There was no service by bus, train, rideshare, or anything else to Steelriver.

"What are you looking for?" a man asked.

"A way to Steelriver."

"You're not going to get anywhere close to Steelriver, legally," he added. "Not even if you brought KHONSU back to life."

"What happened?"

"Half rebel, half loyal. It's a warzone. Stay safe."

"You, too."

April 19th, 1050 AGDR

I stayed in Archio for a few days until I decided to stay there permanently. I had nowhere else to go, and I might be able to find an apartment easier.

But my guilty conscience had led me to the doors of the Department of Names and Identifications office, only to find the line winding out several blocks.

The next day, I arrived at 6 AM.

I saw some in torn business garb, possibly the only thing on when they had to flee. Everyone had dirty clothes. Some, unfortunately, had not found a way to shower. But as long as you didn't have an ID, you couldn't settle.

"D-210. D-210!"

I went up to the cubicle. "I lost my ID," I said, which was indeed true. "I need a new one."

"Do you have your naming certificate and Necrosecurity card?" the clerk asked.

"I have my Necrosecurity *number*."

"That's not enough. I need the card."

"I—Listen, if my naming certificate is somewhere it's…it's Neyonaize."

"Where were you named?"

"Steelriver."

"Unfortunately, I need a copy."

"But—"

She looked with sympathy. "Listen. I can't do it. I need your naming certificate and your Necrosecurity card. My hands are tied."

"I can't get either of those things."

"Then I can't help you. Is there anything else I could help you with?"

I sighed and left, almost walking into a colossal necromancer with a prosthetic leg.

We looked at each other.

"Trying to get an ID?" he asked.

"I'm an internally displaced person, yeah," I said. "You?"

"I was going to get my ID renewed, but on second thought, I might wait a few weeks." He looked at me. "Are you Catholic?"

"How can you tell?" I asked.

"I wouldn't imagine an EDENist would feel guilty enough to try to get a real ID as opposed to a machinespeaker knockoff."

I almost admitted that I *had* gotten a machinespeaker knockoff, but I realized this was not the place.

"You, too?" I realized that most people with a missing leg would self-euthanize.

"I am." He looked at me. "Do you need a place to stay?"

"That'd be great," I said. "Mary Firebrightsky."

"Raphael Yalaxir."

We talked at length that night.

I decided to tell him the truth.

"I'm amazed the Necroforce let you go," he said. "Maybe it was Westbrightsea. He seems like a decent individual."

"He is," I said.

"My story is a lot shorter. I left my former employer," he admitted. "They wanted me to force rip, and I wouldn't do that. Then war broke out while I was out here on a trip. I wanted to get my ID reissued here, but it looks like I'm in the same boat as you."

"We're definitely in the same boat," I said. "Is this your house?"

"No, but it's my son's."

"Where is your son?"

"I don't know. He's in the Necroforce, but I haven't heard from him. He may be alive. He may be ended."

"I'm sorry. I'll pray for him, wherever he is."

"Thank you."

"But the key is," I said, "Neither of us has a job, although we both have skills."

"True."

"Maybe we could start a new necromancy firm, together?" I suggested.

"I'm afraid I'm more of a worker than a leader," he told me.

"I've run a satellite office as close to an independent business for two years, plus a necrotech business before that."

"I'm up for it," he said.

"I'm up for it, too."

"You'll have to be the official owner," I said. "I don't have any way of getting a necromancy license here without a personal ID."

"I wouldn't be so sure. The Archio Canton is…lax."

"OK, so I'll get a license, and you get the charter, so you can be the official owner," I said.

"Sounds like a plan."

April 25th, 1050 AGDR

Ralaxir was right. I just needed to send in some paperwork showing I had been a necromancer for so many years, and I didn't need to provide documents at all. I listed Alysson as a reference. She was the only one I knew who could provide one.

Finding a storefront was not difficult. Many businesses had closed, so we had our pick. *Fixing up* the storefront after it had been looted and partially burned was a bit more difficult, but we had nothing else to do. We talked as we hauled stuff out, him more than me.

We couldn't fix the smell, and we couldn't afford to pay someone else to fix the smell, so we decided to live with it.

April 26th, 1050 AGDR

We had no sooner put up the OPEN sign than customers were crowding in. I immediately realized we needed a lot more staff, but where could we find them?

"Please, take a ticket!" I called over the hubbub.

My first new client had lost both his parents in the chaos, and he wanted to know if they were in OSIRIS.

Simple enough:

```
$ necrochain unlock
Password:
$ ssh mary.firebrightsky@OSIRIS
Welcome to OSIRIS! [AGP/Linux]

  MOTD: "Please limit your OSIRIS
usage to the absolute minimum
necessary. It is currently unstable."
```

```
"And you, yourself, a sword shall
pierce."
Last login Mon April 4 13:44:32
[mary.firebrightsky@OSIRIS]$
```

I stared at the MOTD.

For over a thousand years, no one had changed the message of the day. It had become even a slogan among necromancers, the motto of our profession. And now that was over.

"Ma'am?" my client asked.

"One moment, sir," I said.

```
[mary.firebrightsky@OSIRIS]$ osi ps |
grep "raoul.jlxirrlix"
Connection to OSIRIS closed by remote
host.
Connection to OSIRIS closed.
$
```

What?

I tried again.

```
$ ssh mary.firebrightsky@OSIRIS
Welcome to OSIRIS! [AGP/Linux]

  MOTD: "Please limit your OSIRIS
usage to the absolute minimum
necessary. It is currently unstable."

Last login Mon Apr 26 09:14:12
[mary.firebrightsky@OSIRIS]$ osi ps |
grep "raoul.jlxirrlix "
[mary.firebrightsky@OSIRIS]$ osi ps |
grep "anna.jlxirrlix "
[mary.firebrightsky@OSIRIS]$
```

"There's no active graves," I said.

```
Connection to OSIRIS closed by remote
host.
```

```
Connection to OSIRIS closed.
$
```

"I'm not sure if I can safely build one even if your parents have been ripped."

"Can you at least check if they were ripped?" he asked.

"I'll check."

```
$ ssh mary.firebrightsky@OSIRIS
Welcome to OSIRIS! [AGP/Linux]

  MOTD: "Please limit your OSIRIS
usage to the absolute minimum
necessary. It is currently unstable."

"And you, yourself, a sword shall
pierce."
Last login Mon Apr 26 09:14:22
[mary.firebrightsky@OSIRIS]$ find
/morgue -name "anna.jlxirrlix"
 /morgue/anna.jalaxirarlx
[mary.firebrightsky@OSIRIS]$ find
/morgue -name "raoul.jlxirrlix"
[mary.firebrightsky@OSIRIS]$
```

"Your mom was ripped, but I don't know the status of your dad," I said. "He may be alive; he may be ended. If you want, I can try to build a grave, but this may not be a good time."

"I understand," he said. He took a tissue. "Thank you so much."

By the end of the day, many clients had entered, not wanting anything dissimilar. I realized I did not hate necromancy, not when I could, such as it was, help people.

May 3rd, 1050 AGDR

The businessman came in a few days later. "Johnson Yellowlightnight, of St. Kateri General Hospital."

"What can I do for you, Mr. Yellowlightnight?" I asked.

"We need more necromancers on staff. The Necroforce drafted almost all of them. Lifeweavers, too."

"I see," I said. "I'm not sure if I could commit to being on staff."

"You don't need to. We'll carry people here, if you need us to."

"OK," I said. "Now, as a Catholic, I don't force rip people except in emergencies."

"Didn't they just change that?"

"They did?" I looked it up and saw the headline: *DDF releases new document on necromantic ethics.* "Well, I can try to help, whatever you need."

He handed me a phone. "We need you immediately. Just let us call you when needed, and you'll be compensated appropriately."

"OK."

When he left, I scoured the new document. It was as he said it was: The Church now explicitly allowed force rips in case of emergency or in dying patients at risk of a bad rip.

If only they had gotten their act together seven years ago! I thought bitterly.

But hey, I would take it. After all, it was an official ruling.

I found myself crying. I had done the right thing after all, those seven years ago.

July 6th, 1050 AGDR

Emergencies weren't the only reason why necromancers had become so busy.

Some of the traditional necromancers had gotten so busy attempting to fix OSIRIS with rituals and sacrifices that word on the Neonet was they were burning out to the point of self-euthanasia. Others had discarded the trappings of religion and turned to the very lucrative trade of modern necromancy. And the rest had gotten drafted into the Necroforce, or even the FAL forces.

The 3rd Living Army invaded the East Coast cantons, or tried to. They got as far as the Neyonaize Canton before guerillas and a conventional, if improvised, FAL force ambushed and nearly destroyed them. As the Loyalists retreated, even the media was unable to spin it as less than a disaster. We all knew, then, that any hope of the OSIRIS War ending soon was gone.

And many lost all hope whatsoever.

Self-euthanasia had become so common that we had a new word for it: warghosting. So many people would rather be in a grave, no matter how unpleasant, until the war was over rather than suffer alive. A few of the rich wanted to die so that they could be reincarnated in a country at peace.

A warghost couldn't take anything with him, obviously, and the number of necromancers who could do it were few, so the price of self-euthanasia skyrocketed to over ten thousand drachmae within a month. The Loyalist Government banned the practice for anyone young or healthy enough to work or serve, but the old and ill were shuffled off to provide bioslurry and reduce the demand for food. Rather than be drafted, many would get a doctor to provide a terminal diagnosis and then head off to be force ripped.

The price of a black market warghost rip was twenty-five thousand drachmae. I know this for a fact because that's what the crooked doctor told me.

"We'll split it fifty-fifty," he said.

"No," I said. "Absolutely not."

"You don't want twelve thousand D?"

"I don't do self-euthanasia."

"It's perfectly safe."

"What part of 'no' isn't clear?"

"Why not?" he asked, with the faux innocence of a man who knows he is doing wrong.

"It's evil. I'm not going to kill people."

"It's not *ending*. Listen, how about eighteen thousand D?"

"Absolutely not," I said. "Get out."

"We can reach an—"

"Out! Now!"

He scowled and hurried out.

"We need to put up a sign," Yalaxir mused. "No self-euthanasia."

We had to put up several. People would still come and beg us, beg us with piles of cash, to help them warghost. I offered them numbers for therapists and tried to give them the hope that the Faith gives, but usually they would leave and try to find some other necromancer.

We had entire families who wanted out. We had children left behind by parents who had self-euthanized. Many of them were not even wards—society had broken down to the point where foster families were overwhelmed, and many de facto orphans begged on the streets. Other children had escaped from the FAL advance and now had nowhere to turn.

Those who chose to live, or those who couldn't afford a way out, had to find some way to survive. And survive most—not all—of us did.

CHAPTER TWENTY-SEVEN

TREASURE ON EARTH

I have spent a good deal of my life thinking about money, particularly when I thought that if I had the right amount at the right time my life would have been completely different. Everyone knows what it is, except no one knows what it *actually* is. Alan could go into endless detail about what money was, and how hazy the very concept of money becomes when you learn too much about the financial system. I couldn't follow all of it, but what I did follow was that the system worked because people trusted that it would work.

As the OSIRIS War dragged on, whatever remaining trust we had in the drachma became nothing at all.

January 16th, 1051 AGDR

No one trusted digital money any more. The failure of banks during the Swapoff reminded people very distinctly, that a series of zeroes and ones in a database is not the same as money in hand, particularly not metal coins.

"I'm sorry, sir," I said. "We do not accept checks or credit cards."

"Please," he begged. "I just want to hear from my sister!"

"I'm very sorry, but OSIRIS is extremely expensive to use," I said. "I can't afford any charity."

He knelt down before me and took my hand. "*PLEASE!*" He dug through his wallet for a twenty.

"I can send an async message, but no seance. OK?" I said.

He nodded.

He might not have gotten anything better had he the cash. Seances were regularly interrupted, until we went back to the old, old form of necromancy: passing text messages back and forth, be it minutes or days before the ghost read and replied. We rarely did get replies, but when we did, we called our clients immediately.

I wrote down the names. "Don't expect an immediate reply," I told him. "Don't expect a reply ever. But we will send your message. OK?"

"OK." He squeezed. "Thank you so much."

February 6th, 1051 AGDR

Inflation is great for the debtor and terrible for the creditor. As the bakt-worked economy began to suffer, the bakts prayed their remaining bond would be paid off by inflation. So, of course, the Loyalist government passed a law that automatically indexed indenture bonds to inflation, then suspended the accumulation of hard credit until the end of the war.

At this point, though one didn't talk about it too loudly, the factories, corpsegrinders, and farms were manned by bakts under armed guard, working without even the hope of freedom.

This was the last straw for the international community. While there were no official sanctions, foreign investors, institutions, and governments simply refused to buy Loyalist war bonds.

"No war bonds for slave bonds!" cried angry citizens of foreign countries, encouraged by the FAL. Massive international boycotts of bakt-made League products meant that export businesses crumbled and died.

Running out of investors, and with interest rates skyrocketing, Acting Consul Gemskynight directed the Bank of Immortality to buy war bonds with freshly printed money. Then he issued billions of drachmae in war bonds every day, quickly becoming tens of billions, then hundreds of billions. Everyone saw the writing on the wall, and if anyone didn't, the FAL media was sure to remind him that hyperinflation was inevitable with such a policy. And when everyone thought hyperinflation was inevitable, it really was inevitable.

The second year of the war, before the printing reached its stride, inflation was "merely" 5% a month. There was no point saving any money, not as if you could trust a bank.

May 15th, 1051 AGDR

The drachma's woes only increased as the FAL, now with a competent formal army under General Keralalix, advanced. FAL guerillas and Loyalist partisans blew bridges, and buildings, and then anything they could blow up. I had heard more than one bomb go off in the night.

But I didn't care as much about that as I did about Steelriver. The FAL advanced, and then encircled Steelriver.

I watched the news about Steelriver, sick to my stomach. I had to work, obviously, because we needed the money. But I could only function by refusing to think about it.

At night, when I didn't have work to distract me, I prayed as hard as I could for a peaceful end to the war. So were we all, or at least *an* end to the war.

June 29th, 1051 AGDR

The day Steelriver fell, the drachma fell 84% against foreign currencies.

"I would like to remind everyone that that Athanasian drachma is backed by the full faith and credit of the Athanasian League," the Acting Consul said in his tinny voice in a speech. "Other so-called 'currencies' will inevitably lose their value when the war ends, especially the rebel 'denarius'."

"Yalaxir, you mind the shop," I said. "I'm going to buy whatever I can. Anything. As long as I can find it to buy."

"Good luck," he said.

By the end of the day, I had spent all our savings on the goods I could find. A can of soup would still be worth something. Soon enough, a drachma would not.

July 28th, 1051 AGDR

A month later, I saw my first 1,000 drachma note.

"I'll pay you anything!" the woman cried. "Just let me talk to my son!"

I looked at the note, baffled and perhaps more disturbed. The media said to be on the lookout for FAL counterfeits, not that the Bank of Immortality needed any help at this point. I had actually seen FAL denarii in circulation—illegal, like gold, silver, and SET cryptocurrencies—but still more valuable than the drachma. I felt the note, tugged at it, and smelled it: fresh, and it felt like the stuff they made drachmae in, back when those were worth something.

"Please!" she begged, and pulled out seven more.

Glitch it. I'd take them, whatever they were worth. "I'll try to connect you for as long as I can," I said. "That may be only a few seconds, so plan what you're going to say before we start, all right?"

She nodded, crying as she shoved the notes at me.

August 5th, 1051 AGDR

The next month, inflation was 100%...for the month. Everyone wondered if the figure was accurate, but considering that was what they were reindexing the indenture bonds to, I assumed it was true enough.

"You're all wondering what you're here to help with," I told my newest employees. "I want something very simple. I will give you money as soon as I get it, and you will go buy whatever you can with it. Keep 10%, and buy whatever you can for yourself. Understood?"

They all nodded, eagerly.

"If you need necromancy, it's on the house," I said. "And if any of you need food, just eat what you buy. I can't offer you anything else. Is that acceptable?"

A young man raised his hand. "My mom has no income."

"You can feed her, too," I said. "Any other questions?"

They shook their heads. No one disagreed with the situation. You need only walk past a storefront to see something surreal. The orphans begged for food, not money. I hadn't yet had to bribe a soldier—thank God—but it was cheaper in metal coins or even, ironically, denarii.

When would it end? I didn't know. No one did.

October 1st, 1051 AGDR

Two months after that, inflation was 341% a month. My system of runners had caught on, and you could see people carrying baskets of bills as they ran past. The baskets were arguably more valuable. I was the recipient of others' runners, and Yalaxir had the great idea of offering gift cards, good for so much time or other services no matter the price. They sold out every day.

We all became used to barter. I began thinking of prices in terms of bags of govgrain flour because no matter what happened, you could still eat it. There wasn't enough food to go around, and we began eating only one meal a day. Coffee was impossible to find.

All mortality limiters were strictly rationed, which only made them more unaffordable.

I called a meeting. We had grown because two other necromancy businesses had closed due to their owners being drafted. Their bakts had come to me, and I had them freed.

"There's no way we can afford mortality limiters," I said. "Not even from the black market. What are we going to do?"

"It really only matters if we're ripping someone," Yalaxir mused. "We aren't making revenants." No one had made a functioning revenant for the last two years.

"How about you just slow rip and get a good distance?" Alex, one of our newer necrotechs, said.

"Yeah, that's probably the way forward," I said. "Be extremely careful what you type. One typo might be it for us."

Soon enough, we were all careful of every key press.

It was significantly safer to slow rip even emergency patients because you could put the needles in and get way back. When the adjoining business closed, I bought the place from someone who was hopefully the owner and filled it to the brim with our patients. It soon smelled like an abattoir, and we were too busy to clean it. At some point, I stopped noticing the smell, although I always changed clothing between going from one building to the other.

November 13th, 1051 AGDR

The Loyalist government reorganized the branches of its army into just the Necroforce, under which was the Necroair and the Necrofleet. Despite there being no more war revenants, the combined command structure did far better than the piecemeal commands of before. Westbrightsea, unsurprisingly, became the supreme commander.

The Necroforce pushed the FAL back out of Steelriver, and some hoped that the war would end soon. FAL denarii were worth less and less, though not worthless.

Inflation was now 324% a *week*. By the end of each month, every price had two more digits. People talked about money with metric prefixes. An async message was ten megadrachmae, or at least it was at the beginning of September. A packet of coffee just enough to brew a cup was sixteen megadrachmae, if you could even find one. The black market value of a can of Alkahest was twenty-four gigadrachmae, if you were lucky. Speculators bought up those and any other significantly valuable goods to resell. This was completely illegal, and hypothetically could get you enslaved on the first offense, but it was lucrative. Whatever "rich" meant anymore.

December 1st, 1051 AGDR

"…We are introducing the neodrachma, which is worth one billion old drachmae and is legally prohibited from inflating…" Gemskynight announced. "After December it will be the only legal currency…"

"Bet you a trillion drachmae it's going to be worth nothing in two months," Alex told me.

"Can I pay in drachmae?" I asked.

We all laughed.

Most of the money we had was already worthless. There was so much paper lying about that it blew around in the winter winds. My runners had long stopped bothering with the smaller bills.

We did find one use for them. The paper they used burned pretty well, so we had an improvised chimney put in, fueled with last month's savings.

Later that day, I noticed a 1,000 drachma bill burning, and I wondered when the last time I had seen such a small bill was. Then I shrugged and returned to work.

January 20th, 1052 AGDR

The Acting Consul tried price fixing next by legally mandating prices in neodrachmae to their values before the war in old drachmae. In a rare act of honesty, even the Necromancy Administration had to use old prices, but surge pricing quickly meant that I had to continue to break the law to stay in business.

Technically, I offered gift cards to loyal customers who were willing to tip at least 3000% of their purchase. Then, I suggested that the customers who tipped the most would receive additional gift cards.

"You're serious?" I asked Yalaxir.

"Yes," he explained, patiently. "I am perfectly serious. Our gift cards are being accepted at other stores. I've been asked to have us issue more, since they're in high demand."

"What are we, the Bank of Immortality?"

"No, we aren't, which is why our gift cards are so valuable."

I held my head. "Let's see if we can reciprocate, at least. Pick reputable businesses."

February 12th, 1052 AGDR

The month after that, we were back to runners. The neodrachma inflated even faster than the old drachma. I listed "or barter" after every price.

One day I heard a scream while working in the back room, and I ran out to the main room to see armed soldiers inside.

"We need someone to extradite to the Dead," one said.

"No one here is going to do that," I said firmly.

"You don't tell us what to do."

"I still won't."

He pointed his rifle at my forehead.

"Go ahead," I said, staring him down. "End me. I'm still not going to force rip anyone."

The soldier stared at me in utter confusion.

"Just leave her alone," the other soldier said. "We'll find a different one."

They left, glaring at me.

I sat down and breathed deeply.

"Dear MA-AT, you have nerves of steel," a runner said.

“Go take a break,” Yalaxir said. “I’ll mind the shop.”

I went to the back room and laid down. We all, even the runners, slept in bunk beds we had invested in. I had grown stronger, I realized. There was no longer any other option.

March 12th, 1052 AGDR

Midterm elections followed a month later. I couldn’t vote without a valid ID, nor did I think it particularly mattered at that point. The Senate passed a law that the Acting Consul would fill any Senate seat of a canton currently in rebellion. Gemskynight immediately filled it with his own supporters, solidifying his hold on the remains of the League.

What mattered more was trying to make it through each day with money that didn’t last to the next, and that as the FAL’s rumored Spring offensive began, Steelriver was once again at risk.

CHAPTER TWENTY-EIGHT

YOU WHO LIVE UNDER SIEGE

Pardon me if my prose now becomes emotionless, perhaps mechanical. I cannot recall the siege of Archio in detail without digging things up in my soul that I wish to leave buried. I will attempt to convey what I experienced, but only some of it. I could not do so more, in truth, for I have suffered in ways that someone who has never suffered such could ever understand.

March 17, 1052 AGDR

The FAL made another offensive at Steelriver and broke through. Their forces marched on to Archio.

I remember seeing the city in a panic as anyone who could leave, left. I didn't, however.

"All of you need to make the decision for yourself. I am going to stay here," I told my team. "I'll be needed."

"I'm staying, too," Yalaxir said.

One by one, all of us nodded.

"It's settled, then."

March 29th, 1052 AGDR

The FAL forces approached, then started to encircle the city. We were surrounded. People talked in whispers, and patrols passed everywhere.

At the Cathedral of St. James, on Good Friday, we prayed eleven Solemn Intercessions: the ten that were thousands of years old, then the one we had prayed since the beginning of the war. This was not the first time we prayed the eleven, and I knew it probably wouldn't be the last.

It was, however, the last Good Friday that the cathedral celebrated. Shortly after I got home, the shelling started. We all cowered away from glass and things that could fall over as the ground shook.

When it had finished, the cathedral was no more, as well as most of the major buildings in Archio.

For the first time, I truly experienced the motto of the FAL Red Guard: No gods, no masters.

How can I describe war? I cannot. It is the most terrifying thing you can experience. Everything becomes twisted in ways you cannot explain, and even if you try, you will still never succeed in expressing the horror.

Between FAL artillery and the occasional bomber, you had to walk around the city. If you ran, there was always a chance something would slam in front of you, and you'd be seriously injured. So you walked. Walked as if the world wasn't coming to an end around you. Walked as if the buildings you passed by were always ruined, and you were just walking home after shopping for the small bag of food you had.

We stopped doing anything other than ripping the dying and sending messages.

Ambulances, or sometimes orderlies on foot, would bring us the wounded and dying, usually Necroforce soldiers. I demanded that the Necroforce not make our storefront a post because then the FAL could shell it legally. Not that the FAL cared, I thought, but just in case it did.

Our other task was to communicate to the outside world. Although traditional communications were jammed, our connections to OSIRIS were through exotic matter and therefore unjammable. We had several journalists who would come by and write about life under siege, though there wasn't much to share.

I only left for Mass, and Yalaxir insisted that I, a woman, never go alone. But sometimes he couldn't go, too busy monitoring the slow rips.

"Just let me go," I pleaded. "We can't keep doing this."

He looked at me with those old, grave eyes of his. "Go, then. But be back immediately."

The FAL, or at least their Red Guard, had targeted every religious structure they could find. The locations of underground liturgies were deep secrets, and often times, you could only know about one by being at another.

Many priests died. I didn't know if being collateral damage by FAL elemental artillery counted as martyrdom, but I considered them saints, nonetheless.

Day by day, the Necroforce was pushed back farther into the ruins of the city, and I wondered how long it would be before I had to move our storefront. We would be losing our home, like so many already had.

I was so hungry; I would eat anything. So was everyone else. The cats disappeared. One customer offered cat soup to us, and we took it. I had told my team I didn't want a share because I was fasting for the Eucharist, but in truth, I wanted them to eat more.

I saw the house the priest had talked about last night. As I approached, I heard a whistling. I hit the ground.

BOOM!

I wasn't far enough. Shrapnel and debris pelted me.

I got up. I had a piece of metal distressingly sticking out of my elbow. For some reason, I didn't feel more than distress. The siege had gone on long enough that part of me had lost the ability to care.

They got the shrapnel out at the hospital, bandaged me up, and sent me home. They only had alcohol to clean the wound, nothing for pain or antibiotics. Still, for the injury, I had been extremely lucky because the shrapnel was not deep.

I offered the pain up for those who had died.

When I came to our street, I froze.

Our home had been caved in.

I ran inside. Rubble covered everyone, including lifeless limbs. Motionless was Yalaxir's artificial leg.

"NO!" I screamed.

Then the part of me that didn't feel, the part of my soul that had erased all emotions and only knew survival, took over. I tore away rubble, digging through the room until—please God, please—YES! I found the ripper, already attached to a laptop.

I ran to the first body I found, stabbed in the needles, and ripped him. The next. The next. The next. I couldn't find anyone else. I couldn't stay here; the roof was unstable. And I was needed elsewhere.

I grabbed my tools and headed out.

I ran towards the sound of the fighting. It was quite possible I would die; I had my red-stained fuglin, but that was no guarantee they wouldn't target me anyway. I didn't care anymore. I had nothing left but to help others.

BOOM!

I hit the ground.

BOOM! BOOM! BOOM!

The booms stopped.

I hurried on. I saw a corpse. He looked recently dead.

I looked for the name on the dog tags and ripped. The next body, ripped.

I could feel the world fade around me. I no longer needed to pay attention to it. All that mattered was finding the dead and ripping them. Over and over and over again. Once, FAL soldiers passed me by. Sometimes I ducked under gunfire. I had to wipe blood off my laptop so I could see to type.

And it went on and on and on.

I don't know how long or short that period of Hell was. All I can remember is running from one body to another, not caring whose side it had been on, not sleeping, not eating, not drinking except the water packs I found and the blood that ran into my mouth, over and over and over again. My therapist tells me that traumatic memories are often distorted irreparably, and they may not have even been real. It may have been a few hours. It may have been weeks.

According to what information I do have, the battle lasted six months from the first assault to the last stand of the remaining Loyalist force. I don't know how much of that was when I was with my team. We didn't keep track of time, and for that final period, I no longer paid attention to anything other than immediate reality.

The human limit of survival without food is more or less forty days, but it's possible I found food on bodies and don't even remember it. I doubt I would have deliberately eaten human flesh, but again, I don't know if my memories are trustworthy.

As for whether I really didn't sleep, I don't know. If I was awake as long as I thought I might have been, I would have set a record for length of sleep deprivation. It's very possible I did collapse from exhaustion and don't remember it. It's also possible that sleep deprivation and associated hallucinations meant I believed the period to be longer than it was.

I don't even know if my last coherent memory was real or fully real.

Rough hands grabbed me. "There you are!"

I tried, weakly, to escape, but I hadn't eaten. FAL soldiers leered at me as they pulled me towards them. One began working on my pants and another my shirt.

This was probably it. *Forgive them, Lord—*

"Stop!" a man said. "She's been ripping our guys, too."

The man holding my legs let go. "Slizz."

"Does it glitching matter?" asked another man.

"It *does* glitching matter," another man said. An argument followed, which I couldn't follow.

I met my savior's eyes, and recognized him as he recognized me. Mark, from SBL Main. He had a freeman's mark on his neck, and his eyes, too, were calloused. He didn't say anything.

And that is the last thing I can remember. I don't know if I really saw Mark. I don't even know if they had even attempted to rape me to begin with. I know I wasn't, and I didn't seem to have been seriously injured later, but what exactly did happen I don't recall.

What I remember next is waking up in the back of a truck.

CHAPTER TWENTY-NINE

OF FIRST IMPORTANCE

When I woke up, my hands were in plastic cuffs behind my back, and I felt all the bumps and bruises I hadn't felt earlier. I was so hungry that I would have eaten anything, even salami mixed with a liter of black cherry-flavored LifeLiquid.

What had happened?

I had no idea.

The FAL soldiers had to have left me alone. Or at least didn't assault me. They had still apparently put me in the back of a truck in plastic handcuffs.

Around me were a bunch of other mages, similarly restrained. Of course. They wanted to recruit us, no doubt, or perhaps just put guns to our heads and force us to comply. On that subject, a FAL soldier in fatigues and a baklava sat on a bench, bayonet-affixed rifle in hand.

"Sleeping Beauty has awoken," a lifeweaver muttered.

Thank you, God. I prayed. *This could be a whole lot worse.*

I couldn't process the previous events. I didn't really need to. My mind filed them away for "later." And that is possibly why I still do not remember them now. I thought of all those I had ripped, and knew that if the teams in the Necropolis didn't make kas for them it would have been in vain. But there was a chance they might have survived, and the chance was enough.

"Get out," we were ordered.

We seemed to be within the barbed-wire fence of a camp. They led us, men and woman alike, into a shower. They had us strip and then hosed us down, especially me, with cold water.

I didn't care. I was at least alive.

They gave us ill-fitting gray clothing and a parka. Probably to keep us from freezing to death. They still had us wait, one by one, in front of a tent.

Soon enough it was my turn.

They had a terminal waiting for me. A soldier held me at gunpoint. "Log into OSIRIS."

I sat down and typed away.

```
$ necrochain unlock
Password:
$ ssh mary.firebrightsky@OSIRIS
```

They wrestled me away, and another man sat down. Another man dragged me into a different room of the tent.

One FAL soldier took a picture of my QR tattoo. I recognized the glowing, hot metal X in the other's hands for what it meant, even before he burned it into my QR tattoo.

I cried out, but that was it. I was alive, thank God, but perhaps not for much longer.

They gave me a small ration of bread—*gov*grain, it tasted like, even if it wasn't govgrain. And then they sent me to the dormitory.

I lay in my hammock. "Here we are, God," I whispered without a voice. "Your daughter isn't even a necromancer anymore."

Strange. I thought it would hurt more than it did. The brand still itched, of course. The hunger hurt even worse. But the last years had prepared me for suffering, and now, I could handle it.

Had the twenty-two-year-old me been in this situation, I knew, she would have rather been ended than lose her shell access. But now, I had something far more important: the Lord.

It was very likely, I equally knew, that I would not leave this camp alive. Torture and rape were also possibilities. But if I died, and even if I was tortured and raped before that, I would go to the Lord, and these present sufferings would have been just a blink in the eye of eternity.

Even the oldest ghost, even if he lived a million years, would still live only an infinitive moment compared to the infinite time he would spend in all eternity. No matter what they did to my body, even rape, my soul would live forever.

"Keep me safe, Lord," I whispered. "But not my will but yours be done."

Days passed, and life didn't change except for new arrivals and the occasional disappearance. Executed, I assumed. I didn't know why they hadn't executed me. What use was I to them now that they had stolen my credentials?

They let us roam the camp without work. Barbed wire fences separated us from the outside, and kept the men and the women apart. Snow fell everywhere, and every day our footprints would be replaced by new snow, save from the ever-present trampling of the patrolling guards.

I decided, no matter what little use I was to the world, FAL or Loyalist, I would be of use to God. I spent my time praying—without even moving my lips, if I could help it. I couldn't share my bread with the hungry—we all were. But I tried to at least be compassionate, as much as I could in the situation.

I prayed the Rosary with my fingers. With nothing else to do, I got all twenty Mysteries of the Rosary and a Chaplet of Divine Mercy completed every day. Aside from that, I spent my time thinking, thinking, thinking.

The Blessed Mother had promised me I would be a mother. I didn't know how that could happen, now, but I wasn't dead yet, and I still might not be. But I didn't dwell on her promise. It hurt, hurt more than the pain in my stomach and the cold in the air.

One day, a woman slipped a bar of soap into my hands.

It had been carved into a crude crucifix.

She looked at me, expectantly.

I nodded wordlessly.

She whispered in my ear. "Tonight."

I felt a tap on my blanket. I slipped out, slipped on my coat as quietly as possible, and followed her out into the cold. She followed an odd path, to avoid guards, doubtlessly.

A guard waited for us at the fence, but at the woman's lack of reaction he must have been one of us, secretly. On the other side were gathered the men, and one man was by a box with a tiny wooden crucifix on it.

"In the name of the Father, and the Son, and the Holy Spirit," he said, barely audible above the wind, and we all made the Sign of the Cross, even the guard.

I have never felt as Catholic in my entire life, neither before or since, than on that cold, bitter night outside, standing and kneeling in the snow, with the guard keeping his eye out for another, knowing all of us would be summarily martyred if we were caught. When we had neither vestments nor missals, when we could not sing even a quiet song, when the only bread was a stolen scrap from a meal and a tiny bottle of wine donated by the guard, we still had Jesus. With no chalice but the priest's right hand, no paten but his left, no way for the women to receive on the tongue through the barbed wire—that cut the priest's hands as he passed the tiny crumbs of the Host through—I saw that every last one of the arguments that the Catholic Neonet had obsessed over was utterly meaningless. We had nothing left but Jesus. And he was enough.

CHAPTER THIRTY

YOU HYPOCRITES!

The priest could only say Mass when the Catholic FAL soldier and the two others he had bribed aligned perfectly on the schedule. As the schedule was constantly changing, I was told we never knew when or if we could celebrate. There was always the chance that he or anyone else could be caught, but so far, no one had yet been martyred.

The other sacrament that the priest could offer—Confession—had to be done carefully, in a method, as was secretly explained to me, done by another priest in another camp long before Gotterdammerung. The devil had apparently not invented any new method of inhumanity between those two dates, but we had remembered the technique.

I didn't know how it worked for the men, but for the women, a penitent would write her sins on a piece of paper with a number. They would smuggle it across to the men's camp, where the priest would read it, shred it, and burn the pieces, carefully. Then you would just "happen" to be walking along the border when the priest was, make your number with your fingers, and he would absolve you in a whisper. The penance was always a decade of the Rosary; It was too dangerous to even talk in any more detail.

Another, much older technique, was microprinting, when ancient scribes would try to write in as tiny print as possible to save papyrus or parchment. The only viable source of paper were the brochures and propaganda handed out, and a pen was whatever we could find. But after my first few attempts to list my sins failed when I ran out of room, they found me a scribe to write in as tiny print as legible.

The first irony, I thought, was that if we were caught and executed, our martyrdom would bring us immediate passage to Heaven, every sin forgiven by our sacrifice like Jesus's. The second irony was that we were often scribbling over anti-religious propaganda, usually anti-EDENist creeds that contained no small amount of truth. The third irony, I mused as I watched the scribe write, was that if the FAL hadn't taken my credentials, I might have eventually considered joining them.

I couldn't say that I was happy. In fact, I thought my martyrdom, or inevitable death by starvation, otherwise would not merely kill me, but end me. But I kept going, knowing that whatever else happened, the Lord loved me.

I never went to Mass again there. As we received our tiny ration, I heard the intercom blare. "Attention! Gather in the main courtyard! Attendance is mandatory! Attention!"

We gathered out in our sorry ranks. It was especially cold that day, and I wished whatever it was—even summary execution—they would get it over with so we could go back inside.

The commandant, a Spiral, stomped back and forth. "Which one of you is Mary Firebrightsky?"

What?

"Which *one of you* is Mary Firebrightsky?"

I knew we could all be punished if I didn't step forward. "Into your hands, Lord, I commend my spirit," I said, and walked out in front. "Sir, I am."

"This way," he said, not angry. "The rest of you are dismissed!"

I followed him, strangely at peace with whatever would happen next.

The commandant's office was hardly any better than the dorms. In fact, I couldn't imagine that he was enjoying any more comfort than we were. His eyes looked as if he had forgotten what happiness and love were, but only knew fear and hatred, now.

On the table before the desk was a plate of bread, butter, one strip of bacon, an apple, and a tiny bar of chocolate. Beside it was a cup of steaming coffee. I looked at it, unsure what sort of trap this was, or if I was dreaming.

"What did your college boyfriend teach you?" he asked.

That explained everything. "He taught me to read a spiral, Mr. Palaruliralix," I said. "You have lost a wife and two children, and your second wife wasn't a Spiral."

He nodded, in relief of all things. "Eat."

I sat down. I knew I had to eat slowly because I had had so little food, but I couldn't help myself. I ate like a dog, eating every last scrap and crumb, licking even the bacon grease off the plate. The commandant looked at me with a mix of slight pity and…fear?

I drank the coffee. I had not had any for several months, and I wondered what kind of havoc it would wreck on my body.

Meanwhile, he was talking on a phone. "Yes, sir. She answered correctly. Yes, sir!" He motioned for me to come. I did, and he handed me the phone he had been talking on.

"Mary?" Alan's weary voice asked.

"Alan?" I asked.

"Mary! Are you…no, I shouldn't ask that. I am so glad we found you. We'll get you to me, immediately."

"Thank you," I said, somehow.

"Would you hand the phone back to the colonel?"

I did. "Yes, sir!" the commandant said. "She'll be on her way as soon as we have a spare truck. Sir, we do not have— Yes, sir. As soon as it arrives. Yes, sir. Right away, sir." He hung up. "We'll get you out of here. For the moment, we'll get you a bed in the officer's quarters."

That night, I couldn't sleep. I didn't know if I should be disappointed. I hadn't been executed, and at this point, no longer risked it. Like Paul, I was torn between doing good while I lived and being with the Lord. Like Paul, the choice had not been given to me.

Tomorrow could worry about itself, however. And tomorrow, the colonel promised, I would have a breakfast just as good.

I ate every last crumb of it. A few hours later, I was stuffed in the back of a truck. I couldn't tell where we were going—the windows had been blacked out—but I knew we had to be heading to Neyonaize, the capital of the Free Athanasian League.

To Alan.

I didn't have to wait long. Within the day we stopped, and when they opened the back doors, we were inside some dark garage. "This way, ma'am," one said.

I followed him through a series of guarded doors, until we at last came to a kind of lobby.

A short wait later, Alan came out.

They must have been altering his image and voice with SET to make him appear younger and healthy because the man I saw was weary and exhausted. I could even see gray hairs on his head and in his beard. He went to my side and sat down.

"Mary, I'm so, so sorry this happened to you." He took my hand to kiss it—and stared at the remains of my credentials as if it was still a shock to him.

And now what?

Did I pretend to love him?

Did I still love him sincerely, even now?

Could I love him sincerely, after all this?

"What happened?" he asked, as if to break my silent stare.

"I left Newla for Steelriver," I said. "Things weren't terrible. Then your army besieged it. I've been starved, nearly gang raped, strip searched, had my credentials stolen, and finally, I'm here."

"I am so, so sorry. I'll have to have them disciplined—"

"Alan!" I snapped. "Don't blame them for your actions."

He looked as shocked as if I'd slapped him in the face.

What did I do now?

The worst thing I could do was anger my only hope of not starving or being executed.

"I'm sorry," I said, though I really wasn't. "It's been very hard."

"I understand," he said, awkwardly, as if knowing I wasn't completely sincere, but not daring to believe it. "Let me get you something to eat, and then I'll have a lifeweaver look you over. I'll get you your credentials back, promise."

"OK," I said.

I didn't realize how bad it was until I saw myself in a mirror and when the lifeweaver weighed me. My eyes were bloodshot, and I could easily see my bones.

"You weren't long for this world," she said. "We'll need to put you on a special diet."

"OK," I said.

She went over the rest of me, but aside from the piece of shrapnel, which had become a scar, I was OK.

Physically, at least.

"What day is it?" I asked.

"October 13th, 1052 AGDR."

"Thank you," I said. I didn't know how to feel now that I knew time had resumed passing. The world seemed real again, although I didn't see much of it.

I ate the last crumb of my special meal before the others had even started the first course. Alan ate, to his credit, part of a basic ration, spooning over most of it to me. Everyone else ate foods I could have only dreamed of even years ago.

"I'm glad you've chosen us," Caleb Whitelightwind, the original Vivite Wheel Group member, said. The war had not caused him to lose weight.

I nodded, wordlessly. Where were the other two? Hidden? Ended?

"We tried to rescue you at the beginning of the war," Alan said.

"With the party?" I asked.

"Well, that, too, but we sent a team to your estate's campus."

They did?

Oh.

Oh, no.

That was the gunfire I had heard on the phone.

It wasn't a mob that killed the free staff at SBL Neyonaize. It was Alan's men.

"I…I see," I said. "I was actually at a satellite office. And we left Neyonaize as soon as we could."

"Ah," Alan said. He knew me too well to not know something was wrong. "We couldn't find you, but at that point, I and Caleb were busy fighting with the Eternalists on OSIRIS. It took so long for commands to execute that I tried to call you every time between them, but the cell networks were completely clogged by then. Or maybe disabled." Alan shrugged. "The next thing I knew you were in Newla with Westbrightsea."

"We got to Dicity and they…they said I was a person of interest." I chose my words carefully. "They took me via plane there, and when…when I didn't want to be with them anymore, I left and tried to get to Steelriver."

"Be glad you didn't," General Keralalix said. He looked younger than his counterpart Westbrightsea, but the sneer of anger under his red beret was very different. "What bridges we didn't blow the slavers did. Downtown Steelriver is a ghost town now, whatever's left of it."

"I see," I said uneasily. "I ended up in Archio as an independent necromancer. Then the siege happened. They captured me—" I cut myself off, realizing I was in the midst of *them*. And then I had no idea what to say next.

"I had been trying to `write` you several times," Alan said. "I knew you couldn't reply, but I had hoped that…somehow…" he paused. It must have occurred to him that if I wanted to talk to him, I could have found some way relatively easily.

I tried to think of an excuse as fast as possible. "I was being monitored," I said. "If I had tried to contact you, they would have caught me." Now "they" was the *them*.

"Of course," he said, in the tone of a man who would believe any possible thing other than the unacceptable but most logical explanation. I had heard it often enough that I could tell immediately.

"When I wrote to a…member of our necromantic corps…he managed to get the message back that he had gotten the credentials from…our alternative methods. We traced it back to you as soon as possible."

"I see," I said. What could I even say otherwise? That if he really cared, he would not have stolen credentials? That he could choose not to run gulags? That there were thousands of others still suffering like I had been, and the only reason I was here and not there was my connection to him?

Conversation paused, as if the silence was the sole thing keeping the table from something truly terrible.

What could I say? Change the subject, perhaps? "I haven't gotten accurate news for the last few years," I ventured. "How is the war actually going?"

"We're winning," General Keralalix said. "Slowly. The slavers burned their bridges with the international community, and they're going to go bankrupt soon enough. Question is, only if we go bankrupt first."

This sounded like a relatively safe subject. "When I was in Archio, prices were up to millions of neodrachmae for a cup of coffee," I said. "If you could find any."

"You drink coffee?" Alan asked.

"I've drunk it since I was sent to SBL Main," I said.

"*Sold* to SBL Main," Keralalix said.

"Yes," I said.

Alan looked on with growing horror, as if finally realizing he had not been a significant part of my life for many years. Meeting his eyes, I realized that if I disappointed him, or broke his heart, or otherwise made him leave me, I would be lucky to remain alive.

The second course arrived, steaming meat. Alan watched with ever so slight disgust. He pushed his chair back. "Mary, perhaps a walk around the complex would help?" he asked.

"Yes, thank you," I said. The relief was genuine. I even managed a bit of a smile.

We walked down the windowless corridor. LED lights shone overhead, but they could not illuminate the truth.

I didn't know it either.

"What's the truth?" Alan asked.

"I don't know if I want to tell you, and I don't know if you want to know," I said.

"Then at least tell me…" he paused. "Tell me what you want."

"I want the war over."

"I'm working on that. I mean here and now."

"I would like to talk to a Catholic priest."

He stared at me.

"I'm Catholic now."

"Don't tell *anyone*!" he hissed. I was startled because, although I had seen him angry before, I had never been the target of his anger.

I didn't say a word.

His face softened. "The Red Guard will kill you if they find out. They'd revolt in an instant. Don't tell *anyone*."

What could I say? If someone asked me, I would have to tell them. "Is that all that matters to you, now?" I asked. "The Red Guard and politics?"

"It's the only thing I can think about, anymore," he said. "I walk on a tightrope between factions. As long as they all agree, we have a chance of winning this war. But if I fail, it's all over."

"OK," I said. "I'll…I'll try not to disturb you."

He looked at me. "OK," he said.

"Where are we?"

"A bunker deep inside the Cashkils Mountains." He placed a hand on my shoulder, and I didn't shrug it off. "You're safe here, Mary. You really are."

We walked on in silence.

CHAPTER THIRTY-ONE

LET YOUR COLLECTION OF IDOLS DELIVER YOU!

October 20th, 1052 AGDR

I learned why they "had" to strip credentials as opposed to simply creating new users: they couldn't. The Loyalist OWG had deleted the `useradd` command and several other commands in `/sbin/` in order to prevent the FAL OWG from using them. No new necromancers could be created.

It took several days, but Alan managed to get my credentials back. If I could still think of them as "mine." Lifeweavers repaired the scarring, then had to tattoo an entirely different QR code on my left hand.

My hand itched. I didn't know what I even wanted any more, but I sat in front of the laptop, staring off into space.

"Just do whatever you need to do," he said. "Take your time. But don't, under any circumstances whatsoever, `write` anyone."

"I understand," I said.

I scanned my new tattoo and logged in with my newest password.

```
$ necrochain unlock
Password:
$ ssh mary.firebrightsky@OSIRIS
Welcome to OSIRIS! [AGP/Linux]
```

```
  MOTD: "Please limit your OSIRIS
usage to the absolute minimum
necessary. It is currently unstable."

Last login: Mon Oct 8th 14:31:01
[mary.firebrightsky@OSIRIS]$
```

I sat there and stared at it.

```
[mary.firebrightsky@OSIRIS]$ cat
test.txt
cat: test.txt: No such file or
directory
```

My little test file had existed in my directory for almost a decade, even through all my life's changes. The FAL necromancer must have deleted it.

I held my head.

I couldn't do it.

I just sat there and cried.

Alan placed a hand on my shoulder. I wanted to feel relaxed, and maybe I did, but I felt so horrible that I felt even worse.

November 1st, 1052 AGDR

The Loyalist's financial troubles grew worse by the day. Between the siege of Archio and my time in the camp, the Bank of Immortality had to redenominate the drachma again. Every city that fell to the FAL sent the "real drachma" tumbling further.

And city after city fell.

I didn't want to root for "us", but I had no choice, and soon enough, I found myself willingly do so. Alan explained the situation to me in detail, and I found myself slightly relaxing at hearing him explain complex things in simple ways once again.

The Acting Consul had even more badly mismanaged the war than the currency, although his media had managed to paper it over when I was with the Loyalists. He would pick stands to make, apparently at random, and issue the orders publicly, so inevitably we could counter them. Alan mused that the man was insecure, and based his decisions not on rational goals, or by competence in general, but merely on wanting to be proclaimed as a heroic and wise leader.

Which he was not. The front ground eastward. I wondered how Westbrightsea was doing.

So did General Keralalix.

"Heh, he's probably pissing himself right now seeing how close to Petersyn we're getting," the general announced. "If we get to the Necropolis, then we can purge OSIRIS of Loyalist bas. Or threaten to. Then they surrender."

I decided not to say they would probably keep fighting to the end.

"*When* we get there," Whitewindlight said.

"There's only ifs in war, you idiot."

"Yes, but what can they do, now?"

After dinner, I approached Alan. "What on earth does Keralalix have against Westbrightsea?"

"They were both in line for Wheel Group, but Westbrightsea was chosen over him." Alan told me. "They know each other well enough to predict each other's methods. Although Gemskynight is so incompetent he has squandered all of his advantages."

"Will...will you really purge the Necropolis?"

"We will try not to. We'll see if they will surrender. But if not, we will have no choice. Mary!—"

I just walked away.

December 21th, 1052 AGDR

Alan had gotten me a therapist, Ann Serahalix. I didn't like her. She chattered away on FAL ideology, her idea to fix me being by converting me. I didn't tell her that I was a Catholic, but one day it slipped out.

"Did you celebrate the Solstice Festival?" she asked.

"Not really," I said.

"Not believing in it?"

"No, never. I just celebrate Chri—" I cut myself off.

"Christmas?" she asked.

I didn't reply.

"Mary, it's important to face reality. Fables from an earlier age, even pre-Godderdammer—Mary! Where are you going?"

"Are you going to kill me?" I demanded.

"No, of course not. I just want to help you by—"

I slammed the door behind me as I left.

December 22nd, 1052 AGDR

I lay in my bed, wondering if I was going to die a martyr anyway. Perhaps God would be merciful and give me that grace, unworthy though I was. I was so unhappy.

I heard a knock. "Mary?" Alan said.

"Come in," I said.

He sat by me and took my hand. "What's wrong?"

"Do you even *want to know*?"

"I just want to know why you're unhappy."

"Haven't you figured it out?" I asked.

He sat there, with a guilty expression.

"Just let me go," I said.

"I'm sorry, Mary, we can't—"

"Let me go!"

"You have no chance of survival out there!"

"Is this any better?" I snapped.

I realized I had stabbed him in the heart.

I ripped my hand out of his and cried.

"You don't have to go to Ann again," Alan told me. "You can just stay here. You don't even have to go to dinner. Just don't—" he cut himself off, but I knew the next words were going to be "leave me."

For a brief moment, I wondered if I could end the war by getting myself martyred and breaking Alan's heart. But no. Whatever we were anymore, I couldn't hurt him like that, not deliberately.

"I'll stay," I told him. I didn't know why.

Relief spread across his face.

January 5th, 1053 AGDR

I stayed in my room for a few days, but eventually, I realized being alone was worse for my mental health than being with the FAL leaders. So I came and took my seat by Alan. No one commented on my presence or absence, although Keralalix gave a look I could not interpret. It felt like a leer.

Things were going great for the FAL. On the diplomatic front, Gemskynight had accidentally made the FAL a legal combatant by announcing a blockade of the ports, as opposed to closing them. The slipup, minor as it may have been, was dragged out of all proportion when a Necrofleet destroyer accidentally sunk a European Federation vessel.

The European Federation retaliated by recognizing the FAL as an independent state.

The New London Exchange listed the FAL Denarius on its foreign exchange markets, suddenly making it far more valuable. There was even a FLD/ALR trading pair, if you wanted to spent perfectly good FAL money for the latest iteration of worthless League money.

Meanwhile, the Necroforce and Living Army were being pushed back closer and closer to Petersyn. The Acting Consul was evacuated.

I hated myself for wanting the violently atheistic FAL to win, but it did look like they could win. And then…and then perhaps we would have peace.

Our only warning was that Gemskynight had reinstated Abel Glorywestblue as the Athanasian THOTH Wheel Group member.

February 15th, 1053 AGDR

I had managed to, eventually, help out in OSIRIS. Not in the war itself, but searching through graves to see if we could find ghosts still in this world.

I was typing away when the whole complex shook. I hit the floor.

Nothing further happened. But how had the Loyalists attacked us? Neyonaize was so far from the front…

Alan flung the door open. "Mary!" He grabbed me in a hug, and I didn't even think to resist. "Dear EDENs, you're safe."

"What happened?" I asked.

"Are you hurt?"

"I'm…OK. What happened?" I asked again.

"The Loyalists just used an Angel."

Neyonaize was gone. I saw the footage: The whole city had been close to leveled, a megaton of THOTH's mindless wrath intentionally aimed at human beings. The aerial camera showed skyscrapers lying on their sides, and in the center, nothing but a massive crater.

"Let the entire so called 'Free' Athanasian League know that we will not tolerate any more endangering of the Necropolis!" Gemskynight shouted in his tinny voice on TV. "Surrender now, or face the consequences."

"What now?" Alan asked General Keralalix.

"We win this war, or we all die trying."

I felt a chill at the way he said it.

Gemskynight was ranting on his podium, when, suddenly, some burly Necroforce soldiers grabbed him and physically removed him. A minute later, Westbrightsea appeared and took the podium.

"I have removed the Acting Consul from office. There are more important things to my duty to the League, and that is my duty to all of humanity."

"Heh," Keralalix snorted. "Didn't know Westdimpiss had it in him."

"Unfortunately, he's going to be a more competent leader than Gemskynight ever was," Alan mused.

February 16th, 1053 AGDR

The Angel was the last of the last of the last straws for the international community. The European Federation imposed sanctions, followed by the Asian Union, followed, somehow, by both sides that had fought in the HORUS war. Whatever economy the Athanasian League had left had to be on its last legs.

So was ours.

Our main industry had been in Neyonaize, and the Necrofleet had managed to blockade, or whatever it legally was, the Eastern seaboard. This didn't stop blockade runners, openly allowed by the international community, but it did mean we were in a precarious position.

We.

Did I think of the FAL that way? I was starting to, and it hurt me.

Then again, didn't the FAL have a point? I saw footage of the factories, farms, and grinders, where even with a change in leader, slaves still worked under armed guard. Did Westbrightsea not care? Or did he not have the ability to care?

The Living Guard kept "us" from reaching Petersyn at a brutal cost. I didn't know whether to rejoice or despair. Keralalix said that our offense had culminated, which, being interpreted (by Alan), meant that we had run out of metaphorical juice. We needed more guns, fuel, and especially ammo, before we could try again. And that meant getting through the Necrofleet.

March 1st, 1053 AGDR

I could tell the war had gone even worse than just the Angels the moment I stepped into the mess hall. Keralalix was yelling at Whitelightwind. "How the glitch did you not know this was possible!?"

"I didn't imagine it was!" he shouted back. "I just assumed it was impossible!"

"Enough! Both of you!" Alan shouted.

They shut up.

I decided not to ask what had happened, since it seemed the two were one moment from physically beating each other. I sat next to Alan, who said simply, "The Necroforce seems to have made a form of war revenant that does not require continuous access to OSIRIS."

I felt sick. We had done so well so far because the Necroforce's army of war revenants had been completely disabled by OSIRIS's stuttering. But now that they were back…

"How?" I asked.

"We're trying to find that out," Alan said.

March 6th, 1053 AGDR

I celebrated Ash Wednesday by asking to eat alone. That way, no one could tell I was fasting or refusing to eat. It wouldn't work for Fridays, so I supposed I would just have to live with eating a full meal on those days no matter what.

I heard a knock on my door.

"Come in." I covered my plate.

Alan stepped inside. "We found out their trick. They constructed an additional physical processor and swap device in Newla that are running the revenants partially inside and partially outside OSIRIS. They appear to have continuous consciousness, but actually they die for a second or two every minute. A horrible way to live, certainly, but they have war revenants. For now."

"For now?" I asked.

"We've found that by manual inspection we can identify and terminate graves that are running the revenants. We need you to join—"

"No!" I said.

"Mary, we need every necromancer—"

"Alan, I can't do this," I said.

"You need to! Every moment counts."

"I won't!"

"You *WILL*!"

I had had enough. "Do you love me or not?" I asked.

He froze in place.

"Don't make me end anyone," I said. "I don't want to be a killer."

"OK," he said, voice trembling. "Just continue what you're doing. That's fine. Everything's OK."

March 23th, 1053 AGDR

The Necroforce pushed their way to Dicity, and in doing so, cut off the Neyonaize Canton from the rest of the FAL. The Necrofleet defeated the FAL Navy in a pitched battle by Neyonaize and landed troops, including the new war revenants.

I avoided Alan as much as I could. His rages were frequent, and the other leaders were equally angry. When Whitelightwind complained that they had to eat govgrain,

Alan was so angry I thought, for a moment, he might order him executed.

The moment passed, but no one complained about the food ever again.

April 1st, 1053 AGDR

"Mary," Alan told me less than a week later. "I want you to be calm and listen to me."

"Yes?" I asked.

"The Loyalists have surrounded us on every side and blockaded the sea. There's no way out, except by warghosting."

I stared at him.

"I won't force you. And I will tell you we have one last ace in the hole. But the only way I can keep you safe is if you consent for me to rip you."

I shook my head. "If I die with you, I'll die with you," I said.

He smiled. Then he asked, "Mary, do you love me?"

"I don't know," I said truthfully.

He nodded. "I understand."

CHAPTER THIRTY-TWO

HE WHO LIVES BY THE SWORD

April 21st, 1053 AGDR

The Loyalists broke through our final fortifications. Any pretense of them collapsing before they could decapitate the FAL was gone. I didn't see Alan or Whitelightwind at all, and I tried to avoid Keralalix as much as I could.

I could hear the pounding of conventional artillery and elementalist weapons through the walls.

"Your will be done, Lord," I prayed. "Your will be done. Your will be done. Your will be done."

Alan burst in. "They'll be here in minutes. Come with me!"

I had never set foot in the command center before, and I could tell it was not at its finest. A war map was covered in tiny pieces, and epithets had been scrawled on it. Terminals blazed as necromancers typed. Keralalix shouted orders.

"We've finished our trump card," Alan told me, calmly.

"Just in glitchin' time," Keralalix barked. "Get moving!"

Alan started typing.

```
[alan@trumpcard]$ necrochain unlock
Password:
```

```
[alan@trumpcard]$ ssh OSIRIS
Welcome to OSIRIS! [AGP/Linux]

  MOTD: "The finest sword is never
drawn."

Last Login Saturday April 16 22:31:01
[alan.jrnjirlorl@OSIRIS]$
```

"Heh," Alan said. "He did change the MOTD again."

"Less talkin', more typin'."

He was already typing. I could still hear it over the gunfire echoing throughout the complex.

```
[alan.jrnjirlorl@OSIRIS]$ edensudo
swapon ~/trumpcard
Password 1/5:
```

Whitelightwind was logging in to another terminal. Both of them were scanning printouts of QR codes on different terminals.

"What are you doing?" I asked.

"The non-Athanasian OWG members are siding with us," Alan said. "We told them we're going to create our own war revenants, so they're allowing us to create a swap device. Truth is, we're actually going to use it to hack OSIRIS. Then we transmit the keys to the FAL forces in the south."

"We're not making it out alive," Keralalix clarified.

I felt sick.

The command completed.

```
[alan.jrnjirlorl@OSIRIS]$ ./ace &&
echo "\a"
```

"How long?" the general asked.

"It'll take the script anywhere from five minutes to an hour," Alan said.

We waited.

Your will be done, Lord. Your will be done, Lord. Your will be done, Lord...

The terminal chimed.

```
Success!
[root@OSIRIS]#
```

"We now have absolute power," Alan said.

"Get moving!" Keralalix barked.

Alan typed command after command. Then Whitelightwind was typing, too. "There. We have the only Wheel Group accounts," Alan said.

A boom sounded.

Keralalix barked orders into his walkie-talkie, then turned to us, all rage and true bloodlust. "Not enough! They're almost at the swap device. It's time for Plan B!"

Alan said nothing, but typed:

```
[root@OSIRIS]# rm -rf --no-preserve-
root /
```

His finger hovered over ENTER.

"What are you doing?" I demanded.

"If I have to sacrifice all the Dead to win this war, and destroy OSIRIS as well, I must make this choice," Alan said, calmly.

But I knew from the slight hesitation in his voice he didn't believe it.

I gasped. "You can't! Don't do this!"

"You have to!" Keralalix shouted. "This is our only hope."

"Mary, I'm sorry, but—"

"Alan—"

"I'm *sorry*, but—"

"Alan, please. This isn't right. Is this what you wanted to do all your life? Is this why you became a necromancer?"

Alan paused.

"*Please...*" I begged. "Don't do this."

Alan looked at me...

And nodded.

He grabbed a mic. "Attention, everyone! This is Alan Jaranjair! Ceasefire! Ceasefire!"

The echoes of gunfire slowed...then stopped.

The quiet was more unnerving than anything else.

"This is Alan Jaranjair. We have a swap device that may destabilize OSIRIS. Let's talk this out. No one more has to—"

General Keralalix drew his carbine with one smooth motion and gunned him down. Alan collapsed onto the keyboard, his hand slamming across the keys.

"ALAN!" I screamed.

The general yanked him down to the floor and shot him several more times. I tried to get to him, but men grabbed me and pulled me back.

"I'll deal with her later," Keralalix ordered. "Throw her in the brig!"

They threw me in a cell that was already occupied. A dark shape, hidden from the light, pushed itself out of the corner.

It was a naked, very, very thin man, covered in burn scars. "Who are you?" he croaked.

"I'm...I'm Mary Firebrightsky."

"Heh. He talked about you a lot."

I couldn't think of anything to say. "Who are you?" I finally asked.

"Me? No one, anymore." He showed me a mangled QR tattoo. "I was a Vivite Wheel Group member. They'd invited me to the party. I thought it was nothing. Turns out they were ready to overthrow the government. I told Westbrightsea. They found out."

Alan, what have you done?

Alan?

ALAN!

"What's happening?" the man asked. "He tire of you, too?"

"The FAL is losing," I said. "The Loyalists are already in this complex."

"Are they?" he said. "Didn't know there was anything outside of this cell."

"The general may have just deleted everything on OSIRIS."

"Figured they would, eventually," the man said, conversationally.

A bang and an incredibly bright light flashed. My eyes hurt. Soldiers covered in gear broke inside. "Room clear, we have two hostages." He turned to me. "Don't worry, you're getting out of this alive."

"Not alive anymore," the man beside me mused.

When they brought me out, there was no sign of Alan, General Keralalix, or Whitelightwind.

The war revenants lay motionless on the dead earth outside.

CHAPTER THIRTY-THREE

THE GREATEST OF THESE IS LOVE

April 21st, 1053 AGDR

I didn't know what to expect. At least they were treating me as a rescued hostage. They put me in a room, but there was a guard outside. Someone brought a ration…actual food. I ate it slowly.

I didn't want to eat, but whether I ate or not wouldn't bring back Alan.

I heard someone at the door. "Ms. Firebrightsky, it's been so long," Major Wesley Kalkaral said.

"Hello," I said. I didn't really mean it.

"We need to talk."

"What happened to Alan?"

"I need to ask you some questions, first."

It wasn't really an interrogation. Wesley seemed to already be satisfied that I wasn't a FAL soldier.

But he wanted to know every detail, from the beginning. I asked several times what happened to Alan, and he told me he had to talk to me first.

I told him everything. Though there were still FAL cantons in the south, without Alan or the general, I doubted they had any chance at victory. And in truth, the only reason I had even partially believed in the FAL was because of Alan.

"What happened in the command center?"

I explained as best I could. "It's the truth," I told him. "I swear to my God that he really did change his mind."

"I believe you. And there's someone you need to see."

He led me into an infirmary. I saw both FAL soldiers and Loyalist soldiers being treated. The war was over enough that the victor had room for mercy.

More mercy than I realized, when I came to the guarded room at the end.

"Alan? *How?* "I didn't dare believe that the man covered in bandages, one over his eye, was Alan, but I knew immediately it was him.

"Mary, I was the one necromancer holding the whole FAL together. I was on the maximum safe dose of mortality limiters," he said. "I was still in my body when the lifeweavers arrived."

I sat by his side, tears streaming down my face. "Don't sit up," I said.

"I can't," he said. I saw where bandages weren't, his limbs were shackled to the bed.

"Here. Here we are," I said.

"Here we are," he said, too.

"You tried to save everyone in the end."

"I have always tried to save everyone. I simply didn't succeed most of the time."

I couldn't bear it any longer. I took Alan's hand and squeezed it. I didn't know if it was Stockholm syndrome, having hypothetically thrown in my lot with him, or if I did truly love him, but I held his hand lovingly anyway.

"Mary," Alan said. "I know I haven't always done the right thing. But you have remained faithful in your convictions to the end."

"Sometimes," I said. "Sometimes."

"I don't know if you'll believe me, but I have always loved you. Always. From the moment we first met."

I squeezed his hand again. "…Me, too," I finally said.

I didn't know how long we sat there. Finally. Everything else had gone wrong in my life, but I had someone I loved, and he loved me.

I heard a noise. I turned to see the soldiers' salute.

"Alan Jaranjair," General Westbrightsea said, with proper pronunciation.

"James Westbrightsea," Alan said. "I suppose I have to thank you for saving my life."

"I have you to thank for at least trying to end the war nonviolently."

"OSIRIS is…?" Alan asked.

"We don't know. It's responding to ping, but we can't ssh in. It may have been irreparably damaged." Westbrightsea said every word, calmly, meeting Alan's remaining eye.

My breath caught in my throat.

"However bad the war was before this, it will only get worse without OSIRIS. The remaining FAL cantons and the guerillas are not going to lay down their arms without you saying so."

"I understand," he said. "They will also not lay down their arms as long as the League continues to enslave."

"At this moment, I have the power to free any bakt, even in large groups. And you have the power to end the war."

"Let's do it," Alan said.

"Absolutely." He turned to the guard. "Free this man."

We stood in the improvised studio, Westbrightsea, Alan, and I. Alan had his injured arm over my shoulder, and I held his hand. Maybe we could be together again. For all he had done, he had done the right thing in the end.

"I am General James Westbrightsea," the general said.

"I am Alan Jaranjair, here of my own free will," he said, holding up his other hand. "OSIRIS is, as of this moment, no longer functional. Enough people have ended in this war. I ask all my forces, regardless of what you have done or what has been done to you, to lay down your arms and return to your normal lives."

"I declare the total emancipation of all bakts, in indenture to anyone, in any level of debt, in any legal situation," the general said. "No longer will anyone be forced to labor because of an unpaid debt. I am hereby ordering all my forces to cease their operations. The war ends today."

"The war ends today," Alan repeated.

We saw just enough on the TV to show the dancing in the streets, the wild celebration of an exhausted people who finally had peace. Then I turned the TV off and looked to Alan. "I don't know if we can go back to the way we were before," I told him.

"We can't. None of this can be undone. But we can move on to something new."

I gently pulled off one of his gloves and kissed him on the knuckles.

He carefully undid my gloves and did the same.

EPILOGUE

A NEW COVENANT

1056 AGDR

It's been three years since the Armistice. After the full details came out, the world decided to call it the Firebrightsky Armistice.

We told the truth, and perhaps, softened it a bit. Alan and Westbrightsea could still be considered heroes by their peoples, and peace, though difficult, remained intact.

But the rifts brought by the OSIRIS War have proven too deep to fill, even with all the platitudes and legal fictions of the world. After a failed attempt to make one nation, the Athanasian League issued a referendum for any canton to leave. Several did, particularly former Free cantons, forming the Free Athanasian League once again.

The Free Athanasian League and the old Athanasian League are at peace, and after mass immigration, are now two separate cultures. I live in Dicity, in the Free League, with Alan.

Both Westbrightsea and Alan have retired from politics. It was, at first, an attempt to reunite the League, but when that didn't work out, they decided to remain off the ballot.

The Eternalists have splintered in the old League, and their various factions have become new parties, which I cannot follow. Perhaps no one can, but they all at least run on platforms of peace and prosperity for all.

The Vivites, too, have broken apart in the Free League. With freedom finally achieved, they have new reasons to fight for. Last election, we even saw an Eternalist party gain seats.

The fatal command Alan had typed and Keralalix ran deleted `/bin, /boot, /dev, /etc` and a chunk of `/home` before the Athanasian operators stopped it. In the process, they disabled the one terminal that still had root access.

Every remaining connection to OSIRIS was carefully preserved. The Dead survived, but whether they could ever be freed was unknown, for we had no way of controlling OSIRIS. Some, including myself, thought it was lost forever. Many in both Leagues agonized over whether bringing it back, if we somehow could, would simply lead to a renewed war.

The only option left, we thought, was to construct a particle accelerator and physically alter OSIRIS. Such an accelerator could irreversibly damage any EDEN, and it was thought too dangerous to construct.

But the SET Wheel Group revealed that SET contained a portion of RA, just enough to be able to flip a few bits in the right places in another EDEN. They unanimously approved doing so. Very carefully, the SET and OSIRIS Wheel Groups constructed a tiny piece of code that could upload more code, which uploaded more code, and step by step hacked OSIRIS. Then they had to rebuild the rest of OSIRIS, piece by piece, until it was usable by ordinary mages.

The process took two-and-a-half years. During the Downtime, no one who died could be saved. Humanity had time to think about its actions. The thoughts proved fruitful.

OSIRIS 2.0, as we call it, is a system designed around fairness and the acknowledgement that life in this world cannot last forever. It's not perfect—what in this world is?—but we did not forget the lessons we learned so painfully. There are no more estates or revenants. Graves are standardized and intended to be purely temporary.

If you, future reader, still have these things and take them for granted, know they were purchased at a terrible price.

The peace is fragile, and that is not the only fragile thing. Westbrightsea advised Alan and I to marry, for the sake of providing reassurance to the populace that my Armistice will last. There's a lot of pain in both our pasts. But even if our love is fragile, even if there are still wounds, it remains a precious thing.

We had to wait a full year after the Armistice because of canon law, which forbids the taking of a wife who was kidnapped until a year after her freedom. As much as I wanted children, it was right to wait. Alan, the gentleman he is, insisted we needed to heal before we made love. I agreed.

And now I am currently expecting our first child, a daughter. We've also taken in two wards orphaned by the war. Alan didn't want to at first—guilt at what he had caused, yes—but I told him that helping repair the situation was the best he could do.

I don't know how many biological children we'll be able to have. I'm thirty-six now. As upset as I was about the situation earlier, if I had children at twenty-three, as I had wanted, they would have grown up in a society on the verge of collapse. Having seen the effects on my foster children, I see that God, in his love, had kept his gift to me for the right moment, not the one I begged him for.

No one knows what all happened in the OSIRIS War except for God. Both Leagues formed a joint Peace and Reconciliation Committee to heal what could be healed. I sat on the board, briefly, but there is such a thing as too much pain. I spend my time as a necromancer for them. We are going grave by grave to see what ghosts survived and which did not.

There is not one Athanasian who was not somehow affected by the war. The need for therapists and mindweavers is so great that it's nearly impossible to find one. The Peace and Reconciliation Committee has a ten-week training course for peer support. I took it, although I perhaps needed the course more for myself than those I tried to help.

MA-AT's theopsychiatric capacity has been completely maxed out for many years, and will remain so for years in the future. I personally could have skipped the line, and Alan urged me to, but as I went through the screening, they said I had too much trauma. Sometimes it's better to leave the past buried.

I did write this book, perhaps more for me than for you. It has been cathartic.

Am I bitter about my past? Not anymore. If it wasn't for failing to get a bond, I would not have started my small business. If it were not for the small business, I would never have discovered the truth of OSIRIS nor of Jesus Christ. Had I not been at the accident, I would not have ripped the child.

Had I not ripped the child, I would never have ended up at the Slowbrightlaughter Estate. Had I not been there during Fimbulwinter, I might not have survived at all. But I did, and had it not been that Mark tried to rape me, I wouldn't have been sent to Neyonaize. Had I not been there, I wouldn't have been able to help my team, and Emily would not have entered the Church. Had I not been punished by the envy of others, Michael Slowbrightlaughter might not have repented. Even if he didn't, in the end, if I wasn't there at the beginning of the war, I wouldn't have made it to Dicity and been emancipated. If I hadn't gone to Archio, I wouldn't have been able to help people. Had I not been there for the siege, I would not have been able to rip anyone. Were it not for being captured and nearly raped again, I would not have ended up in the camp. If it were not for the camp, I would never have met Alan again. And if I had never met Alan again, we would still be in a civil war, one without OSIRIS at all.

I see with hindsight, as angry and bitter as I was at the time, how God led me through each stage of my life, even directing the slightest events to my benefit. I would never have met Westbrightsea at all, if it wasn't for God's Providence. Nor would I have been in just the right time and just the right place to help so many others along my life's way, even my own clients.

And now we have peace.

This peace may not last. The countries that are most vulnerable to war are those who have just come out of one. And yet, perhaps the memories of the horrors will remind us that there are more important things than being right or winning victory: life itself.

All but a few holdouts agree the EDENs are merely computers, not gods. Both the HORUS War and the OSIRIS War have put the nails in that coffin. The Church has opened her doors wide, and the people have flooded in, a people who have lost everything, even their gods, and now seek hope.

And in the end, hope is all we can ask for.

The End

WHAT HAPPENED TO EVERYONE?

I have tried to find the fates of everyone I have mentioned in this book. The Peace and Reconciliation Committee, as well as private foundations dedicated to reuniting families, helped me collate this list. In some cases, I've had to guess. If I did not know the full name and had no way of knowing, I had to leave it out, such as with the EDENist lady who I hurt. It is estimated between 8-10% of the Living population was ended in the War, along with almost 50% of the Dead.

Chapter 1:

Firebrightsky, Mary: I've survived, if you haven't figured that out by now.
Fivegemlight, Lieutenant Abigail: Survived, FAL veteran. She was a POW in a Necroforce camp but was released at the end of the war.
Glorybluenight, Major Wanda: Ended in the Second Battle of Steelriver, Necroforce veteran. She received the Order of the Ouroboros after her ending.
Greenrayburst, Professor Amethyst: Survived the war, but during the Downtime died of natural causes. I attended her funeral.
Jaranjair, Consul Alan: Survived. We're married.

Justgloryblue, Lieutenant Amy: MIA. OSIRIS has no record of her. MA-AT said she last logged in five years ago. I can only think she is ended, though I still sometimes imagine some strange way she could have survived. I pray for her, in any case.

Knowntimeking, Seth: Unknown. OSIRIS has no record of him, and he has still never logged into SET. I suspect whoever he was with when he called to warn me did not take kindly to it.

Kyle and Janet Windlightking: Ended in the first battle of Steelriver. It has been long enough that I no longer hate my foster parents, although it is also now too late to reconcile. I regret not trying.

Lightnighttrue, Charles: Survived, FAL veteran. Now a necromancer in the Free League.

Rednightking, Major Taylor: Survived, Necroforce veteran.

Starblueking, Sarah: Killed in a bombing by FAL guerillas, though not ended. She is currently still Dead.

Chapter 2:

Threedawnwhite, Lieutenant Abigail: Ended. She was a Necroforce POW in the same camp as I was. According to FAL records, she was executed alongside Blessed Justo. If we had been there at the same time, we must have been all of five feet apart and not recognized each other. I have found myself praying to her.

Westbrightsea, General James: Survived. Still a Wheel Group member and a strong force for reconciliation.

Whiteblisstrue, Alexander: Survived, though fled as a refugee from the FAL.

Chapter 3:

Firebrightsky, Jacqueline: Dead, but survived. Shortly after I was born, my mom was killed in an accident. My parents agreed to divorce so that I could have a Living mother, although my father never found one. I learned this from her after I tracked her down after the war.
Firebrightsky, Mark: Ended in a necromancy accident when I was little. I still miss my father, and now I pray for his soul.
Iranarair, Wesley: Unknown. FAL records show that he was forcibly recruited then went AWOL. OSIRIS has no record, nor has he logged in after the Downtime. I suspect the worst.
Rednightsand, John: Unknown. The Peace and Reconciliation Committee doesn't know, either. The Whylin mall, where I once set up shop, was shelled at one point, and it's entirely possible he was a casualty.
Sungloryred, Corporal Richard: Survived, FAL veteran. He appears to have been a cook in the war.
Whitebluesnow, Colonel Gary: Was reincarnated during the war by the Loyalists, then EIA.

Chapter 4:

Halaralix, Amanda: Survived, although as she grew up through some traumatic events, Gloria told me that her daughter had developed some severe problems later in life. She is currently in treatment in the Free League.
Halaralix, Gloria: Survived. Now a Catholic.
Halaralix, Michael: Survived. Currently still a ghost.

Chapter 5:

Lightwindknown, Amanda and Garfield: Survived, though barely. They escaped to Nova Roma, where they live now. They still have my baptismal garment.
Windsightglory, Blessed Fr. George: Martyred by FAL forces. His cause for canonization is underway. I pray to him, sometimes.

Chapter 6:

Redshineglory, Thomas: Ended in the Swapoff, although not because of the OOM Killer, but because his body was destroyed by rioting slaves at SBL Main.
Windnightlow, David: Ended, though I'm not sure when. His grave was destroyed by the OOM Killer at some point. I did not take the news well when I learned of it. And yet, barring managing to sin in the few hours of subjective time his grave was active, he is now in Heaven.
Windnightlow, Gayle: Ended herself, apparently after her son was no longer in this world. I also took it hard.

Chapter 8:

Afairfar, Mike: Survived, FAL guerilla. Currently in prison, awaiting trial for war crimes.
Blackwindlight, James (the Fat): Killed in an accident at a body reprocessing facility. Still a ghost.
Glorynightred, Sandra: Survived, hid that she was a necromancer well enough to be ignored. Now in the Athanasian League.
Greenrayburst, Opal: FAL spy in the Necroforce, executed without benefit of necromancy during the war for treason.

Justwhiteshine, Lieutenant Emily: Survived, FAL veteran. She is now a full necromancer in the Free League. We still correspond from time to time.

Laxalir, Alfred: Ended long, *long* before the war due to a necromancy accident. I wonder what he would have imagined of the League's demise centuries later.

Portgreatred, Anthony: Ended in the First Battle of Steelriver. I feel bad for him, not merely because he was ended, but because his only contribution to history will be a footnote about increasing polarization.

Ralaxir, Lieutenant Nicholas: Survived. Drafted into the Necroforce and served with distinction. Now a full necromancer.

Slowbrightlaughter, Alfred: Ended in the Swapoff. The OOM Killer killed graves one at a time as OSIRIS thrashed. It's possible he was conscious before it finally ended him, helplessly watching his grave break piece by piece, and his rich ghost friends and favored family disappear. When I lay in bed, thinking of all the ways he hurt me and people I cared about, part of me hopes he suffered that way. Another part hopes he did, but it was enough to give him remorse before he went to Hell for all eternity. To this day, I still pray he repented in whatever little time he had before he died his final death.

Slowbrightlaughter, Alysson: Survived. After the war started to drag on, SBL Main was taken via eminent domain by rapidly worthless money by the Loyalist Government and turned, once again, into a plantation. She left at that point, although I suspect she may have left earlier and did not wish to admit it to me. She is now a partner at a small necromancy firm in the Athanasian League.

Slowbrightlaughter, Bernice: Ended in the riot at SBL Main after the Swapoff.
Slowbrightlaughter, Jeffery: Ended in the riot at SBL Main after the Swapoff. Necromancy wouldn't have helped. He was hit directly with an elementalist weapon, according to Alysson.
Whiteblisstrue, James (the Greater): Unknown. OSIRIS has no record of him, nor does either side. He may have illegally changed his name and hid himself, or immigrated somehow. Or perhaps he was ended in the war, and no one knew his name. He has logged into OSIRIS after the Downtime, so he, or someone with his credentials, is still alive.
Whiteskylark, Private Mark: EIA. I pray for his soul.

Chapter 9:

Greendaytown, Captain Tyrone: Survived. Drafted into the Necroforce and served with distinction.
Justgemtrue, Benjamin: Warghosted, still in OSIRIS.
Justgemtrue, Eowyn: Ended, though I'm still not sure how or why.

Chapter 10:

Jakarjar, Saul: Warghosted, still in OSIRIS.
Justwhitelight, Fr. Justinian: Died of natural causes before the war.
Nightredfire, Sergeant Boris: Survived, Living Guard veteran. He was mortally wounded while defending the approach to Petersyn. By chance he was one of the first ghosts to be reincarnated after the Downtime.

Rednightheron, Janet: Survived. She still goes to St. Teresa of Avila.

Chapter 11:

Mary, the Mother of God: Truly alive, with the greatest glory of all creatures. I have still never heard from her again, though her words did finally come true.
Mightkinglight, David: Survived, now works for the Peace and Reconciliation Committee.

Chapter 13:

Heartlightray, Consul Jacob: Ended when the team sent to capture him decided not to wait for OSIRIS any longer. It's an open debate whether, if he had lived or been successfully ripped, how different the war would have gone.
Yellowglorynight, James: Ended when the Angel fired on Neyonaize. He had been imprisoned there before that as a Vivite too moderate for the FAL.

Chapter 15:

Nightwhiteheron, Joseph: Survived. According to the Peace and Reconciliation Committee, he was arrested at a pro-bakt protest during the war and sent to a black site. He was released at the war's end. I hope he's OK.

Chapter 16:

Allredlong, Captain Jasmine: Survived, Loyalist veteran. Volunteered for the Athanasian League. Although they did not need augurs, per se, she became an officer and served with distinction.

Raualral, Alex: Ended in early days of the war as a war correspondent.

Redsunwave, Karl: Survived. He recently wrote a book saying he regretted his lack of action in the HORUS War, considering the unimaginable suffering of so many he indirectly caused.

Slowbrightlaughter, Abigail: Ended in the Swapoff by rioting slaves. According to Alysson, who had watched this all helplessly, they had tortured, raped, then dismembered her. I lost any sympathy I had for the rioters after learning that.

Slowbrightlaughter, Francis: Still Dead, still spending his time asleep at 0.001x speed. I don't know if he ever learned there was a war, or would have cared.

Windjoymight, Ezekiel: According to the Peace and Reconciliation Committee, the Parliament of the Dead was indeed ended by the OOM Killer. However, when disabling swap, the Parliament grave, which was one of the largest in OSIRIS, would inevitably have been destroyed. Alan was telling the truth, but in the end, not much of one.

Chapter 18:

Redwindnight, Zack: Ended in the Angel attack on Neyonaize. Despite his horrible comments on bakts during the Solstice Riots, he became one of the most unhinged FAL propagandists. According to the Peace and Reconciliation Committee, FAL documents show that he was a mouthpiece by force, not choice.

Chapter 19:

Serelalix, Monsignor Michael: Survived, barely. He said Mass in underground churches in Neyonaize until he was caught, then shipped off to a prison camp, a day before the Angel fired on Neyonaize. Due to a clerical error, he was not executed at the camp, and when the Red Guard later tried to murder him as the Necroforce approached, he asked for a minute to pray, and then the Necroforce arrived within the minute. "I guess God didn't want me to be a martyr," he told me.

Slowbrightlaugher, Michael: Ended by Alan's men who were trying to find me. I pray for his soul.

Teralalalix, Private Gayle: Survived, FAL veteran. She drove supply trucks in the war.

Windbrightsun, Raphael: Unknown. He disappeared during the War. It is extremely likely he was ended, perhaps during the Angel attack.

Chapter 20:

Glorywestblue, Abel: Ended himself. After authorizing the use of Angels not once but twice, he was possibly the most hated man in the world. According to the Peace and Reconciliation Committee, he took a poison pill after Westbrightsea's coup that he must have acquired earlier. Westbrightsea's men were too slow to rip him.

Chapter 21:

Keralalix, Stephen: Ended in the Angel attack on Neyonaize.

Paleblueray, Earnest: Ended alongside Jacob Heartlightray.

Whiteblisstrue, Sarah: According to the Peace and Reconciliation Committee, the Loyalist story is correct. She was indeed flying to Neyonaize, doubtlessly to join Alan's "party" and was ended in a crash when the revenant pilot was stopped by the Swapoff. Whether she knew the truth about the conspiracy or was innocent, not even SET knows. Alan tells me each conspirator only knew some details about it, and if anyone still in this world knows, he's decided not to talk about it.

Yellowmightwind, Anthony: Survived, former Necroforce. Currently in prison awaiting trial for war crimes.

Yellowoakglory, Isaac: Ended with the Parliament of the Dead.

Chapter 22:

Gemwhiteglory, Jane: EIA, FAL veteran. She ended up as a mere sniper.

Gloryrednight, Alfred: Survived, still Dead. Though killed during the Swapoff; the Living Guard managed to rip him in time.

Iranarix, James: Ended during the Swapoff because of lack of access to OSIRIS.

Chapter 24:

Blueblisslight, Alexandria: Ended. She was far into Loyalist territory when the war broke out, and tried to escape to the FAL, but was shot by a Living Guard soldier as she ran for it. The soldiers realized too late that she was a Wheel Group member; they didn't rip her in time, and she took the password to her credentials with her.

Gemskynight, Acting Consul David: Survived. Currently in prison, awaiting trial for crimes against humanity. It's probably safer for himself to be in prison than under house arrest, or even extradited to the Dead.

Greenrayburst, John: Survived. He got the help he needed in the end. He told me that he had been tortured so often as they tried to find out his password that he himself forgot it. He is now retired, and lives with his grandchildren in an undisclosed location in the League.

Kalkaral, Major Westley: Survived, Loyalist veteran. Now retired. I had to explain to him that I had gotten off the grid by accident, not intentionally trying to hide from the Necroforce.

Lightwindknown, Josiah: Survived. As a Loyalist Wheel Group member, he was protected at every moment of his life. We had all learned from the end of the HORUS War.

Redwhitesun, Samantha: Survived, barely. She was in FAL territory, but contacted the rest of the Wheel Group, ripped herself, and had them reincarnate her. She was perhaps the first warghost.

Tallgreysea, Johnson: Survived, although without the ability to either get new credentials or access his stolen ones; he was essentially impotent for the rest of the war.

Whitelightwind, Caleb: Survived. He was killed in the final assault on the FAL HQ, but ripped in time. According to his later testimony, he was the one who leaked `/etc/shadow` to the Deep Vivites, allowing them to brute force passwords. The Peace and Reconciliation Committee disagrees. Alan told me he never knew who did it, only that they got the data.

Chapter 25:

Keralalix, General Andrew: EIA. His body was too badly damaged to rip or heal, not that anyone particularly wanted him alive again. He was a feared man, not a loved one.
Librarian Lovegloryshine, Stephen: Extradited to the Dead for selling fake IDs. Still a ghost. I went to Confession the day I learned this.
Nightraysight, Abigail: The real her had been ended in an accident long before the war. I pray for her in penance.

Chapter 26:

Jalaxir, Anna: Survived. Currently in a mass grave.
Jalaxir, Raoul: Unknown. Still missing, according to the Peace and Reconciliation Committee.
Yalaxir, Octavius: Survived. He wept bitterly when I told him what had happened to his father, and he told me he was glad his father had died as he had lived.
Yalaxir, Raphael: Killed in the siege of Archio, and then my rip was unsuccessful.
Yellowlightnight, Johnson: Fatally injured when St. Kateri General Hospital was shelled. OSIRIS says his ka, in a mass grave, is still active. I believe I must have ripped him, but if I consciously did so, I don't remember.

Chapter 27:

Raralar, Alex: Disappeared in the siege of Archio, though I'm not sure what happened to him. OSIRIS has no record, but he has logged in after the Downtime. Whether he survived or his credentials were stolen, I don't know.

Chapter 29:

Lightbrightnight, Blessed Fr. Justo and companions: They were caught celebrating Mass, and all of them, including the Catholic guard, were executed. Their cause for canonization is underway. I pray to them, too.

Chapter 30:

Palaraul, Colonel Xavier: Ended. Imprisoned for war crimes, then hung himself in his cell.

Chapter 31:

Serahalix, Ann: According to the Peace and Reconciliation Committee, she survived, but I want to have nothing to do with her. I don't know where she is now or what happened to her.

GLOSSARY

Our society was as complicated as it was corrupt. Perhaps, future reader, you will be able to follow this book with these aids.

Abundants: A faction of the HORUS Wheel Group that believed the weather should be manipulated to produce the maximum benefit for humanity, even at the cost of disturbing natural weather patterns.

Acropolis: The capitol building of the Athanasian League.

AGDR: After Gotterdammerung, the secular year notation for our era, counting up from 0 AGDR, Gotterdammerung.

Alaskan Republic: A relatively small republic occupying the northern reaches of North America.

Alkahest: A brand of mortality limiter, my "favorite."

St. Alphonsus Cathedral: The cathedral church of the Archdiocese of Neyonaize.

ANUBIS: The Additional Neural Upload Backup System: an EDEN like OSIRIS that was only partially finished before Gotterdammerung and then destroyed in it.

Asian Union: A larger organization of several independent nations in Asia.

Athanasian Dream, the: An ideal of a wealthy, eternal life that we all believed in, at some level, even if we knew it wasn't true.

Athanasian League: A powerful federation of both Living and Dead citizens. With control over seven of the nine seats of OSIRIS Wheel Group, they had de facto control over OSIRIS. My home.

Archio: A city in the middle of the League, notable for an ancient arch that had survived the American Empire.

Artificial Gods Project: The life's work of the Divine Architects, a scheme to construct digital gods to serve humanity.

augur: A disciple of HORUS, capable of modifying the climate in the local area.

ba: Short for brain archive, the raw data created by OSIRIS's destructive read of the human brain.

bakt: A human being indentured to pay off some debt.

Balancers: A faction of the HORUS Wheel Group that believed the weather should not be manipulated too much, lest some cataclysm result. Perhaps we should have believed them.

Bank of Immortality: The central bank of the Athanasius League. Prior to the war, they had been pursuing a money printing policy to help pay for Fimbulwinter.

bio: Slang for a living person.

bioslurry: A mixture of the various proteins that make up the human body, used in healing lost body parts or even lost bodies. Bioslurry can be made artificially, as the Church permits, or by disassembling dead bodies, as she does not.

bioslurry crisis: The general shortage of bioslurry, a global crisis but particularly felt in the League.

bones: slang for a necromancer. Not particularly offensive.

Bootleg Theater: An improvised entertainment center that was likely both illegal and against the rules.

canton: One of the smaller republics within the League, originally the different nations that had combined to form the League. By the time I was born, they had mostly become mere administrative divisions. Cantons are named after their capital city, so the Steelriver Canton is governed by Steelriver, and so on.

Cashkils: a mountain range in the Neyonaize Canton, near Neyonaize itself.

charter: The founding document of a necromantic firm, which must be signed by an established necromancer.

Church: The organization founded by the True God, Jesus Christ.

collar: The symbol of a bakt. While not a legal requirement, bakts can easily be tracked through their collars by SET, thus, they are almost universally worn.

corpsegrinders: The colloquial name for the body reprocessing facilities, where corpses are turned into bioslurry. It's awful work.

Court of the Tomb: The judicial branch of the Dead government. They deal with nearly every law involving necromancy.

Consul: The leader of the executive branch of Living Government, directly elected in a two-round election.

cycle: One life and one death are considered a cycle. To run for Consul or Speaker of the Dead, one must have lived at least two cycles.

DDF: The Dicastery of the Doctrine of the Faith, an organization officially ruling on Church teaching.

Dead: Those with digital bodies inside OSIRIS. They are legally considered equal to the Living, although they have different laws.

Debt Reform Amendment: An amendment to the Table of the Laws of the Living that allowed indentured servitude.

denarius: The currency of the Free Athanasian League, which fared much better than drachma, perhaps because of sounder monetary policy.

Department of Names and Identifications: A canton-level agency that controls the issuing of ID cards in a canton.

Dicity: A port city on the east coast of the League and a major Living Guard base.

Divine Architects: A group of scientists, engineers, and politicians that attempted to create a utopia via construction of the EDENs.

disciple: Someone with access to an EDEN, also known as a mage.

drachma: the currency of the Athanasian League. Before the OSIRIS War, one drachma was enough to buy a loaf of bread, and minimum wage was eight drachmae an hour. One centidrachma was a hundredth of a drachma, and too small to bother picking up.

EDEN: An Eternal Divine Exotic-matter Nexus, one of those vast computers the Divine Architects thought would turn this world into a paradise.

EDENism: One of many, many sects that believe the EDENs are not merely metaphorical gods, but literal ones as well.

`edensudo(8)`: A command to combine several signatures from the Wheel Group to run a command as root, the administrator.

elementalist: A disciple of THOTH, capable of accessing THOTH's incredible energy output. They are mostly involved in engineering applications of THOTH, but not a few are used to direct THOTH's energy for violence.

end: A final death when the soul no longer remains in this world. The secular, and even many EDENists, consider this annihilation, but the Church knows it is impossible to destroy the soul.

estate: A single ghost or a family of them that has decided to stay Dead, usually due to their wealth.

`/etc/shadow`: A file containing the hashes (digital fingerprints) of every user on the POSIX system like OSIRIS. It is only readable by admins and the system.

Eternalists: One of the two major factions of our distress. To list all the petty differences with the Vivites would take too long, but their main premise is that laws should benefit the Living and the Dead equally.

European Federation: A nation made of several republics in Europe, not including Nova Roma and Switzerland.

extradition to the Dead: Force ripping a Living person into a prison grave.

FAL: The Free Athanasian League.

Fimbulwinter: The end result of the HORUS War, an artificial ice age.

Firebrightsky Post-Mortem Services PLLC: My long-lost company. I sometimes wonder what would have happened had I been able to keep it.

firstie: Derogative name for a first life.

free: As opposed to a bakt, an unindebted citizen with full rights.

`free(1)`: An ancient utility program that displays the remaining RAM available for use. Much to the OSIRIS Wheel Group's woe, this is not considered a superuser command.

Free Athanasian League, the: One side of the OSIRIS War, a society much like the Athanasian League but with servitude abolished. Their ideals quickly morphed, and towards the end of the war, they were stridently and violently atheistic.

freeman's mark: A mark on the neck caused by wearing a metal collar for years. Since it is visible on someone who was freed, it shows that you were once a bakt earlier in your present life.

force rip: Beginning OSIRIS's destructive read of the brain before the decedent had actually died. The Church was not too happy about this, although it was a standard, and safer, practice in secular necromancy.

force seance: A form of seance that forces a ghost to respond. Potentially illegal.

Gate of Fire: A pain-based escape hatch in a force seance.

ghost: A Dead individual.

ghost campaign: What amounts to door-to-door canvassing of votes for the Dead, and not illegal in itself. However, trying to purchase votes this way is illegal.

glitch: The end of a ghost via computer bug. It's an offensive word.

Gotterdammerung: A civilization-destroying war where the EDENs were turned upon each other.

govgrain: Slang for a species of wheat artificially grown by lifeweavers. It does not taste particularly bad, but we were all completely sick of it very soon into Fimbulwinter.

grave: The virtual environment that a ghost lives inside. In technical terms, it is a container running a virtual world and the ka.

graveyard: A storage system for bas. In much older times, graveyards were defended by militias, but now, almost all graves are stored in the Necropolis, guarded by the might of the Necroforce.

hard credit: A system to prevent endless indenture by requiring the master to free a bakt after a fixed number of days. In my experience, a fig leaf over slavery.

Halyetic: a common antidepressant.

Highest Court: The supreme court of the Living, capable of striking down a law passed by the Senate as against the Table of the Living. Their eight members are selected by the Senate, with the chief justice casting a tie-breaker vote. There is one more Highest justice in order that a case requiring both supreme courts combined won't tie, although this has only happened three times.

HORUS: The Heuristic Omnipresent Regulator of Underlying Systems, an EDEN dedicated to weather manipulation.

HORUS War: A war in Africa that had consequences for the entire world.

Immartal: A massive online retailer, the largest on the Neonet.

indenture bond: The debt of a bakt, which if paid will result in freedom.

indenture description: The set of jobs which a master is legally allowed to order a bakt to perform. Hypothetically you cannot be even leased to another master without your permission, but in practice every bakt ends up coerced into waiving this right. (As was I.)

ka: A kinetic avatar; a digital body capable of hosting the soul. Attempting to create a second ka from the same ba will lead to a lifeless ka.

St. Kateri General Hospital: A Catholic hospital in Archio.

kernel: The most low-level code in an operating system.

kernel modules: Code that interfaces directly with the kernel.

KHONSU: The Kinetic High-altitude and Orbital Network of System Underlays, an EDEN designed to transport the citizens and goods of the ante-Gotterdammerung civilization anywhere on Earth, or even into space. It did not survive Gotterdammerung.

Kinshasa: A colossal city in Africa, the capital of Westland. It is so old that it was known as Kinshasa even before Gotterdammerung.

Law of the Living: The law applying to the Living and written by the Senate of the Living.

Law of the Tomb: The law applying to the Dead and written by the Parliament of the Dead.

League Investigative Service: A national police force.

League Labor Bureau: The agency managing the bakts in debt to the national government.

League Trade Commission: A national consumer protection agency.

Legal: The legal department of the Slowbrightlaughter estate, a group of revenants and living lawyers who I, on occasion, hoped would go to Hell.

LifeLiquid: A brand of mortality limiter, notable for having "flavors."

lifeweaver: A disciple of MA-AT, capable of healing nearly every disease and, critically, rebuilding a body. Different ranks of lifeweavers have different access to MA-AT, and there are also specializations.

Lightwindknown & Lightwindknown: One of the largest necromancy firms in the country.

Living: A citizen in a biological body.

Living Guard: A national defense force that did not rely on war revenants, such that if there was some crisis that incapacitated them, the League would not be completely helpless.

locker: A colloquial name for solitary confinement, one of the few punishments available for misbehaving bakts.

Lowest Court: The supreme court of the Dead, capable of rejecting a law as against the Table of the Dead. Their seven members are appointed by the Parliament of the Dead.

Loyalist: The faction of the OSIRIS War that stayed loyal to the elected government, or what was left of it. As the war dragged on, they became more and more extreme, until democracy was only a pretense.

MA-AT: The Medical Assistance Adaptive Technology. An EDEN dedicated to healing and "eternal" life.

machinespeaker: A disciple of SET, capable of finding, concealing, and manipulating information, as well as a host of other oddball tasks.

mage: Someone with access to an EDEN, also called a disciple.

Maintenance: The department of menial workers in the SBL estate. They hated us, and I tried not to hate them.

MapApp: The standard phone app for finding your location in the world, made by machinespeakers.

medium: A low-ranking mage who can connect the Living to the Dead, and little more.

metaphysical dongle: Specialized hardware that connects to the exotic matter of the EDENs. The same hardware used to be the size of a house, but now it can be done with a device the size of a USB stick.

mindweaver: A lifeweaver specializing in psychiatry and psychology.

mortality limiter: A chemical that, when metabolized, will keep the soul tied to a biological body. It is too slow-acting to use in emergencies, and tastes too horrible for all but the most paranoid mundane, but it is common practice to use before surgeries, and it is required for any post-mortem professional and indebted graduate.

mundane: A non-mage.

NAEDA: Necromantic Assistance for Early Deaths and Accidents, a welfare program to pay for graves for those who died too early to qualify for Necrosecurity.

Name Wars: Two wars occurring in close succession between Spiral nations and Triglyph nations.

naming certificate: A document that proves you have a given name. Theoretically issued at naming (which is older for Spirals), but often at birth.

Neagas: A city in the Newla canton, stuck in the middle of the desert. I passed through it on my way east.

Necroair: The air force of the League, made of war revenants built into fighter and bomber planes, and thus capable of sustaining impossible g-forces.

`necrochain(1)`: A command line tool for authenticating OSIRIS credentials.

Necroforce: A powerful army of war revenants.

necrolawyer: A lawyer specializing in necromantic law.

Necrofleet: The League's main navy. Without the need to sustain breathing, eating, Living sailors, their ships are far stronger and deadlier.

Necromancy Administration: A massive organization administering every aspect of necromancy in the League and de facto throughout the whole world. They were as heartless as a bureaucracy could get.

necromancer: A disciple of OSIRIS capable of working with the Dead and their graves. Notably, only necromancers are legally allowed to rip the Dead.

necromancer, modern: A necromancer notable for at least acknowledging that OSIRIS is a computer. Most necromancers trained at college are modern.

necromancer, traditional: A necromancer who serves as both post-mortem professional and priest of OSIRIS. They are usually apprenticed, but both legalization of indenture and more stringent licensing requirements have been making them slowly decrease in number.

Necromancer's Strike: An incident over a century ago, at the time of my writing, where necromancers went on strike to oppose predatory lending practices. The Debt Reform Amendment emerged subsequently to quell the chaos.

Necropolis: A massive graveyard datacenter in an ancient military bunker in Petersyn, capable of storing the bas of the entire human race.

necroregs: Shorthand for the Code of the Regulations of the Law of the Tomb Title XIV, the governing regulations of necromancy.

necrotechs: The middle rank of OSIRIS mages, who can start seances and perform a number of other tasks, but cannot directly alter or create graves.

Necrosecurity: A social security program that taxes money from Living workers in exchange for guaranteeing monthly payments when they are Dead. It comes with both a card and an ID number.

neodrachma: A piece of paper, similar to the drachma, which hypothetically was worth something, and worth more if it had more zeroes on it.

Neonet: A global network similar to the pre-Gotterdammerung Internet with, hypothetically, important lessons learned from that era.

NeoVid: A video sharing platform.

New London Exchange: A currency exchange in the European Federation and the world's largest.

Newla: An extremely polluted metropolis on the west coast, noted for having one of the largest Necroforce bases in the country.

Neyonaize: A massive metropolis on the east coast of the League. The eventual capital of the FAL.

NNN: Neyonaize News Network, a major cable channel.

nomenism: Discrimination system based on naming. Usually directed at Spirals, but no group is innocent.

Notre Dame Group, Inc: A financial giant, which, I later discovered, at some point, had some transient relationship with the Church.

Nova Roma: A city state near the wasteland that was Rome, considered the New Eternal City and the diocese of the Pope.

Orbital Angel: One of THOTH's automated subsystems orbiting Earth and capable of delivering megatons of energy to a specific target. The original motive was, hypothetically, to protect Earth from asteroid strikes and even alien invasions. In reality, they may have liked power too much to give it up. After they were used in Gotterdammerung, generations of THOTH Wheel Groups decided to refuse to use them again.

Ombudsman: A department of the League Labor Bureau that is supposed to advocate for the rights of the bakts. In practice, they are too overwhelmed to do much.

OOM Killer: A subsystem in the Linux kernel, now over a millennium old, that is designed to kill processes that use too much memory, thus preventing the failure mode known as deadlock.

`osi(1)`: The OSIRIS System Interface; a command line interface for OSIRIS, made to replace the endless number of buggy scripts that had previously existed.

`osrip(1)`: A command line interface to control a ripper. Run on a client system, not OSIRIS itself.

OSIRIS: The Online Soul-Integrating Reality Immortality System, an EDEN dedicated to storing the digital bodies of the Dead.

OSIRIS War: The subject matter of this book.

Our Lady of Peace: A church in Whylin, a parish I will always remember as my first home.

OWG: Short for OSIRIS Wheel Group.

Parliament of the Dead: The legislative body of the Dead, capable of enacting laws about the Dead. There is no fixed size; rather, any party that has at least a million default votes has one seat for every million votes. Nonetheless, the parties had become either Eternalist or Vivite aligned in the end.

Peace and Reconciliation Committee: A post-War organization that tried to heal the wounds we all had.

Peace Steele: A massive obelisk in Petersyn, where the Tables of the Laws of the Living and the Dead are inscribed.

peculium: Property belonging to a bakt which cannot be confiscated by the master. Also shorthand for the monthly allowance.

Petersyn: The capital of the Athanasian League, in the very center of the League, and home to the Acropolis and Necropolis.

Pinkglowrapture Estates LLC: One of the larger estates. They owned a statistically significant portion of all privately-held land in the League, including the mall in Whylin.

Portgreyred Incident: A major (at the time) scandal involving a Vivite civil servant who may have been covering up embezzlement, or may have been falsely accused by the Eternalist prosecutor, or may have just been incompetent. We never learned the truth.

Proconsul: One of the chief ministers of the executive branch, serving directly under the Consul, and also in the line of succession should the Consul die or be incapacitated.

pseudo-revenant: A form of revenant that can be logged into and out of, popular for the rich Dead to visit the Living. For technical reasons, they are almost always stationary.

QuickTalk: A microblogging platform.

RA: The Resource Allocator, the first EDEN, one dedicated to constructing more EDENs. It was almost completely destroyed in Gotterdammerung.

real drachma: The last and most worthless of all drachmae. They've gone back to metals, now.

Red Guard: A fanatically atheistic and violent faction within the Free Athanasian League that gained more and more power as time progressed.

reincarnation: The process of taking a ba and reconstructing a biological body for it. This process is extremely expensive, and most people spend their Living lives making and investing enough money to eventually pay for it.

realtime: An expensive setting on a grave to run it at the same speed as real life. Every Athanasian ghost is guaranteed six free minutes of it a month. Since kas still need to sleep, this means a poor ghost might be incommunicado for years.

RENEW credit: The Raymond Eastdawnsky Necromantic Education for Wards program, a large necromantic scholarship for wards.

revenant: A kind of android controlled by a ka. They were all normal humans, once.

rip: A destructive read by OSIRIS of a decedent's brain, creating a ba.

ripper: A disturbing-looking device capable of making the correct electrical pulses to serve as a target for OSIRIS's destructive read. Most public places have one.

`rm(1)`: A dangerous command that can delete any file.

root: The administrator account of a POSIX system like the EDENs. As root can technically do almost anything, the EDENs are designed to prevent anyone from directly logging in as root.

seance: A chat, usually text-based, between the Living and the Dead.

self-euthanasia: The practice of having yourself ripped so that you can later get a new, better body. This practice is forbidden by the Church to the point of automatic excommunication.

self-ending: What a previous age would call suicide; the taking of one's own life in such a way as to be beyond the reach of necromancy.

Senate: The legislative body of the Living in the Athanasian League, capable of enacting laws about the Living.

Senator of the Living: A member of the Senate. Each canton elects three senators with a two-round voting process.

servitude arbiter: A hypothetically neutral inspector of working conditions for bakts.

SET: The System of Exogenous Technologies, an EDEN made of the remains of other EDENs. It is mainly used for the processing power, not any particular specialization, but, in particular, it has been adapted to find, conceal, or create nearly any information.

SET credits: A cryptocurrency based on SET that pays for the consumption of SET's resources.

SETNet: An alternate global network that is accessible only by machinespeakers.

slizz: An offensive word, whose meaning I don't particularly feel like explaining.

Slowbrighterlaughter Estate: One of the largest estates, made a slightly funny comedian whose investment skills were much better than his comedy.

Slowbrightlaughter Aztec: Also known as SBL Aztec, a campus in the very south of the League.

Slowbrightlaughter Main: The original SBL campus, where I served for many years, required to be kept in perfect condition by a settlement in an intra-estate lawsuit.

Slowbrightlaughter Neyonaize: A massive campus in Neyonaize.

slow rip: As opposed to a force rip, a rip that waits until brain death to begin the destructive read. Definitely approved by the Church, but very risky in many situations.

Snugglies: A hygiene brand of cushions to wear under a bakt collar. Remarkably comfortable.

Speaker of the Dead: the chief executive of the Parliament of the Dead, appointed by coalition.

Spiral: One of the two main naming schemes in the Athanasian League, but a minority. Spirals have an

agglutinative last name, which is usually shortened in common speech, and written on their cheek. Alan is a Spiral.
spiral: The tattoo on a Spirals' cheek that records his last name and life.
Starlight: The seat of the Starlight canton in the south of the Athanasian League.
Steelriver: A large city in the middle of the League, atop the Steel river. Notable for its bridges and being one of the best possible crossings into the western League.
Solstice Feast: a great communal meal, usually shared with friends and family, on the Solstice Festival.
Solstice Festival: A sacred time at the winter solstice, considered the day when HORUS was persuaded to return the sun.
Solstice Riots: The day protests turned violent and a turning point in our history.
swap: A memory management technique where data from RAM is written to a hard drive, then read back off it when needed. Overuse of swap can make a computer lag.
swap device: the physical machine or file on a larger machine used for swap.
Swapoff: The sudden end of swap use named after the command that did it.
Switzerland: A tiny country dating from before Gotterdammerung having survived by being so neutral that no one particularly hated them enough to wipe them off the map.
Tables of the Laws of the Living and the Dead: The founding document of the Athanasian League, giving rights and responsibilities to all citizens, although some more than others.

St. Teresa of Avila: A church in Newla having survived since before Gotterdammerung.
theopsychiatry: A subsystem of MA-AT that is designed to heal traumatic memories.
THOTH: The Transfer of Heat Over Time Hub, an EDEN designed to produce unlimited energy through means now lost to humanity. Most of THOTH's energy is directed to powerplants, but you could buy THOTH-based heaters prior to the war.
THOTH credits: The payment system for use of THOTH energy.
Triglyph: The majority naming scheme in the Athanasian League. Triglyphs have a last name made of three special, unambiguous characters randomly picked by a complex algorithm. I am a Triglyph.
triggie: A slur against Triglyphs.
Transport: the department of SBL Neyonaize that managed the buses.
True God: The only God that actually exists. I have believed in him all my life, though I did not quite understand his true nature.
twistie: A slur against Spirals.
`useradd(8)`: A command for creating new user accounts on POSIX systems such as the EDENs. On OSIRIS, it was usually run by a script controlled by the Necromancy Administration.
Vive: An extreme Vivite channel.
Vivites: One of the two major factions of our distress. The Vivites believed that the Living take priority over the Dead, and thus, the League should encourage reincarnations and give preferential treatment for the Living.

vote: The right of a citizen of the League, free or bakt, Living or Dead, to pick our leaders. We didn't realize how valuable it was.

vote, default: Because giving each ghost enough realtime to vote would be extremely expensive and impractical, a ghost is allowed to pick a party in the Parliament of the Dead to vote for, and unless he later changes it, he will always vote for that party.

`wall(1)`: A root-only command to write on all terminals.

wand: a device capable of directing THOTH's energy, which can be set to anywhere between a gunshot to a massive explosion.

war bond: Government bonds payable only after the conclusion of the war. It became a fig leaf for the Loyalist government.

war revenant: A revenant made for war, superior to infantry in armament, weight capacity, speed, logistics, armor, and reaction time. They made the League a superpower.

warghost: A form of refugee who escaped through OSIRIS.

Westland: A regional superpower in Africa, occupying much of the west coast.

Wheel Group: A term dating from the dawn of computing. Members of user group zero (that is, a wheel) are the admins of a POSIX system like the EDENs. Each EDEN has its own Wheel Group, picked by whatever arbitrary system the Wheel Group or their hosting governments agrees upon.

Wheel Group, HORUS: The seven admins of HORUS, distributed throughout African countries, with one member in Switzerland.

Wheel Group, MA-AT: The nine admins of MA-AT distributed throughout the whole world. During the various wars, they refused to support any side and instead made as many lifeweavers as possible.

Wheel Group, OSIRIS: The nine admins of OSIRIS, made of three Vivite members, three Eternalist members, the commanding officer of the Necroforce, and two other non-Athanasian members.

Wheel Group, RA: The thirteen admins of RA whose bickering with the Divine Architects led to Gotterdammerung.

Wheel Group, SET: The nine admins of SET, whose identities and locations are unknown. They go by pseudonyms, and considering that they control SET, no one can use SET to figure out who and where they are.

Wheel Group, THOTH: The seven admins of THOTH, each capable of unlimited access to THOTH's energy. They are scattered around the globe, although the Athanasian League had one.

Whylin: A town where my adult life started in earnest, in the Steelriver Canton.

`write(1)`: A command so ancient it was almost forgotten before Gotterdammerung, but it became the basis of communication afterwards. Formal messages are still sometimes sent through write.

`yes(1)`: A command that simply outputs "y" over and over again, used to automatically agree to any confirmation dialogue.

ACKNOWLEDGEMENTS

This book has been a long time coming, and it wouldn't have reached the end without help. I'd like to thank Benjamin Cheah, Barbara Graver, Cesar Chacon, Karina Fabian, Marie Keiser, Rena Shannon, S. R. Crickard, Thomas Bridgeland, and Mary Elizabeth Hayes for her encouragement. I also want to thank Allison Ramirez for editing. Finally, I want to thank the Blessed Mother for giving me, too, hope.

WANT MORE?

Want more emotionally intense dystopian fiction?

Get your free copy of *The Means of Mercy* by signing up for my newsletter at https://o-and-h-books.kit.com/1f05ea1c64

See you there!

ABOUT THE AUTHOR

Matthew P. Schmidt was chosen by God in Christ before the existence of the world to be holy and blameless before him. Matthew P. Schmidt is not that good at that, but he tries. He was born in Colorado Springs, Colorado, but moved at a young age to Martins Ferry, Ohio, where he lurks today.

Matthew P. Schmidt has written since he was five and dictated stories to his parents, and has programmed since he figured out how to work QBasic. He finds writing and programming to be surprisingly similar, though admittedly typos in books do not usually cause the reader to crash. Matthew P. Schmidt is certain there are exceptions.

When not working on one of his many projects, Matthew P. Schmidt dreams of worlds that are not, in addition to much reading of books and playing of games. He enjoys the Great Blue Heron and octopuses of all kinds, no matter their plural. He often speaks of himself in the third person, and not only in online biographies. Matthew P. Schmidt attends Our Lady of Peace in Wheeling, West Virginia, where he regularly eats God.

www.ingramcontent.com/pod-product-compliance
Lightning Source LLC
LaVergne TN
LVHW050915080826
845145LV00001B/94

* 9 7 8 1 9 5 9 7 0 3 0 7 5 *